A DAYSTAR OF FEAR

Geoffrey Jenkins graduated from a highly successful Fleet Street career in journalism to that of a bestselling author of sixteen titles published worldwide. Three of his books – *A Twist of Sand*, *The River of Diamonds* and *In Harm's Way* – have been made into major films.

Geoffrey Jenkins now lives in Pretoria.

By the same author

A TWIST OF SAND
THE WATERING PLACE OF GOOD PEACE
A GRUE OF ICE
THE RIVER OF DIAMONDS
HUNTER-KILLER
SCEND OF THE SEA
A CLEFT OF STARS
A BRIDGE OF MAGPIES
SOUTHTRAP
A RAVEL OF WATERS
THE UNRIPE GOLD
FIREPRINT
IN HARM'S WAY
HOLD DOWN A SHADOW
A HIVE OF DEAD MEN

GEOFFREY JENKINS

A DAYSTAR OF FEAR

HarperCollins*Publishers*

HarperCollins*Publishers*
77–85 Fulham Palace Road,
Hammersmith, London W6 8JB

This paperback edition 1995
1 3 5 7 9 8 6 4 2

First published in Great Britain by
HarperCollins*Publishers* 1994

ISBN 0 00 617639 9

Typeset in Sabon by
Hewer Text Composition Services, Edinburgh
Printed in Great Britain by
HarperCollinsManufacturing Glasgow

Author's Foreword

Lake Bangazi is a small star-shaped lake in wild swamp-forest country on the coast of northern Zululand, or Maputaland, about 320 kilometres north of Durban. Until recently, it was part of the northern extremity of a major army missile-testing range, but at no stage was it the site of a floating missile-tracking facility, as outlined in my story.

Bangazi is not to be confused with another lake of the same name, Lake Bangazi South, which is situated about forty kilometres to the south near the great lake and estuary of St Lucia.

The British transport *Nova Scotia* was torpedoed in these waters on 28 November 1942. She was carrying civilian refugees, mainly women and children, and some troops, from East Africa. Her sinking resulted in the death of 750 men, women and children, the highest casualty figure in South African waters during World War II.

For the purposes of my story, I have taken a small liberty with the actual position of the wreck site.

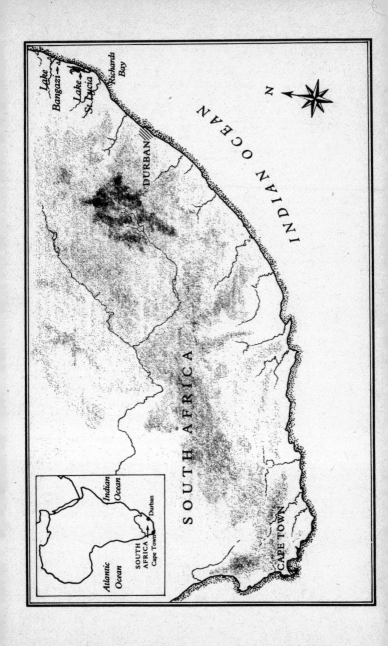

Revenge is a kind of wild justice

Francis Bacon

Prologue

The livid scar of the sabre-cut across the tall man's forehead flashed a murderous danger-signal as a flush of rage rose from his bull-neck through his jowls and cheeks to his temples. The venom behind it distorted the knotted tissue at the corner of his right eye where the sword-slash had healed, giving the whole face an evil cast.

'Give it to me!' he demanded thickly. He raised his silver-mounted Prussian officer's cane and pointed. On the workbench, between himself and the two smaller men in jeweller's aprons, lay the exquisite object, its beauty seeming to hold the combatants at bay. 'Give it to me!'

The glowing, greenish-yellow opalescent gemstones caught the flash of the sun from beyond the door. The light came off the sea rippling against the long iron pier which ran out from the land and nearby German colonial-style lighthouse.

The Italian brothers' workshop was no more than a lean-to against the wall of the adjacent bakery. The tall man, wearing the uniform of the Kaiser's *Deutsche Schutztruppen*, complete with polished jackboots, gleaming leather weapons belt and big Service revolver clipped into a shining holster, seemed to fill the place.

'*For the last time, give it to me!*'

He lifted the cane threateningly.

'Your offer is absurd.' One of the craftsman-brothers moved forward a pace, reaching protectively towards the necklace. His movement shadowed the luminous stones, fashioned in the form of a cross, setting in train the near-century of dark events which was to follow from that moment.

The big German officer, as if fearing the masterpiece would be snatched from him, struck like a mamba. In one swift movement he pitched down the cane, snapped open his revolver holster, and lashed the advancing craftsman across the face with the gun.

The heavy muzzle bit deep into the cheekbone. His victim reeled back semi-conscious against the far wall, blood spurting through hands held to his face.

The other brother, his free movement hampered by his apron, flung himself at the Prussian officer like a terrier at a bull mastiff.

'So – you dare attack a German officer! Foreign scum! You have no status here! Who do you think you are!'

He attacked with the heavy pistol. Again, he went for the face. The big foresight did the damage. One moment the smaller man was coming at him, muscles and sight intact, the next, he was jerking out wild animalistic sobs, holding what had been his right eye now hanging on a bloody string trailing from the socket from which it had been ripped. He spun like a dervish, turning eccentric rings as the blindness overwhelmed him, then dropped to the floor.

'Scum!' repeated the Prussian. 'Filthy foreign scum! That will teach you!'

He clipped the revolver back into its holster, stood looking for a moment at the glowing necklace-cross, then picked it up along with the soft chamois cloth on which it had lain, and slipped it into his pocket.

A thin, skeletal whisper, like a malediction from the underworld, filtered between the blood-soaked fingers of the eyeless man.

'May it curse you forever! We Arnoldis will have our revenge, even if it takes five lifetimes . . .'

The words choked off in a half-scream as the heavy

jackboot crashed into his ribcage, and he toppled forward unconscious, still pawing the remnants of his eye.

The Prussian checked his immaculate breeches for any flecks of blood. Then he picked up his silver cane from the workbench, and stalked into the sunlit street.

1

The shock jarred his mind like a missile blast-off – a body!

The impact was as nerve-jangling as one of the weapons once fired from the strange structure now close under the belly of the helicopter.

Gareth Ridpath leaned forward abruptly in his seat past the pilot's shoulder. He craned through the front window to try to penetrate the murky green shadows clustered under the legs of the floating steel platform. It was there that he had spotted the face-down spreadeagled figure.

But the man's line of vision was lost as the pilot, instead of heading to put the Bell Jetranger down on the helipad, gunned the engine and pulled clear. The machine sidled round the tropical shore of the lake, lush with impenetrable trees and sultry, deep green vegetation, in order to make a new landing approach.

The complex resembled a scaled-down oil rig with its central 'drilling tower', helipad, heavy-lift cranes, steel latticing, welter of heavy pipes, gantries and walkways. But it was not a rig – until recently it had been a missile test-firing facility. A firing gantry scaffold, a long, reinforced openwork steel ramp, projected from a flat, empty deck close to the helipad. Its base and the adjacent steel wall of the module were stained black with explosive gases – a sombre contrast to the garish colours of the floating platform.

Gareth could see the slate-blue helipad deck centred with a white-and-blue leatherback turtle logo, and the adjacent red and white tower capped with a bright radar tracking antenna cluster, now unused. Two ex-missile-handling cranes towered in ochre yellow against the vivid primrose of the catwalks and external stairways clamped from base to summit to five storeys of shining champagne-coloured steel. Lower down, three mushroom-pink lifeboats hung from davits, but the launch ramp asserted dominance over the whole with its finish of spotless, gleaming white. The supporting legs of the platform were painted black circled with white, and where they plunged out of sight into murky green water they resembled a can-can girl's gartered fishnet stockings disappearing into her crutch.

'What is it?'

He switched focus and found himself looking into the wide-set eyes, too eloquent to be blue, too vivid to be grey, of the girl sitting alongside the pilot. As the machine lifted, it caught the sun above the forest margins, and burnished the fair hair falling carelessly over her forehead. The eyes were quizzical, a little puzzled, almost as if they had sensed something of what he had seen in the water. Or thought he had seen.

'Some sort of grotesque light effect, I guess, down there in the shadows under the platform's legs,' he parried. He remarked to the pilot, 'I thought you pulled clear because you saw it, too.'

The pilot shook his head. 'No way. I had all my attention on the helipad. No. I thought we'd clatter round the lake and shake up all those tired executives lounging below.' He stabbed a thumb downwards at the structure now receding behind the machine. 'Heaven for those threatened with executive burn-out,' he mocked. 'That's the selling slogan Ken puts over for Bangazi Lodge. Seems it gets across. Place is always full.'

'How about taking another look-see?' Gareth Ridpath suggested.

'Okay. You've seen the setting before . . .' He gestured widely at the small cloverleaf-shaped lake surrounded by lush vegetation which blanketed the land as far as the eye could see. 'The water's deep under the platform. The defence guys originally dredged it out to make the site a missile-testing facility.'

Bangazi Lodge.

From the Jetranger as it circled to make a fresh landing approach, the place looked like a travelogue advertisement. Floating on the lake was the incongruous man-made structure of pipes, modules and steel latticing, in complete contrast to the dense natural forest which reached out at it from every quarter; thinner on the seaward side, where a narrow tonsure of bush-covered land divided it from the brilliant white of dunes and beach; beyond, the so-blue of the Indian Ocean, untroubled except for a cornet of cloud on the farthermost eastern horizon.

Bangazi is one of an extensive chain of freshwater barrier lakes, lagoons and swamps which join hands behind a rampart of heavily overgrown dunes separating them from the sea. Long ago, it seems, the lakes were submarine canyons which, when the sea receded, were sealed off against the ocean by sand. In time, the wind built up barriers on top of this base to give rise to some of the world's highest coastal dunes.

At Bangazi's face in the east is the Indian Ocean, and at its back, forty kilometres inland, the Lebombo mountains, of profound geological and ecological significance. The low-lying land between is subject to heavy summer flooding caused by tropical cyclones working southwards through the Mozambique Channel and wreaking havoc along the coast. Regiments of sauna-hot swamp forest, evergreen tropical forest, bush, ferns and grass, march through swamps alive with malaria, wild animals and deadly snakes.

There are no roads, tracks, or other communications into or out of Bangazi, although under sufferance the authorities allow a few four-wheel-drive vehicles by permit to use the magnificent beach below the high-water mark – the breeding-ground of the rare leatherback and loggerhead turtle. Otherwise, it is out of bounds. The whole area is a wildlife sanctuary and, until recently, part of a missile-testing range operated by the South African Defence Force.

Lance, the pilot, brought the helicopter round in a right-hander for his new landing approach, which threw open an incomparable vista of ten kilometres of green swampland to the south, and, far away, the waves of the ocean spitting light, like a distant platoon of bayonets.

Had it been mere hallucination, a reflection of the inner anxiety tugging at him, that had made Gareth imagine he saw the outline of a body there underneath the platform's gaudy legs? After all, the assignment he had accepted could easily end with a bullet in the back. And what exactly had made the envoy who was due to meet him at a rendezvous thousands of kilometres away a week or two hence suddenly deviate to remote Zululand, leaving a cryptic, urgent message to meet instead at Bangazi Lodge this very day? Had it not been for the floods which had held him up, Gareth would have intercepted the man in person to find out what had caused such a radical change in their agreed schedule.

He had been lucky to get booked in at Bangazi Lodge at such short notice, especially as the radio-telephone, its only link with the outside world, was about to shut down for the weekend. Lucky, too, that the Lodge helicopter was bound for Durban to collect a VIP and could pick him up on its return flight.

The helicopter banked; the girl's eyes dilated slightly and turned a deeper shade, as if she somehow identified with his anxiety. He imagined that they would always reflect her inner feelings and he found that exciting. Gareth could hardly believe that the tall, slender girl in pale lavender slacks and baggy red jersey was the VIP he had been told about. Her welcoming smile had taken possession of those

16

striking eyes, and time had vanished in the easy exchanges between them as the helicopter had clattered northwards. Her name was Pernelle Clymer and he guessed she was in her late twenties, but Gareth was unaware of what brought her to Bangazi, or what endowed her with VIP status.

The helicopter headed, purposefully now and faster, towards the strange structure afloat on the lake. It began to drop.

Pernelle swung round in her seat to say something to Gareth, who was concentrating on the side of the platform where the 'flare boom' projected. Here he had seen the mysterious object in the water whose colour, reflecting the steel wall above, was impalpable as sifted cinnamon. She saw a man in his mid-thirties, his face darkly tanned as were his strongly muscled hands which had hefted his kit-bag so lightly aboard at Richards Bay. She still retained a vignette of his eyes, squinched against the sun, the generous, full-lipped mouth relaxing its strong line to smile briefly as he had lifted his hand in salute. Now the wide eyes filmed with withdrawal as hers fixed on his, but for a moment, it seemed, she looked down a deep shaft into a troubled mind, which had not been apparent in their previous easy conversation. She turned back, unspeaking, but felt that for a brief flash she had explored a profound sensitivity or grief, maybe, which had helped cast the firm lines into his jaw and cheekbones.

Gareth said to the pilot, 'Down there near the right leg of the platform – on a line between the lifeboat and the boom.'

'Tricky,' commented Lance. He was now at very low altitude, giving the impression that the helicopter was about to crash into the flotel on a level with the twenty 'portholes' of the luxury suites.

Almost at the last moment, it seemed to Pernelle, he juggled with the controls and the machine hung back on its haunches like a reined-in horse. Then, as close as he dared go without tangling the rotors with the plethora of pipes, Lance let the machine sink down. A fish eagle, perched on the extremity of the boom where it overhung the water, rose with a raucous cry of protest, as if it had already staked a claim to the object which floated on the lake beneath the steel walkway.

Gareth put an arm on Lance's shoulder and pointed.

Pernelle sharply drew in her breath.

It looked, from its motionless face-down position and wide-thrown arms, like a floating version of the turtle logo stencilled on the helipad.

It was the body of a man.

2

'He's spotted it! Look, he's going down to check!'

The dark woman, wearing what might have been flowered pyjamas or a very loose jogging-suit, tugged at one of the divided curtains of the porthole to try to track the path of the helicopter in its descent to the surface of the lake.

The man with her twitched the drape back into place. The suite – painted in soft peach and grey – resembled that of a five-star hotel or a luxury cruise liner: thick carpets; twin beds, covers disturbed but not slept in; sound-proof walls over an inner fire-proof skin. Beyond the bedroom was a lounge-cum-office, windowless but lit by discreet concealed lighting, and a bathroom which added a waft of expensive perfume to the scent of an over-large bouquet on the low centre table.

No one would have guessed that sheets of rocket-proof plastic lined the walls over the sound- and fire-proofing. The suite was situated on the corner of the flotel opposite where the body floated, so that the angle of sight from the window-porthole was difficult.

The former rocket launch ramp jutted out above it from the roof, its sword turned to ploughshare by the incorporation of an aluminium sun-awning. A visitor might have thought that several other screens also were anti-sun. They were not. They were anti-bullet. The window glass was bomb-proof.

'Don't be bloody stupid, Romira – do you want everyone to see us peering out? We're not supposed to be aware – the whole business is meant to hit everyone as a shock!'

The woman's wide-set eyes, purple like irises under

a gathering thunderstorm at dusk, were turbulent and resentful. The bracelet of dark hair seemed even blacker against the white skin of her forehead, and although her make-up had been badly, even carelessly applied, perhaps with unsteady fingers, this did not detract from her beauty.

'Shock – that's what you want all the Lodge guests to feel.'

'Call it what you will.' The deep voice lashed out from a brush of close-trimmed black beard, which scarcely veiled the contours of a wide, cynically curved mouth which bit back deeply at the corners and accented the sweep of chin to an aggressive point above the bull-neck. Seasons of hot Bangazi sun had burnished his broad forehead and the too-prominent bones of his nose, jaw and cheeks, had thrown into relief a groove between heavy, threatening brows. Defensive lines seemed to have stencilled the face into a template of reserve and suspicion. The effect was enhanced by the strangely opaque slivers of eyes, which were like tinted one-way glass. He looked any age between the mid-thirties and mid-forties.

'But . . .'

'Listen, Romira –' He made a short chopping movement with the fingers of his left hand, strong and square ' – don't get your knickers in a twist . . .'

'There's a dead man down there!'

'Okay, I know, you know. Nobody else does. Much better that Lance should be the first to spot it while it's still in a state to float rather than the damn thing sinking down to the bottom of the lake and giving us hassles getting it out through the piles and legs.'

'Flood valves.'

He found it hard to credit that the cold words were dropped from lips capable of smouldering into ardent heat when they touched other lips. The right lips. But always, her eyes remained inscrutable and that worried him.

'No need to get bitchy. The flood valves were part of it. As you rightly say.'

She jerked a thumb over her shoulder towards the probing helicopter. 'Flood valves – that's the key to the whole secret, isn't it?' She added, a rasp of anxiety sandpapering her voice, 'You're sure the whole operation went okay, Ken? What if he tried to claw his way out after you opened the valves and the post-mortem shows scratches on his hands, maybe on his back and arms as well, that can't be explained . . .'

The heavy furrow between his eyes appeared deeper to Romira. Not a face to play around with, even playful-tender in bed.

'The cover is watertight, if I may mix metaphors.' An undisciplined muscle jerked the sharp corner of his mouth into the semblance of a grin. 'This is the cover story. Against all the regulations, a newly arrived visitor decides to take a walk in the middle of the night along the old boom walkway reserved for bird and animal watchers – by day. He ignores the big warning sign at the end of the platform which states clearly, "Strictly no entry. Danger. Keep out." He slips and falls into the water. Maybe he does have scratches. He got them when he fell – huh? Perhaps he had a nightcap too many . . .'

'The post-mortem will show he had nothing to drink. You know that as well as I. You didn't offer him a drink – before.'

The one-way traffic out of his eyes was sinister.

'You don't offer drinks to someone who threatens to blow your world sky-high. And has – had – the means to do it.'

'You mean that document? But it didn't have your name right. Not your present name, Ken Ziegler. Remember, I bestowed it on you – a little love-gift in place of a wedding present.'

'We mutually sank the name Kentrat Dehn as deep as

the *Nova Scotia* when we got out of Namibia. You agreed to that.'

'Anyway, the man was a rat, a dangerous rat. He meant to bite. If you play his sort of game, you must expect the trap, sooner or later.'

'He wasn't playing the game alone.'

Ken Ziegler stopped on his way across to a table on which lay a page of damp notepaper, placed under the strong desk light to dry it and weighted down with a couple of heavy ashtrays.

'Wasn't he? That's what bugs me, Romira. Eats me up. On his own admission when we cross-examined him – '

'*You*, Ken, not *me*. You grilled him silly before you finally disposed of him. I just stood by. It was sick-making.'

'If you were so squeamish, why didn't you intervene?'

She remained silent, but thunderclouds swirled in those turbulent eyes.

'I'll tell you why, Romira. You're up to the ass in this, just as I am. If I sink, you sink. If I swim – and I intend to, even more so once I get the wreck business on track – you swim, too.'

'Like a goldfish in a bowl. Beautiful, but un-free.'

His cynical mouth twisted at the taunt. He threw at her: 'Diamonds are a rough game, Romira. Not just a flash-flashy necklace above a pair of beautiful tits . . .'

'Thank you for the compliment. I don't get so many these days from you.'

'How did he know about me, Romira? How did he *know* – about this?'

He indicated the typewritten, water-crinkled document on the desk-top.

'It's your receipt, and your signature, Kentrat Dehn. Large as life.'

'He unearthed this at the dark end of the pipeline. In Angola, he said. Yet somehow he knew to come straight *here*. Here to Maputaland, thousands of kilometres away from Angola. How? Who was he teaming up with, *here* – at Bangazi Lodge which has nothing to do with diamonds . . .'

Her laugh was a grenade-burst of derision. 'Says who, Ken? It's the smoothest operation in Africa south of the tenth parallel.'

'He came to meet someone – *here*,' Ken repeated. 'Or someone was coming to meet him – *here*.'

'You've always encouraged the upmarket clientele, Ken. Take a good look at Bangazi Lodge's guest list.'

Her flippant tone needled him and he almost ripped the paper. As he started to give it a final nervous smoothing, he delved into his trouser pocket and drew out a banknote. It seemed an almost unconscious action, since all his attention was on the typed paper – he doubled the note, creased it between square-cut fingers, and drew it through his front teeth as if using dental floss.

The grotesque idiosyncrasy fired the fuse to the time-bomb of tension which gripped Romira.

'For Pete's sake!' she burst out. 'If you indulge in that dirty habit of yours again, I'll . . . I'll . . .'

Ken stared at the note in his hand as if suddenly becoming aware of it.

He said menacingly, 'Don't threaten me, Romira. It doesn't pay. Ask the guy down there in the water.'

She took a couple of quick, erratic strides towards the window, like a wound-up puppet, then swung round on him, a smile consciously planted on her classically proportioned lips.

She made a throwaway gesture at the window. 'You say he came to meet someone, or someone was to meet him. What about the passengers coming in the chopper? They're the only ones to arrive this weekend.'

Ken took the olive branch as if it were spatterdashed with acid. He thrust the banknote back into his pocket.

'They're okay – I know all about them,' he replied. 'It

couldn't have been either of them. Pernelle is on her way here from Cape Town. She's absolutely in the clear. I can't imagine a well-known marine archaeologist like her and the National Monuments Council's top salvage adviser being involved with illegal diamonds, can you? Anyway, you know her background, you met her when she came here before . . .'

'I know, I know,' retorted Romira. 'No need to throw her career record in my teeth. It's enough that you try and make your marble sweet by giving her a weekend's free accommodation at Bangazi Lodge. Yes, I remember her well. Those eyes.'

Ken let it ride, and went on, 'The other chopper passenger is Gareth Ridpath, the mining engineer. You met him here previously too – remember, he thumbed a ride on our game-spotting flight inland and wanted Lance to drop him off to look at a special ore deposit on the other side of Mkuzi reserve. But it didn't work out – the floods fixed it.'

'What, then, is he doing here again?'

He sighed long-sufferingly. 'Don't try and pin anything on him, Romira – it won't stick. He's simply a harmless mining engineer from Richards Bay. It's possibly something to do with another chopper trip – I don't know. I didn't speak to him. You know the radio-phone is off at weekends. It just happened to be easy for Lance to pick him up after fetching Pernelle from Durban.'

'You paid her air fare from Cape Town to Durban, too?'

'If you want the sort of knowledge and advice she can offer, you have to pay for it. And I need it, if the *Nova Scotia* wreck is to play the part it is meant to. And time is getting short. When it comes to wrecks, there's no one to touch Pernelle Clymer.'

It may have been the sound-proof wall which damped her laugh to flatness. She came across to him, hands outstretched.

'You're a devious bastard, Ken. And I admire you for it.'

He didn't respond but glanced at his watch. 'Listen, the helicopter is pulling clear of the legs now – I guess Lance is heading for the helipad to report his find to me – to us. You get up there to reception to clock in the passengers, the way you normally do. There must be no hint in the routine of anything out of the ordinary to show we know about the body already. I'll come too, to welcome Pernelle as a VIP. All sweet and natural. We will be duly shocked when Lance breaks the news to us. This – ' he waved the paper ' – goes into my safe, along with other special valuables.'

'Special valuables!' she echoed. 'Special safe. You made enough fuss about getting it from Namibia here to Bangazi. An old beat-up safe which looks as if it's been kicked around in government departments for years because no one could be bothered to throw it out.'

'It worked impeccably in World War I and it worked again at Namibian independence. I wish I still had the old ammunition boxes that went with it. But it works again now – for Ken Ziegler. Coming?'

They passed into the lounge-cum-office suite adjoining the bedroom, their feet making no sound on the thick mushroom-coloured pile carpets. It looked like a successful Johannesburg businessman's office: two big desks, a brace of word-processors and photocopiers, filing cabinets matching the decor, an electric typewriter on a swivelling stand.

Ken went to a cocktail cabinet built into the steel wall at chest level, fiddled with a combination lock behind the sherry bottles, and pulled the whole device wide. Behind, like an ageless Buddha, sat a battered, old-fashioned black-grey safe. The once-shiny, now tarnished plate screwed in under the brass handle bore the maker's name, 'Hoppner, Berlin, 1910', plus a big brass keyhole. The ancient contraption looked as secure from the attentions of a modern-day safebreaker as an open city from an atom bomb.

A burglar would have been disappointed at the contents of the safe — a few handfuls of banknotes held by rubber bands, some flotel accounts and ledger books, bills, chequebooks and other hotel management bric-à-brac.

A concealed button lurked behind the scuffed cash-box, but exactly where, Romira never quite knew. Ken did a kind of sleight-of-hand act which confused her. In an almost contemptuous way, as if compensating for the safe's other deficiencies, the steel back slid forward.

The hard light from the overhead fluorescent strip was transmuted by the jewellery, which lay there in greenish-yellow glory. Each opalescent stone of the necklace took on individual illumination, stretching down to a pendant at the extremity in the form of a cross. The stones were more stunning than diamonds. They were heliodore, the rarest gemstone in the world. The masterpiece did not need the handful of uncut diamonds, lying loose alongside, to show it off.

Romira leaned over Ken's shoulder as he thrust the typewritten sheet he had taken from the dead man into the safe, smoothing it down and weighting it with a couple of little diamond bags to prevent it from curling.

Her eyes were fixed on the necklace. 'It does things to me, deep inside. I can imagine myself walking into a room wearing it and everyone struck speechless.' Her voice caressed the words. 'The Stones of the Sun,' she breathed. 'The Stones of the Sun.'

3

'Maybe he was a suicide bungee-jumper – tried to leap off the helipad overhang in the middle of the night and his cord broke.' Lance threw the sarcasm across the polished desk at Romira. In front of her was a big hotel-type guest register, pens, and a pile of tourist brochures, behind her a pigeon-cote of cubby-holes with guests' names on them.

Romira's eyes flickered; playing the innocent was not new to her. They travelled from Pernelle, and then on to Gareth, as if trying to enlist support for her apparently incredulous reaction to Lance's news after his quick landing and the scramble by the three occupants out of the Jetranger. Romira had been duly on station behind the reception desk in a small steel module adjoining the helipad, to which it was connected by a roofed-in passageway. She could find no fault with the lovely figure which was masked by slacks and a loose sweater. Her laser-scrutiny knifed in turn over Gareth: a strong body without a superfluous gram of fat, she could see the way his shoulders filled the washed-out blue bomber jacket. But there was unfathomable tension there; maybe he needed a rainbow at the back of his brindled brown head in the form of a woman . . .

Romira broke in on her split-level thoughts with a banal comment to Lance.

'Dead? Are you sure?'

'Do you want me to fly you down there for a closer look?'

She dropped her seething eyes at his tone. The long manicured nails fiddled with the register-pen. They could also be claws.

'Ken has got to know about this right away,' she responded levelly. She paused as she picked up the intercom and said to Gareth and Pernelle, 'You saw this – body – also?'

Gareth replied: 'No doubt about it. In fact, I spotted it first, on our initial landing approach. Lance went back the second time to look, when I told him.'

'What does the body look like? I mean, young, old . . .?' She added what she thought was a neat touch: 'He's wearing what? Pyjamas? I mean, if he fell from his room – but then he couldn't have. When Ken renovated Bangazi Lodge he made sure that none of the windows of the suites could open because it's such a sheer drop to the water.'

'He's fully dressed, shoes, wearing a flowered Hawaiian shirt,' responded Lance tersely. Romira remembered the way Ken had gripped the shirt by the collar when he had manhandled him into the buoyancy tank . . .

'Get on with that call!' the pilot went on sharply. 'We need Ken quickly – he's the boss and he's got to decide what's to be done. But the sooner we get that body out of the water before it sinks, the better. We've no idea how long it's been in the lake.'

Three hours, four hours, how long does a dead body float? It had been dawn when she and Ken had pushed him clear, not light enough for any sleepless guests' eyes to have seen what they were up to.

Romira dialled a number which she knew would not reach Ken. All these procedures had to appear natural, so everyday, in line with shocked reaction, and beyond suspicion.

She said, as the instrument buzzed without response, 'Ken could be around anywhere, getting ready for the scuba-brunch out to sea this morning.'

She tried another number, the kitchen. 'Is Ken there? No? Any idea where?'

She dialled a third number. She knew in advance, of course, that Ken would be waiting at his office desk phone for her call.

'Ken? Can you come up right away to reception? We've got a serious problem.'

A curious, tense silence insinuated itself between four people who were essentially strangers but were now irreversibly handcuffed to one another by virtue of the object riding on the slight swell of the lake, lifting gently between the steel legs of the flotel. There was no sound except the creaking of the whole unlikely tophamper, like a futuristic life moving through the tracery of steel beams and pipes, plus the distant throb of the electric generators and the more muted susurrus of the air conditioning, which operated day and night in the soggy environment.

Gareth saw that he had been correct in his assessment that Pernelle's eyes would always be the barometer reflecting events: they were veiled now as she stood immobile, unspeaking. As he glanced at her withdrawn face, the slightly irregular contours at the corners of her mouth and eyes, his mind projected itself into the future and he told himself that neither anxiety nor time would ever chisel those faint lines into anything but their present unstudied loveliness. At her feet was her suitcase and kit-bag which he had hefted out of the helicopter; the kit-bag puzzled him, however; it was wrapped round with squared green nylon mesh. Tied to each square was a numbered white tag, following in consecutive order, to over twenty. He could not guess what the purpose of the net was. Its unusualness alone put her outside the rich executive category frequenting Bangazi.

Lance paced along the front of the reception desk, his eyes seeing but not registering the plethora of blown-up animal shots, birds, underwater views of coral and the inevitable wash of rainbow-imitating fishes.

His tanned face was tight with tension. 'What the hell

is keeping Ken?' he demanded of Romira. 'He must have guessed something was wrong, the way you spoke.'

Romira replied enigmatically, 'He guessed.'

'Then what – '

'Morning, folks!' Ken threw his overhearty mine-host voice across the helipad like a Scud missile. 'I hope Lance saw you right – ' He advanced on Pernelle and Gareth with his hand outstretched but his heartiness failed to erase the lines of effort and anxiety it cost. His opaque eyes took no colour from the bonhomie of his words.

'Can the crap, Ken,' snapped Lance. 'We've got a dead man on our hands.'

Ken's greeting hand stopped in mid-flight towards Pernelle as if it had slapped on air brakes. His ardent stride checked likewise.

'*What's that?*'

He's acting it out well, Romira told herself. But the pressure's not really on him – or me – yet.

Lance explained quickly. 'I was coming in to land the first time, but I didn't see it. Gareth here did. Down under the platform, among the legs. I pulled clear, really only for a bit of a joy-ride round the lake, but we shot back to check. There's no doubt about it, Ken. There's a man floating down there on his face.'

'It could be that he's unconscious and not dead.'

'No one floats face downward in water and lives.'

Gareth added, 'The sooner we get him out, the better.'

'I'm sorry to subject you to this, Miss Clymer . . .' Ken's unctuous tone to Pernelle was at odds with his other ragged, jerky utterances.

'I've seen drowned men before.' Something in her response made Gareth wonder if she were reliving a past event.

'Where – where exactly is this body? We'll have to make a plan . . .'

'Under the bird-watching boom,' replied Lance.

Romira said, 'Maybe he took a stroll in the night and fell off.'

'Let's first take a look from the helipad overhang right here next to us. You can point it out to me then,' answered Ken.

'I doubt whether it'll be visible,' said Lance. 'The overhang will block the view, so will the bulk of the flotel.'

As if the thought had newly struck him, Ken blurted out, 'Bangazi can't afford a scandal! We've got to keep this thing away from the guests! People – top people – come from all over for peace and relaxation – A body! We can't go and fish it out in full view of everyone!'

Before he had finished, Ken reached the barrier of landing-lights demarcating the edge of the helipad. Below was a stiff drop to the water. He was trying to peer over.

'Watch it, or you'll find yourself in the drink too,' said Lance. 'You can't see the body from here, as I thought.'

'Where is it?' Ken's voice emerged tense and thick from the black growth of beard around his mouth.

'About on a line with that lifeboat hanging near the entrance to the bird-watching boom,' replied Lance.

'We can't have all the palaver of launching a lifeboat – everyone will be out to see and the story will be all round the Lodge like wildfire!' Ken went on. 'Today is to be a special day – a brunch on the charter craft out at sea, a diving competition to the coral reefs . . .'

'Spot the coelacanth, spot the wreck.' There could have been an overtone of mockery in Romira's interjection.

Ken continued, quoting his own sales talk, 'Yes, this and much more. And if we're seen fishing for a body here in the lake beforehand . . .' He rounded on Lance. 'You're still okay to fly the party out to the coral reef this morning?'

'Why not?'

Gareth broke in: 'Have you a rope, a long rope?'

Later, he was to wonder what compulsion had made him volunteer and so precipitate the stormwind of events which was to sweep across the lives of the group standing there in the bright sunlight on the helipad. But it was too late and maybe he should have stayed uninvolved much further back in time, as long ago as Dr Nikolai Vize's offer from Glavalmazzoloto . . .

As it was, he heard himself repeating, 'A rope, long enough to attach me to the helicopter skid and lash round the body to secure it. Lance and I can get down there – now – and bring it up.'

'Now?' echoed Ken. 'Now . . .' The words came slowly as if they were the output of an inner computer checking time against factors unknown to anyone else. '. . . now-would-be-splendid.'

Lance said, 'There's all the rope you need in the chopper, as well as the steel cable for the horse-collar. It's part of the rescue gear. But what sort of experience have you had in this kind of thing?'

'I've done quite a bit of rock climbing and abseiling. What we're about will only be a variation.'

Pernelle intervened. 'You could kill yourself.'

He looked at her, but the sunlight shut out what was happening behind her eyes. 'You can kill yourself crossing a street.'

'I'll take the chopper as low as I dare,' said Lance. 'You can get to water level by means of the horse-collar. Then fix the rope round the body and I'll pull clear.'

'A rope by itself won't be enough,' replied Gareth. 'The arms and legs will hang loose. We need something like a blanket. The skid is very narrow.' He eyed Lance. 'The weight distribution will be tricky.'

'I know, I know,' the pilot answered tersely. 'There's a rug in the chopper for VIP knees. There's also a grapnel among the rescue gear.'

Gareth's mind was racing to the logistics of retrieving a limp, inert object like a body from among the massive steel legs of the flotel. These went far down to the floor of the lake (how deep?) at a slightly splayed angle. On them, like a house of cards, balanced the whole conglomeration of modules, booms, platforms, ramps, gantries and pipes which made up the Lodge. Lance would have to keep the machine's rotors clear of the miscellaneous objects which could bring disaster, such as the bird-watching boom projecting at the base of the platform, or the pink-painted lifeboats in their davits hanging nearly above the body . . .

He pulled his concentration back to the silent group. 'Okay, he'll play it by ear. Ready?'

Pernelle wondered whether she could bear to watch the body pick-up. She said: 'Don't slip on the skid. But I see you've got the right shoes for it.'

He glanced down at his feet and then grinned swiftly back at her. They were soft moccasins with thick soles and outsize tongues which covered his instep. 'Climbing, hiking, beach-bashing, you name the terrain.'

'Good luck, Gareth.'

Lance started to edge away towards the Jetranger.

Ziegler repeated, 'Lance, remember to carry out as much of the rescue where it can't be seen from the VIP windows. I wouldn't like to offend . . .'

'I'll do what the situation demands,' the pilot rejoined curtly.

Ken didn't seem to hear but rambled on: 'You see, today's my day for the special coral reef picnic brunch, on board the charter craft, like I told you. The main attraction is abalone – I flew up cases of it specially from the Cape. Lance, you remember you picked it up in Durban? There's caviar and champagne as well . . .'

'Gareth and I will discuss the menu when we get back,' retorted Lance. 'Ready, Gareth? Ken, while we're down there I suggest you make a plan as to what you're going to do with the body when we bring it back.'

Romira said, 'It'll have to be a police affair, whatever.'

The two men turned, strode across to the Jetranger and swung themselves aboard. Lance indicated the rear of the machine, the thin wire cable of the horse-collar, a long coil of nylon rope and a blanket.

'Better get the collar on before we take off. I don't want to mark time amongst all that clutter of pipes down there longer than I have to.'

'You think you can get close enough?' Gareth held the grapnel attached to a short length of rope. It resembled a fisherman's gaff.

'That's the only means we have of bringing the body close to the machine. But you can't lift it with that hook. It'll tear loose with the weight.'

'How close can you get to the surface of the water?'

'A couple of metres. Flying a chopper over water at zero feet isn't a recommended procedure. I've got to keep my eye on the legs of the platform and all the other projections at once. I won't have time for you. Right?'

Gareth fixed the awkward horse-collar under his arms. 'Got a knife?'

For answer, Lance slipped a long knife from a sheath by the pilot's seat and passed it to Gareth.

'If things go wrong you may have to cut him loose, even if you do hitch him to the skid. We can't airlift a corpse like a dead cowboy over a saddle.'

Lance fired the motor and gave a thumbs-up signal in the direction of the reception area, to which the others had withdrawn.

The machine rose quickly above the helipad and dropped again like a lift towards the water.

Gareth wrenched his eyes away from the spinning rotors, which seemed to be about to remove their tips on the steel latticing of the boom. He slid open his side door. The surface of the lake was being reduced to fine spray by the slipstream. Gripping the inside grab-handle, he lowered himself until he felt the skid under his thick soles. He stood balanced.

Lance yelled above the racket of the rotors: 'That's about as far as I dare go.'

Gareth assessed the distance to the lifeboat and boom. Both seemed within touching-range.

He launched himself.

His first instinct was to hook anything that could be grabbed with the grapnel. What he hadn't bargained for was the marked pendulum-like swing on the short length of cable. He was precipitated bodily towards the corner leg of the platform. As it neared he kicked out both feet and steadied himself against the slippery, weed-and-slime-coated surface.

Lance was magnificent. Instead of holding position, which would have swung Gareth away from the platform, he somehow found an extra metre or two of manoeuvring room and held the Jetranger like a shying horse so close to the steel structure that every bolt, every red-leaded rivet-hole, was visible close-up.

If they had rehearsed together a hundred times, it couldn't have worked better. Gareth took a deep breath, then eased himself down the outward-stretching steel leg with its white-painted depth rings to within half a metre of the surface.

The body, flowered shirt and all, had lodged itself between the main beam of the leg and an ancillary strut on the inside.

Gareth hefted the grapnel on its short rope, aiming for the corpse's belt. The helicopter canted inward towards the danger area of the legs and platform edge. A lifeboat davit leered enticingly at the spinning rotors.

Lance corrected. The manoeuvre was minimal but enough to wrench Gareth free of his precarious foothold. He went clawing and pawing his way towards the water, sliding on the metal's slimy surface.

Lance's judgement remained impeccable. His hands were as sensitive as a showjumper's. A masterful touch brought the skittish machine to heel; Gareth had lost only about a metre of foothold.

In a flash, Gareth saw his opportunity. He aimed, and cast the grapnel at the corpse's belt. He paid it in slightly so that it caught. Then, with a strong pull, he steered the body away from the platform and the rotors moved clear of their proximity to the deadly clutter of projections.

Gareth was down on his knees on the skid, only slightly wider than a man's hand-span, clinging to a supporting strut with one hand and juggling the grapnel rope to the corpse's belt to keep it taut. If it slipped, they would lose their prize.

Lance leaned over in his seat and signalled: he would head round the outside edge of the bird-watching boom, out of sight of the VIP windows, and make for the rear of the flotel, in accordance with Ziegler's wishes.

The dead man's belt served as a fulcrum at the end of the grapnel rope, and Gareth paid out more slack as Lance came clear of the various overhangs and picked up a few metres of altitude.

Now – they had to get that body up to the helipad!

His ongoing plan was formulated in an instant. He needed the rug from the cockpit. Caught in the rotors' slipstream and deafened by the roar of the engine, it was impossible for Gareth to communicate with Lance other than by hand signals.

Gareth gestured to Lance to descend. Using his hands and fingers like a deaf-mute, he tried to convey his plan to the pilot. He carried out a rolling, tieing, fastening mime, then edged to the side of the cockpit, still slackening and tautening the grapnel rope as if playing a gaffed marlin. He leaned through the open door, snatched up the rug, and ducked back to his perch on the skid.

Lance comprehended his meaning once again and eased the machine down.

Gareth kept the grapnel rope taut: almost at water level, he leaned over as far as his arm would reach, did a turn with the rope's end to secure the body, threw the rug over the head and, still working with one hand, made a rough envelope round the head and shoulders. He followed it with a slipknot dropped into position, pulled it tight, effectively pinioning the body at the shoulders. He got a couple more turns round it, so that the arms were fast to its side, and masked the bloated face with an end of rug.

The machine was too high above the water for him to complete the operation. He signalled Lance once again: down, down! Still more!

Zero feet!

The water churned white under the slipstream. The spray half-blinded him.

Now!

All his back muscles cracked as he hefted the corpse's dead weight clear. Using his left hand, he shortened the rope so that it held the body half across the skid, got hold of one loose leg and laid it along the runner. He lashed it fast with the short end of the grapnel rope. Holding the knife between his teeth, he now found some slack from the main rope, and sawed off a short length. He grabbed an inert leg below the knee, doubled it back, roped it across the crutch, and then to the skid.

The job was done.

Gareth crawled back into the cockpit.

'Okay?' shouted Lance above the roar of the engine.

'Okay as he is for a short while. Out of here – fast!'

The machine lifted rapidly, hovered above the helipad. The body now hung half-on, half-off, the skid. But the ropes were slipping.

'Check, will you, Gareth – I don't want to put the chopper down on top of the body.'

'It'll pass.'

Lance put the machine down.

As the engine cut, Ken Ziegler came at the double from reception. Gareth caught a glimpse of Pernelle and Romira standing uncertainly in front of the desk.

The rotors were still swinging their last revolutions as Gareth and Lance jumped out of the cockpit.

Gareth pulled back the wet, shroud-like cover. The face was purple and the eyes wide, terror engraved in their stare. The last screams of the open mouth had been stifled by water.

'Know him?' asked Gareth.

'He arrived yesterday,' said Ken Ziegler. 'His name is Nadim Samsonov.'

Samsonov!

This was the envoy who had been assigned to rendezvous with him. But not at Bangazi. Half the continent of Africa away.

That open mouth would never confide its secrets to Gareth now.

4

At least the body was unmarked, thought Pernelle. Yet it had been the sight of the drowned man which had ricocheted her mind back to that traumatic day fifteen years ago when her world had come to an end on a remote white beach under a cloudless blue sky, with nothing to show that the devil was loose underwater . . .

She stared unseeingly through the micron-thin white marquisette shrouding the big square window which faced eastward across the lake towards the far sea. To mask its original functionalism, the steel frame had been side-draped with cascades of pink net down to the carpeted metal floor. This was the Coelacanth Suite, in Ken Ziegler's book the cherry on the top of Bangazi Lodge's accommodation, converted at a cost of many millions from the utilitarian living quarters previously occupied by the military personnel who had manned the missile platform.

Ziegler himself had conducted her there from the reception area. Samsonov's body had been discreetly tucked away out of sight under Romira's reception counter, after Gareth and Lance had carried it from the helipad deck. Ken's gesture towards Pernelle was in itself the measure of the importance he attached to her. On their way along the previously stark corridor, now softened by the skill of interior decorators, they had passed other VIP suites with tourist-luring names – Leatherback and Loggerhead, after the unique great turtles which trundled up and down the beach beyond the line of coastal forest dividing the sea from the lake.

During her last stay at Bangazi she had been accommodated further down the corridor in the Angelfish Suite, suitably decorated with denizens of the coral reef. There, at least, thought Pernelle, she had been spared the present cascades of pink net, embossed with scarlet, prancing seahorses which drifted down to the wall-to-wall carpeting – if you'd had a gun, you could have picked them off for target practice. Ken had remarked, when putting down her kit-bag wrapped in its odd covering of nylon mesh, that the decor had been Romira's idea; the box-like steel of the window had, in Romira's view, been softened by a lambrequin of watermelon satin. The overall effect was like a whore draped in a Pierre Cardin creation.

How much, she wondered now that she could collect her scattered thoughts in isolation, had the whole business of Samsonov rocked Gareth? Only now could she marvel fully at his nerve-stretching, death-defying rescue of the body from the water. Delayed reaction made her knees feel weak. There had been no time to say anything about it to Gareth, no time even to arrange another meeting, before Ken Ziegler had solicitously bustled her away from the helipad. Would Gareth contact her? She eyed the internal telephone by the bedside.

The air conditioning ululated softly like a Zulu dancer. The recent sight of Samsonov's body forced itself to the front of her mind; she wandered aimlessly round the suite, idly inspecting a shelf, its original steel carefully hidden by grained mock-timber, which seemed to boast everything from a Bible to Professor J.B.L. Smith's classic on South African fishes.

Samsonov's body had precipitated the trauma of that other drowned man. She thought the pain had died, it had all been so long ago . . .

'. . . I was fourteen at the time,' she told Gareth, when he had indeed come to the Coelacanth Suite as her intuition had told her he would. 'The dream ended, there on the beach. The golden years were dead.'

Her voice was shot with tension. For the first time since the tragedy, she had not repressed her feelings of grief and, for once, she had not wanted to be alone. She had almost willed him to come, so that she could tell him, a stranger. She had hardly paused to analyse the fact that a few hours before Gareth Ridpath had been unknown to her.

Now he was here. There had been a kind of quizzical, unspoken question in the tight lines of his jaw and cheekbones as he had thrown a laser-quick glance past her into the garish suite.

She said tightly, without preliminary, 'It isn't the first time I've seen a drowned man.'

'You said, it was fifteen years ago,' he responded. 'Fifteen years is a long time. It must have been quite something not to have healed in that period. You also said, the dream ended. The golden years were dead. Yet you must have been only a schoolgirl.'

'I wasn't a schoolgirl,' she replied offhandedly. 'I never went to school, until after that day when he was drowned. That was the dream – a strange, wonderful, beachcombing sort of life, living in a caravan on remote beaches at the site of wrecks. Golden years, I said. I mean just that.'

'You've given me the ending first,' he chided her quietly. 'It would help if I came in at the beginning. I don't know who "he" was. I don't know what your job is.'

Her lovely eyes were veiled now, shut to the world. She gave a self-deprecatory laugh. 'Sorry, I somehow half expected you to know. Maybe it'll help you to understand. I am a marine archaeologist.'

'That's a pretty unusual occupation, especially for a woman.'

She replied abstractedly, 'Cape Town University. Attached to the Cultural History Museum and the National Monuments Council.'

'The body on the beach,' he prompted.

'It's part of my present scenario,' she answered. 'If it hadn't been for him, I wouldn't be what I am.'

He said, 'I hadn't heard that Bangazi Lodge advertised any wrecks amongst its tourist attractions.'

'It could.'

'That's pretty cryptic.'

She went across to the wide, draped window and looked out across the lake to the line of dunes and the ocean in the far distance.

'My father, Sean Clymer, was crazy about exploring underwater wrecks,' she went on. 'That was in the 1970s, when very little was known about the precise locality of many of the thousands of wrecks round the South African coast. Remember that then diving techniques were in their infancy. It was this passion for undersea exploration that cost him his life.'

She stared unseeingly past Romira's drapes. The heavy steel framework of the flotel seemed to relay along its endless bolts and plates the faraway sounds of the life of the Lodge, the throb of diesel generators, the air conditioning, the muted sound of human activity in the levels below.

'That doesn't make it your dream.'

'It was, it was!' she exclaimed. 'We used to take the caravan and set up camp at the site of wrecks on isolated beaches, wrecks and sites which we had researched first in old newspapers, books and maps in archives and museums. I used to help him; that was part of the dream. It might take days, weeks, sometimes months. Then off we'd go to pinpoint the wreck offshore on some remote reef or part of the coast, and set up camp. It could have been anywhere on the Atlantic coast in the west to the Indian Ocean in the east.

'To set off and discover an unlocated wreck had a compelling fascination of its own – all the anticipation, all the thrill of setting up camp at the site, the wild stimulation of that first dive — would you or wouldn't you strike it lucky?

'I can see my father still, running up the beach dripping wet, shouting and laughing, with his collecting bag in his hands, which might have contained anything from golden pieces-of-eight to eighteenth-century Mexican silver pillar dollars, from silver buckles to golden teaspoons, from porthole rings to flintlock pistols.

'The fun of it never lessened for me. Sitting on the beach in the sun, spreading out the loot on a cloth, words of excitement cascading out of my father, while we sifted and sorted what he had brought up from under the waves. He was a child at heart, and remained that way until the end — exploring wrecks was fun, it was laughter, it was life.

'I hardly ever went to school until I was a teenager, but by then the golden years were dead. My father taught me history as he found it underwater — at ten I was familiar with all the great voyages of exploration round the Cape. I could quote chapter and verse — ships, admirals, captains, explorers' names. I was particularly intrigued by the account of the Phoenicians circumnavigating the Cape and by some rare maps my father had located drawn by Chinese 150 years before Bartholomeu Dias. When finally I went to school and I trotted out obscure knowledge like this, I was told by my teachers not to be precocious.'

'I could almost feel sorry for them,' said Gareth dryly.

Pernelle rode his comment. 'Even as a teenager, my knowledge of subjects like history, geography, climate or anything relating to ships or salvage far outdid that of most above-average university graduates. However, when it came to run-of-the-mill subjects like maths and languages, I was abysmally ignorant — nor had I any wish to learn.'

'It must have been a kind of out-of-balance relationship having no mother,' Gareth observed.

Pernelle gave a brief laugh. 'Oh, I had — have — a

mother all right. Neither my father nor I took any notice of my mother's pleas to lead a "normal" life, which to her meant a comfortable pad in suburbia. What started really as isolated salvage expeditions gradually hardened into a way of life. She came along on a few of the early ones and then point-blank refused. She hated it. Father promised her that one day when he struck it lucky with the treasure trove he always believed he would find, he would buy her the home she craved and give her the kind of life she wanted.

'Our beach-boy life by contrast was fun, it was exciting, it had its own rewards, apart from the occasional haul of coins and artefacts which my father sold to museums which were only too willing to snap them up – those were the days before the official clamp-down on such sales.

'It was obviously impossible for my father to dive without an expert to help with the handling of the boat, the diving gear, the air lines and so on. Father had a partner for some of the time on his dives, a Hollander named Gil Witte. Gil was a splendid amateur diver as well as an artist. He lived at Hout Bay – do you know the Cape?'

Gareth nodded, and she went on, 'He had his own cottage on a cliffside overlooking that wonderful bay; he had learned his diving in the bay itself. He was first-class. Gil was a gay. He and my father understood one another. I suppose you could say they were very close. Their friendship – it was no more than that – put a further strain on the relationship between him and my mother. In the period before my father's death, tension became very severe. I wonder sometimes whether his death didn't come as a release for her because in less than a year she had married a wealthy Johannesburg executive and had the kind of social life she had always yearned for. For me, her way of life was utter misery. I mourned my father not only for himself but for the life that I loved. To me, it remains utterly precious.

'I was put firmly into a "proper" school in Johannesburg after his death. I became an anti-social introvert, detesting my schoolmates and longing for those unforgettable days and starlit nights on the beach in our old battered caravan.'

She paused, and Gareth asked quietly, 'You haven't said yet what caused your father to drown. When. Or where.'

'I told you, I was fourteen at the time, that's fifteen years ago – 1977,' she replied. Her head gave a slight tremor of anguish. 'It was at a place called Arniston, which isn't very far from Cape Agulhas, the southern extremity of South Africa – of the African continent itself, for that matter. It was named after a British transport named the *Arniston* which was wrecked in a storm there about the time of the Battle of Waterloo in 1815 with the loss of some 370 people on their way home from the East.

'Up to the time my father started to explore the wreck, the *Arniston* hadn't been investigated or explored to any extent, although it has been thoroughly covered since.

'It was a clear, calm, lovely day and I was sitting on the deserted beach waiting for him to come back from his dive. There was nothing on the surface to show that the devil was loose underwater. But it was. The inquest found that Father had apparently been knocked unconscious underwater by a massive rogue groundswell which came out of the blue, as it sometimes does on that coast.

'The first I knew was a big wave out of the calm sea which tossed his body up on the beach almost at my feet. When I said Samsonov's body was not the first drowned man I had seen, I meant it. There he lay, drowned, dead, mutilated.' Her voice died as she made a helpless gesture.

Gareth asked, 'You've said you are a marine archaeologist – isn't that connected with salvage also?'

His eyes were intent on her. She liked the way this warm stranger was walking into her world, and she found herself telling him things which had remained locked away inside her for all her adult life.

'Everything to do with wrecks.' Her smile broke momentarily through her introspection. 'You see, when the bit and bridle of suburbia was clamped on me, I became a social introvert as I said, longing for my other way of life. Although I detested routine school subjects, I took a long shrewd look at my future and made up my mind that if I wished again to enjoy a taste of what I had had with my father, I needed a university degree in the field which would give it to me – marine archaeology. The only university which offered such a course was Cape Town.

'I found out all about it from Gil. Our communications were secret; my mother disliked Gil for being a gay and having such an influence over my father's life.

'My choice of career – when it became known – aroused the most bitter opposition from my mother, who refused to allow it. But I had pre-empted her objections by winning several scholarships and bursaries. The effort of applying myself to subjects which I loathed in order to get the money was almost too much for me.

'I simply announced to my mother that I was going – and I went. I stayed with Gil at Hout Bay in his lovely little cottage among the oaks and mountains overlooking the sea. Being with Gil was like having something of my father back again, but I soon realized that Gil was a sick man. I didn't know he had incurable cancer.

'One Sunday, Gil told me he was going diving off Bloubergstrand, a well-known area not far north of Cape Town within sight of Robben Island, where there are a score of unexplored wrecks even now. There was something off-beat about him that morning which should have warned me. Blouberg is a place noted for its treacherous groundswells, which race in from a dead calm sea. He pooh-poohed my reservations about the area and turned down my suggestion that I should go along and keep a weather eye open from the boat – he used to hitch it to a trailer behind his four-wheel-drive truck.

'With hindsight, I realized that his instincts told him what could happen, and he wanted it to happen.

'It did.

'The inquest found that his body had been severely mauled by a savage groundswell, not unlike the one which had accounted for my father, and that Gil had been knocked unconscious before he had drowned.

'I knew he had chosen his favourite pastime as a means of suicide.

'Generous always, Gil bequeathed me his cottage at Hout Bay, where I now live.'

Gareth wished he could see her face as she stood staring, oblivious to the idyllic lake below.

He said levelly, 'I've never heard of marine archaeology as a career for women.'

'It isn't,' she replied without turning. 'I'm the only one I know of.'

He tried to lighten the intensity of her conversation.

'So now you're back among the pieces-of-eight, the doubloons, the pillar dollars and all those other magical piratical-sounding things?'

She turned now and came nearer to him: her words sounded like a sleepwalker's returning to reality.

'As I got deeper into my marine studies, the old thrill of the chase for those sort of things began to dim in favour of a new concept which began to take place in my mind. Cannons, portholes, spoons, and other intriguing artefacts are the bones of a wreck, but what of its spirit – the people? The people who went down with it, the people who survived? What sort of social strata did they come from, what was their place in the historical setting of the age in which their ship went down, their lives, hopes, fears? Still more fascinating, what *happened* to them after they survived a shipwreck? How did they *feel* about such a traumatic event, where did they go, where did they settle, are any of their descendants still living? This approach brought a whole new concept into my researches.'

'I didn't know there were any wrecks in Lake Bangazi, Pernelle.'

The tight, vulnerable lines along her cheekbones eased at his gentle mockery.

'There aren't,' she responded. 'And the offshore wreck that there is isn't mine. It's Ken Ziegler's – I'd never heard of it until he brought it to my attention earlier this year in Cape Town. You'd have thought from the magnitude of the tragedy that it would have been widely known – almost as many people were lost in it as in the famous liner *Lusitania* in World War I, and in the *Athenia* in World War II.'

'What does Ken Ziegler want with a wreck? He's a hotelier.'

'That's just it, he wants to make it an offshore scuba-diving attraction for his guests. If he can locate it, that is. That's the reason why he's brought me here all the way from Cape Town.'

'Surely its position must be known if it was such a tragedy!'

She took a stride towards her kit-bag enveloped in the nylon mesh and stirred it with her toe as if she were involuntarily trying to will it to tell her something.

'Fifty years ago, on a clear early summer's night, you could have witnessed close out to sea off Bangazi one of the most brutal and vicious U-boat attacks of the Second World War,' she said slowly. 'You would have seen a holocaust of fire and blood as 750 men, women and children either drowned or burned to death in a sea of flaming oil after the U-boat loosed three torpedoes into a civilian transport. For weeks afterwards hundreds of bodies, many half-eaten by sharks, were washed up on the beaches of Zululand and Natal, even further south than Durban, which is over 300 kilometres away. It was the biggest loss of life in South African waters during the war.'

Gareth stood silent as she outlined the brutality of the sinking.

'The ship's name was the *Nova Scotia*. She was bound for Durban from East Africa. The passengers were mainly civilian internees, men, women and children, plus a troop of South African soldiers homeward bound from the Middle East war theatre.

'I don't understand why Ken Ziegler is so fixated on the ship. There is very little detailed documentation on the sinking available in South Africa, only facts in a broad general way, and I want more than that.

'Another thing is the wreck's exact position. She went down, we know, about four sea miles off the coast, but as yet it remains unpinpointed. It's another of the mysteries surrounding the *Nova Scotia* which brings me to Bangazi.'

5

'That's the second saga of death Bangazi has presented me with this morning.'

Gareth was tight-lipped. He had pushed Samsonov on to the back burner of his mind while he had listened to Pernelle; now the immediate tragedy rose to the surface again.

'First, one individual, Samsonov, and now human slaughter on the grand scale in the *Nova Scotia*,' he remarked.

'It was a long time ago,' said Pernelle. 'Though the screams of those unfortunates choking to death in burning oil must still seem to reverberate across the sea and among the trees.'

Gareth made a wide gesture at the scene. 'It all seems so unlikely – like blood splashed across a tourist poster.'

'Don't be deceived by the soft lying face of Bangazi, Gareth. I wasn't aware of the *Nova Scotia* when it first came to my attention, but I did know of another hideous tragedy north of Bangazi on the beach. Death again. She choked to death in the sand.'

'She?'

'It happened far longer ago than the *Nova Scotia*,' answered Pernelle. 'Over four centuries ago, to be exact, but the horror of it is every bit as bad as the torpedoing. There was a group of survivors from a Portuguese ship which had been wrecked further south on the coastline. Among them was the captain's wife, young and exceptionally beautiful, with her children.

'The blacks tried to strip her, but she defended herself and said she would rather be killed before appearing naked in front of them. There is no doubt that the Africans would have murdered her there and then had not her husband begged her to let herself be stripped, saying that all humans were born naked and since this was the will of God, she should submit.

'Her children formed a circle round her and she stripped, but she covered herself with her waist-length hair and made a pit in the sand in which she buried herself. She never rose from it alive. Her husband and children joined her suicide pact, and died in the sand about her.'

Her eyes were refined almost to translucence in reliving the horror. She said quietly, 'So, when I say, don't be deceived by Bangazi, I mean it.'

'I haven't got it straight in my mind what your job involves beyond being a marine archaeologist operating out of Cape Town.'

'Not out of, in.' She smiled. 'I don't usually flip all over the place enjoying myself diving to exciting wreck discoveries, much as I would like to. That would be something like a return to the good old days with my father. I have to concentrate on much sterner stuff than that.'

'Such as?'

'I'm afraid I'll have to burden you with more personal biography to answer that,' she answered diffidently. 'You see, in order to make sure of getting what I wanted by the time I left university, I threw myself so whole-heartedly into my studies that I came to the attention of my professor. He liked my work so much that even before I graduated he offered me a job in his department. I also had something no other student had, and that was all my deep practical knowledge of wrecks. My job at the university was a foregone conclusion, but because I had a wide working knowledge of the laws governing the salvaging of wrecks, I pretty soon found myself vetting applications made to the National Monuments Council . . .'

'Where does the National Monuments Council come in?'

'The system works this way. Before my time, anyone wanting to explore or salvage a wreck had only to obtain a permit from Customs and he could remove anything he wanted, subject only to having to pay a small percentage of its value to the state.

'Now matters are different. The same salvage permit as before is still required, but in addition an excavation permit from the National Monuments Council is needed, if a wreck is more than half a century old. The person who applies must also be affiliated to a recognized museum – at present only thirty-five permits entitling salvors to work on wrecks round the coast have been granted, and of those twenty are in conjunction with the Cultural History Museum in Cape Town, with which I also work very closely.

'We also have to have assurances that the would-be salvor is trustworthy and well-meaning. This is a very important condition. If the National Monuments Council sees fit to grant permission, it is subject to a number of lesser conditions I won't bore you with, such as the affiliated museum getting a share of the value of the salvage, and so on.

'But, before we will even consider a permit, we have to have information from the salvor about the exact situation of his wreck, background of its identity, and how and when the ship was lost.'

'I like the way you say "we",' remarked Gareth. 'It seems you're a king-pin in the whole set-up.'

'I hadn't thought of myself as such,' replied Pernelle. 'But I suppose you could call me that. This is how I came to be involved in Ken Ziegler's wreck. He thought that all that had to be done about scuba-diving to the *Nova Scotia* was to obtain a Customs permit and he could go ahead. When his application first came to us – it must have been as long ago as nine months now – it was so scrappy and lacked so much of the kind of

52

detail we required that we simply threw it out then and there without further ado.

'It upset him very much at the time. He flew to Cape Town and was directed to see me. That's how I became involved. He finally persuaded me to come here to Bangazi, and I went out to sea with him, but he couldn't even pinpoint the *Nova Scotia* wreck site. As I told you, I hadn't heard of the ship before, and the magnitude of the tragedy made me interested.'

'Surely with all that loss of life involved, warships and aircraft must have been sent to the scene of the sinking next day . . .'

'Oh, the general area where she went down was well known, it was about four or five sea miles off the coast. But a general fix is something quite different from a pinpoint of an exact spot. And if you want to dive to a wreck, you have to know where it is – precisely.'

'I still can't understand it,' repeated Gareth. 'Search craft must have been sent out from Richards Bay.'

She shook her head. 'You've forgotten the date, Gareth – 1942. There was no such thing then as the port of Richards Bay. The nearest naval base was Durban, although they did fly some long-range flying-boat patrols from a mangrove-lined lagoon which was to become the heart of the present-day Richards Bay. In fact, you won't find such a place as Richards Bay listed in publications such as the Admiralty Pilot even in the early 1950s.'

'It doesn't seem possible!' exclaimed Gareth. 'Richards Bay is where I'm based – a huge modern coal port!'

'Lack of information is something which is bedevilling Ken Ziegler's application still, and he's getting very worried about it. It took more than twenty-four hours before the first warships got to the area where the *Nova Scotia* sank.'

'Again, I can hardly credit it!' said Gareth. 'Surely the *Nova Scotia* had radio and got off a Mayday signal!'

'Those U-boat captains were professionals,' answered Pernelle. 'The skipper who sank the *Nova Scotia* went for the jugular and put his first torpedo into her side exactly under the radio cabin. It was blown to bits before another two reduced her to a flaming wreck. There was no question of an SOS, as they called a Mayday in those days.

'The first anyone knew of the tragedy was when the *Nova Scotia* didn't turn up in Durban late next day and an emergency signal was received from the neutral Portuguese saying they had been tipped off about a dreadful sinking and they sent a sloop to the scene.'

'So they had the ship's position,' interjected Gareth.

'No more than that there was a huge oil slick, wreckage and bodies about four or five miles offshore. The landmarks they had to go by were three hills – look!' She pointed. 'There's the southernmost of them opposite Bangazi, and the other two are out of sight another two miles to our left. That's enough for a general fix for wreckage and bodies – which were being dispersed all the time by winds and currents – but not when the hulk itself is what you're looking for . . .'

'Seems you've done a lot of Ken Ziegler's homework for him,' observed Gareth. 'What did he have to say about the *Nova Scotia*'s position when he first applied?'

She laughed. 'He didn't. His application merely said, "the *Nova Scotia*, sunk by a U-boat off the coast of Maputaland". It really was a most amateurish effort.'

'Then why does he keep at it? Why bring you into it again – after all, you were the judge who rejected it.'

'As I said, he came specially to Cape Town to see me. I don't normally give interviews to unsuccessful applicants – in fact, there's hardly any need, because they know in advance what is required in the way of facts and figures. Unlike Ken Ziegler. It was only because he told me something about a tragedy which somehow seems to have got lost in the past that I became interested. It was then that I gave him some tips about how he should apply.'

Gareth nodded in the direction of her mesh-bound kit-bag.

'Is that part of the guidelines?'

She laughed. 'I've noticed your eyes straying every so often to my kit. Yes, it is. It's a model of a grid system which is laid out over the site of a wreck, both for the benefit of the divers themselves and for the museum involved. It is of major value to a museum in evaluating artefacts and pinpointing whereabouts they came from underwater.'

'And those odd bits of numbered plastic?'

Pernelle went to the case and untied the mesh. She laid it out on the mushroom-coloured carpet.

'This is not the real thing. It's just a scale model to illustrate the idea. A full-scale grid is made from nylon rope, big enough to cover the whole site of a wreck. It's spread out on the surface of the sea. As a find is made underwater, it's logged by the support boat in a special book according to the check number in the square. Eventually the whole wreck site can be reconstructed from the grid pattern. I brought this along to demonstrate to Ken, but as far as he's concerned it's jumping the gun – he doesn't yet know where to look for the *Nova Scotia*.

'I'm also at a loss to understand his insistence that his pampered guests must dive to the *Nova Scotia*. Why? There are other wrecks hereabouts, although not as close to the shore as the *Nova Scotia* and in deeper water.'

'Perhaps he's counting on providing his jaded business-men with the sight of a real torpedoed ship.'

'Then it's another example of his naivety about the whole diving business,' she replied. 'No way is he going to find a sunken hull sitting upright on the bottom with three neat torpedo holes in her side.'

'But that's what you said, isn't it? That the U-boat put three torpedoes into her?'

'Yes and no,' she answered. 'If the *Nova Scotia* is lying three or four miles offshore – say, about seven kilometres – then she's in pretty shallow water, according to the charts. There are several splendid coral shoals lying in successive ranges out to sea, and the wreck could be resting on one of them. They're not well charted.'

'That still doesn't answer my question.'

'What I'm saying is that where you get such shallow water, a wreck takes a tremendous pounding – a southwesterly gale in these waters is enough to throw whole sections of it around underwater. The rocks of the shoals also help to break it up. The net result is that after half a century, I'd say all that's visible of the *Nova Scotia* underwater would be some of the solid bits of metal such as the engine block, the propeller, some boilers and other heavy gear. In shallow waters like here, oxidation's also very quick and ordinary objects become quite unrecognizable. Of course, copper and brass fittings are not affected. I'd say that the hull was smashed into chunks and scattered about all over the sea bed.'

'Was the *Nova Scotia* carrying any valuables? Is that why he's so keen?'

'Not that I know of, but then, as I've told you, there's a great lack of information about the ship, which I'm busy now trying to sort out.'

'For Ken Ziegler?'

'No, for myself. It's a puzzle which teases me, and I want to know more.'

'Will you dive to the wreck, if it's located?'

'Yes, providing the water is not much deeper than ten metres.'

'Why ten metres?'

'That's the safe limit for scuba-diving. Below that depth, to an ever greater extent, the deeper they go, divers are liable to the bends.'

'What's that?'

Her reply was shadowed, remembering her father's death.

'Nitrogen narcosis. It's the gas from a diver's breathing accumulating in his bloodstream and then, if he ascends too rapidly, the gas forms bubbles which can lodge anywhere in his body and cause a blockage. In varying degrees, the outcome can be like a stroke or a heart attack, and can be equally fatal.'

'The *Nova Scotia* seems a pretty poor tourist bet, all things considered.'

'Ken Ziegler knows all about it, but it hasn't stopped him going ahead – he's got a luxury privately owned fishing and diving charter craft called the *Sea Urchin* anchored over Gold Reef right now . . .'

'Gold Reef?'

She shrugged and laughed. 'That's it – Gold Reef. He's a master at hatching up tourist-luring names. Gold Reef satisfies both his Johannesburg moguls and the description of the wonderful corals and fishes. The more they pay, the more they can boast that it costs 500 dollars a day to laze on the *Sea Urchin*'s deck. I happen to know that Ken Ziegler pays 9,000 dollars a day to hire the ship.'

'How often does she come – I presume she's not out there at anchor all the time?'

'For a week at a time. She's there right now. She's been over the reef several times during the past six months, ever since he started his *Nova Scotia* applications in earnest.'

'How does he transport his guests out to the ship? There's no landing-place for boats.'

'Lance in the Jetranger shuttles from Bangazi. There's a helipad on the *Sea Urchin*.'

The intercom rang and Pernelle answered. The infinite

blue of her eyes was upon him and he had already guessed from their expressiveness what the message was before she put down the receiver.

'We are invited to a champagne brunch aboard the *Sea Urchin*,' she told him. 'Bring diving gear. I accepted for us both. Lift-off in half an hour.'

6

'What about Samsonov?' Although Gareth asked the question of Pernelle, he also inwardly asked it of himself. Should he reveal to Pernelle his involvement in something which had begun innocently enough as a challenge to his expertise but now seemed to be exploding into something far more serious? And more dangerous, too – if one saw Samsonov's death not as an accident but a cold-blooded killing. Had the Russian really gone for an out-of-bounds midnight stroll after a few drinks too many and fallen into the lake, or had he . . .?

Gareth got a grip on his cartwheeling thoughts. He was a mining engineer, not a cop or a secret agent, he reminded himself. A mining engineer with a specialized knowledge of diamonds, which was what had led Dr Nikolai Vize of the Russian Academy of Sciences to him all those years ago in the first place; then, more latterly, from his position on the central committee of Glavalmazzoloto, the Department of Diamonds and Precious Metals under the USSR Council of Ministers, as it was before the new revolution. This was the Russian counterpart of De Beers.

It was a pity that he had ever left Namibia and taken a position with an outfit dune-mining titanium along the beaches of Zululand and Maputaland – it was, after all, simply a euphemism for the ecological rape of one of the world's most beautiful environments. Yet, he had seen the red light in time, and was in fact staging via Namibia to rendezvous with Samsonov in Angola before going overseas when he had received the Cryptic message to meet him instead at Bangazi.

Who *was* Samsonov anyway? He had never met him, he was only a name. All he had found was a bloated corpse floating in a lake; death had stopped a mouthful of information which could have been dynamite. To acknowledge any link with the dead man would be sticking his neck out – and Pernelle's also if he mentioned it to her, much as he wanted to reciprocate her trust in him.

'What *about* Samsonov?' she echoed.

He had hardly noticed that she had started to gather together the bits and pieces of the demonstration grid from the floor, and was looking hard across at him, as if waiting for something. Even though she had freely confided in him, and their relationship had bypassed a whole series of conventions, he knew he couldn't tell her – yet.

'I mean, what will Ken Ziegler do with the body? This is a police affair, and he'll have to notify the authorities, instead of organizing a champagne brunch.'

Even to himself he sounded like an off-camera teleprompter saying the right things at the right time. He *would* tell her, when the time was opportune, but meanwhile he didn't have to clam up entirely. It had been a long time since he had talked to a woman about himself. Too long . . .

Her left eyebrow gave an amused quirk as he squatted beside her on the floor.

'Did you know Samsonov?' she asked.

'I never met him.'

That was true enough.

She recalled his daring and perilous retrieval of the body and her glance went automatically to his strong hands. She noticed that his fingers were clenched. Did they reflect the tight intensity in his face? And what message did that heavy gold signet ring on his left small finger convey? Why should it concern her?

'Bangazi doesn't look any more like your scene than mine, Gareth. You haven't told me what brings you here.'

It seemed to her that he relaxed.

'It's a sort of farewell visit,' he said. 'I've been here before, but the first time didn't work out because of the floods. You know, Cyclone Mary-Lou?'

'The media went to town over it.'

'Apparently these cyclones work their way down the Mozambique Channel and once in a while strike inland, and when that happens, there's chaos. The whole country-side from Bangazi to St Lucia to Maputo was swamped. Unfortunately I chose that time to do a little exploring.'

'It's still pretty wild, isn't it?'

'Between here and the Lebombo mountains you can get a potted scenario of Stanley and Livingstone's world, if you want.' He grinned. 'The lot – heat, malaria, swamps, rhinos, crocs, black mambas, gaboon vipers.'

'Did you want?' She seemed vaguely disappointed at his response.

'I didn't. I was looking for a mountain. A legendary mountain of green stones. Which in my book could indicate radioactivity.'

'What *is* your book, Gareth?'

'I'm a mining engineer,' he answered. 'I work – did work – for the mining company which is the villain of the piece in this bitter controversy raging over whether the unspoilt beauty of this coast, and St Lucia in particular, should be sacrificed for commercial ends. Big money versus nature.'

'I signed the "Save St Lucia" petition, along with hundreds of thousands of others.'

'The controversy is one of the reasons why I threw up my job. I'd only been there a few months, but I couldn't stomach the idea of having any hand in St Lucia's death-blow.'

'Good. Good for you.'

He warmed to her approval, and went on, 'Titanium-mining in particular and dune-mining in general isn't my scene. I sometimes wonder why I came here in the first place. You see, diamonds are my sphere.'

'There aren't any diamonds in Zululand.' The sudden soft intensity of her laugh upstaged his seriousness.

'I'm not so sure. My previous job was with the Rössing uranium mine in Namibia, which is the biggest uranium mine in the world. I was there for a couple of years, but uranium and radioactive ores haven't the mystique for me that diamonds have.

'But while I was in Namibia, I latched on to a curious historical fact. The German trader Adolf Luderitz who originally secured what is now the territory of Namibia for Germany, had an intuition about diamonds in Zululand. So much so, that some years before the turn of the last century he sent one of his agents, another German named Einwald, to these parts and bought the lake of St Lucia and 100,000 acres of land surrounding it for fifty pounds' worth of trade goods.'

'Was he serious?'

'He was serious all right. To such an extent that Einwald ceremonially annexed his purchase to Germany, just as Luderitz had done with Namibia. The deal aroused a stink in the diplomatic dovecotes of the Great Powers and provoked some sharp exchanges between Britain and Germany. Finally, after a display of gunboat diplomacy by Britain, Germany withdrew Einwald's claim and the place became British. It keeps teasing me, though, Pernelle. What convinced Luderitz that there were diamonds here? I'd become bored with uranium-mining at Rössing and the Luderitz story triggered my restlessness to get out.'

'Is your mountain of green stones part of the diamond legend?'

Gareth shifted his weight from one knee to the other.

'No, it has its own legend. A gory one. The story goes that somewhere in the wild hot bush country between the Lebombo mountains and the sea there is a Mountain of Green Stones, which could well mean radioactive ores. It ties up with another strange legend about one of Shaka's tribes. They were skilled metal workers and lived some way away to the south.

'They were known as the Lala miners and their metalwork was famous throughout southern Africa. They worked small deposits of gold, silver and copper. From these they crafted some highly original personal jewellery for the Zulu élite. There was one armband with a very striking design, and Shaka hijacked the sole right to confer them on his favourite warriors.

'However, the magnificent armbands carried a fatal penalty – the warriors who wore them developed a vicious and obscure skin complaint which was beyond the skill of even the best Zulu medicine men. These witchdoctors threw the bones and pronounced that the Lala tribe was taking its revenge against Shaka's warriors in retribution for previous butcherings of their own clan.

'Shaka was never one to do things by half. He ordered the whole Lala tribe to be exterminated, every man, woman and child. Their bodies were thrown into mass graves, along with their special jewellery. The place was declared taboo, and lost sight of, except the general area.

'What I would like to know is, did the radioactive ore originate from the Mountain of Green Stones and was it transported to the Lala craftsmen? Did the unfortunates suffer from radioactive burns? The legend gave me another reason to come to Maputaland. What I didn't bargain for was being drawn into the dune-mining controversy.'

'Are you now headed back to Namibia, then?' She quickly completed tying the net and stood up.

'Yes and no,' he replied. 'Not to Rössing, if that's what you mean.'

'Why not?'

He stood up, looking far beyond the tinsel drapes as if trying to recall things he hadn't thought of in years.

'I think I was drawn to Rössing and its radioactive ores in the first place because of my father – he's an expert in the radiological treatment of cancer at the College of Medicine, Saskatchewan, in Canada. I thought it might broaden my professional horizons, but as I said, uranium isn't diamonds for me. However, I did get in some wonderful hikes and rock climbing in the mountains north of Rössing . . .'

She pictured those strong hands which had kept his balance on the helicopter skid doing the same thing on some perilous rock-face in the Namib desert; her glance went automatically to them again. They were still tight with tension.

'. . . My bachelor flat was on the outer edge of the mine's perimeter and at night I used to have fun welcoming the little desert creatures when they came looking for scraps and water – gerbils, geckos, and the occasional sand-viper. I made a friend of a jackal which had been injured – I used to leave the dustbin lid off at night for him – until one of the mine hands shot him for "sport".'

The vibrations from the helipad, as the first batches of brunch-goers prepared to leave in the Jetranger, penetrated the silence which fell between them. There was more to the man, Pernelle knew innately, than the picture he had so far presented of a rudderless bachelor working off superfluous energy by challenging rock-faces in desert mountains, or stomping a path through tropical, malarial swamps in Maputaland.

So she asked, 'If you're not returning to Rössing, Gareth, where are you going in Namibia?'

'Nowhere. Namibia is merely a staging-post on my way to Switzerland.'

'Why Switzerland?'

If he were to tell her anything about himself, it had to include Russia – and diamonds. But there would be no mention of that Siberian spring – the pain of it lingered, even after ten years.

His generous, full-lipped mouth relaxed its strong line to smile briefly.

'What do you know about Glavalmazzoloto?'

Her response was that characteristic sudden, quiet emphatic laugh of hers.

'Nothing. You'll even have to spell it.'

'I always think of it myself as Glaval for short. Under the old Russia, it was the Department for Diamonds and Precious Metals. Now it has been taken over by the new Russian Republic under the worse name Rossalmazzoloto, but in fact it's just the same cat in a different skin. A sort of Russian De Beers, if you like such an analogy.'

'Go on.'

'I'm friendly with the present head of what I still call Glaval – about ten years ago he was a leading member of Glaval's central committee, and I did him a service.'

'In connection with diamonds, I suppose?'

'Yes.' Gareth seemed unwilling to amplify, in spite of her glowing eagerness to hear about his early life.

'You didn't simply pick up your special knowledge of diamonds from textbooks, Gareth.'

He laughed and shrugged. 'Don't get me on my hobby-horse of sea diamonds or else we won't get to that brunch at all. We'll have to hurry,' he sidestepped.

'Are you going to take part in today's dive to try and locate the wreck of the *Nova Scotia*?' she asked

'Is that what the party's all about?'

'Suitably wrapped up in salmon pâté, caviar and champagne,' she replied lightly. 'Yes, that's what it's all about. I'll check my gear quickly.'

She tugged at the drawstring of her kit-bag. It contained a diver's long-john and long-sleeved jacket, boots, hood and gloves and other diving paraphernalia.

'Aren't you going to be rather warm in all that?' he asked.

'Not really – it gets pretty cold once you get down below the surface. Did you notice if there was any wind today?'

'Lance compensated a bit towards the southwest as we made our landing approach.'

'That's okay, then. A southwester clears the water.'

'Why should that be?'

She thrust her diving gear back into its bag. 'It blows clear water from the Agulhas Current towards the land. Diving so close to the coast we don't need an offshore wind – it'll stir up murk.'

He smiled. 'I'm clearly not in your league, Pernelle. I'll bring along a pair of trunks and splash around on the surface near the ship.'

While he went to fetch them, Pernelle thoughtfully pulled the red sweater over her head and slipped off the S-shaped earrings. Gareth's 'keep off the grass' signals were clear for her to read. What had she said to make him clam up? He had confessed his fascination for sea diamonds and then suddenly back-tracked . . .

There was a quick knock at the door. Gareth came in carrying a pair of bathing trunks, a towel and a remarkable piece of headgear.

Pernelle's eyes fixed on it.

'Apologies for this, but it's my favourite sun-hat,' he grinned. 'Specially woven by local Hottentots from the reeds and sedges of Sandwich Harbour near Walvis Bay.'

She took it from him, perched it on the side of her head and pirouetted in front of the mirror. They began to laugh. The phone rang.

A surly, guttural voice at the other end killed the moment.

'Take-off in ten minutes. And don't keep the pilot waiting. He's got a tight schedule.' The assertive voice wasn't Ken Ziegler's.

'Buks – Buks van As.' The introduction spilled as reluctantly as his politeness. Buks sported the manners of a sergeant-major, and a cotton singlet which displayed his powerful shoulders, hairy chest and short stocky build. He wore old ankle-length army boots, no socks, and khaki shorts.

Lance was already waiting at the helicopter door.

Buks hefted a cardboard carton from the reception desk and grunted. 'Chopper's already packed full of these, this one last, says the boss.' There was an implicit sneer in his use of the word, as if he did not acknowledge superior ranking.

'What's in it?' asked Pernelle.

Buks yomped ahead across the helideck and tossed the words back over his shoulder.

'Your brunch, lady. You VIPs call it abalone, but give me the good old Cape word – *perlemoen*. Flown specially here for the VIPs. Iced. Do not touch, keep frozen. The caviar and Pierre Jourdan are already aboard. There's hardly room for your pretty backside amongst all the goodies.'

There wasn't, Gareth established as the Jetranger lifted above the trees, heading east towards the sea. The inside of the machine was packed with insulated cool-boxes and icy cartons breathing steam into the muggy air. Most seats were occupied with the picnic, as were the clear spaces between them.

Buks had balanced the box of abalone like a precarious booby-trap on top of several others on the seat next to him.

Lance gunned the rotors harder than he needed out of anger and frustration.

'My trip after this one will be full of fun,' he jerked out ironically. 'I'll have the pleasure of Buks' company heading for the police station at Richards Bay. Plus a corpse.'

The discrepancy between air uplift over the lake and the narrow land barrier separating it from the sea asserted itself and tossed an air pocket at the aircraft. With its impact both Lance and Pernelle shot up in their seats and their heads almost collided with the roof.

Gareth, who had been unable to strap himself in because of the cartons, was pitched sideways out of his seat on to the metal floor. The insecurely balanced abalone carton crashed down, burst open and scattered him with shellfish, like small rough hand grenades.

One of them smacked into the stay supporting Pernelle's seat and broke open from its securing label within a few centimetres of his face. It held no luscious flesh – the hollow of the shell was polished, dry. What lodged there was small and insignificant, almost like a sliver of mother-of-pearl.

To Gareth's trained eye it was something different.

It was an uncut diamond.

7

Abalone. Abalone. Abalone.

The word thrummed through Gareth's brain in sync with the beat of the rotors overhead as he sprawled face-down, half under Pernelle's seat.

A diamond stashed in an abalone shell!

And an uncut diamond drags a tail behind it of one thing only – a racket.

The ploy was hellishly ingenious. Most diamond tricks are, from a dung-beetle's pat to sewing a strip in a donkey's backside. The ear-shaped shell had been prised open along the line of the breathing-holes, the flesh partly removed and the uncut diamond insinuated. Then the shell had been resealed, using a striking double-purpose blue-and-yellow adhesive label. It bore the drawing of a half-clad dancing girl swathed in mist and the words: 'Dare the taste of exotic male strength and feminine mystery' – emphasizing the popular belief that abalone is an aphrodisiac.

The enormity of the implications left Gareth motionless for a moment, his head amongst the clutter of intact abalone shells, the diamond pinched between his fingers. Broadside after broadside of thought crashed through his mind.

Who was smuggling diamonds? *From whom*, in Maputaland? *To whom*? There were no diamonds in this part of the world. The nearest fields were probably in Lesotho, 1,000 kilometres away! Only a laboratory test could determine the origin of the abalone diamond.

Did diamonds – these diamonds – somehow link up with the unheralded materialization of Samsonov in Zululand when he should have been waiting halfway across Africa in Angola? What had homed him in on Bangazi Lodge? Samsonov was diamonds because Glavalmazzoloto was diamonds, and so was he, Gareth. What that involvement was, he still had to find out. All he had learned from Dr Nikolai Vize, Glaval's spokesman and his mentor, was that Glaval was unhappy about developments in Central Africa; he would be fully briefed on what it was and what was required of him when he reached Switzerland. The plan was that he was to have staged in Angola, where he was scheduled to rendezvous with Samsonov for a preliminary briefing. He knew no more than that. It was an open secret that there was a huge smuggling racket going on out of Angola of its own local diamonds, supplemented by a flourishing pipeline from neighbouring Namibia. During Namibia's pre-independence years of war, and the complementary Unita bush and civil war, this pipeline had netted fortunes for the unscrupulous . . .

'Are you all right?'

Pernelle was anxiously trying to get her safety belt loose in order to find out what was going on under the seat.

The thought banged into Gareth's mind as imperatively as the clattering of abalone shells round his ears – Pernelle must not see the diamond! She was not to be involved. He jammed it back into the loose shell and hastily cobbled it together with the gummed label.

'Okay,' he called back. 'One of the cartons fell and spilled open. I'm trying to put it all back. There are a lot of shells rolling around under your seat.'

'Pass the carton out first and then the shells. I'll fill it here where there's space.'

He mingled the loaded shell with several others and then shoved the carton into the cockpit, creeping forward between the seats as he did so.

'We'd better keep that box safe, from now on,' he said.

Pernelle found herself looking down into his face, and it

seemed to her that his words carried an odd weight – had something fazed him?

Lance came in on the exchange. 'Apologies. My fault. Shows you shouldn't mix prejudice with flying. And flying weather it is, by heavens, corpse-ferrying or not. Look at that!'

He gestured widely.

To the east, the limitless leagues of the Indian Ocean, unsullied by land until Australia was reached; to the north, the dazzling virgin beaches of the shoreline which the early explorers named the Downs of Gold; to the south, the peerless estuaries and languid lagoons of St Lucia.

Lance circled tightly as a preliminary to picking up height, then pointed and exclaimed, 'Look there!'

Three vehicles, two four-wheel-drive pick-ups and a bright red VW Caravelle Syncro, stood on the beach close to the water's edge at a point almost opposite the hill north of Bangazi which indefatigably displayed its nipple-shaped summit to the elements. Five men, blurred to black silhouettes against the stark brilliance of the beach, seemed to be standing on a small rocky promontory which extended out of the breakers and then lost itself, after a narrow strip of burning white, in the interwoven tangle of lush greens which constituted the dune barrier between coast and interior.

Pernelle indicated the rock-shelf. 'There's a deep rocky gully in the sea a couple of kilometres out – I think that's a landward extension of it.'

Lance broke in. 'They've no right to be there! Driving above the high-water mark is banned! This beach is totally off-limits! I'm going to play policeman and take a look-see!'

The machine headed for the group. Two of the men, down on their haunches, seemed to have a long tape measure stretched between them, as if they were busy measuring the size of the rock. The other three regarded the approaching helicopter without concern.

Pernelle said, 'That red truck is from the Natal Parks Board – look at the lettering on the side.'

'Then, whoever they are, they're here with official approval,' said Lance.

'Perhaps something to do with the turtles,' suggested Gareth.

'You don't need a tape measure that length for a turtle,' Pernelle pointed out.

'Whatever they're up to, visitors are a novelty here – we don't get many because of the restrictions,' said Lance.

He put the machine's nose down and hovered over the group, who raised their hands and waved.

Pernelle waved back.

'Strange,' remarked Lance, and headed out to sea.

'Wonderful diving weather,' said Pernelle. 'You can almost see the bottom. Sand. Ideal for Ken Ziegler to locate the *Nova Scotia* – if he had a precise idea where to look.'

'What makes you say that?' asked Gareth.

She swivelled in her seat to talk directly to him. Her eyes were as impalpable as the shifting colours in the sea below.

'If the ship went down in a gully such as that one close to the shore, the rocky formation would break up the ship as it moved around with the wave action, a sort of grinding, tearing action. On the other hand, sand is an excellent preserving medium because it's swirled around by the underwater waves and banks up all over a wreck. It has another big plus, too: it shuts off oxygen from a hulk . . .'

'What's oxygen got to do with it?' asked Gareth. 'The ship's dead, and so are its occupants.'

'You'd be amazed how much life – chemical and marine – goes on round a wreck, almost from the first hours,' she replied. 'Oxygen helps break down the metal, especially when it's ripped raw, like a torpedo hole. Over half a century, if the *Nova Scotia* went down on sand, I'd say she'd be practically invisible by now. That's why I'm so insistent about knowing her exact position.'

'So you think this sort of searching is futile?'

'I didn't say futile, but it's a wild shot in the dark, every bit the needle in the haystack. Ken Ziegler may be lucky. But it's all highly problematical and unscientific. I've suggested a proton magnetometer survey before any diving as such begins, but Ken won't have it. He seems in a hurry. Keeps talking about the fiftieth anniversary of the sinking of the ship.'

'When is that?'

'November twenty-eighth. The *Nova Scotia* was torpedoed on the night of twenty-eighth November, 1942.'

'I expect your proton magnetometer is a pretty pricey piece of equipment, Pernelle?'

Lance broke in ironically, 'I'd put money on it that it costs less than today's champagne-and-caviar lunch.'

Pernelle laughed softly. 'It's not the most expensive, if that's what you mean. A side-scan sonar could be invaluable, and if Ken really wanted to go to town he could invest in a sub-bottom profiler. Highly expensive, highly sophisticated, specialists required to operate it – but very effective. In the supermarket category, though, there's a hand-held metal detector, which we've found quite efficient. The proton magnetometer can be towed behind a support boat, and will record any sort of metal object like chunks of a ship's hull, anchors, engines and so on.'

'But you said that if the *Nova Scotia* had gone down on sand, she'd be well buried by now.'

'True. But the beauty of a proton magnetometer is that it will detect metal through a thick accumulation of sand or mud. I thought I'd sold him the idea – until Buks put in his oar.'

'Buks? What say has he?'

Lance interrupted. 'You'd be surprised. He seems nothing more than a general factotum but in fact he's the power behind the throne at Bangazi. Ken leans on him pretty heavily. Why, I don't know. Can't stand him, myself.'

'What's his background?' asked Gareth. His mind kicked back to the truculent air of the thickset, singlet-clad lout.

'Did you see his boots?' Lance asked obliquely.

'Yes. Ex-army issue, I'd say.'

'You say right,' rejoined Lance. 'Buks was one of the squad who previously manned the platform when it was a missile-firing and -detecting facility. A warrant officer – sergeant, I think. That's where he gets his love of ordering people around. But I gather he was a technician in charge of operating the complicated buoyancy compensation system which corrects slight movements the platform makes on the surface of the lake . . .'

'But there are no waves on Bangazi lake!' exclaimed Pernelle.

'Apparently, when a missile was about to be fired, there had to be a completely steady platform – even movement of a millimetre or two could throw a sophisticated missile-guidance system off course, and off target. The control room and buoyancy tanks are still operative as a stabilizer for the flotel.'

'What's all this to do with a proton magnetometer?' asked Pernelle.

'Buks is an arrogant little bastard and sets himself up as god on anything to do with water,' replied Lance. 'I say it grudgingly, but he must have been good to have held down the job he did with the army. But he didn't like the sound of the magnetometer – he probably didn't understand how it worked – so he scotched the idea with Ken. And that was that. The thought of having to spend the rest of today flying with that little so-and-so, and a drowned man to boot, doesn't appeal.'

'Why not simply report the death some other way – I know the radio-phone doesn't work at weekends . . .'

'How?' challenged Lance. 'No, I'll just have to spring a surprise on the police . . . By all that's holy, I have it! Do you know the Richards Bay police station?' he asked Gareth.

'I can't say I know it – I've passed by.'

'It's got a nice big lawn in front. I'll put the chopper down there, walk over nonchalantly to the Joe on duty and say, "See here, chum, I've got a deader on board. Come and take it away." That'll make them piss themselves.'

It seemed a shabby epitaph for Samsonov. But he had been trusted by Dr Nikolai Vize, and Gareth felt suddenly that a dark mist had obscured the lovely morning. Diamonds. Samsonov had been on a diamond trail, and had found out something vital enough to search him out . . . Gareth jerked upright. There was a diamond right here at his own shoulder, secreted with hellish ingenuity into an abalone shell . . .

'. . . and talking of getting pissed, that's exactly what Buks will do once we're at Richards Bay. He's always sounding off that it was his favourite stamping-ground when he was stationed with the army on the missile platform. The technicians were rotated on the basis of a fortnight's stint at a time. On the platform, no liquor, no women, only hard work. No runs ashore – if anyone were crazy enough to want a run ashore in the swamps and bush. The army couldn't manage to build access roads anywhere near. Even using helicopters was cheaper – as Ken himself has found out. In fact, that's how they built the missile platform in the first place, I'm told. They ferried it all in by Super Frelons as a prefab job and assembled the bits and pieces like a giant bit of Meccano.'

'They must have had *some* land to work on,' Pernelle pointed out.

'If you take a close look at the side of Bangazi Lodge

facing away from the sea, you'll see an area of forest which was cleared. There was a patch of hard land there, but the bush and trees have all come back. Things grow like rockets in this climate. That's how the army did it. Buks told me. He was at Bangazi right from the start.'

'And he chose to stay on, even after the army pulled out?' asked Pernelle.

'Yes, Maputaland has a special facination for him. So he says, at any rate, when he's drunk. The local liquor, the *busulu*, is out of this world, the whores are out of this world, everything in Maputaland is out of this world.'

Pernelle had been sitting with one leg tucked under her so that she faced Gareth. His eyes wandered for a moment past her, beyond the instrument panel and windscreen. The wayward mist was still working magic on the sea ahead.

It parted a little.

He couldn't believe what he saw.

'Look!' he exclaimed. 'It can't be!'

The outline of the Chinese junk was blurred enough by the haze to make him doubt the evidence of his eyes: he was seeing a dragon with open mouth, bristling mane and lashing demon's tail. Between the two, on a raised platform, were the pagoda-like towers of two miniature tea-houses, separated by what looked like an advertising billboard, surmounted by two smaller dragons. They reared into the air above four red, yellow, purple and crimson squares like giant heraldic emblems.

Pernelle was as transfixed by the spectacle as Gareth.

'It's – it's a junk!' she exclaimed incredulously.

'It isn't,' grinned Lance. 'It's a Chinese chop-house.'

'A Chinese chop-house – afloat off the Maputaland coast! Can you beat it!' exclaimed Gareth.

'It's what the abalone in the cartons is all about,' explained Lance. 'Distinguished Chinese visitors, with whom you will no doubt share your repast. Wealthy gentlemen, of status back home, from the trawlers out of sight over the horizon. And I should know – one of this dog's-body's jobs was to ferry 'em in for the party from a factory ship!'

'But the chop-house!' repeated Pernelle, straining to see.

'Romira's bright idea. Let our wealthy guests feel at home,' said Lance. 'Chop-house, abalone, champagne, caviar. Bangazi's going international. When I say your lunch is costing more than a fancy piece of salvage equipment, I mean it. And late this afternoon I have to ferry them all back to the flotel for a special dinner Ken's laying on.'

'Where they will be spending the night, no doubt,' added Gareth.

'No doubt. On the house. Not the Tea-house of the Zulu Moon, either.'

'Come again?'

Lance stubbed a tanned finger towards the gaudy banner strung between the pagoda-like structures.

'That's what the banner says. Tea-house of the Zulu Moon. It's a crib from somewhere, I'm certain.'

The Tea-house of the Zulu Moon wasn't real, of course. It was a confection of painted canvas and plywood, like a stage set. Neither did it float of its own accord, but was carried atop the forward superstructure of a sleek, modern ship. Even from a short distance, the illusion was striking.

'Nice sop to those well-heeled Chinese gentlemen from over the horizon,' went on Lance. 'And I'm sure they're flattered. They were pretty chuffed when they sighted it first from the chopper. The ship underneath the tea-house is real enough. That is, if you reckon 9,000 dollars a day is real. The *Sea Urchin* used to be a government research ship, but she was declared redundant. Sold privately for a song and renamed *Sea Urchin* after the coral reef creatures. Now out on fishing and diving charter along this coast, and she's ideal for the purpose. Look at that low stern deck of hers, it's almost at water level. There's also a hatch which opens

directly into the water – made to measure for scuba divers.'
He addressed Pernelle. 'You can make a full gear entry from
the stern, and recovery is equally easy. See that hydraulic
crane? It was used for lifting gear for scientific experiments.
The new owners wisely decided to keep it: it's perfect to
launch a support boat for divers. No elbow-grease required
aboard the *Sea Urchin*, I assure you.'

The helicopter swung round, lower now. The helipad
looked to Pernelle about the size of a handkerchief.

Lance sensed her anxiety. 'It's tight, about minimum
size. It's okay providing the weather's all right. This is my
fourth landing today. It's about the only item aboard which
there seems to have been some stinting on. She's got every
creature comfort – air-conditioned cabins, even a walk-in
freezer for all this fancy food we're carrying. The Chinese
have to have their abalone,' he added derisively.

The Chinese have to have their abalone! The words
raced through Gareth's mind. Abalone, laced with uncut
diamonds! Trawlers over the horizon!

He asked sharply, 'Where do those trawlers come from?'

Lance gave a slight 'hold-it' gesture with one hand.
The tight landing required all his concentration. He had
the deft hands of a plastic surgeon and gently coaxed
the machine down, the dragon-capped heraldic banners
flapping disconcertingly in the rotors' slipstream.

Then they were safe.

At last, Lance answered Gareth's question: 'Taiwan,'
he said.

8

Taiwan!

Ever since lifting its import duties on diamonds, both rough and polished stones, Taiwan had taken its place as a front-runner in the world's diamond market, eclipsing both Hong Kong and Japan. The object of the open market was to reduce Taiwan's bulging reserves and huge trade surpluses; to make trade more competitive and to encourage the local industry to process more gems. Yet, perversely, most diamonds still continued to enter Taiwan through 'unofficial channels', and what these were was anybody's guess.

Was one of them abalone?

Were the boxes right under Gareth's hand part of a superbly ingenious racket being enacted behind a playboy front, wholly innocent on the surface, yet as crooked as the original Connecticut corkscrew underneath?

Where were the diamonds coming from?

Gareth was conscious of Pernelle's penetrating stare – he had not heard her speak his name from the helicopter door which she was holding open for him to climb out, nor had he been aware of Ken Ziegler's rapid approach.

'All set for the Tea-house of the Zulu Moon?' he boomed. 'My Chinese friends can't wait to meet the finest salvage expert south of the Sands of Gold.'

Pernelle bridled. The words were as brash as the pink curtains and swooning seahorses of the Coelacanth Suite.

Ken didn't wait for a response to his bonhomie. 'I'll get these cartons of abalone out of the sun into the freezer before they come to any harm.'

Gareth dropped to the deck. 'They're in a bit of a mess – one of the cartons fell down and broke open.'

Ken stopped in his tracks, rounding angrily on Lance. 'How did you allow that to happen? You know these boxes are special!'

'Air pocket over the beach,' responded the pilot blandly. 'Pernelle and Gareth shoved 'em all back again. No harm done.'

'Which carton?'

'The one propped up between the seat and the roof,' answered Gareth.

Ken thrust his bulk through the narrow door like an over-zealous scrum half burrowing for the ball. He flipped open the lid, glanced searchingly at the contents, and seemed satisfied. There was an outsize coloured sticker in the form of an abalone shell on the side of the box – Gareth could not tell whether the other twenty-odd cartons had the same logo, or just this particular one.

Ken backed out of the door, carrying the carton.

'This box of abalone is specially earmarked for Dr Chang Zhang, one of the distinguished visitors you'll meet in a moment. There's another for Mr Yu Cheng, who's also dropped in for brunch.'

A tall youth came hurrying forward, his almost white hair the perfect foil for his black and dayglo-orange diving gear.

'Ken,' he demanded in a nasal voice. 'Can't we get on with the dive? Is this who we've been waiting for all this time? I changed about an hour ago.'

'Pernelle is one of the top salvage experts in the country,' Ken retorted, as if that explained everything. 'She arrived at Bangazi only a short while back.'

'Well then, what are we waiting for? Fire the gun, and let's go!'

'Pernelle, this is Brad Harland,' Ken introduced. 'From the Kingfisher Snorkelling Club up towards Sodwana Bay.'

He indicated another sulky-looking youth. 'Darren Peters. He and Brad have quite a joint record of discoveries.' Darren's wetsuit glowed fluorescent in response.

'Cut the credits, Ken. Let's get under starter's orders, huh?' urged the nasal Brad. His eye travelled critically over Pernelle's diving gear – no in-fashion stripes, no incandescences to rival the rainbow denizens of the coral reefs.

Another couple and a middle-aged man closed on Ken from the milling crowd, effectively blocking his way, abalone case on shoulder, to the *Sea Urchin*'s freezer room.

The woman of the couple said loudly, 'Yeah, let's do just that, and cut the fancy stuff until we've had a look-see down below.' She wore a hot-pink wetsuit, and a printed logo encircling her right thigh from knee to hip recorded her port of registration – 'Coral Coast Exploration Club, Sodwana'. Her feet were tinted bright pink, as were the tips of her luminous elbows. Her male companion was less blatantly coral-reef friendly in lime green.

Ken gave Pernelle a glance and said, 'Mircea Cattel, Otto Johnston. If anyone can find the *Nova Scotia* today . . .'

'We will.' The pink incarnation finished Ken's sentence. 'We're going for the jackpot you see there. Reserve it for us. And the bubbly with it.'

Pernelle turned and saw a long table under the scarlet banners set with crockery and champagne glasses. In the centre was a collection of small jeweller's cases containing key-rings, inscribed cufflinks, framed scraps of metal, two in the shape of a miniature ship's propeller, and a couple of medallions. Dominating all was a small scale model of a World War II troop transport. A brass plate read: 'Nova Scotia, 1942'.

'Those aren't made from real remains – yet. They're just imitations to whet your appetites,' explained Ken. 'And I'm going to have the *Nova Scotia*'s propeller sliced up and framed just like that model there.'

'You could be counting your chickens, Ken,' Otto said

with surprising detachment. 'Especially as you expect to hit the jackpot the first time. This morning, no less. You never can tell with the sea.'

'You only have to have a ticket in the lottery and you're in with a chance,' answered Ken ambiguously. He turned to Mircea. 'Go out there and give it a go, honey. I've got some of the top divers on the coast here today, plus Pernelle Clymer as the cherry on top, and if they can't locate the *Nova Scotia*, nobody can.'

Pernelle again bridled inwardly. She felt she was being drawn into Ken Ziegler's salvage circus against her better judgement.

The short, middle-aged man, who had the well-scrubbed look of a fitness fetishist, edged his way to the front.

'Ken, what worries me is the wreck's position. You say she's four or five miles offshore. That sort of information is so vague that if it was a business deal, I'd cry off.'

'Ah, but the sea isn't business – you know that, Stephen.'

'But – '

'Pernelle here is working on it,' Ken added placatingly. 'She'll locate her exact position, for sure.'

Brad Harland called out in an agonized voice, 'For Pete's sake, Ken, the *start*!'

Ken turned to Pernelle. 'Would you mind if we sent the front-runners off, so to speak, and you could follow by yourself as soon as you're changed? You see how everyone is champing at the bit.'

Pernelle gave Gareth a quick glance of relief.

'By all means.'

'It's to be a Le Mans-type start,' Ken explained. 'I fire the starting-gun and everyone runs for their boat or goes over the side . . .'

'Where's the gun?' demanded Mircea.

'Romira!' called Ziegler.

Romira, fetching in figure-fitting beach shorts, left two

men, obviously Oriental, at the long table and handed Ken a pistol.

He raised it above his head and used his booming voice to maximum effect over the gaggle of bright-suited hopefuls.

Gareth's attention wasn't on Ken. It was fixed on the gun.

This was no run-of-the-mill weapon. It was a Makarov automatic – Russian terrorist weapon.

'Remember, all,' Ken proclaimed, standing with one foot on the abalone box, 'the three commandments of reef diving – don't sink down on the reef and damage the coral, it's delicate stuff. Don't touch the coral, and don't break bits off or collect shells. Now – on your marks, get set . . .'

The heavy round exploded. It must have been live, by the sound of it, Gareth thought. One woman screamed with fright, but her voice was lost in the hubbub as the divers scrambled to the ship's side. Brad and Darren were ahead of the pack at the stern. They leapt nimbly into an outboard, gunned the motor, and cast off, heading decisively south and east on an obviously predetermined course.

Ken hefted the abalone carton. 'This has already been overlong out of the freezer,' he said to Pernelle and Gareth. 'But before I take it below, I want you to meet our distinguished guests.'

Near the long table, in gaily coloured South Sea shirts, stood the two Chinese.

Ken advanced, box on shoulder, Makarov in hand.

One of the Orientals said, 'It looks like you're guarding something very precious in that box, Ken.'

Was there a touch of irony, of double-speak, in the bland voice? Gareth wondered. Was Ken's responsive laugh, too, not a little forced? But years of experience made Ken's introduction as sleek as the seafood pâté due to be served with the champagne, and gave no hint of any inner disquiet.

'Dr Chang Zhang, head of Specialized Seafoods Import Corporation in Taipeh, and Mr Yu Cheng, Dragon Jewellery and Allied Crafts, also from Taipeh.'

Abalone equals seafoods; diamonds equals jewellery.

Gareth only half reacted to Dr Zhang's polite query.

'Mining engineer, eh? What in?'

'Titanium. Dune-mining on the coast.' It was only part of the truth, but it was enough.

Ken came unwittingly to his rescue. All at once he seemed in a hurry.

'We don't want all those other divers to have too much of a head start on our star, do we? Pernelle, there's a cabin below specially reserved for you to change in. I'll show you the way. I had them clear out one of the officers . . .'

Pernelle felt again that she was being smothered in false hospitality and bonhomie. She said, 'Please don't expect too much from me. I'm sure some of the other divers have far more experience on this particular coast. I can't conjure up a wreck where there is no wreck, you know.'

'There *is* a wreck – it's only a matter of nailing down exactly where it is.' Ken smiled ambiguously. He put his free hand chummily round her shoulders and started to lead her aft towards the entry to the 'tween-decks area.

Gareth fell in behind with Pernelle's gear, the harsh smell of cordite still stinging his nose.

They had agreed to meet at the stern hatch and Gareth deliberately skirted the tea-house brunch area and guests to get there. Pernelle hadn't arrived so he sat down to wait. It was a turtles' *dolce vita* world. The sky was brilliant blue, like Pernelle's eyes, the sea a deeper complementary shade, the swell too languid to heave itself above the *Sea Urchin*'s waterline. Of the gaggle of divers, there was no sign. The soporific ocean had swallowed them in an intricately sculptured half-lighted dream world of corals, sponges, algae and waving seaweed, the moving currents of shimmering fish providing a continual scene-shift of illumination.

Gareth stared unseeingly. Men, women and children had died horrible deaths, 750 of them, here, in this water, where Ken's glitzy charade now took place. What was there behind Ken's fixation on the *Nova Scotia*, or was it no more than the drive of a go-getting publicist? Samsonov – was there another side to the story beyond what appeared on the surface? An uncomplicated drowning – or? He left the question unanswered. He, and only he – and perhaps Dr Nikolai Vize in Moscow – might know what dark forces could have clustered round Samsonov's unfortunate head. Diamonds – it all came back to diamonds! And the sight of that uncut stone bursting from the abalone shell there on the floor of the helicopter had delivered a punch from which he had not yet recovered.

'Diving's supposed to be a major remedy for stress.'

He had not heard Pernelle come up behind him. He swung round. The severe black Lycra figure-hugging wetsuit showed a body honed to perfection by a thousand dives since girlhood. Seawater had modelled those beautiful breasts; seawater had been the masseuse for her hips and thighs. She had given her body no chance of display under the loose jersey and pants during the up-coast helicopter flight. Now, crowned by her loose fair hair, it was released to its element. She carried a mask, fins, snorkel and weightbelt. Her only concession to colour was the purple and orange pouches on the belt.

She sat down beside him and started pulling on her fins. Everyone else seemed either to be diving or chatting at the brunch table.

He asked, 'Do you think you will locate the *Nova Scotia*, Pernelle?'

'No. I repeat what I said, this isn't the way to set about it. Today all I hope to spot is an emperor angelfish . . .'

'Emperor angelfish?'

'It's one of the most beautiful fishes on this coast. He's got a blue snout and exquisite yellow-green lines along his body, like a tiny underwater zebra with delicate tracery. A bright yellow tail into the bargain – no, I can't describe it. I wish you were coming along, Gareth. These Sodwana system reefs are utter perfection.'

'You seem to know a lot about them.'

She reached for her diving cap and shook her hair clear of her forehead, so that it fell into new and disturbing patterns round her face.

'Not really. I wish I knew more. There are actually seven reefs in the Sodwana system, and the longest is some way south of here, called Leadsman's Shoal . . .'

She broke off and asked abruptly, 'What are you sitting here thinking, Gareth?'

She leaned down to make an adjustment to one of her fins, putting a hand on his shoulder to steady herself.

'Two things, Pernelle. First, the *Nova Scotia*.'

'What about the *Nova Scotia*?'

'I wish I knew. Do you think this whole elaborate – and expensive – diving fun game is solely in aid of locating a pretty worthless old wartime transport, carrying no bullion or specie or valuable cargo, or passengers' personal jewellery? They weren't that sort of passenger – they were internees. Even her metal fittings can't be worth much. The ship wasn't in that league. She wasn't another *Titanic* or *Lusitania* or *Athenia*, or any one of the big famous names.'

'I can't give you the answer – yet.'

'Why not?'

'I'm busy doing some research – perhaps you might even term it ferreting – into the loss of the ship. As I mentioned, there's so little known about her, in South Africa at any

rate. I'm trying to sort out the *Nova Scotia*'s background.'
She readied herself to go overside.

'And the second subject of your thoughts?'

'Samsonov,' he replied briefly. 'Samsonov.'

She hesitated and lifted the snorkel free of her mouth for a moment.

'What about him?'

'Samsonov didn't die naturally, Pernelle.'

'If I knew something of his background, I might be able to help answer that.'

He had almost stepped into a self-dug trap. He back-pedalled. 'Nor do I.'

She eyed him for a long moment, then leapt into the water.

Did she believe him, he wondered, watching the circle of bubbles vanish. If he wanted to keep her trust and their relationship to develop, he would have to confide his knowledge of Samsonov's background. And more than just Samsonov. He would have to include other things which had lain hidden for so long. He crushed down his line of thought. There were enough problems in the present, and one current one was, how soon could he manage to get the news of Samsonov's death to Dr Vize? How would his own plans be affected?

His musing was interrupted by the rapid clatter of feet on the ladder from the upper deck. It was Ken Ziegler.

'Was that Pernelle?' His voice had lost its mine-host boom and was dry with tension.

Gareth indicated the last ripples which were still visible from Pernelle's dive.

'She's just gone in.'

Ziegler pulled a banknote from his pocket and unconciously ran it through his teeth like dental floss. Gareth found the trick almost as odious as Romira did, but the tension it reflected was patently clear.

'She's the star diver. If anyone can find the *Nova Scotia*, she can.' He plucked again at his teeth. 'She's the only one who really knows what to look for underwater. She thinks the wreck could be in pieces all over the place . . .'

Gareth said, 'Brad Harland and Darren Peters also seem to know what they're about. You said so yourself.'

Ziegler didn't seem to hear. 'Pernelle could be away anything up to an hour, then. Trouble is, all those pieces of metal could be so encrusted with calcium deposits, seaweed and so on, even coral, they've been there half a century . . .'

'Is that so important?'

Gareth's question seemed to bring him to a realization of something else.

'Not really, but a wreck's a wreck, and if I could show my guests something that truly *looked* like a wreck . . .'

'Like the *Titanic*, you mean?' Gareth mocked.

Ziegler ignored him. 'Tell me the moment Pernelle comes back aboard. I'll be on the restaurant deck. I want to know what it looks like down there . . .'

He turned abruptly and went quickly up the companionway, sticking his professionally smooth smile back into position and the banknote into his pocket. He pushed past Romira on the way, hardly seeming to notice her.

She said, 'Mind if I share your sun?'

She was sure enough of Gareth's answer to sit down and arrange her legs and shorts to show just the right amount of untanned flesh above the hem-line.

'Do you know that turtles' sex is determined by the sun?' she went on. 'Females hatch from eggs laid in a warm, sunny place on the beach, and males from eggs laid in the shade of vegetation on the margin of the sand.'

Gareth grinned and moved into a shadow cast by the ship's upperworks.

'Now we're in our right places, sexually speaking.'

'Sun for me, shade for you.'

This was the sort of suggestive banter at which Romira was adept. Skilful make-up had restored the damage done by the trauma of dealing with Samsonov, but her eyes were the colour of rusty violets at dusk, cold dusk, and did not run in tandem with her flippant words.

'Ken seems pretty uptight about the search for the wreck,' Gareth observed.

'He's spent a lot of money on all this.' Romira's broad gesture took in the *Sea Urchin*, the Tea-house of the Zulu Moon, and the sea's surface hiding the divers. She went on, choosing her words carefully, 'Also, Ken has set himself the goal of locating the *Nova Scotia* before the anniversary of its sinking. It'll be fifty years ago at the end of November.'

'Why is that important?'

She turned her head away and gazed far out to sea, leaving her thighs to do the talking.

'You ask a lot of questions, fellah.'

'Idle curiosity, that's all.'

'Romira!' It was Ziegler from the deck above. 'Come, will you? I've got a problem.' He addressed Gareth. 'No sign of Pernelle, I suppose?'

'It's only minutes since you asked last. She's scarcely had time to get down to her operating depth.'

'I suppose not. But as soon as she appears . . .'

Romira remained sitting, and Gareth asked, 'Aren't you going up?'

'Ken hasn't a problem, really. Nerves. I can tell from his voice.' She turned away from her contemplation of the sea and said ambiguously, 'My job is to see that Bangazi's guests aren't lonely.'

Gareth said, 'Bangazi is a very small, self-contained world. A kind of locked-in island. You can't be able to move around much.'

'That's what prisons are, too.'

'Is that how you feel?'

'I didn't say that. I meet lots of people. People from all over. They come and go, all the time. It's sometimes interesting to find out what makes them tick.'

'What made Samsonov tick, for example?'

She veered away abruptly from his probe. 'You shouldn't be sitting here alone brooding. You did a wonderful job recovering the body. We all say so. I'll get you some champagne.'

'Thanks, no. I'll wait for Pernelle to surface.'

She eyed him consideringly, then dug into her shorts pocket and drew out a tiny fragment of white stone. She held it out to him.

'Crystal,' he said.

'Stones are therapeutic, you know.'

'So I've heard it said. But I'm a plain mining man. I don't go in for the fancy side of it.'

The timbre of her voice softened. 'Touch it and see. Feel how smooth it is. It's cool, in spite of being close to my body.'

With emphasis on the last word she extended her hand. He took the stone and fingered its surface.

'Cool, isn't it?' she asked.

'When it should be warm.'

'Crystal has immense powers. It makes me feel fey.' She took the fragment back from him and asked, 'You haven't seen my shop at Bangazi yet, have you? I call it Touchstones. I've got all kinds of fascinating gemstones – rose quartz, agates, tiger's eye, amethyst, jade, jasper. I'd like your expert opinion on my collection.'

'You don't get any gemstones from this part of the world.'

'No. Mine come from all over. I've got good contacts. Agate from Botswana, aventurine from Zimbabwe, paua shell from New Zealand – ' she chuckled at some inner memory of the New Zealand contact ' – snow quartz from Namibia, you name it.'

'Who are your contacts in Namibia? I know the country. It's probably the richest of all places for gemstones.'

She stood up abruptly, and thrust the crystal back into her pocket. 'Ken will be getting fussed. I've lots of things to fix.'

As she started towards the upper deck, Ken appeared again at the railing.

'Romira! For crying out! What's keeping you? The divers will be back soon . . .' He called to Gareth, 'Any sign . . . ?'

Without waiting for a reply, he disappeared from sight.

Gareth remained on the hatch-deck, standing by the hydraulic crane. Within minutes, it seemed, Ken Ziegler was back alongside him.

The man was in an inner ferment, but doing his best to maintain his mine-host smile.

'Any divers in sight yet?'

He reached into his pocket, but withdrew his hand empty.

He must have run out of banknotes to gnaw.

'What do you expect to do if and when anyone does locate the wreck?'

'First, I'll have to get proper marker buoys down to establish my exclusive claim to it. The *Nova Scotia* is *mine*. I'll get Pernelle to obtain validation from the National Monuments Council so that no other salvors can stake a claim . . .'

Gareth eyed him. 'You'd think she was carrying a million in treasure.'

'There's treasure and treasure,' he replied ambiguously. 'I need the *Nova Scotia* as a special adjunct to Bangazi Lodge. There'll be nothing like the combination anywhere. Strictly tourist treasure, you understand.'

Gareth didn't understand, nor did Ziegler give him the

opportunity to ask. He went up the ladder to the tea-house deck, two rungs at a time, his bull neck cutting a passage through the languid air.

Gareth could almost feel his continuous anxiety drumming down from above via the decking plates.

There was a splash alongside the stern hatch. No need to identify the diver – the pink leg thrown on to the planking said it all, 'Coral Coast Exploration Club'. Mircea followed.

Ziegler was at her side before she had time to pull off her goggles and mask. His voice was thick; stress sewed together the furrows between his eyes.

'Yes?' he jerked out. 'Yes? What luck, eh? You found her . . .'

'Hell,' Mircea exclaimed. 'I've never seen anything like it . . .'

'She's intact – just as she went down?'

Romira was there, too. Gareth had been unaware of her until he felt her hand on him steadying herself against the ship's motion. The sea was flat calm.

'Dammit,' went on Mircea. 'I've never seen a marine garden like it, ever before. And we've got some beauts up near Sodwana. Sea anemones, the biggest I've ever seen. Banded clown fish all mixed up amongst the anemones' tentacles – if it had been a human, he would have been half stung to death! And a potato bass – whew! You'd never guess his size! Here, Otto, tell 'em!'

Her lime-green diver-buddy was in the process of hauling himself on to the hatchway. 'Squirrelfish, moorish idols, swallow-tailed rock cod! And the coral – staghorn, brain and plate! Ken, this is the biggest treasure house south of the Mozambique Channel!'

Ziegler asked slowly, 'No – ship?'

'What more do you want, Ken?' Otto retorted. 'What can some bloody old wreck add to that paradise down there?'

Romira's gaze lasered Ken's face. Pull yourself together, it said, get a grip!

'A wreck's a wreck,' she told Mircea and Otto diplomatically. 'And we're thrilled about your underwater garden. Just think what we have to offer our guests in future!'

Ziegler managed to smooth some of the disappointment from his face, but it still lowered like a distant cyclone approaching the coast.

Romira stepped into the breach again. 'We'll organize night dives down into your garden, Mircea.'

Otto broke in. 'We even saw a leopard-shark asleep on the sea-bed.' He grinned. 'He didn't wake up; we didn't wake him.'

'Hell, no!' added Mircea. 'Ken, I tell you it's paradise!'

Her enthusing was cut short by the arrival of more divers. Air-time ran out almost simultaneously for all.

Ken fired his question again at the newcomers. 'Any sign of the wreck?'

Stephen, the well-laundered fitness fetishist, said, 'Ken, I told you before we started off that we needed more information about the wreck's position. To say four or five miles offshore is like a bum steer for a deal.'

Romira broke in urgently. 'Look out there! Brad Harland and Darren Peters! Look at their boat belting it! Like a bat out of hell!'

'They're waving. That's Brad in the bow! He's got something in his hand!'

It looked like a crucifix, a rusty crucifix. Darren was at the tiller, gunning the engine.

As the boat neared, no one had time to pay attention to another splash alongside the hatch except Gareth. It was Pernelle. He gave her a hand aboard. The others lined the ship's rail, attention riveted on the approaching support boat.

Brad stood balanced in the bow and waved the rusty object. He cupped his hand. His shout came across the water.

'We've found the *Nova Scotia*!'

9

Brad's boat slowed, eased in towards the stern-deck. Eager hands reached out for it.

Ken Ziegler stood rooted, his eyes fixed on the object in Brad's hand. The line of his cheekbones was sketched with a patina of sweat. He had only a metre or two of decking to cross to reach the support boat's bow, but he seemed unable to get going, as if the consequence of handling whatever Brad had salvaged was too great to stake on a single step. A couple of gulls which had been squabbling around the stern fell silent, as if they, too, caught something of Ziegler's tension. He started to say something, but the words foundered in his throat.

Then, abruptly, he dashed across the planking and seized the crucifix-like object in Brad's hand.

'What is it? Where did you get it? Where is the wreck?'

Brad shook drops of water out of his so-white hair.

'Say, give us a chance, Ken! Let's go back to the beginning. Darren . . .'

The discovery had cleared Darren's face of its sulks. He said, 'It was a piece of luck – '

'*What is this, for Pete's sake?*' Ken boomed.

It looked like a dagger, about twenty-five centimetres long. The haft, which could have been of wood or leather, had been largely eaten away by years of submersion. There was a metal cross-piece with slots. The weapon looked formidable still, even though the blade was pitted and encrusted.

'The wreck – you say you found her – whereabouts does this come from, whatever it is – '

Pernelle's voice broke in unexpectedly. 'I'll tell you. It's a Second World War bayonet.'

Brad turned to Darren. 'See? We were right – the ship's there somewhere close, for sure.'

Ken rapped out, 'Did you find the *Nova Scotia*, or didn't you?'

Brad indicated the bayonet. 'The *Nova Scotia* was carrying a contingent of South African troops, right? So they had rifles, right? And those long old-fashioned bayonets went with the rifles, right?'

Pernelle added quietly, 'The South African bayonets were in use for years longer than other armies. They weren't like the modern short bayonet.'

'I don't want to know about bloody bayonets!' burst out Ziegler. 'I want the *Nova Scotia*!'

'We're trying to tell you,' went on Brad in a long-suffering voice. 'It was pure luck, finding this bayonet – if that's what it really is. It was all by itself on a spur of coral. I guess Darren and I spotted it all at once, both together. The spur is on one side of a deep gully – in fact, the water's deep there, I don't know how deep. We didn't go down.'

Ziegler revolved the weapon in his hands while the other divers crowded close to get a glimpse. 'So you found a bayonet, and that makes you say the ship is there, too.'

'She's there all right,' Darren asserted. 'We just didn't have time to look further. Our air was almost finished.'

Brad said, 'The ship was torpedoed, eh? A torpedo makes a hell of a mess. Blows everything around. So it's logical that this bayonet belonged to one of the troops on board and the force of the explosion blew it clear of the ship.'

Ziegler turned to Pernelle. 'Can that happen?'

'I'd say it was more than likely.'

Ziegler's mood somersaulted. He grabbed Brad's hand

and pump-handled it. Darren moved clear, as if he half-feared a kiss on the cheek.

The blood rushed up Ken's neck and into his face as the full impact of the find stirred an inner reaction of which the rest were unaware.

He said hoarsely under his breath, 'I've wanted this all my life . . .'

Then, taking a grip on himself, he assumed his usual heartiness.

'Congratulations! We'll celebrate this! The champagne's already on ice! And you two will get the first prize, that model of the *Nova Scotia* there on the table! Tell us more about the find!'

Romira took the rusty bayonet and made an odd lunging movement.

'It's one way of getting your man,' she said. Her words gusted like cold wind across the warm day.

Brad took the weapon back and used it as a pointer as he explained, 'Darren and I had a hunch right from the beginning that there wasn't much wreckage under the *Sea Urchin* here,' he said in his nasal voice. 'Eh, Darr?'

'Yeah. Pretty coral, I guess, but not what we wanted.'

'Mighty pretty, boy. Paradise. You've never seen anything like it,' Mircea enthused.

'There's a series of small reefs running parallel to one another out there where we were,' Brad went on. 'If the *Nova Scotia* had come down on any of them, she would have broken her back for sure, if the torpedoes hadn't done that already. Very difficult to tell which is reef and which wreck.'

'Sand?' asked Pernelle. 'Was there sand, or just coral?'

'Lots of sand. Even the small fish puff up clouds of it, which makes visibility very tricky. When a big 'un like a ray passes, it's like an underwater dust storm.'

'That's good news for preserving the wreck.'

'Yeah, in a way. But it's tough on an eyeball search.'

'What are conditions like down there?' persisted Pernelle. 'Any turbulence? Currents?'

'Naw,' replied Darren. 'I was half-expecting some underwater movement – one of those tricky sets that come in from the Agulhas Current.'

'Everything as calm and quiet as a cathedral,' added Brad.

Ziegler's voice was rough with tension. He fired his question at Brad. 'We're on the edge of a discovery, but we aren't there yet. Agreed?'

'Yeah,' said Brad.

'You two – will you dive again after brunch?' He swung on Pernelle. 'Will you go with them?'

'I thought we'd come for a party,' Brad whined.

'Yeah, sure,' agreed Darren, 'but it would be a hell of a thing if we missed out, just for the sake of some fancy food and drink.'

'Okay,' said Brad. 'I go along with that. We'll dive.'

'And you, Pernelle?'

'I'm out of air. If someone can lend me another cylinder, I'll go. The eats can wait, too, for my part. The wreck's much more exciting.'

'*If* you locate her,' added Romira from the fringes of the group.

'You know where to look for the bayonet area – you put down a marker buoy?' demanded Ziegler.

Brad eyed him contemptuously. 'Don't start teaching us kindergarten stuff, Ken. Sure there's a buoy.'

Ziegler addressed Pernelle. 'That's the exact fix you've been demanding for the salvage permit, Pernelle. Exact! I'll get Captain MacDonald to work it out – this is an ex-survey ship, and full of hi-tech equipment. By all that's holy, you shall have your precise fix, Pernelle!'

'The wreck hasn't been found yet. All we have is one rusty World War Two bayonet. That doesn't give you the right to claim you've found the *Nova Scotia*. The bayonet could have originated anywhere – this area is right on the shipping route. Hundreds of ships must have passed this way during the war. That bayonet could have come from any of the troopships either going to or coming from the Middle East. One swallow doesn't make a summer.'

'Don't try and talk it down, Pernelle.' A black look suffused the big man's face. 'We've got the *Nova Scotia* in our sights, and I intend to bag her. Are you backing out of the other dive now?'

'Just the other way round. I want to *know* – from seeing the wreck myself – that you *have* found the *Nova Scotia*. I've told you before, there are other wrecks in this vicinity.'

'It is the *Nova Scotia* – it *must* be the *Nova Scotia*!' he asserted, then hesitated. 'Brad,' he said more quietly, 'that buoy – is it outside territorial waters?'

Brad shrugged. 'How should I know, Ken? I'm a diver, not a geographer.'

'Will you accept Captain MacDonald's position for my official application?' Ziegler barked at Pernelle.

Romira saw the danger signs looming. She said in a conciliatory voice, 'Brunch, dive, in that order, people! These are all nit-picking points – let's find real evidence of the wreck, and then we can go from there, eh?'

Mircea, the pink mermaid minus tail in a wetsuit, broke in. 'Don't crowd us – give us all ten minutes to change, will you? Boy, this is going to be a day to remember!'

Ken presided masterfully over the top table, playing genial host to his assembled guests, the mounted gilt model of the *Nova Scotia* taking centre stage before him. Scarlet banners flapped overhead as the company feasted on a shell-pink salmon pâté, mounds of glistening black caviar, succulent turkey set in champagne aspic and, of course, the long-awaited abalone. Iced Pierre Jourdan flowed freely until at last Ken rose rather unsteadily to make an effusive speech of welcome to the Chinese and to present the scale-model of the *Nova Scotia* to Brad and Darren, who had sat patient and abstemious at his left throughout.

After coffee, Brad, Darren and Pernelle climbed into the support boat and were waved off with many exuberant shouts of good luck.

The afternoon passed in a haze of champagne and laughter until at last someone spotted Pernelle's fair hair like a beacon in the sun out to sea.

Ken Ziegler led the crowd to the entry hatch at the stern in order to be the first to hear the news.

For news it was. Brad was standing in the bow gesticulating, pointing at Pernelle.

His hail came across the water.

'We got it! Pernelle found the wreck!'

As the boat drew alongside, Ziegler threw out a hand to help Pernelle inboard. Gareth noticed that her eyes were a little blue and swollen, as if she had ventured deeper than she should.

'Brad's exaggerating. I didn't find the wreck proper, or any identifiable piece of wreckage to show it was the *Nova Scotia* . . .'

'She found the ship's gun!' interjected Darren.

'Gun? The *Nova Scotia* wasn't a warship . . .' Ziegler's words stumbled like a loggerhead turtle making for the surf-line.

Brad went on. 'I'd never have recognized it as a gun. It was the wrong way up, stuck in a gully.'

Darren added, 'It looked more like a chunk of boiler-room equipment. Then there was the stern itself . . .'

'What!' burst out Ziegler. 'The stern!'

Pernelle said quietly, unsmiling, into the circle of flushed, excited faces, 'There's too much jumping to conclusions going on here. There's nothing to show at this stage that what I've located belonged to the *Nova Scotia*, neither the gun nor the chunk of wreckage. But it's hopeful, I won't say more than that. First, there was what I think could be the type of small-calibre stern gun which was fitted to most World War Two merchantmen. Second, what might be part of the stern, but the metal is heavily encrusted and mixed up with coral . . .'

'Isn't the ship's name on it?' demanded Ziegler. '*Nova Scotia?* And on the gun, some marking identifying her?'

'There is nothing visible at this stage,' replied Pernelle. 'There should be other sections of the ship scattered around if she broke up as I think she must. They could be some distance away, but heavy machinery – boilers, engines, and so on – wouldn't move very far. There's a lot of work to be done.'

'How deep is this wreckage? Why didn't you check when you were down . . .'

'Give us a chance, Ken,' Brad burst out. 'The gun's stuck in a narrow gully, it's rusted, encrusted, oxidized. Only someone with Pernelle's experience could have spotted it.'

Darren added, 'You could easily mistake it for a coral pipe.'

'How deep?' Ziegler rapped out.

'Maybe twelve metres, maybe a bit more,' replied Pernelle.

'How could the ship's gun have got there? Where's the rest of the ship?' demanded Ziegler.

'I'm trying to explain. I'd say that one of the torpedoes caught her in the stern. The stern was a favourite target of U-boats, in order to draw the enemy's teeth at first blow. Right on track for the engine-room, to start with. I'd guess the explosion blew the whole gun – mounting, barrel, everything – clear of the ship.'

'In which case, the body of the ship is close by.'

'Depending on a lot of factors,' Pernelle answered. 'The chunk of stern is a good omen. But for the rest, fragments from the explosions could have been distributed hither and thither by other means such as currents, underwater storms and so on.'

'Come!' Ziegler hurried on. 'Come with me to the bridge. I want you to explain where the wreckage lies so that Captain MacDonald can make an exact satellite fix . . .'

'No need,' replied Brad. 'We put down a buoy. That, plus the other one for the bayonet, are more than enough.'

'No!' retorted Ziegler. 'I have to have MacDonald! Anything could happen to the marker buoys and then we're back to square one.'

Lance, who had now joined the group, said, 'Before you start shifting the ship, remember that I've got a lot of people to ferry back to Bangazi Lodge before it gets dark.'

'We'll talk about that later.' Ziegler brushed the pilot aside.

'There are other things to talk about,' Lance said cryptically. He addressed Gareth: 'That involves you.'

Ziegler started to propel Pernelle up the ladder leading to the upper deck and towards Captain MacDonald on the bridge. Brad and Darren followed, still clad, like Pernelle herself, in diving kit. Gareth fell into step alongside Lance, who was last up the companionway. The rest of the guests stood about in animated knots on the stern deck.

'What involves me?' Gareth asked.

'Samsonov.' The flier's usual flippant tone was sombre. 'My little jape of landing on the police station lawn at Richards Bay with a cadaver didn't come off. The cops took a dim view – a serious view, in fact. They thought we might have killed Samsonov. And having Buks around didn't help.'

'That's ridiculous,' said Gareth. 'You and I had nothing to do with his death. We merely fished his dead body from the water.'

'That's what the fuzz want to question you about,' went on Lance. 'They don't believe that anyone could have risked his neck the way you did simply to retrieve an unknown body from the water.'

'Not to mention your neck,' replied Gareth. 'It was as dicey a piece of flying as I ever saw.'

'They spent a hell of a lot of time cross-questioning me, getting statements, trying to trip me up on any nit-picking point,' said Lance. 'Buks played the know-all tough guy, which seemed to make them only more suspicious.'

'Suspicious? Of what?' asked Gareth.

'The whole Bangazi set-up,' he said acidly. 'This.' He swept an arm to encompass the *Sea Urchin* and its tea-house. 'I insisted that I had to get back here in time to ferry the guests back to Bangazi. A brunch? they demanded. Who gives an eats-party kilometres out to sea just for the hell of it? Ken Ziegler does, I replied. It's his style. I even proposed that the sergeant who grilled me – a guy called Joubert – should come back with me in the chopper and see for himself. He cried off, but he's waiting at Bangazi now. If you've any plans to leave this area, you'd better forget about them for the moment, at least until after you've seen Sergeant Joubert.'

Samsonov. Namibia. Angola. Switzerland. Dr Nikolai Vize. Glavalmazzoloto. His onward plans clicked through his mind like a computer. He was only half-sorry to be forced to stay at Bangazi. Pernelle – she was a new factor to be taken into consideration as far as he was concerned.

His mental computer, however, was nothing to the electronic marvel Captain MacDonald sported in the chartroom adjoining the bridge. They found the bearded skipper with basset-hound eyes toying with a program in preference to toying with the social frivolities of Romira's lunch.

'Can that thing give a spot-on fix?' Ziegler demanded without preliminary. 'On two buoys these divers have put down – so we can find our way back exactly to the place again?'

He jabbed a switch and lights came on. A screen lit up.

'This is an integrated navigation, weather and communications system,' said the skipper. 'It's called INWAC. This system is so accurate that I can give you a position within long spitting distance.'

'Then up-anchor and get over to the buoys and work out their position from your box of tricks,' snapped Ziegler.

'Not today, Ken,' interjected Lance. 'I'll just manage to ferry everyone back in time for your dinner tonight. It's not on, moving the ship today.'

'Then tomorrow. First thing,' replied Ziegler. 'Anything could happen to spoil things – the weather – '

MacDonald jabbed a button and indicated a screen. 'The weather's fine. No hassles ahead. But, I don't move the ship tomorrow.'

Ziegler eyed him. 'I said, I want that fix.'

'This ship is on charter only until sunset tonight. The charter fee lapses then. That's the contract. It'll cost you another day's charter fee to do what you want.'

'Get on with it – damn the expense,' retorted Ziegler.

'I'll want your signature for that – it costs plenty, as you know.'

'You heard what I said. Now, are those two buoys outside South African territorial waters?'

'Well inside,' replied MacDonald. 'The limit is twelve kilometres offshore. We're just under seven kilometres at this spot, near on four sea miles.'

'You're wrong,' Ziegler insisted. 'The limit is three sea miles. So the buoys and the wreck are *outside* territorial waters.'

'You'd better update your facts,' retorted MacDonald. 'Since shortly after the end of World War Two South African territorial waters have been twelve kilometres offshore, along with most other nations of the world. Three miles goes back to the days of the old-fashioned muzzle-loading cannon. Maximum range about three miles. That range determined the territorial limit.'

Gareth watched the flush mount Ziegler's neck.

'The wreck of the *Nova Scotia* is outside territorial limits,' he said harshly. 'I say she's lying in international waters. So she's mine, and I can take what I like from her without a lot of – of – '

Pernelle interjected decisively. 'Any wreck inside territorial waters is subject to the law. No salvage can be undertaken and nothing removed without the consent of the National Monuments Council and the Controller of Customs. I can quote you the legalities, if you wish.'

'You mean to say, after all my trouble and expense to locate the *Nova Scotia*, I can't take what I want!'

'Everyone goes to a lot of trouble and expense to find their own special wrecks,' replied Pernelle. 'Tough, but it's the name of the game.'

Gareth eyed Ziegler speculatively. What did it matter to scuba-loving tourists whether the *Nova Scotia* was inside or outside territorial waters? He felt certain that Pernelle must have cautioned him before, so why did he now choose to forget and make his point in front of others?

Pernelle underscored his thoughts. 'I did make this quite plain to you, Ken.'

Ziegler suddenly backtracked and rushed on. 'Okay, let's leave that problem for the lawyers to sort out later. What I must have now is a fix, even an approximate one.'

MacDonald regarded him with his hound's-eyes. 'According to the buoys, her position is approximately four sea miles, or seven point two kilometres, from the shoreline.'

Ziegler said tightly to Pernelle, 'I need to know, and you need to know for the sake of my application, the exact location of the wreck. Will you dive again tomorrow? And you too, Brad? Darren?'

'Yeah.' Their answer was immediate.

But Pernelle said, 'I found only a gun and what could be part of a ship's stern. I don't even know yet whether it was the *Nova Scotia*'s stern.'

'You're saying you won't dive?' The rasp in Ziegler's voice was like steel plating scraping against a reef.

Pernelle answered levelly. 'I didn't say that. I will dive. But I'm here in an official capacity, not for the fun of it. I'm not obliged to locate a wreck in order to back up anyone's claim.'

Ziegler backpedalled again and, with an effort, stretched his mouth into the semblance of a smile. He was conciliatory. 'Of course not. And I for one value more than I can express what you have already done.'

Lance broke in impatiently. 'Listen, Ken, keep the compliments on ice. I've got a lot of flying to do. Let tomorrow take care of itself. Let's get the first batch of guests together into the chopper, and I'll get going. My last trip will be around sunset.'

Pernelle and Gareth were the last to leave the *Sea Urchin* on Lance's final shuttle. On the short haul home, the pilot seemed preoccupied and morose. His mood infected them both.

As they approached the flotel, Gareth glanced down. The smell of early summer was in the air and a slather of scarlet burnished the sun-doped waves as they moved languidly towards the necklace of lush green forest enveloping the shoreline. He knew that eventually he would have to tell Pernelle about himself and then what would be would be . . .

10

Night comes early at Bangazi on the eastern littoral of Zululand, and it was already dark, the alcoholic witching-hour between cocktails and dinner, when Ziegler and Romira entered the office adjoining their suite.

Ken went through the drill of opening the old-fashioned safe concealed in the cocktail cabinet, and disclosed the secret compartment behind its innocent façade. The only other witness to the ritual was the Makarov pistol lying atop the cabinet within easy reach of Ziegler's hand.

The necklace of green-yellow stones lay resplendent among the piles of uncut diamonds, glowing in spite of the patina fogging its true potential. Romira reached out. 'Let me wear it – only once, Ken! It's safe enough in here out of everyone's sight.'

Ziegler struck her hand roughly aside. 'Leave it, you little fool! Do you want to spoil everything? It's taken months of submersion in sea-water to get even that amount of encrustation! Or oxidation, or whatever it is! Leave it, I say!'

Ziegler was too preoccupied to notice the angry lightning which flashed across the great violet sea-pools of her eyes, wide-set beneath the thundercloud of her hair.

She held the powder-keg of her temper under control. 'I thought you said gold doesn't rust underwater.'

Ziegler's reply was patiently long-suffering. 'You can go and check in any museum which has salvaged gold coins from old wrecks, if you don't believe me.'

'Then why . . .' She indicated the necklace.

'There has to be some tarnishing or discoloration, an

indication that the thing has been underwater for half a century. You can't just go and haul a necklace like that out of a wreck with it looking as if it had just come out of a jeweller's showroom. That's why I rigged up that special sea-water tank in the flotel buoyancy chamber.'

'In other words, to salt the wreck of the *Nova Scotia* with the Stones of the Sun you have to make the fraud convincing, eh, Ken?'

'There's no need to spell it out. You're pretty bitchy this evening,' retorted Ziegler.

'I'll keep it away from the guests at dinner,' she snapped back. 'And you can do the rounds in your cummerbund and Bavarian mine-host shirt, charming them out of their dollars.'

Ziegler did look striking – a fine figure in black evening trousers and fancy shirt with a scarlet cummerbund round the waist matching his scarlet string tie. At thirty-five, his heavy-boned structure cast its shadow ahead to middle age, but as yet his body was lithe and in surprisingly good shape.

Her eyes fell on the water-crimped document which had cost Samsonov his life. '"*South West Africa Diamond Directorate. Tintenpalast. Windhoek. 10 October 1989 . . .*"' she read.

'Go on.' His voice burred with overtones of a mother-tongue which wasn't English or South African – German, probably.

'Tintenpalast – Palace of Ink,' repeated Romira. 'I like the name.' Her voice held a hidden taunt. 'Always did, when you were working there. It has the ring of bureaucratic civil servants at work.'

'I had a nice office in the Tintenpalast,' observed Ziegler. 'Overlooking the gardens. The view gave full scope for what civil servants are supposed to do – sit on their arse and gaze into the middle distance.'

'But you didn't let the grass grow under your feet, did

you, Ken? You were one of the top guys in the Diamond Directorate. You couldn't have had the authority to issue this document if you hadn't been.'

'It's not the original — it's a photocopy.' As if that mattered, thought Ken, when a man had been killed for its contents.

Romira went on. 'October 1989 — that's three years ago now, about six months before Namibia's independence, eh?'

'The whole country was in a ferment,' supplied Ziegler.

Romira gestured at the little piles of diamonds. 'And that's part of the pay-off.'

She silently read through the rest of the document. 'You made it sound good, Ken. You even used your own name. That was before you hijacked mine. Rick fell for it, and he was no sucker.'

'Some of those diamonds in the safe are still his.' Ziegler's voice was hard.

'Dawn Diamonds,' murmured Romira reminiscently, with a shade of provocation in her words. 'Rick was always a romantic.'

Ken threw her a penetrating glance, but her face was inscrutable.

'Without your good offices, we might not have brought Rick into the net,' said Ziegler. 'That was a nice little offshore diamond barge outfit of his. Well run, too. Pity it had to fold up, later.'

Romira laughed cynically. 'By courtesy of Kentrat Dehn.'

'You were in with me, don't forget. All the way. Let's get the necklace into position. We've time before dinner.'

Romira seemed reluctant to pull herself away.

'What is it worth?'

'About fifteen million dollars.'

'Where'd you get that figure from, if you've never risked putting it up for sale?'

'From my father. He gave me the figure shortly before

his death. He'd already had one heart attack. Perhaps he felt instinctively that there was a second one coming.'

'I thought his death had something to do with a terrorist attack.'

'That was my mother. As you know, the family farm was called "Allesverloren" – everything lost – in a remote area on the edge of the Kalahari desert. It was right in the path of the terrorists who used to raid from Angola into Namibia – then known as South West Africa. I reckon it was the shock of my mother's murder which triggered my father's heart attack.'

'If I'm to go along with your fake salvage charade of the Stones of the Sun and the *Nova Scotia*, I've got to know more about it and its true background so that I can keep up my story when the news breaks. And break it will, with a dollar-soaked masterpiece like that. How did you get hold of it in the first place?'

'I inherited it.'

'You inherited it!' she echoed. 'A thing like that, just lying around, waiting to be inherited! From whom?'

'I've told you, it's a family heirloom.'

'Tell me more. Not every family has fifteen million dollars lying around. I'd never heard of heliodore until you told me, and I thought I knew plenty about gemstones, after running your Touchstones shop in Windhoek while you were sitting hatching diamond schemes in the Tintenpalast. You've never told me the full story before.'

'Heliodore is a rare kind of beryl. You've heard of Rössing, of course?'

'Of course. Everyone in Namibia has. It's the biggest uranium mine in the world.'

'Good. Move to the top of the class. Okay. Rössing is a little over forty kilometres into the Namib desert from Swakopmund. In early German colonial days it was merely a remote railway siding which some loyal officer named in honour of his superior in Berlin.

'In 1912, German prospectors were electrified when the stationmaster at Rössing found a handful of very beautiful semi-precious stones on a barren mountainside near the station, and called in experts to identify them. They classed the gemstones as a completely new variety of beryl, not found anywhere else in the world.

'The tiny deposit lay on the mountainside amongst a lot of meteorites. The prospectors believed that the stunning yellow-green opalescent stones – ' Ziegler gestured at the necklace ' – had fallen from the sky along with the meteorites. So they officially named the mineral "Stones of the Sun".

'Nothing like it had ever been seen before and the stationmaster got the idea that the stones he had collected should be properly cut and mounted and crafted into a necklace which would be presented by the territory to the German Empress as a token of the colony's loyalty to the Fatherland.'

Ziegler picked his words slowly and carefully, as if not wanting to be tripped up. 'This was done, and that – ' he indicated the necklace '– was the result.'

'So that belonged to the Empress of Germany before the First World War? Which makes it stranger than ever that your family should have got possession of it.'

'Not so fast – you're jumping the gun,' replied Ziegler. He reached nervously into a pocket to find a banknote with which to pick his teeth, but caught Romira's cold glare and thought better of it.

'My grandfather, an officer in the colonial Schutztruppe, was selected by the German governor to act as special emissary to present the necklace to the Empress.

'The Kaiser and the Empress were at their hunting-lodge in East Prussia, a place called Schloss Allenstein . . .'

'More than ever, I'd like to wear an empress's necklace,' said Romira, who seemed captivated by Ziegler's story. 'When was this?'

'The summer of 1914, just before the outbreak of the First World War. My grandfather travelled via Berlin to Schloss Allenstein and joined the royal entourage. In fact, that's where he met my grandmother.'

Ziegler paused, as if marshalling his thoughts.

'Who was she?' asked Romira.

'A lady-in-waiting to the Empress,' answered Ziegler emphatically. Too emphatically. 'She fell for the handsome, debonair Prussian officer from the outpost of empire. In fact, they were married in Allenstein and she returned with him to South West Africa.'

'The Stones of the Sun! What happened to the Stones of the Sun?' demanded Romira.

'But you must know the background to understand what happened next,' he remonstrated. 'The necklace was duly presented to the Empress, who was enchanted. But Europe was going up in flames – in fact, the first shots were fired while the ceremony was going on at Allenstein.

'The Empress was fearful that in the event of a world war – which everyone recognized as inevitable – the priceless masterpiece would be lost. So she entrusted it to my grandfather to take back to South West Africa and put it in the safekeeping of the colonial governor until the war was over. His loyalty and devotion to the Kaiser were unquestionable.

'Back home, my grandfather suggested to the governor that because a South African attack on the territory would surely come at any time and the necklace would be in danger of being seized as war loot if the German defence failed, he himself should secrete the necklace at "Allesverloren", his remote farm on the border of the Kalahari desert. This farm had come to him as a grant of land from the government – all officers of the Schutztruppe were given such bounty as a token of their loyalty. This was agreed.

'My grandfather was killed in action against the invading

South African forces, and the governor was drowned when the German ship in which he was returning home – he had been recalled to Berlin by the government – was sunk by the Royal Navy in the Bay of Biscay.

'The only other person who knew the secret of the Stones of the Sun was my grandmother, and she was a forgotten woman out there in the wilderness.

'She had a hard life. She had two children, a boy and a girl, but she never remarried. My mother used to tell how, in order to keep up civilized standards, my grandmother used to dress for dinner every Saturday night, and wear the Stones of the Sun. It was quite safe to do so because no one ever came near "Allesverloren". She finally died of cancer of the throat in the 1930s.'

'But why didn't she come clean about the necklace?' asked Romira. 'Even if she hadn't received its full value, what she did would still have been a fortune.'

'No, it wouldn't, and she knew it,' replied Ziegler brusquely. 'Following the German collapse after World War One she knew the victorious Allies would confiscate it, if they learned about it.

'My father used the same argument – it was equally valid after World War Two – and so he kept the necklace at "Allesverloren" all his lifetime. I doubt my mother – a girl from Namibia he married in the fifties – was aware of it. Both my father and grandfather still felt a lingering loyalty to the once-mighty German Empress. It kept them from handing over the masterpiece to the British, or Americans, or whoever. It belonged to their empress – and so it remained.'

'And you feel no such quixotic loyalty?' Romira's smile was supercilious, mocking.

'Listen!' replied Ziegler abrasively. 'This is a different time and age, a completely new ball game. Things like unswerving loyalty until death us do part are old hat. It's every man for himself. I came to that conclusion when my father told me the history of the Stones of the Sun. He was very ill still, after his first heart attack. I think he needed to get the secret off his mind. He was also right about the main issue. If he – or I – revealed that we had kept the necklace in our possession for three-quarters of a century when it rightly belonged to the German government, we wouldn't have had a leg to stand on. The authorities would have had the first claim, and a very legitimate one.'

'Three-quarters of a century!' echoed Romira. She bent closer to the necklace in the safe. 'Fancy this beautiful thing lying out there in the bush all that time!'

'You don't want to start getting sentimental about it,' said Ziegler briefly. 'That's the danger of a thing like that. For me, it simply represents cash – hard dollars.'

'Fifteen million of them,' added Romira. 'Where'd your father get that valuation from?'

Ziegler shrugged. 'He was very cagey about it. I don't know. My main concern after my father had told me the story, and shown me what the Stones of the Sun looked like, was to get it on the market and cash in as soon as possible.'

'You'd never seen it before? Never?'

'I never knew about it,' answered Ziegler tightly. 'It might have been a different story if I had. No Bangazi Lodge, for instance.'

'You always had a yen for pretty stones,' said Romira. 'Think of Touchstones. It was probably the best gemstone shop in southern Africa.'

Touchstones! It had been Ziegler's first essay into running a front and where he had first gone wrong. Gemstones are only one small step from diamonds, and Ken couldn't resist using the flourishing little shop as a front for his illicit diamond racket in and out of Namibia into Angola, torn apart by civil war, but nevertheless a nest-egg of small diamond mines and wide guys. There was also the terrorist war along the no-man's-land border between Angola and South West Africa, where a couple of quick in-and-out runs with packets of diamonds filched by the light-fingered Ovambo workers from the biggest diamond fields in the world, Consolidated Diamond Mines at the mouth of the Orange River, were enough to net a fortune. Ziegler himself had had the perfect opportunity to cash in on the situation – one of the top men of the government Diamond Directorate, which entitled him to free passage across the Angolan border as he wished. And he did wish.

When Romira had taken over Ziegler's shop – and his bed – she soon found that Touchstones, with its innocent touristy facade, was the perfect cover for Ziegler's racket.

But his diamond scam paled into insignificance, dollar-wise, alongside the golden egg which had dropped into his lap in the shape of the Stones of the Sun.

'Heliodore!' Romira rolled the word on her tongue. 'At Touchstones, as I said, I'd never heard of it.'

'You're not the only one,' retorted Ziegler. 'When that first small deposit at Rössing was worked out, the name practically disappeared, except in mining textbooks as a rare one-off mineral. If you asked anyone at Rössing now, I'd lay a silver dollar they'd never heard of heliodore. The same thing goes for dealers.'

'Dealers? You showed the necklace around?' asked Romira in surprise.

'Don't be a fool!' snapped Ziegler. 'Of course I didn't show it around. After I'd inherited it, I put out a couple of tentative feelers on the world's auction markets in London, Geneva and New York. Heliodore? they demanded. What's that? What is the background of this necklace? Who is its rightful owner? I realized then that I would never be able to dispose of it without authenticating its pedigree, all the rest of it. My story of it being hidden away on a remote farm for the greater part of the twentieth century simply wouldn't wash. No, there had to be another way.'

'Salt the *Nova Scotia*!' Romira mocked. 'Open a second front at Bangazi!'

For the first time, Ziegler seemed a little defensive. 'It works.'

'Maybe. We haven't got to the crunch yet. By the way, what made you choose the *Nova Scotia* for your wreck racket? There are plenty of others.'

Once again, Ziegler's hand reached nervously towards his pocket for a banknote to pick his teeth, then dropped it self-consciously. His eyes were opaque, giving away nothing.

'I heard about the ship in Windhoek, when I was looking for a way to dispose of the stones,' he said.

He's lying, thought Romira. I know the symptoms.

'It's quite famous in its own way,' he hurried on.

Even Pernelle the expert, considered Romira, had not yet established the *Nova Scotia*'s history beyond the bare essential facts. Certainly, it wasn't famous.

'Pernelle is working on it,' he hastened on. 'She'll be able to fill us in for my salvage application . . .'

Romira didn't want to hear. She'd gone in with him, hook, line and sinker, when he'd burned his boats getting out of Namibia incognito in a hurry. Even changed his name as part of it, taking over her own surname as cover. She was involved in Ziegler's double racket, his diamond-smuggling first, and now, second, the 'salting' of the *Nova Scotia* wreck which would make them – him – millionaires for life at a single stroke.

'Okay, okay,' she replied impatiently, her anger directed against herself for being a sucker in more senses than one. 'Let's get on with what we came here to do. I hope it works.'

'The necklace has been submerged off and on for months in the tank downstairs. We should get away with it – we *must* get away with it. There's even sand and coral along with the sea-water, just as conditions would be if the necklace had been underwater in the *Nova Scotia*. Let's get going.'

From a small metal drawer under the steel shelf on which the necklace lay he took a short length of what looked like a cut-off section of fishing rod, through the top of which was threaded a loop of nylon cord with a plastic hook at the end. Without fingering it, Ziegler dextrously manoeuvred the hook through the necklace's gold chain and then deposited it carefully in a small square white plastic box. Neutral plastic could not have any effect, or leave any tell-tale deposit or patina on the gold or the stones, if they were checked, as they would be, under a microscope for authentication.

They gathered up the Makarov and Stones of the Sun and walked over to the far wall, where Ziegler pressed an electric button. There was nothing else to show that the outline in the steel was a private lift which went to the lowermost deck of the flotel where the former missile platform's 'facility wing' was situated, housing the fire-control and buoyancy-control centres.

The lift descended quickly and silently, the door opening on to a strange, desolate scene. Inside the big blast-proof, sound-proof and flame-proof chamber were groupings of empty steel desks; computer consoles robbed of their brains; disconnected, neatly insulated multi-coloured wires coming from nowhere, going nowhere. Half a dozen telephone cradles, minus their earpieces, might have been survivals of a world blasted into oblivion by a holocaust. The place was airless, clammy, totally without sound.

'This place gives me the creeps,' said Romira. 'Even the corpses are made of grey steel.'

'Don't be fanciful,' replied Ziegler.

'The buoyancy chamber is at least *alive*,' added Romira.

They vacated the lift and headed half to their left towards what seemed to be a blank steel wall. Ziegler approached and thrust a key into a keyhole. He pulled open a panel and pointed a small hand-held radio impulse switch at a couple of lighted dials next to a continuously burning bulb 'alert'. There was an answering bleep, and Ziegler used a big handle to swing wide a heavy door on oiled hinges. He turned on a light inside.

This was the hydropower buoyancy compensating system. It was the centre from which the computer-measured differences of buoyancy between the four legs of the platform were automatically assessed and compensated for, so that a missile would be assured of a completely level take-off.

It was also alive, alive with the sound of water circulating through pipes, and at the far side, a soft gurgling. Two grey steel consoles, the height of a man, into which led four thick grey pipes, each loaded with double valves like stop-cocks, were flanked by what looked like two pot-bellied brandy stills, whose big transparent stomachs were full of green lake water. These were 'silt domes' to measure the silt content of Bangazi's lake.

At elbow-height, designed for an operator to work standing, were complexes of thin pipes, some plastic, some glass, connected to flasks, through which water restlessly circulated. Above them, in a recess, was an illuminated computer dial capped by a strip of green-and-black plastic.

Between the two consoles was what looked like the cockpit of a luxury car with a seat of black leather set between two 'automatic gear change' levers, one right and the other left. They were fronted by a circular illuminated dial on a white control panel. This in turn was flanked by a dozen lights in green, yellow, black and red. With a hand on either 'automatic gear lever' it was like driving a futuristic car without a steering-wheel, an impression heightened by the 'windscreen' in the mock-mahogany cabin and a side-window of one-way tinted glass.

On the far side of the chamber were several banks of

turbines. Their function was to maintain constant pressure and levels in the platform's supporting legs. From them led four red pipes, each with its own pressure dial, which entered the steel floor via an open manhole cover, about a metre and a half across. From the shaft arose the sound of the soft wash of water. This ventilation shaft accessed the lower-level intakes, and inside was clamped a steel ladder leading downwards.

Ziegler and Romira threaded their way through the complex machinery to a spot next to the shaft where a large glass tank was bolted to the wall. It gave off a curious burbling sound. Ziegler turned on a switch, the gurgling stopped, and an underwater bulb came on, lighting in soft violet the pale green of the water. The tank was more than three-quarters full.

Ziegler waited until the water had settled, then took the plastic box containing the Stones of the Sun, hooked out the necklace with the 'fishing rod' and draped it over a similar hook inside the tank.

Romira stood abstractedly watching the proceedings, her mind turning on other things.

'I wonder how long you're going to go on fooling Buks,' she said suddenly. 'He surely doesn't believe that story of yours about this being a header sea-water tank for the real fish tank in the lounge upstairs.'

'We've only about a month more to go,' answered Ziegler. 'Lance brings the drums of sea-water in the chopper and Buks taps them into the tank upstairs.'

'That doesn't answer my query,' went on Romira. 'Surely with the knowledge he has of operating the buoyancy-control system, he isn't convinced.'

'Yes, he's suspicious, I think. Buks is a water expert and he can't see the object of this tank set-up. He doesn't know about the necklace, of course.' Ziegler's lips twisted cynically. 'Nor have I the slightest intention of letting him know.'

'Rightly so, but why do you allow him in here at all, even when the necklace is upstairs in the safe?' Romira was carping. The confined air of the chamber was starting to work on her.

'Buks was an army technician and he worked here,' answered Ziegler. 'If I shut the place up and locked everyone out, he'd be more suspicious anyway.'

'I don't trust Buks as far as I could throw this whole damn platform,' rejoined Romira.

'The moment I saw this set-up, I realized just how much it fitted my purposes,' said Ziegler. His self-congratulatory air irritated Romira. 'The tank was my idea. How to get the effect of years of submersion on the necklace without ever risking it near the sea, or near the wreck itself. Smart, eh?'

'Don't be too clever, Ken,' she said ominously. 'Someone like Pernelle, for instance, who knows a hell of a lot about wrecks and the condition of artefacts underwater, could blow your whole scheme sky-high.'

'She won't get the chance,' he retorted confidently. 'Once she's fulfilled her purpose and sorted the bloody red tape connected with it, she'll never see the inside of Bangazi Lodge again, I assure you. It's only because she's useful to me that she's here now.'

'And the way you intend to produce the necklace like a rabbit out of a hat on the anniversary of the *Nova Scotia*'s sinking, that in itself might look suspicious, too tailor-made. Especially as you'll have to give some explanation how a masterpiece like that came to be aboard an ordinary wartime transport carrying no rich passengers.'

'I don't have to account for why and how it came to be aboard the *Nova Scotia*,' he replied brusquely. 'What you find at a wreck, you find. I've told you the real background of the Stones of the Sun. It is mine. I inherited it. That's all there is to it.'

But it wasn't. Ken Ziegler was lying. Along with the

masterpiece he had inherited a secret time-bomb, its fuse burning inexorably towards the point of detonation from which all the blast-proof chambers of Bangazi would not shelter him.

11

'Shit in high cotton.'

Buks slapped his braces against his singlet in a double gesture of contempt; a tuft of chest hair deputized for a tie. He viewed the dining-room from behind the ornately carved mahogany bar.

Guests at Bangazi Lodge wore formal dress for dinner and Buks's rig stood out like a comic-cut. It was meant to. It was intended as a protest against the Saturday night fashion parade of beautiful women dressed by the finest couturiers in Johannesburg, dripping with magnificent jewels and escorted by men from millionaires' row, their glamour complementing the opulence of the softly lit dining-room.

Buks ran his eye over Gareth's clothes – elegantly cut white jacket, and ink-blue patterned viscose shirt over indigo tailored trousers – and their simplicity seemed to provoke a more egalitarian response. He stretched a brace again, its sharp slap against his protruding right nipple underscoring his words. 'That bloody string-whanger!' he growled. 'Thinks playing a harp makes her into an angel.' He cast his eyes to heaven. Buks had heard of heaven.

Gareth followed his gaze towards the small band playing at the far end of the room and was astonished to see Romira sitting very still, lips evocatively parted, playing a harp. Not wanting to be drawn into Buks's blast-area of contempt, Gareth commented mildly, 'She must be pretty good to play a harp with a band – rock-and-roll and a harp don't seem to mix, somehow.'

'Wait till you hear her go solo,' said Buks. 'Watch, she'll

wow 'em into eating out of her hand or throwing up out of sheer delight. Enrique Granados, Villa Lobos – you name the high-hat.'

Gareth idly wondered how Buks force-fed such composers' names into his memory-box. Perhaps he slapped them in with his elastic braces. Or was there more to Buks than met the eye?

He started to pour the two dry sherries Gareth had ordered for Pernelle and himself and indicated with the neck of the bottle a man sitting by himself at a table near the waiters' service doors. The solitary figure in tweed jacket and unmatched tie (borrowed from the bar) could not have looked more incongruous amidst the elegance.

'That's the guy who wants to talk to you,' said Buks. 'Sergeant Joubert, from Richards Bay. Not amused at the body being dumped on him at the police station.'

'He'll have to wait,' replied Gareth. 'No police business now.'

'Well, don't let him spoil your dinner.' There was an implied leer in Buks's voice. 'He's a suspicious type, like all cops.'

'Too bad,' said Gareth. 'I've got nothing to hide.'

In the hustle of getting ready for dinner and his unqualified pleasure in escorting Pernelle, Samsonov's ghost had taken a back seat in Gareth's mind – now the ghost was walking again and diamonds were the bottom line. He had said he had nothing to hide – a lie, of course – and very soon he would have to tell Pernelle.

He rejoined her at their table in a small alcove where the windows met an intersecting wall, giving them some privacy. She looked wonderful in gold-coloured pants with matching soft chamois jacket, and against the soft swell of her breasts lay a golden Mixtec pendant in the shape of a head in a filigree frame, salvaged by her father from an East Indiaman off the Cape.

After dinner, over coffee and liqueurs, Gareth finally decided to broach the subject.

'I always seem to have been mixed up with diamonds,' he started a little lamely.

Pernelle had felt all through dinner that he had something on his mind, and she wanted to hear it.

'Is that why you came here?' There were shadows in the deep blue pools of her fine eyes.

'Perhaps.' He paused, and then went on more rapidly, 'I graduated at the Witwatersrand University in Johannesburg and had a couple of early jobs at the famous De Beers in Kimberley, and then in Lesotho, which, believe it or not, has diamond fields in those icy, inhospitable mountain ranges. Those were my career *hors d'oeuvres*, so to speak. Inevitably I migrated to Oranjemund, at the mouth of the Orange River. Heard about it?'

'It's famous, that's all I know.'

He smiled slightly. 'It's the heart of the world's biggest diamond fields. However, it's the sort of diamonds you get and how they come to be there which I found just as fascinating.

'You see, Oranjemund diamonds are mined from the Namib desert diamond terraces which adjoin the beach. They yield small, but the world's purest, gemstones. They're mostly one carat or less and much sought after for jewellery. It is their superb quality which makes them unique.

'Diamonds are also won from the sea itself by offshore dredging in what we call the intertidal zone. These operators are small, often one-man outfits using catamarans equipped with suction air-hoses to nozzle out the diamonds from the seabed gravel or from submerged rocks along the shoreline.'

Gareth pulled himself up. 'Sorry, this sounds like a lecture. But to understand what's coming in regard to myself you have to know.'

She smiled. 'I'm listening.'

From the entrance across the room Romira noted the two heads drawing closer, and smiled. Her instinct had been right about them.

'I was – still am – deeply interested in the origin of these Oranjemund diamonds. The weight of scientific and engineering opinion is that they were washed down, over millions of years, from the interior of South Africa by ancient floods and deposited on the shoreline, which was then considerably different from the present. Palaeofloods, they're called.

'Now the Orange River, at whose mouth the great diamond fields lie, flows 2,000 kilometres right across the sub-continent, after rising in the high mountains of Lesotho. The theory is that millions of years ago diamonds were carried down the river to the sea, where they now are. That, as far as the experts are concerned, is that.'

He watched her next reactions closely. 'You've probably heard the long-standing debate on why the dinosaurs on earth suddenly died out?'

'What's that got to do with diamonds?'

'Diamonds – the kind of diamonds I've been searching for at the mouth of the Orange River – may be the strongest evidence yet that the dinosaurs' 150-million-year reign suddenly ended when an object from outer space – an asteroid – struck the earth sixty-five million years ago, causing havoc with the climate.'

'A moment ago we were in Lesotho, now we're back in the Namib.' She smiled.

He grinned back. 'I'm not telling this particularly well. But the second theory on the dinosaurs was that their end was caused by volcanic activity. Up to now, you could take your pick which theory best suited your book.

'But what I found in Lesotho proved otherwise. It's great dinosaur country – some of the beds are even well-known tourist attractions. In one of these areas

I found microscopic diamonds of the same type and concentration as are found in meteorites, which are small asteroids or comets which crash into the earth from space.

'At the same time, experiments I carried out showed that the Lesotho diamonds would have been destroyed by the high temperatures and pressures of volcanic eruptions.

'At Oranjemund I'm still hoping to find similar microscopic diamonds which will have been carried down from deep in the hinterland.'

What was he trying to tell her? The dinner and the setting were hardly the place to expound an esoteric theory such as this, however satisfying it might be to the ego of the person concerned. And Pernelle had already made up her mind that there was more to Gareth than an egotistical scientist. He spoke with quiet exaltation which, at the same time, seemed to hide a half-defined dread.

Her eyes held his across the table, and the candlelight opened deep shafts into his mind.

'Go on. I want to hear more.'

He laughed diffidently, almost apologetically, endorsing her opinion that this was no mere career line-shoot.

'It was called an original and daring proposition. Somehow, it percolated through the old Iron Curtain to the Soviet Union and came to the ears of the Soviet Department of Precious Metals and Minerals, which they called Glavalmazzoloto – it's got a new name since the revolution, but I still think of it as Glaval. It fell directly under the USSR Council of Ministers. There are huge deposits of diamonds in Russia. Next thing, I was flabbergasted to get an invitation to visit the Soviet Academy of Sciences. They called my theory electrifying and asked me to lecture on it at the famous Conference Centre at the city of Novosibirsk, in Siberia.'

'Siberia!' she echoed.

A faint smile illuminated his seriousness. 'Siberia isn't

at all what we imagine – I'll tell you in a moment.' But his face remained abstracted, almost sad.

'How old were you then?'

'Twenty-five.'

'Such an honour for anyone so young must have aroused a lot of feeling back home.'

He shrugged. 'It did. Especially when Glaval broadened the invitation for me to visit Akademgorok, the famed Siberian "village of scientists", thirty kilometres from Novosibirsk itself.'

'But what about the Cold War at that time?' she exclaimed in surprise. 'South Africa was regarded as the pariah of the world.'

'True,' he said. 'But Glaval squared that circle by asserting that science transcends the bounds of geography and politics as well as youth – they wanted me, they wanted to hear my theory. In fact, they lionized me. Very flattering.'

She looked at the strong face, observing, remembering what he was saying, for she still had the feeling that there was more to come.

'And yet,' she said, and her voice held no inflection of disparagement, 'with all that background you're not engaged in diamonds any more but in titanium-mining along the beaches of Zululand.'

'It was ten years ago,' he added. 'But it's all come round in a big circle now, with Glaval and diamonds at the centre of things. Right here at this very flotel.' His brown eyes held hers. 'Samsonov.'

She said acutely, 'Those lost years – there was something else, Gareth. Something cataclysmic for you.'

'Yes,' he said levelly. 'Anstice.'

12

The pounding of the band, with the contralto fibrillations of Romira's harp throwing themselves into the wild
rhythms, built up like a pressure cooker. Several couples,
unable to resist, were cavorting on a pocket-handkerchief-
sized space in front of the musicians.

Pernelle made a little stabbing movement with the fingers
of her left hand, accompanied by a forward lunge of her
head and slight dilation of her eyes at Gareth's use of the
name. It was a mannerism which Gareth had come to know
signalled something of major importance to her.

She said, 'Let's get out of here! We can talk in my
quarters.'

She stood up even before Gareth replied, oblivious
to what Ziegler's guests might think of the prettiest
woman in the room leaving early with an attractive
male escort.

Romira's eyes swivelled towards them as they passed the
dance floor – she thought at first they had come to dance –
and, at the door, there was no doubt what Buks thought.
The snap of his elastic braces against that calloused nipple
said it all.

Pernelle unlocked her door, and said, 'At least here the
seahorses won't shout us down.' She gestured towards the
courtesy liquor cabinet. 'Drink?'

He shook his head.

'Anstice,' she repeated. 'Who was Anstice?'

Anstice! When had he last spoken her name? Perhaps
never, to an outsider.

Pernelle noticed the tension in his clenched fingers as he

chose a low Zulu-patterned pouffe to sit on in preference to a chair, sinking down into what she thought of as his prospector's collecting stance.

'This "village of scientists" was created with the express purpose of settling a population in Siberia. Frozen wastes is the popular concept. It isn't like that at all. In the spring, when I arrived, it reminded me of the Transvaal Highveld, brisk air, wide open spaces, fresh green, animal life. There was even a Cape arum lily in full bloom in a pot at the entrance to the conference centre in Novosibirsk just to make me feel homesick!'

'But the pictures one sees . . .'

'Winter, of course, is different,' he agreed. 'Then the mercury is down to minus forty-five, milk is delivered in solid blocks, and car tyres freeze like old-time solid-rubber types. They're so hard that there's nothing pneumatic left about them.

'But it was all new and exciting and one day, in the Academy's Geological Museum where I was working, the head of the section, Dr Nikolai Vize, brought in a young woman reporter.' He seemed to choose his words carefully. 'Dr Vize and I are still in touch; he has played a big part in my life.'

Connections began to jell in Pernelle's mind over those Russian names – Vize, Samsonov . . .?

'This reporter was writing a feature for a rather avant-garde (for those days) Moscow magazine called *Ogonyok* on foreign scientists to whom the Soviet Union magnanimously threw open its doors – "There are no race barriers or prejudices here." But there were. I am talking of ten years ago, when the Cold War was in full swing, and everything South African was regarded by the outside world as anathema.

'Dr Vize had given her a preliminary briefing on me. To the Russians – and to her – I was something from Outer Space.

'She was about my own age, twenty-five. Her name was Anstice Petrov.'

Gareth could no longer hold his tense pose on the pouffe at Pernelle's feet. He got up and went to the big windows. He went on, speaking to the view.

'Anstice had had an exceptional journalistic career for a woman, even in a country where no career discrimination against women existed. She worked for the up-and-coming new-style magazine and had made her name about two years before we met in a dramatic rescue of Soviet scientists trapped by pack-ice in their Antarctic base. She flew by helicopter from the research ship which had gone to their rescue. Her vivid reports caused a sensation back in Moscow.'

On her return, Gareth went on, Anstice had been lauded by both the state and the media, and had further enhanced her reputation with a number of in-depth reports on Russia's world-wide scientific achievements.

Gareth returned to his seat by Pernelle.

She fingered the mental scars of the old wound gently. 'What did she look like, Gareth? Do you want to tell me?'

What had this woman done to him? Pernelle asked herself. From the lines round his jaw and nose, she knew that he had been into the depths of grief.

He leaned forward and ran his fingers lightly over the fragile instep strap of her Italian sandal. 'She was slender, with shoulder-length, darkish blonde hair, average height. I don't know how her features – high Slav cheekbones and slanting hazel eyes – would have rated in a conventional Western beauty competition, but it was a compulsive, unique face. It created its own attraction when she warmed to a subject which intrigued her.

'That day, the subject was me. The bogeyman South African from Outer Space.

'What started merely as a way-out interview developed – even at that first meeting – into something with much, much deeper overtones. It came to be an interview which neither of us wanted to end, and extended far longer than it should have, rather to the amusement of Dr Vize.

'When she finally left, both of us realized innately that it wasn't goodbye.'

Pernelle inclined her head, but did not speak.

Gareth went on. 'She was back again next day, on the pretext that her English wasn't all that fluent, and that she wanted to check various facts. Actually, her English was excellent. She had a very quick ear for language and spoke both French and German as well, which made her an ideal person to interview the various international scientists gathered at Akademgorok.

'We both revelled in the intuitive recognition of what was happening – in her subsequent series of interviews with other scientists she always found time for me. They were magic times. I think she strung out the Akademgorok assignment to about ten days.

'We met also in Novosibirsk. Our own private world was full of the magical upsurge of that beautiful Siberian spring. That's how I always think of Siberia, none of the cold, traditional greyness.'

He ran his finger along her sandal-strap again and said quietly, 'That was to come, in our lives.

'When Anstice went off to Tashkent, about 1,800 kilometres away to the south west, to continue her series on modern cities in contrast to their time-honoured history, she and I could recognize that we were something very special to one another. She promised she would come back to Novosibirsk, somehow she would fiddle it with her magazine bosses in Moscow.

'She phoned me at Akademgorok from Tashkent, she phoned from Samarkand, and then there was the glorious moment when she rang from Novosibirsk to say she was only thirty kilometres away. We were intoxicated; this was love; we knew it for what it really was.'

Gareth shook his head like a boxer coming back from an eight-point count.

'She had told me her parents lived in what was then Leningrad and now St Petersburg; her father was a teacher. In fact, that's where her rather pedantic name came from. It's a shortened form of Anastasia, daughter of one of the Czars. I never bothered to ask her Leningrad address or phone number – what need was there, when she was right here with me! Leningrad was as far away as the moon, farther away than South Africa even, to me.'

He paused and shivered as if there were Siberian air outside instead of the warm Maputaland night.

He said quickly, as if to get it over, 'Had I known what cards she had played with her Moscow bosses, or if I had understood Russian even, I might have had some insight into what happened.

'Anstice vanished after that telephone call.'

To Pernelle, his voice was that of a man who had agonized a thousand times over insupportable alternatives.

'We had made a date for her to come to Akademgorok next day at ten – she was one of the privileged few with her own firm's car. She, like myself, was elated, excited, full of the world which had opened up for us.

'She said goodbye, hung up the phone.

'That was the last I ever heard of Anstice.

'When she did not arrive next day, I was puzzled but not overly anxious. I went to Dr Vize, who had been sympathetic to our relationship, and asked him to check her hotel. I couldn't phone myself because of the language barrier and, as it turned out, that lack was part of the heartbreak. I was stunned at what he was told – Anstice had left just before breakfast – with a man.

'I couldn't believe my ears – a man!

'But there was something about Dr Vize's reply –

something too bland, too carefully phrased – which made me uneasy. He said that Anstice had stuck her neck out with her fearless articles in *Ogonyok*, and perhaps she was answering some official questions. The way he left the explanation open-ended disturbed me.

'I extracted a rather reluctant promise from him to phone the hotel again that afternoon. I was with him when he did. There seemed strange overtones about the way he spoke, and equally strange overtones to his silences at the replies – like a doctor who has identified terminal symptoms in a patient and doesn't want to disclose the worst.

'Anstice had booked out of the hotel, he told me. The man had carried her suitcase. He wasn't young, he wasn't old. The hotel had no idea who he was. They had driven off in Anstice's car.

'I was frantic, and pressed him for details. All he knew – or would admit – was that she had gone. No, she had left no forwarding address. The hotel wasn't expecting her back.

'It was I who then asked the sixty-four-thousand-dollar question. Remember, those were the days of the Cold War, the pre-Gorbachev era, when the KGB still reigned supreme. There was no such thing as liberal ideas, or the sort of lance-like criticism of officialdom which had made Anstice's magazine a top popular favourite.

'"The KGB?" I asked bluntly.

'Dr Vize remained poker-faced. "Remember," he told me, "you are a South African and come from one of the most hated countries in the world. You and she were very friendly. You have my sympathy, but figure it out, my friend."

'"What Anstice and I feel has nothing to do with politics," I protested. "Will you phone her editor in Moscow for me? I must know!"

'He looked at me gravely. "You know this line could be tapped? You want to see South Africa again, don't you?"

' "I'm due to go back soon! Time is short!"

' "Mine may also be," he responded. "Listen, Gareth, I'm doing this outside the line of duty because I respect your work and like you as a human being, and I know that Anstice is a great girl. That's as far as I can go."

'I stayed with him while he phoned Anstice's editor. Dr Vize's tone was the same flat, give-away-nothing voice he had used with the hotel. The call was short-lived.

' "She has been given an extended assignment in Central Asia," he said.

' "But where? Since when?"

'Dr Vize was very kind, but I couldn't get beyond his bland assurances.

' "Accept it, Gareth," he advised me. "Write to her home."

' "I don't know her address in Leningrad," I told him desperately. "I only know her father is a teacher . . ."

' "What sort of teacher? Of what? School, technical, university – what?"

' "I don't know. But we could look up the name Petrov in the phone book – "

' "First, here in Akademgorok or Novosibirsk – or anywhere else in Siberia – you won't find a copy of a Leningrad telephone book. Second, the name Petrov is as common as Jones in Britain. And how do *you* propose to check? You can't read or speak Russian."

' "I must find out what has happened!"

' "Perhaps she will phone you herself, or write . . ."

'She never did.

'I think I nearly went out of my mind in the traumatic month or so which followed before I was due to return to South Africa. Dr Vize remained sympathetic but wary, looking over his shoulder all the time. He never admitted it, but I knew the KGB had taken her. Where, where, where?

'On my way through Moscow on my return to South

Africa I visited the offices of *Ogonyok*. It was impossible to convey who I was, what I wanted. They all claimed ignorance of English, and the name Anstice Petrov was the signal for a complete switch-off. The editor wouldn't even see me.

'My time ran out, I had to leave. I left Russia stunned, sickened, terrified. I still wake up with nightmares thinking what the KGB might have done to Anstice. Traumatic, lonely years followed.

'Diamonds went sour on me. I decided to get out of them – I associated them with Anstice, in a warped kind of way – and changed my interest to radioactive materials. It was an almost natural step for me to take a job at Rössing, near Swakopmund, the world's biggest uranium mine, in the Namib desert.

'Rössing would have been interesting enough, I suppose, if I hadn't had such a weight on my mind. The area had been bombarded at some time in the remote past by meteorites. There was a historical record of a rare kind of beryl which was named heliodore by the earliest German prospectors who discovered a small deposit of it just before World War One.'

'Heliodore – what does that mean?' asked Pernelle.

Gareth laughed. '"Stone of the Sun". The German scientists thought the mineral had fallen from the sun at the same time as the meteorites on the barren slopes of Rössing mountain. That's imaginative enough, but the local Bushmen came up with a name which is quite poetic as well – "Stones of the Daystar", the "daystar" being their word for the sun. The deposit was so small, in fact, that heliodore is unknown today, and there are no specimens to check and analyse in the light of modern knowledge. I might have gone for heliodore if I could have found out more about it. Heliodore is radioactive and apparently had a glorious greenish-yellow glow, a kind of fire that was supposed to be brighter than a diamond.'

'Stuck out there in the desert doesn't seem the right place for a man with all you had on your mind,' observed Pernelle.

He shrugged. 'Rössing was a splendid jumping-off place for expeditions and climbing trips into the desert mountains. I had a lot of physical exercise, and a crash course in combat methods run by the mine for security reasons. I guess that's what enabled me to retrieve Samsonov's body. I learned to abseil from the Namib's rock-faces.'

'Shall I make some coffee?' asked Pernelle. 'There's one of those self-brewing gadgets right here.'

Gareth shook his head. 'You've been splendid, listening to all this. I'd like to finish. You see, diamonds wouldn't leave me alone, even at Rössing. I'd been there a couple of years when out of the blue came a telephone call from Dr Vize. He'd been elevated to the council of Glavalmazzoloto, and was based in Switzerland. Glaval was deeply interested in a superb diamond which had been exhibited at the international Watch, Clock and Jewellery Fair at Basle, with a price tag on it of five million dollars.

'It created a sensation, and an intense controversy because the exhibitors refused to disclose either the origin or the owner. Apparently it was superb – a thirty-carat pure white, rated as D-flawless.'

'What does that mean?'

'Sorry, I got carried away,' said Gareth. 'D-flawless is the highest possible classification in the diamond world, denoting a complete absence of colour. Only twenty-seven other diamonds in the world have earned the rating D-flawless.

'Diamond dealers in Europe maintained that the origin of the stone could not be determined, but argued that it had been cut in Europe. Even De Beers's name had been bandied around, but this was denied by the company.

'Dr Vize asked me to fly to Switzerland and pronounce on the diamond, which hadn't even got a name.

'The invitation was like a shot in the arm, Pernelle. I was back where I belonged. When I reached Switzerland, my judgement ran counter to that of the dealers. Without boring you with the technicalities, I maintained that it was an Angolan diamond which had been cut and polished in Israel – there were aspects of the pear cut which were typically Israeli.

'I told Dr Vize, who had joined up with me, that the stone had never been worn and therefore whoever bought it would be entitled to name it. The D-flawless rating was correct.

'Glaval was delighted at my verdict, and put in an immediate bid for the stone. And – a typical gesture of warmth from Dr Vize – named it "Welwitschia" in honour of a famous Namib desert plant which has been called a "living fossil" and grows nowhere else in the world. "You are of the Namib, and so is the Welwitschia," Dr Vize told me.

'Although Glaval was delighted, they were also concerned, because there were quite a few questions about the diamond which still remained unanswered. They were worried about its origin, since Angola was increasingly becoming the pipeline for the flow of illicit diamonds. In short, diamonds were simply pouring out of Angola.

'Getting back to Rössing was like having a bucket of cold water thrown in my face. My colleagues there were burned up with jealousy. Although I stayed on, the cold shoulder was really frigid. Finally I got out, and took this job with the dune-mining outfit here in Maputaland. But I can't stomach being party to ruining one of the most beautiful natural environments in the world. So, I'm on my way again. I might indeed have been gone already, had Samsonov not cropped up.'

'Without regrets, Gareth?'

'Not without regrets.' He did not say, because I could love you. His next words might blast that prospect forever.

He added, 'Samsonov came to Bangazi to meet me.'

Her lovely eyes widened, then became veiled. There was a long silence. She said, at length, 'When they asked, you said you didn't know Samsonov.'

He shook his head. 'No, I said I had never met Samsonov. Nor had I.'

'But you knew him.'

'No. We were due to rendezvous at the La Presidente Meridien hotel in Luanda in Angola. The change of plan to meet here came as a complete surprise to me.'

He could not read her mind behind those masked eyes, but it was clear what thoughts the shock of Samsonov had detonated: had she been swayed by the smooth words of an undoubted charmer, been taken for a ride about might-have-beens which had no reality; and was now faced with a double-speaker who split meanings over the identity of a man who could have been murdered? Why had he risked his neck to go and fish the body out of the lake?

'Did you tell the policeman from Richards Bay about this?' she asked without inflection.

'I told him what I told you, I had never met Samsonov. Which is true.'

He could see what an effort her next question cost her.

'What is your involvement, Gareth?'

He was glad she had not used the word game.

He went on, picking his way through a minefield of words. 'I told you, even at the time of the Welwitschia stone Glaval was concerned about the illegal diamond pipeline racket in Angola. Since the so-called end of the Angolan war and its flare-up again, it has grown, rather than lessened. But then it came to Glaval's ears that their name was somehow being used in connection with the racket. Something about bogus receipts or guarantees — there was no certainty what.

'Dr Vize telephoned me, here in Zululand at Richards Bay. He offered me a commission to go to Angola — or indeed anywhere the trail might lead in Central Africa — and get to the bottom of how Glaval was being implicated. Dr Vize's offer came at the exact moment I had decided to get out of an outfit which I regarded as desecrating a unique and splendid coastline. I am, in fact, on my way. I am working off my final weeks as leave.'

'You haven't explained Samsonov.'

'Samsonov has — had — been Glaval's man in Angola-Zaire for some time. But, Dr Vize told me, he lacked my expertise on the origin of diamonds. Still, Samsonov had an unparalleled knowledge of the ins and outs of the smuggling pipeline route. He and I were to work it out together and find out how Glaval was being dragged in. As I said, we were due to meet in Angola. He must have hit on something startling for him to completely change the nature of his brief from Glaval. Dr Vize knows nothing about it, of that I am certain. Samsonov came personally to tell me something too big, too dangerous, to commit to paper. His body in the lake proved that.'

'You think he was murdered?'

'I know.'

'What makes you say that?'

'I am convinced that Bangazi is the tip of a diamond-smuggling iceberg. I saw the extreme tip of the iceberg this morning in the chopper on our way to the Tea-house of the Zulu Moon.'

Her eyes were very wide now, in alarm.

'You remember how that case of abalone fell and broke open? How I was a long time on the floor fishing around for them? One of the abalones had split open along its natural seam. Something fell out — maybe to anyone else it would have looked like a chip of mother-of-pearl. To me it wasn't. It was a diamond. More than that, from the quick look I had, I reckon it was a sea-diamond. You only get sea-diamonds in Namibia. That meant it had been smuggled out of one place only, Oranjemund.

'Do you also remember how when we landed Ziegler wouldn't be parted from the case of abalone? It was a gift for his Chinese guests, he said. Later it was to be flown out to a Taiwanese trawler offshore.

'Pernelle, that was a carton of doctored abalone, loaded with illicit diamonds. It is clever, very clever.

'Bangazi is the front for a hellishly ingenious diamond scam. The mastermind behind it is Ken Ziegler.'

13

'*Where is Samsonov?*'

Gareth looked into the special Smith and Wesson sights of the Colt 45 and behind them into the hard brown eyes of the man holding the heavy automatic. The shock of being confronted by the killer weapon, with its blatant mouth, photoflashed into his brain the die-stamped words cut on the side of the gun: 'Colt's government issue'. His stunned mind took in the irrelevant fact that the butt was of wild olivewood, with a tiny monogrammed silver shield. There was no chance of the intruder missing at a range of a couple of metres. But if he did, he had a lethal back-up in his other fist – an Excalibur fighting knife with a fifteen-centimetre blade. The words spilled like venom. '*Where is Samsonov?*'

Gareth found that all the security combat techniques he had learned at Rössing had been blown clean out of his mind by the stark reality confronting him. He said lamely, 'If you pull that trigger, you'll never know.'

The man lifted the gun, as if it required still finer targeting on the centrepoint of Gareth's forehead. His inner tension was clear in the way the knife-blade made small arcs in the air. The bristles of his short black beard pushed out droplets of sweat.

'Don't try and sell me any soft-soap crap. Answer my question!' His voice was slightly overlaid with foreign vowels.

They were in Gareth's lounge-cum-office in his quarters at the Richards Bay mining company.

It was mid-Tuesday morning.

A whole lifespan of time seemed to have passed since

Lance and his helicopter had picked him up at Richards Bay and he had found himself sitting next to a girl with great blue-grey eyes and fair hair, and had been whisked away to a never-never-land in the middle of a lake. It was, in fact, only three days before. The rest of the weekend had had a strange air of unreality, of wonder encapsulated into a make-believe setting – plus a beautiful woman.

Plus a dead man.

He and Pernelle had talked in her suite until late that Saturday night about Samsonov and the possible reasons for his breaking their pre-arranged rendezvous in Luanda – they had come to no conclusion. Gareth had given Pernelle all the facts, down to the tiniest nuance which might cast light on the mystery. He found this self-confession therapeutic; by the time he had left her, he knew innately that their relationship had deepened. She had been shocked by his revelation that Ken Ziegler was the mastermind behind a diamond-smuggling ring; where, however, they both asked, did the wreck of the *Nova Scotia* come in? From Ziegler's relentless pressure to discover it, they concluded it must have a major role – but what?

Gareth's full interview with Sergeant Joubert the next day, Sunday, had been less pleasant. He felt as if he were threading through a minefield. He knew too much about Samsonov which he hadn't previously revealed, and although he was sure he had let nothing slip, the policeman must have picked up a certain guardedness in his terse replies. Sergeant Joubert insisted that Gareth must not leave Richards Bay until after the inquest on Samsonov, and simply shrugged when Gareth told him his plans to leave – he would have to stay. A second statement would also have to be made at Richards Bay police station on Monday.

The policeman also interviewed Pernelle, who had little to add to Gareth's account of spotting Samsonov's body floating under the flotel. Nonetheless, Sergeant Joubert insisted that she 'be at the disposal of the police' for the next few days in case further questions arose, before returning to Cape Town. Ken Ziegler was jubilant and immediately offered to let her stay on at Bangazi; he saw the delay as an invaluable chance to get Pernelle's expert guidance in the formulation of his application to the National Monuments Council for exclusive salvage rights to the *Nova Scotia*.

Ken Ziegler had also come under Sergeant Joubert's searchlight. He maintained – and there was nothing to show to the contrary – that Samsonov must have fallen off the bird-watchers' boom after taking a forbidden stroll in the middle of the night. Ziegler further exonerated himself by stressing the 'no entrance' signs on the bird-watching vantage point.

Ken wanted another dive to the *Nova Scotia* wreck that day, but the police interviews took up most of the morning. Pernelle, Brad and Darren, with Gareth accompanying the flight, went out to the *Sea Urchin* in the afternoon. It was an unrewarding dive. They found no new artefacts, and no fresh chunks of wreck. They put down more marker buoys and got an exact positional fix from Captain MacDonald, but Pernelle reckoned that months of exploratory work lay ahead.

Gareth, that Tuesday morning, had been on the point of reaching for the phone to speak to Dr Nikolai Vize in Moscow (he commuted between there and Switzerland) to inform him of Samsonov's death when his office door had been flung open by the gunman. The man's clothes were crumpled, as if he had travelled hard and far, his face lined with fatigue.

'What have you done with my half-million and my diamonds, eh?' he jerked out savagely.

It flashed through Gareth's mind that he might pull the trigger solely to discharge the colossal build-up of tension tearing through his body. Any hedging, any trying to talk the man out of lowering the gun at this stage would, Gareth registered, be futile. It might only precipitate action.

He threw the punch straight from the shoulder: 'Samsonov is dead.'

The fighting knife in the gunman's left fist made a couple of wild oscillations in the air, but the Colt's sights remained fixed unwaveringly between Gareth's eyes.

'You killed him. You . . .'

'Don't be a fool,' Gareth snapped. 'I never met him.'

'I didn't break my balls to get here just to be told you don't know Samsonov.'

An uncontrolled muscle jerked back his lips on the right side of his mouth to show a line of fine teeth. They had the risibility of a corpse's gape.

'You're lying! Samsonov told me himself in Luanda he was coming to see you. He gave me your address and your phone. That is how I knew to find you here. But you double-dealt the poor bastard and killed him . . .'

Gareth half-rose from his chair and the gunman's trigger finger tightened. He sank back.

'Listen!' snapped Gareth. 'Just listen for a moment instead of throwing around wild allegations. First, Samsonov was only a name to me; second, Samsonov drowned — or was drowned. I don't know which.'

'Where? How?'

'I would like to know. The police would like to know.'

'You didn't drag the police in!'

'They weren't dragged in. A body in a lake at a luxury lodge invited the police.'

'Who killed him?'

'No one, it seems. He went for a stroll in the middle of the night along a bird-watchers' vantage point and fell into the lake. He drowned. End of Samsonov.'

'But not, by all that's holy, end of story!' he snarled. 'I know the flotel lay-out. You shut Samsonov's mouth because he knew too much — he told me only a little in Angola, and it was enough to know that he'd opened a can of worms, all right. He rushed here to tell you and you stopped his mouth because he was on to something big . . .'

'For Pete's sake!' exploded Gareth. 'Stop accusing me of killing Samsonov! I'm involved only because I fished his body out of the lake. I was in the chopper coming in to land and we spotted a body floating amongst the flotel's support piles. I didn't know it was Samsonov until the Lodge people identified him.'

Gareth noted that the barrel of the gun had started to droop, as if it were becoming too heavy for the suntanned hand to hold. If he could keep the gunman talking . . . His eye travelled past the man's shoulder to the wall. On it hung a climber's rope and some karabiners on a heavy belt. One quick back-hander from that across the side of the head before he realized what was happening – Gareth's leg muscles flexed under the desk.

'How did you know that Samsonov was at this lodge? He told me you were based at Richards Bay, and he was on his way here to see you.'

'Because Samsonov informed me,' retorted Gareth. He eased a tiny slip of paper from the corner of his blotter and pushed it across to the gunman. 'Read that. I missed Samsonov here: I was held up getting back by the floods. That's his note asking me to meet him at Bangazi. He had something big to tell me.'

The man used the fighting knife as a claw, drawing the slip of paper to him with its deadly point. When he had read it, the blade did not resume its lethal arcing, and the intruder's face clouded with doubt.

He said, after a silence, 'Samsonov was coming back to Luanda to me, after he had interviewed you. I think it was his plan to bring you back with him. I waited only as long as the money held out – you see, Samsonov was paying my way at the Presidente Meridien. I was – am – broke, have been ever since that shit double-crossed me . . .' His voice was rough, his accent prominent.

A spasm of rage shook him. 'What have you done with my diamonds? Five hundred thousand dollars! Hell, how I sweated, day and night, and drove the catamaran to get them together so that they'd be ready before Independence Day! She was a little beauty, was the *Namib Dawn*, and I was forced to flog her in the end because I was broke, made to go broke!'

'You're confusing me,' said Gareth. 'Start at the beginning by telling me your name, and what Samsonov came here to tell me. Then perhaps we can talk sense.'

The gunman laid the Colt on the edge of Gareth's desk, butt facing himself, and the knife next to it. Five minutes previously Gareth would have tried to jump him, but it was rapidly becoming unnecessary.

The man groped in the inside pocket of his scuffed old leather jacket and finally pulled out a rather grubby plastic-coated folder containing a sheet of paper.

He started to pass the wallet across the desk but suddenly withdrew it.

'I gave Samsonov a copy of this to bring to you. This is the original,' he said slowly. 'If what you say is true, you never saw it.'

'I still don't know what it is.'

'It's a receipt,' he went on. 'A receipt – for half a million United States dollars.'

'In respect of what?'

'Diamonds. My diamonds. Sea-diamonds.'

'Legitimate?'

'I told you, I worked my arse off in my offshore catamaran outfit day and night to beat the deadline of Namibia's independence. I did. I scoured practically every offshore pot between Luderitz and Hottentots Bay. Yes, it was legitimate, all right. Half a million at going prices, but I would have got more elsewhere on the black market. That's where everything blew up in my face. It was clever, Dehn's scheme was, but I was the sucker. Taken for a ride – half a million's worth! But, by all that's holy, I'll get them back yet! Samsonov was my only hope, but now he's dead, you say . . .'

Gareth said, 'I was working with Samsonov, and was due to rendezvous with him in Angola. Now you appear.'

The gunman pushed the Colt and the knife to one side. 'The name's Rick Arnold.'

He eyed Gareth searchingly, as if expecting a reaction. Gareth knew he had won.

Rick indicated the document in the plastic wallet. 'I'm going to read this to you. I don't trust it out of my own hands.' He nodded at the two weapons. 'Don't try anything funny while I'm doing so. And keep your hands away from the phone.'

'That's not such a good beginning for co-operation between us, is it?'

Rick's teeth showed white under his untrimmed moustache.

'Maybe not, but it'll have to pass. See here, Gareth Ridpath, when you've been taken for a ride like I have, and lost everything, so that today you're down on your uppers and forced to keep body and soul together by doing a job you were trained for but still hate, it makes you suspicious. That's all.'

'Okay, okay.'

Now the words bled from his mouth as if they hurt.

'The letterhead is, South West Africa Diamond Directorate, and the date is October 1989. I collected this myself from the Tintenpalast.'

'Before Namibia's independence.'

'That's the kicker. It had to be before independence. Everyone in the territory was mining diamonds like hell, to have a nest-egg stockpile when the hour came. Including De Beers.'

'Consolidated Diamond Mines,' Gareth corrected him.

'Yeah, CDM. Same thing. Samsonov said you knew a hell of a lot about diamonds.'

'Technically, maybe. Market-wise, not so much. I worked for CDM once.'

Gareth did not elaborate. It was Samsonov who had had the knowledge of the devious underground channels of the diamond set-up once the parcels of illegal stones crossed the border from Namibia into Angola and Zaire then on into Central Africa and beyond. He had been set to learn from Samsonov. Death is a rough teacher.

Rick went on. 'I told you I had a flourishing little offshore catamaran outfit called the *Namib Dawn*. That's the reference in this document.'

He continued, holding the paper with one hand, the other drifting close to the Colt.

' "This instrument, duly authorized by the above Department of State . . ." that's the Diamond Directorate,

and secured with full collateral by Glavalmazzoloto of the USSR, Department for Precious Metals and Minerals under the USSR Council of Ministers, Moscow, and its Africa office at 130 Avenue President Jose Eduardo dos Santos, Luanda, Angola, acknowledges raw diamonds to the value of $500,000 (five hundred thousand US dollars), the property of Namib Dawn Diamonds (owner Mr Rick Arnold) operating offshore in the Luderitz-Hottentots Bay concession area, for onward delivery to the said Glavalmazzoloto in Luanda, and guarantees full payment of the stated amount within 4 (four) calendar months of the territory of Namibia becoming independent after March 21, 1990.

Signed on behalf of the Diamond Directorate,

Kentrat Dehn,
Chief Executive Officer,
SWADD'

The formal words of the document sank deep like an acupuncture needle into Gareth's brain. Glaval! Named as the co-conspirator in a racket as murky as any he had as yet encountered and perfectly scheduled at a time when the guns along the Namibia–Angola border were starting to fall silent. But the smoke of battle still masked a thousand sins! No wonder Samsonov had taken off like an out-of-control missile to get to him across the width of the African sub-continent, leaving Rick comfortably ensconced at his expense in the Presidente Meridien to await his return. The document would be a wall-to-wall nightmare for Glaval. In that half-page of typescript was almost all the basic information Glaval had commissioned him to find out. It would, he knew, stun Dr Vize as much as it did him. It had all the outward sanction of authority; the man who had thought up the use of Glaval's name must have had nerves of steel. No wonder Rick had fallen for those smooth legal-sounding words . . .

Gareth pulled his thoughts together: Rick was talking fast and had not noticed his abstraction.

'Do you really know what the situation is there in Angola still? Organized crime syndicates . . .' he slapped the typescript in front of him '. . . are stealing diamonds worth hundreds of millions of dollars a year from the mines in Namibia, and they're like bees round a honeypot since the peace accord between Unita and the Angolan government collapsed. Millions! There are twenty to fifty thousand diggers working in the diamond areas of Angola! Diamonds are second only in importance to oil . . .'

'You seem to know a hell of a lot about it,' interjected Gareth.

'If you don't learn and learn fast who and what you are dealing with, you finish up the way Samsonov has. I'm interested only in tracking down my half-million referred to in that receipt, not in present-day rackets. My nose is clean.'

'It wasn't so clean at the time of that receipt. I'd say you were either very naive or very greedy to have fallen for a racket like that.'

Rick stiffened, then gave an apologetic half-grin. Gareth began to think he could like the man.

'Five minutes ago, that remark could have cost you a forty-five slug. My people originally came from Sicily – we're a hot-blooded lot.

'Yeah, I tried to cut corners, and a lot of guys did, at that steamy time.'

'When was this?' demanded Gareth.

'About mid-1989 and on towards 1990 – independence was in March 1990. It was the period just before the Untag forces took up their positions, and there was plenty of coming and going between Namibia and Angola, which gave the wide guys all the cover they needed for a bit of diamond-running. The small guys with pint-sized marine diamond outfits like mine, or maybe a one-horse show on land, knew that we'd catch the rap if politically things went sour. At that stage, the cat could have jumped either way. We, the small guys, were shitting our pants with all kinds of fears.'

'They turned out to be unjustified,' said Gareth.

'I – we – weren't to know that. Then along came this smooth bastard Kentrat Dehn.'

'You make him sound like a superman,' observed Gareth.

'He was in a position of authority in the pre-Namibian administration as one of the top guys in the Diamond Directorate. He could fly a helicopter, and was one of the privileged who were allowed to move backwards and forwards into Angola after the ceasefire had been arranged, but before the peace came fully into operation. The border was a wild, hairy place, and Dehn had the nerve to cash in on it.

'Dehn briefed us small guys secretly about what he called the government's "trusteeship" scheme. This is what it was. In order to safeguard the state's currency, he said, the government would buy up all the diamonds it could as a collateral to back the currency issue. No money would change hands but a fully pledged receipt would be given. Payment – ' Rick indicated the paper in front of him ' – was guaranteed for four months after independence. Dehn went further: Glaval, as we all knew, is the Russian counterpart to the De Beers-backed World Selling Organization – '

Gareth intervened. 'Times have changed radically since then.'

'I know, I know,' retorted Rick impatiently. 'I'm telling it as it was. Everyone was aware that the emergent Namibian regime and its Swapo fighters had been backed militarily, financially and politically for many years by the Soviet Union. So, what could be more natural than that Glaval should be willing to back the small diamond man against the Western diamond giant, and offer higher prices than the WSO would? It all sounded kosher, one hundred per cent watertight.

'Moreover, Glaval had been genuinely operating in war-torn Angola buying free-market diamonds at bargain basement prices and Dehn, so he said, was the official go-between from Namibia who was allowed to move freely across the border.

'As a top Diamond Directorate official he had access to official letterheads in Windhoek; he must have faked the rest of the receipts himself.

'The logistics of the scheme were that I brought my diamonds secretly to his Windhoek office and handed them over – hell's teeth! Half a million's worth I passed over to him and watched him lock them away in his safe! I still remember the battered old thing! I was given my "trusteeship" receipt in return. Trusteeship! It wasn't worth the paper it was written on!'

'You could have gone to the authorities afterwards and told the whole story – plus the receipt to prove it.'

Rick snorted. 'You're saying exactly what Dehn said when I went back and confronted him after independence when my half-million was due. Go, he told me to my face. All that receipt will show is that you cheated the state of substantial tax income, failed to declare your output, and were up to your neck in a major scheme to defraud the state. I will be shown to be in the clear by holding on to the diamonds and being ready to hand them over to the authorities in due course.

'I pulled this same gun on him and told him to open up his safe and hand them over. Dehn is a tough cookie. "I don't have them," he said, "Glaval has. Go and ask Glaval." No need to tell you what else happened at that meeting, but I didn't get my money, I didn't get my diamonds.'

'But you still had your offshore marine outfit,' Gareth observed.

'In a sense, yes. I still hoped to get my half-million, but the *Namib Dawn* was bleeding to death. I started to become strapped for cash as operating costs continued to rise. Most of all, I wasn't able to market my output by returning to the orthodox De Beers-backed WSO channels since awkward questions would have been asked about my previous output and how I disposed of it.

'I faced ruin, and decided to confront Dehn again. I flew to Windhoek and found he had disappeared without trace. I met with a blank wall at the Diamond Directorate. The new political regime had purged and rejigged the whole structure; everyone was tight-lipped about Dehn and the pre-independence members of the department – shady deals were known to have been put through but nothing could be proved.'

He shrugged. 'That was the end of *Namib Dawn*. I shut down and started to look for a job.'

'In diamonds?'

'No, I wasn't trained in diamonds. I'm a specialized type of engineer. I'm with the Cape offshore oil-from-gas platform at Mossel Bay. I was trained in oil rig engineering in Italy. As a matter of fact, I was one of the men who helped build the Bangazi flotel for the army when it was a top-secret missile-firing platform. I'm not sold on that sort of work. My interests are in diamonds. Losing the *Namib Dawn* broke my heart.'

The tight face trembled like a squall rippling over the surface of the sea.

Gareth believed him. He asked, 'What did you hope to get out of Samsonov? Or me?'

'The route to Glaval,' he replied without hesitation.

'Your quarrel isn't with Glaval,' Gareth answered. 'Why don't you locate this Kentrat Dehn? He's your man.'

'You don't have to tell me,' he hurled back. 'I tried everything I knew to track him down. Dehn brushed out his tracks – but completely. You're my last hope. The way I reckon is, Glaval could lead me to Dehn. It's Dehn I want to get my hands on! And if I do, by all that's holy, I'll kill him! I meant to do so when I went that second time to Windhoek, but the bird had flown! Him and his bloody little whore along with him. When it comes to names, you'd think *her* name would be easy enough to trace!'

'What was it?' asked Gareth.

The words spilled like acid from his lips.

'Romira.'

14

'Romira Ziegler?'

The sun-tanned face in front of Gareth blanched. He never saw Rick move, but found himself once more locked in the blue stare of the Colt's muzzle.

'Brunette? Small? Violet eyes? Plays the harp?' Rick's words rattled out like a volley of small-arms fire. '*Where is she? Damn it, where is she?*'

Gareth got up, leaned over the desk, brushed aside Rick's gun hand. 'If we're going to hold an intelligent conversation, you're bloody well not going to stick a gun in my face every time I say something you don't like! Got it?'

Rick's lips were open, his breath coming in short pants.

'Tell me! If I can get my hands on that little bitch, the way is open to Dehn! Where Dehn is, she is!'

Still leaning across the desk, Gareth said, 'Pull yourself together, man! I'll tell you – Romira is at Bangazi Lodge. I saw her there last weekend.'

'And Dehn! It's Dehn I have to have!'

'There's no Dehn there. Now get a grip of yourself. Where does Romira come into your trusteeship racket?'

'Romira was Dehn's confidential secretary-administrator. In Windhoek. It was she who – ' he stumbled over the words ' – was responsible for finally putting through the deal with my *Namib Dawn* diamonds. If she's around, then so is Dehn.'

'Let's deal with Romira first. You said just now that you delivered your diamonds to Dehn himself at the Tintenpalast. You didn't mention Romira.'

Rick dropped the Colt and the knife heavily on the desk.

'Look,' he said more reasonably, 'I'm not dumb. I didn't simply take the *Namib Dawn*'s output and hand it on a plate to Dehn. I admit I was sold on his trusteeship scheme when I first heard about it. But there were snags, major snags in it for me and *Namib Dawn*.'

'But you bought the idea in the end – why?'

'Would you say Romira was attractive? To men, I mean?'

'Very.'

'Okay, we're men of the world, you and I. I didn't buy Dehn's scheme and told him so. So she came to see me about changing my mind. At that stage, I hadn't said yes, and I hadn't said no.'

'But you said yes . . .'

He grinned, a little sheepishly. 'It was Romira who said yes. We clinched the deal – in bed. Quite a girl, is Romira.'

Gareth recalled those violet eyes, with no heart at their core.

'That little lay cost me half a million dollars. Dehn had the documentation all ready on stand-by – I don't know whether he and Romira had hatched up the seduction together. I wouldn't have put it past either of them, even if Romira was his live-in lover.'

'See here, Rick, if I tell you what's going on in the back of my mind about Romira and Bangazi Lodge, I want an assurance from you that you won't start throwing your hardware around.'

Rick pushed the weapons further across the desk so that they lay midway between the two men.

'I've told you, Romira is at Bangazi Lodge . . .'

'From what you say, she couldn't afford a place like that without a sugar-daddy.'

'Or your diamonds.'

That brought Rick up like a left cross to the jaw.

'The cap would fit, living way out in the bush where no one knew her.'

Gareth cut across his surmises. 'You say you couldn't trace Dehn when you went back to demand your half-million? The second time?'

'He'd brushed out his tracks completely. Not even an address, not a hint.'

'Did you consider he might have changed his name?'

'I thought of it, but where does a man start with a thing like that? "I'm looking for a man who has changed his name and haven't a clue as to his whereabouts . . ."? Try it and see how far you get!' He shrugged.

'The man who owns and runs Bangazi Lodge – has the name Ken Ziegler. What if Dehn simply hijacked her surname when they put the dust of Windhoek behind them? And Ken sounds near enough to Kentrat to get by. Ken Ziegler, alias Kentrat Dehn. Your man.'

Rick stood up, his muscles jerking. 'How do I get to Bangazi? Quick!'

'Listen, damn you! I've got something else to tell you.'

Rick stared at Gareth wildly, the legacy of his Sicilian blood pulsing hotly.

'Sit down!'

Rick obeyed.

'From what you've told me, I'm sure that Ken Ziegler and Kentrat Dehn are one and the same.'

'Romira being there too makes it certain,' added Rick.

'So does something else. Much surer. I know that Ken Ziegler is conducting a diamond-smuggling racket to Taiwanese trawlers lying offshore with Bangazi as a front. I had proof of it flying out to a charter pleasure ship anchored off the coast. Abalone . . .'

Gareth explained how the case of abalone had fallen and strewn its contents, how one of the shells had broken open, spilling a diamond. A sea-diamond. From Namibia.

When he had done, Rick exclaimed, 'Sea-diamond! You must be a very smart bastard to be able to recognize a sea-diamond. Very smart indeed! There can't be more than a couple of men in the whole territory who can do that, and then maybe not without a laboratory and microscope test to back up their verdict. I can see now why Glaval wants you.'

'My brief from Glaval is a pretty wide one,' replied Gareth. 'They want to establish how they are being implicated in the diamond scam in Angola–Namibia–Zaire. That –' he indicated Dehn's fake receipt ' – goes a long way to explaining. That's why Samsonov rushed off and left you at the Presidente Meridien. He'd have been back all right, bringing me with him, probably.'

'You've blown Dehn's whole racket sky-high!'

'No, I haven't, Rick. There are lots of loose ends. Kentrat Dehn–Ziegler is up to something else which I can't yet put my finger on. I wouldn't say he was the type to be interested in wreck-hunting, would you?'

'Ken Dehn? Hell, no! Not unless there was some spin-off involved for himself.'

'And it's just that spin-off that I'm interested in. He says he wants the wreck as a pleasure-spot for scuba-divers from Bangazi. But there are other wrecks whose position is known that he could have gone for. He's spending a packet of money and effort on locating this particular one. I ask myself, why? What's he up to?'

'I've got to get to Bangazi Lodge!' Rick burst out again. 'How do I organize it?'

'Forget it,' answered Gareth. 'You can't get into Bangazi except by courtesy of Ken – or Romira. The Lodge is virtually inaccessible from the land. The only way in is by a helicopter service owned and operated by Ziegler himself. There's one pilot only and Ken does a bit of stand-by duty. There's a radio-phone link at the Lodge for reservations, but it doesn't function at weekends. You'd kiss goodbye to any hope of nailing down Dehn–Ziegler by trying to get into Bangazi by announcing yourself in advance. Forget it.'

'I don't intend to forget half a million dollars in diamonds!' retorted Rick.

'I'm not asking you to. Bangazi is like a fortress shut off behind a moat. You need a strategy – and time. You haven't got either, it seems.'

Rick jumped up and took a couple of nervous steps towards the door. He seemed to have forgotten the weapons on the desk. They were Gareth's for the taking, had he wanted them. But he didn't. Rick could be a valuable ally.

'Unless I fly back to Mossel Bay and be at work by tomorrow, I'll lose my job,' he said. 'I simply can't afford that. I told you, I'm down on my uppers, flat broke.'

Gareth came to a sudden decision. 'Look, Rick. Just before you burst in here with your gun I was on the point of phoning the head of Glaval in Moscow, Dr Nikolai Vize, to tell him about Samsonov. Since your visit I've a lot more to tell him. I still intend making my call – now. You can stay and listen, if you wish.'

'You must be in a hell of a good position to be able to phone the top brass of Glaval, just like that.'

Gareth indicated the 'trusteeship' receipt still lying on the desk.

'That's worth its weight in diamonds to Glaval. You and I could do a deal, before you go and throw yourself away by trying to get into Bangazi Lodge and at Dehn's throat.'

'What deal?' Rick said sharply. 'Don't try and buck the blame off on me for that.' He indicated the receipt. 'I don't intend finishing up in an Angolan or Namibian gaol.'

'I'd say at a guess that Glaval will be only too glad to indemnify you.'

'Maybe, maybe.' Suspicion clung to the bearded face like a halo around a medieval Italian painting. 'You must have pretty high status to make a promise like that.'

'I didn't make a promise. I only said what I thought Glaval might do.'

'That doesn't satisfy me. I'm putting a lot on the line, even half-trusting you.'

A new thought struck him. 'How can you simply pick up a phone and speak to a Russian state department in Moscow? Do you know Russian? How – ?'

'I don't speak Russian, beyond a few words. I have a private, direct line to Dr Vize, when he's not in Switzerland. I couldn't cope with a Moscow switchboard, or the language. Satisfied?'

'Go ahead. I'll listen. But – be careful.'

Gareth consulted a diary from his desk drawer and dialled. He felt that Rick was keeping himself within close reach of the Colt.

'Dr Vize? It's Gareth. Gareth Ridpath.'

'Gareth?' The deep resonant voice vibrated with pleasure. 'I didn't expect to hear from you! Are you in Luanda? Has Samsonov – ?'

Gareth chose his words, watching Rick's dark, brooding face.

'I'm still in Zululand, Richards Bay,' replied Gareth. 'There have been radical developments. I need to talk to you.'

'Good,' replied the Glaval chief. 'Samsonov will be glad to hear from you when you get to Angola. He'd rather run up against a dead end when we spoke last.'

'Samsonov won't hear,' answered Gareth. 'He's dead.'

In the following silence, Gareth thought he heard the sound of a distant motor horn in the street outside Dr Vize's office.

'Dead? If he died in Angola, how did you get the news half Africa away in Zululand? We agreed on the strictest secrecy.'

'Both Samsonov and I observed it. He came here to see me. What about, I shall never know. I hauled his body out of a lake from a chopper. Drowned. So it looked. But I reckon he was killed.'

There was a hard note in Dr Vize's voice. 'Explain yourself, Gareth. I don't understand.'

'I'm not sure I understand a great deal, either. But the hard fact is that Samsonov left me a note to meet up with him at a place called Bangazi Lodge, which is in the middle of a lake . . .'

Gareth sketched the setting of Bangazi Lodge, and all that had happened there.

'Where does this get us?' demanded Dr Vize. 'All it says is that someone has broken open our lines of communication, someone ruthless enough to drown Samsonov. For what?'

'That's what I wondered, until this morning,' answered Gareth. 'A man burst into my office here with a gun – ' He watched Rick tense, his glance going compulsively to the Colt. 'He demanded to know what I had done with Samsonov.'

'So our lines of communication were penetrated,' commented Dr Vize.

'No,' said Gareth. 'The man's name is Rick Arnold. He's standing here with me at the phone.'

'With the gun?'

'It's lying on my desk between us, right now. Plus a fighting knife. He says he is a Sicilian – at least South African of Sicilian descent. He met up with Samsonov at the hotel Presidente Meridien in Luanda, and what he showed Samsonov made him up-anchor at the double and make for me here at Richards Bay. Unfortunately, he missed me but left a note to rendezvous at Bangazi Lodge. He left Rick Arnold behind at the Presidente, saying he would be back in a few days.'

'What did he show Samsonov? How does it affect what I commissioned you to do?'

'I'm going to read the document to you.' Gareth held out his hand.

Rick hesitated, then slowly passed over the 'trusteeship' receipt.

'Wait a moment,' said Dr Vize. 'If this document is worth all you say it is, have you a copy?'

'No.'

Rick was eyeing him. Gareth felt that if Dr Vize waited much longer, he would lose Rick.

'I'm recording it. Read slowly,' Dr Vize said.

Gareth heard the recorder click on and started to read through, giving the name Kentrat Dehn as the signatory at the end. He added, 'Dehn sold it as a state trusteeship scheme in collaboration with Glaval.'

Gareth pushed the paper back to Rick, who pocketed it.

Dr Vize said, 'I can understand why Samsonov wanted to see you in a hurry.'

'Rick says he gave Samsonov a copy. However, nothing was found in his pockets, or amongst his luggage, according to the police.'

'That's bad.' Dr Vize was grave. 'Do they have a lead on who killed him?'

Gareth laughed. 'I think I'm their Number One suspect.'

'What!'

'All I've told them about Samsonov is that I have never met him. You, Glaval, diamonds – I kept my mouth shut about it all. They can't understand how I could have risked my neck to fish a body out of a lake perched on a chopper skid.'

'You did *what*?'

Gareth explained quickly, and added, 'I had a hunch when I saw the body floating face-down in the water that it might have some connection with Samsonov. Sixth sense, call it what you like.'

Rick scrawled something on a slip of paper and shoved it under Gareth's eyes. It read, 'What about me?'

He said into the phone, 'Rick Arnold – what do we do about him? He's been squeezed. The "trusteeship" racket broke him financially. He's got a job he doesn't like far away on the Cape coast, at Mossel Bay, with the oil-from-gas project. Unless he gets back by tomorrow, he'll be fired.'

'He's the key to the whole situation. We mustn't lose him, Gareth.'

'I don't think we will, if he's careful. You see, I reckon I've tracked down the man who signed that receipt and took Rick's half-million.'

'Kentrat Dehn?'

'He doesn't go by that name any more. He's now Ken Ziegler. He's the owner of this luxury resort on the lake I'm telling you about. By chance, I found out that he's conducting his own different kind of diamond racket from here.'

'Zululand?' Dr Vize was incredulous.

Again, Gareth explained briefly and quickly about the abalone. When he had finished, Dr Vize said, 'Tell Rick we'll try and see he doesn't lose his half-million. I naturally haven't thought it through yet and there's no legal or moral obligation on Glaval to underwrite his loss, but we'll work something out. But make it clear, it's a one-off understanding, a gentlemen's agreement. If we assume responsibility for Rick's half-million, others whom Dehn did down may show up as well.'

'Quite likely.'

'You can tell Rick he can start helping Glaval by getting us a list of all the other small outfits, offshore and on-shore, whom Dehn swindled during the pre-independence period.'

'That's a tough assignment, especially as they were all undercover.'

'That's my proposition,' replied Dr Vize.

'And meanwhile?'

'Glaval can't wet-nurse Rick. Tell him to do the best he can until the picture gets clearer. We can help by your getting back to Angola as soon as possible.'

'Angola?' exclaimed Gareth in dismay.

'Yes. Rick is only one cog in the overall racket – perhaps a fair-sized cog, but still only one. That's Glaval's main concern. We've lost millions.'

Gareth said, 'I'm hog-tied to Richards Bay for the moment. The police made me surrender my passport.'

'That won't be for long. It's simply a precaution. You'll get it back soon.'

Gareth stalled again, eyeing the Italian. 'I think Rick will expect more.'

'Tough. He is to co-operate with you, keep in touch.'

'Mossel Bay is a long way away. So is Angola.'

'So is Moscow. Anything more, Gareth?'

Gareth tried to find some other reason to stave off Dr Vize's instructions to go to Angola.

'Yes. I suspect Dehn is up to some other racket. It involves an old wreck. But I don't know what else comes into it.'

'Don't go overboard about something outside the main-stream of Glaval's interests, Gareth,' Dr Vize came back.

'I haven't established whether the wreck is somehow linked to his personal diamond racket or not. It smells different to me.'

'Don't go opening another can of worms and losing sight of the prime objective. Keep me posted, will you?' he said incisively. 'Goodbye. Good luck.'

'Goodbye.'

Rick asked, when Gareth had put down the phone, 'What's the deal?'

'Glaval won't underwrite your half-million uncondi-tionally. But Dr Vize said they will try and work out something.'

Rick snatched up the gun and the knife and rammed them into his pockets.

'I don't want any more bloody double-talk or half-promises. I'm going to get to Bangazi and sort things out with Dehn!'

'Don't be a fool, man,' retorted Gareth, on his feet

now, too. 'Any way of getting in – or out – of Bangazi Lodge lies in Dehn's hands. You'd simply be throwing yourself away.'

'I want my diamonds!'

'You've been without them now for a couple of years and a little longer won't make any difference. Dehn is a slippery customer and you won't achieve anything by a hard-kill counter-blow. Your approach needs careful planning. Start the ball rolling by getting Glaval that list of small outfits as Dr Vize requests.'

The telephone rang; Gareth answered.

'Gareth?'

Before he had even spoken, the timbre of the voice sounded a warning to his mind. It also seemed remote.

'Pernelle! Where – ?'

She hurried on. 'I'm speaking from Bangazi.' He caught the unspoken hint in her next words. 'The open radio-phone, you remember?'

'I remember. I didn't expect to hear from you so soon.'

'I'm leaving Bangazi, Gareth. Today. I'm flying back to Cape Town this evening.'

A sense of emptiness overtook Gareth. He was hardly aware of Rick's surly, defensive presence. He thought he would have Pernelle near, if not present, for a couple more days.

'Why?'

'Can you come to the airport at Richards Bay about three this afternoon? Lance is flying some guests back to Durban, and he's managed to fit me into the helicopter. I'll explain to you then.'

He didn't reply immediately, and she added, 'My boss at the National Monuments Council, Dr Riekert, phoned me earlier this morning. A crisis has blown up and they have to have me back. He himself is leaving for overseas tomorrow. I've been trying to get hold of you, but your phone has been engaged for a long time.'

Gareth was tempted to explain, but remembered the open radio-phone and pulled himself up.

'Long-distance,' he replied laconically. 'Sorry.'

'Will you come?' Even the technical distortion of the radio-phone could not mask the eager note in her voice. Gareth knew then that her sudden departure had nothing to do with him.

His relief kept him monosyllabic.

'I'll be there.'

'See you, Gareth.'

She rang off.

Rick said suspiciously, 'Who was that?'

'Someone called Pernelle Clymer. Nothing to do with diamonds. She's a wreck and salvage expert.'

Rick seemed satisfied.

'I was thinking while you were busy on the phone,' he said. 'I guess I could still lose everything if I played my cards the way I meant to with Dehn, so it's a deal. I'll try and get the list your Moscow man wants as a start. I won't promise I won't be back here, though. Dehn or Ziegler is my man, and I intend sorting things out with him. You'll be around here if I want you?'

'I've got no option. The police require me here until the inquest on Samsonov. It could take days, or weeks, they won't commit themselves. They're uncertain about the time of his drowning. Only a post-mortem will show that, more or less. Yes, I'll be here.'

'Maybe I'd better get out, too, in case the police find out I knew Samsonov.'

'Leave me your Mossel Bay address and phone.'

Rick scribbled them on a piece of paper taken from Gareth's desk. 'Here, we'll be in touch.' He looked at his watch. 'I'd better be starting back for Durban. My plane leaves this afternoon. Not all of us are lucky enough to be ferried backwards and forwards by helicopter.'

*　*　*

That afternoon, as Gareth stood watching the blades of Lance's helicopter splinter the sunlight into sync on its landing approach, the problem of Pernelle's hurried departure burned in his mind. He was no nearer now to a solution than he had been when she had phoned while Rick was in his office. Three days with her! It seemed so poor a crumb for the gods to toss from their table.

He watched her walk across the tarmac towards the terminal building. The almost imperceptible droop of her right shoulder where it had been broken as a girl by a rogue wave off the Cape coast lent a slight dejection to her coming. He hoped he was wrong.

Then she was in front of him, the hammer of aircraft engines taking off like a seal against the world as he unashamedly searched her face with his eyes.

She smiled and clasped his hands. 'Lance says we can have ten minutes for a cup of tea. He made it clear that even that was a favour.'

They bought two cups from a self-serve counter and sat down.

'You are going.'

'Yes, Gareth. As far as I am concerned, this is goodbye Bangazi.'

'Why, Pernelle? What's happened?'

'Nothing, really. Yet everything. Plus some things down in Cape Town I don't know.'

'Meaning?'

'My boss phoned me this morning. He's going overseas tomorrow. "I want you back here on the first available plane – I've got a crisis on my hands over that wreck of yours," he said. He didn't say what the crisis was, and I know better than to try and cross-question him. He did say that it affects all the work I'm doing in Zululand and that I'm to stop immediately. Apparently a big bundle of documents has arrived from overseas relating to the *Nova Scotia*, but whether they have any bearing on the "crisis" in Cape Town, I don't know.'

'So, what happens now about Ken's application to the National Monuments Council?'

'You know, Gareth, I still can't accept it as one hundred per cent kosher that the wreck *is* the *Nova Scotia*. The discovery could almost have been stage-managed.'

'That suspicion crossed my mind, too, Pernelle.'

'As soon as Ken Ziegler believed he had the wreck of the *Nova Scotia* under his belt, so to speak, he started moving his goalposts,' she went on.

'What does that imply?'

'Look, Gareth, a salvage application has to conform to a number of rather intricate legal requirements, and if it doesn't it gets thrown out. Ken Ziegler is trying to cut his corners. I told him it wouldn't work. He was starting to turn rather unpleasant when fortunately Dr Riekert recalled me to Cape Town. I've been let off the hook.'

'What did Ziegler want you to say?'

'First, he's harking back to his original claim that the *Nova Scotia* lies outside South African territorial waters. It simply isn't so. The territorial limit is twelve sea miles. He maintains it's three. That's long since out of date. But his argument is that because the ship was sunk in 1942, the territorial waters limits which were *then* in operation should apply to the wreck *now*. It's an untenable argument. The *Nova Scotia* wreck is precisely seven point two kilometres, four nautical miles, offshore.'

'What's his insistence on territorial waters?'

'Outside territorial waters, the ocean is classed as open sea. Anything salvaged is finders-keepers. Not so inside the twelve-mile limit. Inside territorial limits, you have to go through all the formalities – and obligations. However, Ken Ziegler is now prepared to make a legal fight of it. He can only lose. I tried to dissuade him, but he's going ahead.'

'Why, Pernelle?'

'I don't know, but the implication is that there's something aboard the wreck that he intends to salvage and does not want to share with an accredited museum.

'That's another shortcoming of Ken's. He has first to obtain affiliation with a recognized museum and it must receive a percentage of all finds. He obviously doesn't care for that. Why? If the ship carried nothing of value, why should he bother?

'The Council also has to decide whether the applicant is a trustworthy, well-intentioned salvor who will respect the historical value of the wreck and its site. He has to carry out scientific excavation methods and he must grant the museum researchers full access to all discoveries he makes. The museum actually takes full charge of these finds, and only later will return them to the salvor. Ken Ziegler hasn't yet fulfilled the *first* condition, to locate and identify the discovery.

'He's trying to short-circuit all this and – again for a reason I haven't found out – he's setting himself a deadline of the anniversary date on which the *Nova Scotia* was sunk. She went down, as you know, on the twenty-eighth of November 1942. I've pointed out that he cannot hope to have an application approved before the anniversary date and that's been another point of friction between us.'

Her lovely eyelids were heavy. 'I cannot wear two hats. Either I am for Ken Ziegler or for the National Monuments Council. Therefore I won't be coming back to Bangazi.'

She stared sightlessly into her cup and sipped the lukewarm brown liquid. After a silence, she said, 'Gareth, is this the end – of us?'

He wanted to feel again the flare of that wonderful incandescent zest of her heart, instead of her grey hurt in this run-down setting.

Without waiting for him to react, she hurried on. 'Will you come to me in Cape Town?'

'The police have ordered me to stay in Richards Bay until after the inquest. That could be at any time. They made me surrender my passport. Also, Dr Vize wants me in Angola as soon as I can get free of the inquest formalities.'

She looked at him with numb disbelief. He thought he would remember always the classic lines of her cheekbones under the fathomless blue eyes which held him steadily.

She said in a remote voice, 'So you won't come?'

Without waiting for his answer, she inclined her head towards the tarmac.

'Here comes Lance.'

She stood up. 'Anstice was torn out of your life, and I am being forced to walk out too.'

She leaned across and kissed him.

He stood and watched her walk away. She did not look back. He watched the filament of her bright hair merge into the reflection of the helicopter's canopy, and then become a faraway flash as the machine surged into the sky.

15

'Is this another Anstice-type eruption, Gareth?'

Dr Vize's voice lost little of its sharpness on its 9,000-kilometre telephone journey between Moscow and Richards Bay. Gareth wondered, as he had dialled Moscow, whether in the ten intervening years since he had last laid his emotional cards on the table the Glaval chief's understanding would have been modified by the cut-and-thrust of international diamond wheeler-dealing and whether he would accordingly find the boss, rather than the man, at the other end.

'That's the second time in a week that her name has been used against me, Dr Vize.'

'It's you who is presenting the ultimatum, not me, Gareth.'

'It has nothing to do with you personally, you know that.'

'Yes, I know that. If it were, we couldn't be talking on this basis – or even discussing the possibility that you intend to throw up everything unless I agree.'

It was Monday of the following week, six days since Pernelle's departure for Cape Town. A complete silence had followed. On several occasions Gareth had thought of phoning her but he knew that, in the end, the gulf between them could be crossed only in person. He had, therefore, to break through the barriers which kept him from her: the police and Glaval's commission in Angola.

When he did not respond, Dr Vize added, 'You can't go very far anyway without a passport – that is, if you are still interested in Glaval's proposition in Central Africa.'

'I've licked the passport ban. At the end of last week, in fact.'

'So?'

'The day we last spoke, I went straight to a lawyer. He agreed with me that it was absurd that the police should consider they had the authority to tie me down like that, with not the slightest evidence to show that I was involved in Samsonov's killing . . .'

'You say killing, still?'

'I don't know how Samsonov's drowning was engineered, but he didn't die the way Ziegler says he did. If I was going on with Glaval, I would find out. After all, he came to tell me something, and it cost him his life. I owe him that, at least.'

'I'm glad you feel there's some obligation to counterbalance your own personal emotions in this matter, Gareth.'

Gareth rode the thrust. But it gave him an idea of how deeply Dr Vize was feeling his pending defection.

Gareth went on. 'The lawyer was drawing up an urgent application to court for the return of my passport. When the police heard about it, they suddenly turned obliging. They returned the document without any more fuss. They saved face by saying they had received the result of the pathologist's preliminary post-mortem on Samsonov which showed he had drowned about six to eight hours before I fished him out of the water. Therefore he could have drowned the way Ziegler said he must have. That let me off the hook.'

'Then what are you worrying about?'

Gareth weighed his reply. 'If I go to Angola as you wish and get involved with the type of underworld character who picks up a living on the fringes of the Presidente Meridien, the odds are that one thing will lead to another, and it could be months, even longer, before I get back to South Africa. It simply isn't a deal for Pernelle. She herself sees it that way – I told you. Bangazi provided a glimpse of a glorious might-have-been, something we both want.'

'Have you discussed it with her?' asked Dr Vize.

'No. Things aren't at that stage. It's all or nothing now.'

'Listen, Gareth. You're the sort of man I need at the heart of the action in Angola. The country is awash with diamonds. The new legislation which was intended to "soak up" the millions of them floating round the country has backfired in its purpose. And, secondly, because of the critical drought, huge lakes, swamps and river beds have dried up, opening vast areas containing alluvial diamonds, simply for the taking. You are the expert who can tell at a glance a sea-diamond from an alluvial.'

'Thanks for the accolade, Dr Vize. But I don't need to go further than Bangazi to uncover a major illicit diamond pipeline. Heaven alone knows how much has already poured out to those Taiwanese trawlers offshore! I don't feel I'm letting you down if I refuse to go to Angola. I've already done my bit.'

'Because of Pernelle?'

'Yes. I feel I'm wasting my time and my life in Central Africa. It'll take several weeks, I'm certain, before Rick can get a list together of the small men who were swindled by Dehn, alias Ziegler. There's nothing I can do here in the meantime. I intend to hurry down to the Cape and see Pernelle, whatever. Angola is out.'

Dr Vize hesitated, then said slowly, 'Pernelle apart, maybe it is a question of the man on the spot being better informed. That means you. Listen, Gareth, if I agree to your taking a couple of weeks off away from Richards Bay, will that satisfy you?'

'That's very generous of you, Dr Vize. I thought I could count on you as I have in the past.'

'On full pay, of course.'

'That makes it more generous still, after my having pointed a pistol at your head.'

Gareth knocked at the small hammered copper door in the white wall of Gil's Cottage at the foot of steep mountain steps.

After a wait, the door opened and she was there.

'*You've come*!' The two words were supercharged, her eyes shining lamps, after days and nights of darkness.

'Yes, Pernelle,' he said gently. 'I've come.'

Suddenly, she was in his arms, her body warm against his. As he held her, he realized that she was wearing only a wet bikini under a thin cotton wrap, and that he could not distinguish between tears and water. They embraced as if they never meant to let go, her beautiful hair damp against his chest.

At length she moved away, pulling the robe about her. 'You'd better come in before the south-easter blows us away.'

He hadn't noticed the near-gale either, roistering down the bracken- and boulder-clad mountainside as if it were a ski-run.

She pulled his arm and led him through the low doorway into a little enclosed courtyard which sheltered them from the plucking wind.

'How – how did you manage to – I mean, the police, Dr Vize? I thought . . .'

He held her face in his hands and kissed her very gently.

'It had to be, and it is. That's all that matters.'

He gazed into the bottomless pools of her eyes and felt her body trembling against his.

She eased away and said unsteadily, 'I've told you so much about Gil's Cottage, now come and see for yourself.' She spoke mundanely, but her eyes told him all he needed to know.

She held out her hand and led him down a flight of stairs into a room overlooking the wide panorama of Hout Bay. Through the leaded windows, Gareth saw to the right The Sentinel, the majestic headland standing guard over the entrance to the bay; on the left, below the level of the cottage, historic old cannon batteries built to protect the anchorage.

'I call it Gil's Cottage,' said Pernelle. 'But Gil had another name for it – San Antonio Cottage.'

'Where'd he get that name from?'

'Here,' said Pernelle, opening one of the windows. 'You see there, right underneath us, that little bay? That was named San Antonio Bay after a slaver which was wrecked there in the middle of the last century after she had been intercepted by a British warship. I never liked the name much. Even when Gil was alive, I called it Gil's Cottage.'

Gareth looked round the big room. 'It certainly has a feel of the deep sea,' he smiled.

Against one wall was a cupboard containing a collection of silver and gold coins, pieces-of-eight embedded in conglomerate from the ocean floor, spoons, buttons, beads of all sizes and shapes, fragments of porcelain, and a tarnished brass telescope.

'I added my own collection to Gil's when I came here; I inherited my father's when he died,' explained Pernelle. 'This is something I really treasure.' She indicated a big, old fumed-oak desk with a striking severity of line which stood near the windows. On it lay a briefcase and a pile of documents.

'This came from a wreck my father and Gil were exploring off the Agulhas Peninsula. The two of them floated it ashore, and then Dad gave it to Gil after they had argued over it. Gil wanted Dad to have it. "Where would I put a desk in a caravan?" he asked Gil. So here it is, a memorial to them both.'

'This room seems full of history,' said Gareth. He went to

where an old-fashioned ship's bell hung by a leather thong from an overhead beam. 'This – '

'Don't ring it!' exclaimed Pernelle as he reached for the clapper. He drew back his hand in surprise.

'Sorry,' she apologized. 'That bell is special. I don't know if I should even tell you: it's something private, something special to me, you may not understand.'

'Try me,' replied Gareth.

'You won't laugh?'

For answer, he went and took both her hands in his.

'No,' she said slowly. 'I should have known you wouldn't.' She hesitated before going on.

'At ten in the morning each July twenty-sixth I hold a little private ceremony. I ring the bell a few times to commemorate the moment, way back in 1909, off the coast of Pondoland, when the crack liner *Waratah* was last sighted by human eyes before vanishing into a super-storm and oblivion, taking with her 211 people in one of the world's great sea mysteries. Nothing has ever been seen or heard of the *Waratah* since – not a stick of wreckage, not a body, nothing.'

Pernelle walked over to the big windows. She seemed lost in thought.

Then she turned and came to him. 'Why do I do it?' she asked. 'Perhaps it is to placate an evil which stalks the face of the waters, who knows? It took both my father and Gil, and in the end it may take me . . .'

'That's curiously fatalistic, perhaps a little primitive,' he said.

'The man who wanted to move into this cottage would have described it as ridiculous,' she answered.

'What man?'

'His name was Stephen Carling,' she said. 'I became emotionally involved with him when he was a final year medical student here in Cape Town. I first met him when he was busy writing a monograph on the types of diet consumed in the early Portuguese and Dutch ships rounding the Cape, based on evidence I had found among their cargoes.

'We found each other attractive and we had an affair, with reservations on my part because Stephen was pushy and acquisitive and rather scornful of the way I kept all Gil's possessions here in the cottage just as they had been during his lifetime.

'I quickly realized two things about Stephen, first, that if he moved in here as he wanted to he would pull the place around and make it his consulting rooms for starting a practice, and, second, that his diet study was only a passing phase, like so many other things with Stephen, including, I think, myself.

'When I started objecting to this planned take-over, we had a row and broke up, on the very eve of Stephen's graduation. He taxed me bitterly with that, and tried to use it as a lever to get his way. Stephen reduced everything to a shabby common denominator. He knew the shape and functions of a woman's body through his medicine, and that's where I ended for him. My passions responded, and so did his. Finish of story. On to the next chapter, whatever that might be. I guessed it would be status and position, plus Gil's Cottage for a roof over his head.'

She gave a small shiver, pulled the wrap closer around her, and went back to the window with its grand view across the bay.

'Was I cynical? Realistic?' Her voice became low, intense. 'You see, I had gone looking for treasure with my father and Gil and, by all that's holy, we found it! But there was treasure in their hearts and minds too, and I need to deep-dive emotionally to find it once more. I need the gold of the heart, not a cargo of worthless scrap-iron.'

He opened his arms and she came to him.

She said softly, 'I can say this to you, and probably to nobody else. Perhaps the sea with its mystique has made me a dreamer; you know my background. I'm always reaching out for something beyond the horizon, perhaps for something that isn't there. Maybe the treasure's lying at my feet and I'll wake up only on the day I stumble over it – Gareth, I think that day is now.'

'Darling – my darling . . .'

He slowly slipped her wrap from her shoulders, her nipples hard against his chest through the flimsy bikini bra. He knew from her lips what she meant by gold of the heart. His hand reached to free her breasts . . .

From the brass knocker on the copper front door a loud rapping echoed through the cottage.

She gave Gareth a wild, disbelieving glance and jerked away. She cupped her naked breasts in her hands, panting and sobbing. 'No, no, no! It's the visitor I came home specially early to meet, but he's an hour too early!'

'Who is he?' Gareth asked hoarsely, shakily.

'He's the leader of the Italian community in South Africa. It's very important! It has to do with the wreck of the *Nova Scotia*!'

16

'We intend getting the *Nova Scotia* declared an official war grave. We will approach the International War Graves Commission. The wreck is sacred. It is *not* to become a tourist playground,' snapped Pernelle's visitor.

'That's why I am here in the first place to make representations to the National Monuments Council and to block any application for salvage rights to make certain that can't happen. There are 750 dead down there. Many of them are our own blood relatives. The *Nova Scotia* isn't a funfair.'

The elderly man rose in agitation from his chair near Pernelle's desk. The sea and the circle of mountains were starting to turn soft, elusive sunset colours, but the magnificent view through the windows meant nothing to him.

When Gareth had answered the front door, the man had introduced himself as Louis Arnold. The similarity to Rick's name made him wonder if they were related. Indeed, he spoke with the trace of an Italian accent, and Gareth thought he could discern a vague facial resemblance. He appeared to be in his mid-seventies, a little old to be Rick's father, though he walked with a spritely step as he followed Gareth into the living-room. He carried a standard briefcase, and a bulkier, square leather-covered box like a salesman's sample case.

Pernelle had soon joined them wearing a cool plain white dress with a blue polka-dot collar. Her eyes held Gareth's for a moment as she entered, and only their luminous sparkle gave any hint of what had passed between them.

'Dr Pernelle Clymer? I am Louis Arnold, president of the South African Italian Society.'

'Not doctor,' Pernelle corrected him. 'Just plain miss.'

'Miss maybe, but certainly not plain,' he said gallantly.

Pernelle smiled. 'Won't you sit down, Mr Arnold?'

Louis found a chair and rushed straight to the point.

'You know the background to the *Nova Scotia*?'

'Until recently I knew only the bare outline of facts, which was surprising for a wreck of such importance. The biggest wartime sinking in South African waters . . .'

'Seven hundred and sixty-five was the number of Italian civil internees from East Africa on board,' he broke in. 'There were also about 130 of your own soldiers, plus the crew. But you say, until recently you knew so little – why?'

Pernelle gestured towards the documents on her desk.

'My work regarding wrecks and salvage entails not only getting impersonal statistics about cargoes, manifests and so on, but obtaining a full picture, if possible, of the people who sailed in a ship, their lives, social background, status – '

'Ah!' exclaimed Louis. 'Good!'

'In other words, a rounded picture of people as human beings, not as cyphers.'

'But you say this was lacking in the case of the *Nova Scotia*?'

'Yes. Perhaps because it was wartime and there was naturally a security clamp-down on human stories to the media. Certainly there was very little about the sinking in the newspapers of the day. The South African War Histories and the Royal Navy later were not very helpful to me, beyond the bare bones of the facts which you've just stated. It seemed to me as if I had run up against a dead end.' She gestured towards the desk-top. 'That is, until recently.'

'So?' he said. 'We will go into the question of survivors

more fully in a moment.' He gave a small secret half-smile. 'Hopefully I can satisfy your thirst for information. First, I want you to know that the South African Italian Society has in train a project for a memorial to the *Nova Scotia* dead on the shore opposite where the ship went down.'

Pernelle asked quickly, 'So you know her exact position?'

'Not exact, but near enough for a memorial site. There aren't so many suitable sites anyway and it would have to be approximate. Rock formations for the base of such a memorial aren't very plentiful on those sandy beaches.'

Gareth interrupted. 'From the air, we saw a group of men on the shore recently.'

'I was one of them.' Louis got up abruptly and started to fiddle with the catches of the square box. 'It's a long time ago now, almost fifty years,' he said slowly and thoughtfully. 'I – we – the South African Italians have always felt the need of a token for the *Nova Scotia* dead. We have had no graves or headstones to visit, nowhere to lay a wreath on the remains of our relatives from among those Massawa internees. There is nothing but that empty stretch of sea, and all the lonely years in which we have had to rebuild our lives without our loved ones. Now, when the memorial is unveiled, there will be words of spiritual comfort which we did not get at the time.'

He opened the lid of the box and unlatched the collapsible sides.

A model cupola, supported on pillars as graceful as only an Italian craftsman could conceive and execute, rose from a base leading via steps to a catafalque on which rested the bronze figure of a recumbent woman, round whose head were grouped four kneeling children, weeping, heads cowled. A man, head bowed in grief, stood at the figure's feet looking down at her. Inside the cupola hung a minute ship's bell.

Louis explained. 'The woman symbolizes all those lost in

the *Nova Scotia*, as well as Doña Leonor, a beautiful woman who was shipwrecked and buried near the spot four and a half centuries ago. The children are hers, weeping and refusing to leave her side. The man is her husband, who chose to stay and die with her. He symbolizes the love of those men who tried to save their loved ones from the oil and flames of the *Nova Scotia*.'

Pernelle said, 'It is very beautiful, very imaginative.'

'When is the memorial scheduled to be opened?' Gareth asked.

Louis replied without hesitation. 'On November twenty-eighth. The anniversary of the *Nova Scotia*'s sinking.'

'That's less than a month away!'

'Yes.'

'But there's an immense amount of work to be done before a memorial like that can be erected.'

Louis smiled. 'It is finished. It is ready.'

'How can that be?' asked Pernelle. 'We flew over the site less than a fortnight ago and there was nothing there!'

Louis sat down, his finger tracing the reclining figure.

'We – the Italian community – ran into what we thought were insurmountable problems right from the word go – and that was a long time ago. A memorial like this costs money, plenty of money. Funds have to be collected, plans drawn, ideas exchanged, and that swallows time.

'Our original concept was to have the cupola of hand-cut marble imported from Italy itself, mounted on a plinth of similar material.' He smiled. 'It appealed to the craftsman in my blood – you see, my father and my uncle were both great craftsmen.

'As soon as I – I say I, because the memorial has always been my special pigeon – had tentatively approached the authorities about building the shoreline memorial, I realized that marble was out. They didn't object to it being on the shore, but to the idea that the memorial would have to be erected by men and machines working on the beach.

'The Natal Parks Board vetoed the plan because of the turtles. You probably know that the beach is one of the few remaining breeding-grounds in the world of the leatherback and loggerhead, highly endangered species. You can understand what sort of threat lorries using the beach would pose to such rare creatures. So, in view of this, the authorities simply threw my memorial scheme out of the window.'

Louis got up, then restlessly sat down again, and Gareth wondered once more about his relationship to Rick. He had the same razor-edge, volatile mind.

'I think that master-craftsman ancestor of mine came to my rescue with a solution.' He smiled. 'After weeks of agonizing, it suddenly struck me – must it be marble? Why not anodized aluminium?'

'What is that?' asked Pernelle.

'It's aluminium coated electrically with a protective layer against corrosion – light, durable, weatherproof, rustproof, highly workable space-age material! In fact, it has a lot of advantages over marble, which would have been weathered and stained by the action of salt and wind and weather. In the event, the lightness of the material has allowed the sculptor to produce a far more graceful, airier structure than he would originally have been able to with marble. Look at those pillars supporting the cupola, for example.'

'I still don't see how lightness overcomes the problem of erecting it,' said Gareth. 'The construction still has to take place.'

'Not so,' answered Louis. 'Instead of building the memorial *in situ*, we decided, with the new material we were using, to pre-fabricate the whole thing in a factory, mainly here in Cape Town. The entire structure has now been manufactured in sections, and even the base plinth on which the cupola and bronze figure rest are ready to be dropped into place.'

'They'll still have to be transported there by truck along that sensitive turtle beach,' remarked Pernelle.

'No,' rejoined Louis. 'I licked that problem, too. The total memorial will be airlifted by helicopter and simply lowered into position. In fact, we have a workhorse helicopter standing by on charter at Richards Bay now to do the job. It will only require a handful of workmen on the beach, also brought in by helicopter – no wheeled transport whatsoever. The bronze figure group will also be lowered from the air. In fact, we shipped it to Richards Bay from Cape Town some weeks ago and it has now joined the rest of the anodized aluminium sections in storage there. It'll take less than a day to do the job.'

'It all sounds very ingenious,' remarked Gareth.

'You said you saw me recently on the beach with some officials: what we were actually doing, under their supervision, was drilling holes in the rocks to take the big bronze bolts into which the base plate will be slotted. That semi-final stage will take place only a few days before the opening ceremony itself.'

'Why not simply go ahead now?' asked Pernelle.

'Merely a precaution against vandalism and to make sure that nothing happens to the memorial meanwhile. It's a very remote and lonely stretch of coast.'

The age lines of his face were ironed out by the intensity of his anxiety, and there were flames deep in his eyes. He ran the palms of his hands down the muscles of his upper arms, as if warding off lurking evil.

His voice rose in pitch. 'We are taking this question of the memorial to our dead very seriously,' he went on rapidly. 'The *Nova Scotia* was a major tragedy in the hearts and minds of hundreds of Italians here in South Africa which seems somehow to have got lost sight of. This – ' he gestured at the model ' – is not just another patriotic monument, to be launched with pretty speeches. It's in our blood, we feel it burning, just as the ship herself did when the U-boat's torpedoes slammed the life out of her. That's why we want the wreck to be a war grave, and sacred, just as the Royal Navy's HMS *Edinburgh* was after she had been sunk in 1942 on her way to Russia carrying gold bullion. She had only sixty men lost; we have 750 souls, the majority women and children. The British War Office refused to give permission for many years for the *Edinburgh*'s bullion to be salvaged, in deference to the fact that it was a grave. We want no less for the *Nova Scotia*.'

Pernelle said, 'The trouble is that so little is known in the public mind about the *Nova Scotia*. If there is a whisper that she was carrying bullion or treasure, nothing will stop the avalanche of adventurers. I know, I've seen it happen elsewhere. I've mentioned the difficulties I've had in getting detailed background of the ship.'

She indicated the pile of documents lying on top of her desk.

'That was, until recently. Now I'm obtaining a fuller picture. You say there will be actual survivors of the disaster at the memorial's opening. Theirs is the kind of background story I specialize in for my type of investigative research. Will you put me in touch with some of them?'

Louis' eyes puckered and he said, 'There is no need. I was there. I was made to walk the plank.'

17

It is doubtful whether Louis was aware of the startled exchange of glances between Pernelle and Gareth, or of his gracious surroundings. He was reliving the fire, the blazing surface of the sea, the screams, the choking, gurgling swimmers drowning in oil, the agony of women thrashing about searching for their children. And, above all, the long, low black casing of the U-boat, an embodiment of death and evil in the nightmare light.

'At least, "walk the plank" is what the U-boat captain called it. The logistics of the act bore no resemblance to the torture old-time pirates practised, although the agony and the final death were the same.'

After a long pause, Louis resumed. 'I escaped death, that is why I am here. It makes the *Nova Scotia* doubly important to me.'

Pernelle got up and started towards her desk, but Louis seemed unaware of her movement. He went on.

'Kapitänleutnant Jost Keller was the most brutal and inhumane skipper of the undersea war, in a sphere of operations where brutality and inhumanity were criteria for success among the young Nazi officers of Hitler's Reich. With Jost Keller, it was compounded by his genes. Alone of anyone that night at the *Nova Scotia* sinking, I knew his Prussian background.'

Louis ran his tongue round dry lips.

'Let me get you a drink,' suggested Pernelle.

He nodded like a man concussed. 'Yes, please. Some wine. Not too dry, though.' He gave a wan smile. 'I am Italian, and like it sweeeter rather than drier.'

'Gareth?' she asked.

'Gin and tonic,' he said. It could, he judged, be a long confession. Here was no rosy wartime reminiscence but an experience which, even after nearly half a century, still seared like acid.

Settled with a glass of wine, Louis resumed his story.

At the end of 1942 he had been one of a party of 134 South African soldiers returning from the Middle East after two years' war service in the requisitioned 6,800-ton transport *Nova Scotia*. On board also were 765 Italian internees, mainly women and children, from Massawa, in East Africa, on their way to South Africa. Louis had volunteered for war service; there was no conscription in South Africa.

The *Nova Scotia*, heading south off the Maputaland coast, was due to dock in Durban next day. Louis had been standing near the stern on the landward side chatting to two or three other soldiers, thrilled about the prospect of getting home. It was a balmy, early summer's evening, and from nearby on his right he could scent the warm smell of the land, dark green in the distance against the bottle-green of the coastal range, broken here and there by an occasional hilly summit cloaked in tropical forest.

The ship was zigzagging at fourteen knots, and one rather prominent hill with three distinct summits caught his attention. Then . . .

'I was told afterwards that three torpedoes crashed almost simultaneously into the *Nova Scotia*, the second of them among the lifeboats at the stern where I was. Fortunately, I was standing on the landward, not seaward side, or else I would have been dead. The first torpedo detonated amidships near the radio cabin and bridge, the third forward.

'One moment it had been calm, peaceful, the only sound being the ship's engines and swish of water past the hull; the next, our world stopped in its tracks in a stunning cataclysmic holocaust. It was like hitting a concrete wall head-on. A river of oil, already afire, gushed flaming from the vessel amidships.

'I saw a group of women who had been giving their children supper up on deck in the summery evening, sailing high into the air with their skirts on fire like flaming parachutes, some upside down, others at grotesque angles with their arms outstretched, high above the ship's masts.

'I don't know how I got into the water; I expect I was blown off the deck by the concussion of the torpedoes. I came to the surface, swallowing and gagging water mixed with fuel oil. The stink of that oil! Even today, the smell of ordinary diesel makes me want to throw up.

'The water was full of men, women and children, screaming, burning, yelling for help. There were lifebelts, rubber rafts and rubber dinghies in the water, but no lifeboats. The demented survivors were flinging themselves at anything which floated, grabbing, fighting others away from handholds, losing their own grip in the slippery oil, and then threshing back like berserk things to snatch at hanging rope-ends or trailing hands. The ship began to list steeply.

'Then, out of the chaos and smoke, a shape rose from the sea like a phantom of doom. It was the U-boat's conning-tower.

'It threw aside oil and seawater, and spewed men in black oilskins. Several of them doubled out on to the half-awash casing like a well-drilled ballet of death. They came to a sudden halt, immobile, riveted by the sight before their eyes.

'From behind me came an ominous tearing, grinding sound – the *Nova Scotia* was about to plunge to the bottom!

'In my state of terror and heightened perception, I noted a couple of rope-ends dangling near the black figures of the crew. I knew that if I could make it to the U-boat and hang on, I might save my life.

'I struck out, and was there before I realized what was happening, because the U-boat was also moving, at slow speed, into the chaotic jumble of debris, burning oil, screaming and drowning human beings.

'The metal casing was rough, just like the skin of a shark, and that terrified me even more. I grabbed a rope, flung it round my slippery wrists and shoulders, knotted it fast.

'One of the U-boat men slashed me across the hands with a boathook. I didn't feel the pain, I was so intent on keeping my hold.

'The man shouted: I rolled sideways to evade another blow. Other crewmen were beating off swimmers who had similar ideas to myself. My vision focused on the gold braid, white top and German eagle cap badge of a Kapitänleutnant in the centre of the group on the conning-tower.

'He was a tall man, with a sharp black beard. I had seen him once before, for a brief while only, but that face had been branded indelibly on my memory for life.

'Then he had been running from one attempted murder; now he was gloating over the killing of hundreds. Before it had been only one woman; now it was women and children by the hundred.

'I looked up into the face of Jost Keller.

'I knew my life at that moment hung on a razor's edge. If he recognized me, he would order his crew to smash my hands loose and leave me to the oil and fire. Sharks had begun to converge on the fast-sinking ship, and from nearby came terrified screams as the swimmers realized that the deadly hunters were massing for a banquet of human flesh and blood.

'Jost shouted at me, in English: "You – what ship?" His Oxford accent was impeccable.

'I buried my head as much as I could to conceal my face.

One of his crew prodded me with a boathook to extract a reply.

'I shook my head, but the man got the hook round my jaw and raised it in the direction of the conning-tower, now lit by the flames of the blazing vessel.

'As he did so, the light was suddenly extinguished, as if by a switch.

'The *Nova Scotia* had taken her last plunge!

'I yelled into the darkness: "*Nova Scotia*! Unarmed transport!"

'"Tonnage? Cargo? Bound for where?"

'I coughed oil from my mouth and called thickly, "Massawa to Durban. Civilian refugees. Italian."

'"Bullshit!" he snarled back. "Armed merchant cruiser, that's what! Carrying troops. How many aboard?"

'"About 130 – South African. Home leave from the Middle East."

'"That's better! Don't try lying to me. So you want to be rescued? You and your pal?"

'Until then I had been unaware of anyone else on the casing. I had been too occupied trying to hide my face from Jost.

'Now I saw my fellow-survivor. A bedraggled, oil-soaked, white-faced figure hung on to a rope a little forward of me towards the bow. The water over the casing was deeper there. The torso washed backwards and forwards as if it were a corpse already. A trickle of oil cut through the blood round the mouth. An overwhelming desire for life made the hands clench the lifeline as if rigor mortis had already set in.

'But he was alive. The bloodied mouth whimpered at me, "Don't let them throw me off, for pity's sake! I can't take the pain! Something's bust inside me."

'I called to the bridge. "Rescue – yes, yes, yes!"

'Jost continued his cat-and-mouse game. "In ten minutes, you mayn't be so sure. But it's your decision."

'He gave an order; the U-boat picked up speed through the water, scattering a dinghyload of panic-stricken survivors who had been making for the craft. They screamed in horror as the steel hull brushed them aside.

'One woman, holding high a baby and a crucifix, cried out in terror as she watched the bow coming at her. "In the name of the Mother of God, captain! Captain . . .!"

'She toppled sideways into the oil.

'The U-boat cleaved onwards through debris, oil and human bodies.

'Jost barked a sudden command. Two of the crew used their boathooks against another dinghyload of determined survivors, up-ending them. Then they hitched the empty boat by its lifelines to the U-boat. A mouthful of oil and water choked any protest I might have made.

'Jost called out conversationally to me, "Once upon a time, pirates used to have fun making their enemies walk the plank at the tip of a sword until they fell off the end into the sea. The principle remains the same today, although the method has changed. If you stay alive in the wash of the bow-wave as far as the land, I promise I'll put you ashore in that dinghy we've just acquired. If you don't make it, too bad."

'"The bastard!" moaned the injured man next to me on the casing. "The unspeakable shit! My side . . .!"

'He gave a sudden scream as the U-boat, moving faster now, rode over a large wave.

'"What's wrong with your friend?" Jost went on sarcastically. "We're quite close to the shore, not more than three or four miles. Doesn't he want to live?"

'I rolled on to my back to get my mouth clear. Jost was standing with his leather-gloved hands resting on the railing round the bridge. He was grinning and pointing.

'I opened my mouth to speak, but the words were aborted by a stream of pressurized water. I choked, gagged into silence.

'It may have been three, it may have been four miles to the shore as Jost said, but to me that journey was forever. It was a calm, clear night and there was a moon, but I never saw its light on the placid line of breakers, or heard Jost's command to slow the engines as the U-boat came within hailing distance of that green, deserted, bland-faced shore.

'Half submerged under the water, I gagged and vomited, non-stop now. I think the fun of the latter-day pirate's trick had gone out of it, even for Jost. Perhaps he realized that his calculated sadism was sapping the morale of his crew.

'He rapped out, "Stop all engines! Get those men into the dinghy. They can find their own way now through the breakers. It's calm enough. If they can't, tough!"

'Two men in sea boots, with hard, shut faces, cut the rope which held me to the mooring-ring and tossed my body like a sack into the rubber dinghy. A child's doll floated in the slop of water at the bottom. I saw blood filtering between the strands of cut rope round my wrists. I didn't realize that the cords had cut deep, very deep. I have carried the scars all my life.

'My co-survivor gave a strangled half-scream as they handed out the same treatment to him. Next moment he lay next to me jerking in agony.

'As we started to float clear, I was just conscious enough to hear Jost giving an order:

'"Make a signal to *Befehlshaber der U-boote*. Sank heavily armed and camouflaged merchant cruiser *Nova Scotia* carrying about 130 South African troops and nearly 1,000 civilian internees ex Massawa. Two survivors taken on board. Still about 400 in boats and rafts. Moved away to the east because of threat from the air . . ."

'My world went black.'

The big lounge of Gil's Cottage had darkened, too, while Louis had been recounting his story. He sat staring fixedly ahead, like a man anaesthetized.

Pernelle broke the long silence.

18

Gareth and Pernelle sat tongue-tied by the fervour with which Louis had recounted the story of the *Nova Scotia*'s sinking. Below the surface of his narrative, however, seemed to lurk a sinister force which had yet to make its power and scope known.

Gareth stood up, as if physically as well as mentally rejecting full acceptance of Louis' dramatic recital.

Playing devil's advocate, he asked, 'You say that the U-boat devil was your brother-in-law, yet a minute before you told us you had seen him only briefly once before in your life. It doesn't add up, Louis.'

'Nothing added up about Jost Keller,' replied the Italian. 'It doesn't add up in ordinary terms that a man should try and kill his sister by a method so outlandish and barbaric that it left her partially paralysed for the rest of her life – '

'Again, more facts please,' interrupted Gareth. 'I – we – cannot simply accept an accusation as damning as that off the cuff.'

Louis allowed himself the ghost of a smile. 'I speak from first-hand knowledge. You see, I married her. She became my wife.'

Pernelle broke in incredulously. 'But how could a brother bring himself to . . .?'

A flush of anger rose from under Louis' loose collar and spread up behind his ears. His knuckles were white where they gripped the arms of his chair. Whatever powerful forces were at work gave his face a rather frightening purposefulness.

'He was a Prussian.'

He spat the word with such hatred that Pernelle's further question was silenced.

'His Prussian genes were bad, bad,' Louis went on. 'His father was a true-blue regular Prussian officer. The von Kellers were involved with the Arnoldis long before Jost tried to kill my wife Ingrid. Captain Hans-Ludwig von Keller pistol-whipped my uncle Louis-Pisani to death, and so blinded my father with the same pistol that one of his eyes was useless for the rest of his life. There was no doubt in my mind that night of the *Nova Scotia*'s sinking that Kapitänleutnant Jost Keller would have drowned me like an unwanted puppy had he known it was me.'

'A moment ago you called him von Keller. Now it's Keller,' said Gareth. 'First, the name of a Prussian officer, and then a U-boat captain. You also speak of the Arnoldis, yet your name is Arnold.'

Pernelle reinforced his criticism. 'You're telling it all backwards, as if we were already aware of the context.' She put a hand over the tightly clenched fingers on the chair arm. 'I'll get you some more wine.'

Louis eased his grip and held up his hands as if for inspection. They were shaking.

'The fire still burns — look!' he exclaimed. 'Because of something which happened so long ago!'

He held the glass unsteadily to his lips and drank deeply.

'My story is overlaid with blood,' he said in a strained voice. 'Maybe it would be better if the *Nova Scotia* were left alone in its grave rather than risk spilling more. Perhaps she should be left undisturbed on the bottom where Jost Keller sent her.'

Pernelle remarked quietly, 'It's too late, Louis. Ken Ziegler has already located her.'

'That's as far as he is ever going to get,' retorted Louis. 'There will be no desecrating the remains of my people. I for one have suffered enough!

'The U-boat casting the dinghy adrift in the breakers and pulling away from the shore that night was really only the first chapter of the nightmare.'

'Do you want to relive it all again now?' Pernelle asked gently.

'I want you to understand!' Louis exclaimed passionately. 'I am not trying to get your sympathy for myself – I want you to *understand* why the *Nova Scotia* means so much to me!'

'Go on,' said Gareth.

Louis shuddered. 'I guess I passed out. I don't remember anything about getting ashore. The darkness of the night and the darkness of my mind were one. When I awoke in brilliant sunlight on that white, white beach, I thought I was dead. The dinghy washed in and out of the waves with my companion in it. He was dead. That beach – ' another convulsive shiver shook him ' – the beach wasn't dead. The first of the jackals arrived, and they watched for the next three days waiting for me to die. The great turtles belly-flopped their way from the forest margin to the sea. Water! I cried out for fresh water, but there was none. The beautiful surroundings had a lying face. It was torture of the worst kind; walking the plank was at least quick.

'I lived off raw baby turtles and drank turtle eggs for liquid. I still want to throw up if I think of the smell.'

'But the authorities must have mounted a search for the *Nova Scotia*,' exclaimed Gareth.

Louis shook his head. 'I heard later, she didn't get off a Mayday – an SOS, as they called it then. It was only when she was overdue in Durban that the first search ships went out.'

'But what about aircraft?' demanded Pernelle. 'It isn't that far from Durban for a plane!'

Louis permitted himself a small smile. 'You're looking at the situation with hindsight,' he said. 'True, there was a long-range flying-boat base among the mangrove swamps of what is today Richards Bay, but then it didn't exist. It took three days for the search to reach the area – three days! I lost all count of time. I only heard the big Catalina flying-boat pass overhead. They had spotted the upturned dinghy and my dead companion, or what the jackals had left of him. The plane dropped emergency supplies to me. By the time a jeep convoy from Durban reached me two days later, I was half out of my mind. I was taken to a Durban hospital, suffering as much mentally as physically. After many weeks, I finally managed to pull through.'

'The *Nova Scotia* incident is one piece only of the von Keller jigsaw,' observed Gareth. 'You're jumping their entire earlier involvement with the Arnoldis you spoke about.'

Louis' eyes lost their distant focus. He said incisively, 'Have you heard of a place called Rössing?'

'Indeed,' said Gareth. 'I worked there until recently. It's the site of the world's biggest uranium mine.'

'You're talking of the present,' answered Louis. 'I'm referring to the time immediately before World War One – 1912, to be exact. Uranium had never been heard of then. Rössing was no more than a remote siding in the Namib desert about forty kilometres from Swakopmund.

'The stationmaster at Rössing found a small quantity of strange and very beautiful semi-precious stones on a barren mountainside near the station and was so impressed by them that he gave them to two Italian craftsmen-jewellers in Swakopmund who were eking out a living fashioning semi-precious stones into jewellery for the wives of German officers.

'The Italian brothers' names were Roberto and Louis-Pisani Arnoldi . . .'

'Later to become Arnold,' observed Pernelle.

'As I said, Roberto was my father and Louis-Pisani my uncle. Their workshop was a very humble affair in a lean-to near the lighthouse. You must not forget that as foreigners, Sicilians, the Arnoldi brothers enjoyed no status or legal rights whatever in the territory. It was the German officers, particularly the Prussians, with their arrogant, brutal, overbearing ways, who were the élite, the *Herrenvolk*.

'The Arnoldis had never seen anything like the Rössing stones and could not identify them. They had a greenish-yellow opalescent glow, which was enhanced once the stones were cut and polished. They guessed it might be a new kind of beryl, and they were not so far off the mark.'

Louis addressed Gareth. 'What do they say today at Rössing about heliodore?'

Gareth laughed. 'They don't. There are no specimens even in the mine museum. All there is is an unsubstantiated legend of a minute deposit on Rössing mountain which was worked out before World War One. Your story fascinates me. Go on!'

'The legend was not unsubstantiated. My father and uncle held in their hands the Stones of the Sun . . .'

Pernelle glanced penetratingly at Gareth, and said to Louis, 'Stones of the Sun – it's a glorious name! It was Gareth who told me how it originated from both the German prospectors and the local Bushmen. Now you're giving it a whole new dimension.'

'The Arnoldi brothers may not have known the mineral they were working, but they knew it was good. They crafted an exquisite necklace, set in the form of a cross. My father used to say that nothing like it had ever been seen before.

'It held the same fascination for a German officer in a crack regiment stationed at Swakopmund at the time. His name was Captain Hans-Ludwig von Keller.'

Louis stopped to regain his composure before going on. 'That name has haunted the Arnoldis for the best part of this century.'

Pernelle let the silence settle before she asked, 'Why?'

'Von Keller was the stereotype, jackbooted Prussian. What I am about to tell you – incredible as it may sound – is not hearsay or second-hand; it was related by the main players involved. It began about four years before I was born, not long before the outbreak of the First World War.

'Von Keller arrived at the Arnoldis' lean-to workshop and asked to view the necklace. The brothers laid it out on their workbench on a chamois cloth and he made them an absurd offer for it. They refused point-blank. Von Keller turned nasty: with true Prussian arrogance he now demanded that they should hand it over.

'My uncle, Louis-Pisani, moved to take the necklace out of the Prussian's reach. Without warning, von Keller whipped out his heavy Service revolver from its holster and struck him a terrible blow across the face. He was thrown across to the far wall, half conscious. He was to die later of a fractured skull.

'My father, who was a small man, hurled himself at von Keller. The Prussian hit him with the heavy gun-sight and the steel tore out his right eye. The agony of that moment, when his whole world went dark, remained with my father all his life.

'The last thing he remembered before passing out was seeing von Keller put the necklace in his pocket. As he did so, my father had strength enough to put a curse upon him: you must remember, we are Sicilians and our blood-feuds can stretch back centuries. We never forgive, we never forget.

'So it was with von Keller. My father cursed him and the necklace – forever.'

Pernelle and Gareth stared awe-struck at the naked hatred in their visitor's face.

He said in a thick voice, 'I have searched for the von Kellers all my life – you see, apart from avenging my father and uncle, I owe them a death for what a von Keller did to me that night of the *Nova Scotia*.'

Gareth said, 'You're jumping the gun. What happened to the necklace?'

Louis seemed to collect himself, and went on in a quieter voice.

'Von Keller's original intention was to get hold of the necklace and present it, as a token of the colony's loyalty, to the German Empress. With this in mind, he approached the German governor who whole-heartedly fell in with the idea. So much so that he sent von Keller to Germany as his special envoy to make the presentation. War clouds were hanging over Europe, and the loyalty of the strong colonial territory to the Fatherland was important.

'Kaiser Wilhelm and the Empress, along with an entourage of several hundred, were due to make a visit to their hunting-lodge in East Prussia, Schloss Allenstein, and Von Keller, who was in high favour, was invited along.

'But von Keller had become obsessed with the necklace and determined to steal it for himself.'

'You're putting thoughts into the man's mind,' remarked Pernelle. 'How could you know all this?'

Louis answered with dramatic understatement, 'From the woman who stole the necklace for him.'

Gareth looked penetratingly at Pernelle and observed, 'We're in very deep waters.'

'They get deeper and murkier still,' remarked Louis grimly. 'The woman was a lady's-maid named Gerda who helped look after the imperial quarters. Von Keller, who had very considerable personal charm when he chose to display it, persuaded her into the theft on the promise of marriage.

'War was getting closer by the day and von Keller knew that very soon he would be recalled to his regiment. Once the necklace was in his possession he could just slip away with it, leaving Gerda holding the baby – literally, for she was pregnant by then.

'The nearness of war took the heat off the search for the

thief, and von Keller returned to his regiment completely unsuspected. Gerda, however, was made of stern stuff and followed him to South West Africa. She confronted von Keller and threatened that unless he married her as promised, she would spill the beans. He might be cashiered, even shot.

'He gave in and was forced to go through with the marriage, then shunted Gerda off to his remote farm on the border of the Kalahari desert.

'The farm was called "Allesverloren" – everything lost. That just about described it. Von Keller stashed the necklace there, knowing it was unlikely ever to be sought in such a wild and lonely place.

'A boy was born, named Jost. A second child, Ingrid, followed. Von Keller was killed in action against the invading South African forces, and Gerda now gained possession of the priceless heliodore necklace.

'It was a hard, pioneering life and Gerda's only concession to civilization was that she used to dress for dinner on Saturday nights and wear the stunning Stones of the Sun necklace. She was unaware that in so doing she was working out the Sicilians' curse – the gemstones were radioactive, cancer-inducing.

'Jost ran wild and made a reputation for himself as a hell-raiser. He started school in South West Africa but longed for Germany. Gerda finally managed to scrape together enough to get him out of her hair and sent him overseas.

'Those were dark, troubled days in post-war Germany: Jost was ripe to join the new Nazi movement along with other hungry, disillusioned, disaffected young men. In the wave of egalitarianism sweeping the country, he dropped the "von" from his name. In the light of his father's previous officer status he managed to get into the reviving German navy and was eventually seconded to the submarine service.'

Pernelle broke in on Louis' narrative. 'This is incredible! Where else could I have tracked down such family information about people connected with the *Nova Scotia*?'

Louis answered tightly, 'The worst is yet to come.'

'Jost?' asked Gareth.

'Yes, Jost,' replied Louis.

He recollected his thoughts, then resumed his story.

'My father Roberto heard that von Keller had been killed in action, but he was totally unaware of Gerda's existence, or that the man who had ruined his life had a wife in the territory at "Allesverloren". Roberto became a naturalized South African citizen with the occupation of the territory by South Africa and changed his name by deed poll to Robert Arnold. I myself was born Louis Arnold.'

'It seems so long ago,' interjected Pernelle.

'To me, it is like yesterday,' responded Louis. 'You see, because there was no money I became a travelling salesman selling household and farm wares. One of these journeys took me to "Allesverloren", where Gerda lived with her daughter Ingrid. Ingrid was twenty-four by then and had led a completely isolated, frustrated, lonely life. It was simply love at first sight between us, and that remained so all our lives. Neither of us had any idea of the blood-feud between our families.

'Gerda had developed cancer of the throat and, on the eve of the Second World War, Jost was given compassionate leave to visit her from Germany. Jost, an arrogant Nazi, was officer material for the German navy and a potential U-boat commander. Gerda was seriously ill, but Jost arrived in time to find her alive. It was her wish that Ingrid should have the Stones of the Sun in recognition of her devotion.

'After Gerda's death there was a violent confrontation between Jost and Ingrid. With typical arrogance, Jost demanded that he, as the eldest son, should have the priceless masterpiece. Ingrid naturally refused. But Jost determined that he would have it, and decided to kill for it.

'Using a poisoned Bushman arrow, he shot Ingrid, grabbed the necklace, and left her to die.'

Louis stirred in his chair and said rather breathlessly, 'Ingrid did not die, however. She was saved by the timely arrival of that young travelling salesman in his car. Such a vehicle was a great rarity in the outback in those days . . .'

'You?' asked Gareth.

'Yes, me,' replied Louis, the agony of the moment evident in his voice.

'As I told you, previous to the sinking of the *Nova Scotia* I had seen Jost once before, and then only briefly. That was the occasion. I saw him running out of the house at "Allesverloren". When I got inside Ingrid was already partly paralysed from the poison, but she managed to gasp out that it was her own brother who had shot her.

'I gave her emergency first-aid treatment and rushed her to a small outback clinic in the car. After many days of teetering between life and death, she survived, but remained partly paralysed all her life. It also affected her child-bearing ability; we thought she was barren, until she had a son in 1958, years after we had been married.

'Ingrid was shocked to the depths by her brother's attempt to kill her; she wanted nothing ever to do with him, "Allesverloren" or the necklace, and all her life she never spoke of it again. We moved to the Cape but she, being German, was interned by the South Africans. I volunteered for the South African forces, and that is how I happened to be aboard the *Nova Scotia* coming home from service in the Middle East. We were married in Ingrid's internment camp and never saw one another again for years, but it made no difference: ours was a great love affair.

'After Ingrid died in the late sixties, I made a few enquiries but the trail had gone dead. All that I could find out was that "Allesverloren" had been sold shortly after the end of the war to a man named Dehn. The sale was negotiated from

Germany, so presumably Jost remained overseas. There was no way of finding out. Finish of story.'

Gareth sensed Pernelle's growing tension. But he could not see her face clearly in the twilight. Now, she jumped to her feet and went swiftly to the big desk and clicked on the light above the pile of documents.

She banged her hand down on them.

'It isn't finish of story,' she said. 'It's all here. The person called Dehn was Jost Keller himself. He had a son named Kentrat Dehn. That man is the present owner of Bangazi Lodge.'

19

The gasping intake of breath and rapid exhalation sounded to Gareth for a moment like the onset of a heart attack. Louis' face first turned purple, then deadly pale, as he hauled himself to his feet by the arms of his chair. There he hung, half-sitting, half-standing, with his eyes riveted on Pernelle.

His voice sounded as if his vocal cords had been scoured by sandpaper.

'What have you got there? I've been trying for a whole lifetime to find that out!' he rasped. 'How could you locate . . .'

Pernelle went to him. 'I think you had better sit down.'

He didn't seem to hear. 'Kentrat Dehn! The son! Right under the memorial's nose! Jost Keller's son! The devil who sank the *Nova Scotia*! What's he up to so close to the wreck . . .' His voice trailed off in shocked disbelief.

Pernelle intervened. 'That's what I ask myself! What *is* he doing?'

Louis broke in thickly, 'What are those documents? Who could know this about Jost Keller?'

'I have good professional friends in Germany at the office of the former *Befehlshaber der U-boote* – the wartime Supreme Commander,' answered Pernelle. 'I told you previously that I was having great difficulties in this country getting the information I wanted about the sinking of the *Nova Scotia*, beyond the bare outline. So I got in touch with my German contacts. For a considerable time I thought I had drawn a blank. But then this arrived while

I was at Bangazi.' She indicated the pile of papers on the desk. 'It lays the story bare.'

'And a lot more besides, if it reveals that this Dehn who bought "Allesverloren" and Jost Keller are one and the same,' asserted Gareth.

Pernelle went on. 'The giveaway was via one of those ridiculous pieces of red tape which crop up in bureaucratic outfits like the German navy. As a wartime serving officer, Jost Keller was automatically transferred to the Officers' Reserve and as such his whereabouts had to be notified.'

She riffled through the papers. 'Here it is – "Kapitän-leutnant Jost Keller, farm "Allesverloren", PO Otjituo, South West Africa."'

'The date!' exclaimed Louis. 'What is the date of that?'

'July 1952.'

'That still doesn't show he changed his name and re-occupied "Allesverloren",' argued Louis. 'The name and address in the German records could merely be out of date and were never altered.'

'Except for this,' replied Pernelle. 'Here is a photocopy of a Government Gazette notice, dated three years before, recording a name change by deed poll of one Jost Keller to Jost Dehn.'

'Why should anyone bother to include such a name change in an official file?' asked Gareth. 'It seems beyond the functions of a civil servant.'

Pernelle said, 'Because Jost was somewhat notorious, and his changing his name drew attention. You see, after the Nürnberg trial of major war criminals, which ended in late 1946, the spotlight was directed on lesser suspects. Jost was one, because of his sinking of the *Nova Scotia* with 750 civilians on board. Here I have a complete record of Jost's trial, which dragged on for months. Finally, he was acquitted on a technicality – a signal from U-boat Command ordering him not to carry out rescue attempts and to carry on operating.

'It was a razor-edge verdict, and Jost was very much in the public eye. It isn't strange that his change of name was noted.'

'I accept that,' said Louis. 'But I still can't understand how he could move back to "Allesverloren" under the name Dehn.'

Pernelle sorted again among the pile of documents.

'Here is the deed of sale, registered at the Surveyor General's office in Windhoek in 1950. There are also copies of legal documents from Germany – the sale was, according to this, financially negotiated between one Jost Keller and the buyer Jost Dehn and finally registered in South West Africa.'

'Surely the name Jost for both parties aroused some suspicions?' asked Gareth.

'Not necessarily. It is quite a common German name,' answered Pernelle. 'I don't know how Jost organized the finer points of the sale at long distance, but the proof of the pudding is here in the deed of sale. Jost Dehn became known as the new owner of "Allesverloren".'

'And so brushed out all his previous tracks so that there could be no connection between Dehn, von Keller and the Empress's necklace,' Louis said bitterly.

'Yet, what did happen to the necklace?' asked Gareth.

'The fake deal over "Allesverloren" was such an elaborate ploy that one can only assume that it had something to do with concealing the necklace,' said Pernelle. 'Wherever it was hidden, Jost lived the rest of his life on "Allesverloren", but not in the style one might have assumed had he disposed of the necklace for the king's ransom it must have been worth.'

'It was incomparably beautiful, I believe,' said Louis. 'It haunted my father.' He turned to Pernelle. 'How do you know this Dehn lived on "Allesverloren" all his life?'

'That was easy to document. In the dying days of the terrorist war before Namibia became independent

"Allesverloren" was attacked by a group of terrorists who murdered Dehn's wife. He managed to give the alarm and escape. The farm came into the news because of the murder. Not long afterwards Jost Dehn died of a heart attack, probably as a consequence of his wife's killing.' She referred to the documents. 'Here is a newspaper account of his death. It also mentions that he was survived by one son, Kentrat Dehn, a senior official in the office of the Diamond Directorate in Windhoek. There is no doubt about it, Kentrat Dehn is the son of Jost Keller, the notorious U-boat commander who sank the *Nova Scotia*, grandson of Hans-Ludwig von Keller, the Prussian officer who pistol-whipped your father and uncle and stole the Stones of the Sun.'

Louis said, 'As an example of thorough investigative research, I think your reconstruction of Dehn's past is magnificent. It tells me everything I want to know. But it all ended over two years ago when Jost Dehn died of a heart attack after his wife's murder by terrorists on "Allesverloren".' He leaned forward. 'You've made an incredible statement that the present owner of Bangazi Lodge is Jost Dehn's son Kentrat. There is absolutely nothing to connect the present owner of Bangazi with the Dehn family. Not even the name is the same – it's Ken Ziegler.'

'You probably know that when the army announced it was abandoning the Bangazi missile-testing platform there was a great outcry from ecologists and conservationists. The army intended simply to leave the half-dismantled platform to rot. Then they proposed to sink it in Bangazi lake, which they had originally dredged to accommodate it. This aroused another storm. The army would not hear of disposing of the missile station by breaking it up and carting it away in sections. Understandably, the cost would have been prohibitive.'

Pernelle found a sheaf of newspaper cuttings.

'At the height of the controversy, an ecological saviour appeared unexpectedly out of the blue. His name – I quote a Durban newspaper of the date – was Kentrat Dehn, from Namibia.'

Louis sat transfixed. 'This is unbelievable . . .!'

Pernelle continued. 'One of the preconditions of the National Monuments Council in granting a licence is that the salvor must be trustworthy and well-intentioned. We always investigate an applicant's background. So the buyer of the missile platform came under our scrutiny. Only once – on that first occasion in the press – did the name Dehn appear. Subsequently, every reference was to Ken Ziegler, the hotelier from Namibia. There seemed something fishy, to say the least.'

'But your Monuments Council isn't – wasn't – concerned with who might or might not have bought the missile platform, it is concerned with the wreck of the *Nova Scotia*,' argued Louis.

'True,' replied Pernelle. 'Except, as it turned out, they happen to be one and the same person. And that leaves us with doubts about his *bona fides*.'

Louis got up. There was anguish in his face, but formidable determination flared in his eyes. His voice was turbulent.

'Touch a Sicilian and you find revenge,' he got out thickly. 'My father cursed the Prussian when he knocked out his eye and blinded him for life, and beat his brother to death. A Sicilian never forgets a vow of vengeance. It is an obligation on the family and descendants to carry on such a feud – in blood. We, the Arnoldis, have waited three-quarters of a century to nail von Keller or his offspring. I personally owe the Kellers blood for what they did to me and to my wife. Now, at long last, I have the von Kellers in my sights. Now . . .'

Pernelle sat appalled at the landmine of hatred and wild revenge which had been fused.

Gareth gripped Louis by the shoulders as if to shake loose the fixed, hypnotic stare which had clamped his eyes.

'Louis! Listen to me! Pull yourself together! Louis – what are you going to do?'

'I am going to Bangazi Lodge,' he spat, 'to finish this once and for all!'

20

'Bangazi is a powder barrel with two lighted fuses rushing to blow it.'

'*Two*?' Pernelle exclaimed. 'Two! There's only one and that's Louis, mad for revenge because of this lifelong blood-feud . . .'

'There's his son Rick, too, equally mad to settle with Kentrat Dehn in blood. For a completely different reason. Heaven help him if either of them gets at his throat!'

'Son? Rick? What's all this about?'

'I got acquainted at the wrong end of a gun. That day, when you phoned from Bangazi to say you were leaving, Rick was there alongside me in my office. When I answered the phone, that gun was lying on the desk between us. Plus an Excalibur knife. A minute or two before, he'd been quite willing to give them a workout against me.'

'Any moment, I'll wake up and find there was no elderly man here at Gil's Cottage telling me about a priceless necklace in his past, no dead-and-gone Prussian officer, no blood-feud . . .' she choked on the words '. . . and no Gareth!'

Louis had stormed out of Gil's Cottage, hell-bent on revenge, deaf to Pernelle and Gareth's pleas to let his anger cool while he thought over the implications of what he wanted to do. Now he was gone and they were alone in the lovely room with only the twilight and the sheaf of damning documents for company.

Gareth took her in his arms, and felt her shaking with horror and revulsion at the stark blood-lust which confronted them both.

'Tell me,' she said hoarsely. 'I have to know! Tell me about this Rick!'

They sat down and Gareth tried to arrange into a semblance of order the tangled skein of events and relationships which had thrown the two Italians, father and son, into their lives.

He said consideringly, 'Rick knew my name and where to find me from Samsonov. They had met in Angola, where Rick was making a last attempt to lay his hands on Kentrat Dehn and half a million in uncut diamonds which Dehn had swindled him out of.'

'But, Gareth, you weren't involved in this, were you?' Her eyes were fixed on his face and, as an awful doubt rose in her mind, they clouded as if a delicate rime of frost had covered them. 'Were you?'

He shook his head. 'No. I've somehow been drawn into all this, deeper and deeper, simply through my previous professional connection with Glaval, which means Dr Vize. You see, Rick had the one solid piece of evidence in his pocket which was worth a king's ransom to Glaval, and he showed it to Samsonov, who rushed post-haste to me.'

'What was it?'

'He had an official receipt, signed by Kentrat Dehn on behalf of the former Diamond Directorate, purporting to be part of what Dehn styled a state-backed trusteeship scheme under which small operators could surrender their diamond output in exchange for a collateral guaranteeing payment four months after Namibia's independence. Rick fell for it. It was as clever a scam as you could hope to encounter. It was the use – or rather misuse – of Glaval's name on the fake receipt which pitched the whole business into my lap.

'I still don't know by what murky path Rick reached Samsonov, but the fact is that they did meet at the hotel Presidente Meridien in Luanda. Samsonov recognized the priceless value of Rick's receipt and flew at all speed to

Richards Bay to meet me, leaving Rick at the Presidente Meridien to await his return. When Samsonov missed me, he left me a note arranging to meet him at Bangazi Lodge. The rest you know.'

'No, I don't. Why did Rick come looking for you so far away from Angola?'

'He arrived in a very dangerous mood – with a gun and a knife. Samsonov was his lifeline, and when he didn't hear from him, he believed I had done him some harm.'

The grey, serious hue of her eyes overtook the blue as they widened in fear. 'You – you're not in danger, are you, Gareth?'

He laughed shortly. 'Not from Rick. Not any more. He, like Louis, wants to throw himself at Ken Ziegler's throat, but for the moment the red light has changed to amber. He's working for Glaval now, compiling a list of names of other small Namib operators who were caught in Dehn's racket.'

'All that you're telling me adds up to one thing – we've got to stop Louis, Gareth! Where is Rick to be found? Can't you get hold of him, tell him the deadly danger at Bangazi?'

'He's quite close to us here, at Mossel Bay. I have his address and his phone number.'

'Gareth, you must contact Rick at once and get him to stop his father! Anything could happen now to Louis!'

'It's not that simple, Pernelle. Rick and his father are completely estranged because of Rick's involvement in the diamond scam. He told me so himself. His father won't have anything more to do with him.'

'But in an extreme situation like this, and with the same man involved? Rick knows just how ruthless Ken Ziegler can be! Look at Samsonov!'

'A phone call wouldn't be the means of discussing this issue, it's far too complicated,' answered Gareth. 'Better if I went in person to Rick's workplace at Mossel Bay.

It's not so far from Cape Town, maybe a little over half a day's drive.'

'You could take my car.'

'That's the way we'll do it, then,' agreed Gareth. 'We've still some time to play with. Even with the most pressing urgency in the world, Louis can't get a flight to Durban and onwards before tomorrow afternoon. If I can put pressure on Rick tomorrow, he may still be able to stop him.'

The next afternoon, Gareth telephoned Pernelle at her Cape Town office.

'Pernelle? I'm sorry to tell you I've drawn a blank on Rick.'

'Where is he?'

'Apparently he was flown out to the production platform yesterday. It's about seventy kilometres offshore, they tell me, and it's right in the middle of an area notorious for heavy seas and powerful currents. They've just had a strong gale which threw something in the platform's buoyancy stability system, and Rick's an expert in that field.'

'How long is he likely to be away, Gareth? Time is vital, in fact more vital even since you left.' Her voice sounded sharp and strained.

'Until the system is fixed – two, three days, maybe. The people ashore wouldn't commit themselves. It could even be tomorrow, if they're lucky.'

'It might be worthwhile waiting in Mossel Bay rather than driving back here, then back again.'

'That's what I thought. In fact, the rig management was pretty sympathetic. They seem to have plenty of casual visitors' accommodation for all the comings-and-goings to the production platform, and they've offered me a bed.'

'It means we'll have missed another day with Louis. He may have left by the time Rick comes ashore again, and anything could happen once he gets to Bangazi.'

Again, Gareth noticed the strain in her voice.

There was silence, and then, with convulsive uncertainty, the announcement spilled out.

'Gareth, I'm going back to Bangazi.'

'*You – are – going – back – to – Bangazi?*'

'Yes. I'm flying on Friday to Durban. My visit may even have a silver lining: I can try and prevent anything happening to Louis if you can't lay your hands on Rick in time.'

Gareth was stunned. 'You are going back to Bangazi, knowing what you know about Kentrat Dehn alias Ziegler? How will you ever get aboard the flotel?'

'Ziegler's invited me, even paid the air fare. Everything on the house, in fact.'

'Pernelle – I'm getting back to Cape Town, now! You can't! It's crazy! It's a trap! You accepted an invitation from *Dehn*!'

'On the surface, I realize it sounds crazy. But Ziegler has changed course – at least, I think he has – and good could come out of it instead of killing. Don't race back, my darling – I'll be gone soon anyway.'

'Pernelle, Ziegler is a crook and a killer, and you're putting your head into his lion's den!'

'Gareth, hear me out for a moment. Ken Ziegler needs to be told, very plainly from the shoulder, that his application to obtain sole salvor's rights to the *Nova Scotia* is a non-starter. The reason he phoned and invited me was to say that he had modified his previous hard-line stance and was now willing to accept the fact that the wreck was inside South African territorial waters, and therefore within the jurisdiction of the National Monuments Council, and subject to our rules. He's also dropped his talk of legal action. Louis' objection on the grounds that the Italian community is having the site declared a war grave is in itself enough to kill Ziegler's chances. Of course he doesn't know about that – yet!'

'Pernelle, you could have told him all this on the phone, no need to risk yourself and *go* there!'

'Before he went overseas, Dr Riekert gave me full discretion,' went on Pernelle. 'I intend getting this whole *Nova Scotia* business off my back once and for all by confronting Ziegler.'

'You don't have to stick your neck out!'

'The worst will be that I will have to endure the Coelacanth Suite for a night.'

'Courtesy of Kentrat Dehn/Ziegler, never forget. He runs the helicopter shuttle. You're a prisoner in a gilded cage. At least you'll be in good hands for the flight with Lance.'

'Lance is off for a few days in anticipation of all the ferrying he'll have to do once the VIPs and others start arriving for the memorial opening. It's only ten days away.'

'Who's meeting you at Durban, then?'

'Not Durban this time, but Richards Bay. Ziegler himself is flying the helicopter. You know he does occasional standby duty.'

'If I can't dissuade you from going, please, please, Pernelle, phone me when you reach Bangazi – I'll be on tenterhooks every moment you're away.'

'Dearest Gareth,' she said softly. 'I'll promise, but it does depend on the radio-phone link at the Lodge. It's not an ordinary telephone connection.'

'That makes me unhappier still,' Gareth replied. 'Pernelle, apart from Ken Ziegler, you could surely say all you have to say to Louis by seeing him in Cape Town.'

'I tried his flat this morning with that in mind, after Ziegler had phoned,' she answered. 'There was no reply. I don't know whether he's already left for Bangazi or not. Rest assured, my darling, that if I can prevent Louis from setting out, I will. I have too much to lose, if things go wrong.'

'I'm having nightmares already, when you speak like that.'

'All that's required is a clear, official, surgical break with Ziegler and an end to all this double-talk.'

'There was no double-talk with Louis,' Gareth observed. 'He's probably polishing his World War Two Service revolver now, ready to spit defiance at anyone who tries to stop him. There was murder in his face and heart last night.'

'Rick *must* stop him!' said Pernelle. 'Louis' life is at stake.'

'It's not the only stake,' said Gareth quietly. 'You are, too.'

'You're over-dramatizing the danger,' she replied. 'I don't believe there's any to me. I'll be back after the weekend, you'll see.' But he didn't know, then, just how long it would be before he saw Pernelle again.

21

They dumped Louis' body on the beach. It had a 500-mm
speargun shaft through the neck. It lay on the rock base
of the memorial site, only a few paces from where he had
staggered ashore from the U-boat after walking the plank.

Ziegler and Buks were careful to leave as few footprints as
possible. They confined themselves mainly to the rock and
the sand below the high-water mark so that the incoming
tide would erase all trace of their presence.

The solution to their impossible problem had been
Romira's idea, down there in the buoyancy chamber of
the flotel. All the blood had been a major worry, and
they had let it drain into the water of the access and
ventilation shaft in which Samsonov had been drowned.
By the time it had stopped – a nerve-racking time while
the life of the Lodge went on in the upper levels – they
were satisfied that it would have congealed enough not
to stain the helicopter's floor. Any residual traces found
on the memorial slab would only serve to reinforce their
story. The rising tide, though, would do a better job than
they could.

Louis' old Service revolver, with one shot fired, was a
liability, and Ziegler had finally decided to stash it away
in the secret compartment of his old safe. There was no
trace in the buoyancy chamber of the spent slug which was
discharged as Louis fell.

Louis' revenge-lust had lent wings to his departure from
Cape Town, and a midnight flight saw him waiting in
Durban on Thursday morning to be ferried to Bangazi
Lodge by Lance in the helicopter. A lifetime's simmering

madness had come to the boil and his intention was simply to kill, to settle the score.

Romira had been at reception when Louis landed with Lance on the helideck. She gave him the usual professional, welcoming smile but noted nothing unusual about the wiry, spruce, elderly man except perhaps a measure of tension in his clipped replies. He had asked immediately for Ken Ziegler. He had the revolver, carefully oiled and checked, right there in his pocket.

'Everyone asks for Ken,' Romira had replied easily. 'But Lance dropped him off at Richards Bay for a business appointment and to collect supplies. He won't be back until tomorrow. Anything I can do?'

Louis licked his dry lips. He wanted the kill – now! Twenty-four more hours of crucifying marking-time in an alien room, alone with the ghosts of his dead and the luminous wraith of that incomparable necklace.

'It'll have to wait.'

It did wait, until the following day, in Ziegler's private quarters.

Ziegler was in the process of getting to his scuffed old safe concealed behind the slick modern cocktail cabinet. By an oversight, he had not locked the outer door of the suite leading to the corridor; through this Louis had entered, silent-footed as a stalking leopard.

'*Von Keller!*' His voice carried eighty years of remorseless Sicilian hatred.

The use of the name, after so long, photoflashed trouble into Ziegler's mind. He straightened up, taking in his wiry little visitor, the heavy revolver, and the savage expression at a hyper-quick gulp.

Von Keller! Not even Keller! Von Keller! The old Prussian form! What pit out of the past had this gun-brandishing apparition sprung from?

He assumed an easy, almost jovial voice in his best mine-host manner.

'You've lost your way, friend. No von Kellers in this establishment. Can I help you? It's obviously urgent . . .' He smiled stagily and gestured towards the gun, moving forward slightly as he did so.

'Keep back!' snapped Louis. 'Listen, Keller, or von Keller, or Dehn, whichever you choose to call yourself. It's a matter of life or death. *Your* life, *your* death.'

'That's very melodramatic talk,' Ziegler said. Humour him, he thought. Talk him out of his gun . . .

'I came here to kill you, and that I intend to do. So cut the crap.'

Automatically, Ziegler took a banknote from his pocket, snapped it through his teeth, like a zip credit card, then let it fall to the floor. He looked at the hard eyes of the elderly man, now unnaturally bright, and knew he wasn't bluffing.

He took a step back, and felt the rough metal of the old safe against his hands. Every man has his price, and there were enough diamonds in there left over from the last Taiwan airlift to buy off even a madman.

'Who are you?' he asked thickly.

'That's better!' said Louis. 'Better you know why I'm killing you, and for what.'

'You've got the wrong man, the wrong name!' broke in Ziegler hurriedly.

'I have not,' retorted Louis. 'You are Kentrat Ziegler, alias Kentrat Dehn, son of Jost Dehn, more properly U-boat Kapitänleutnant Jost Keller.'

'I don't know what you're talking about!' Ziegler got out wildly. 'You should be in an asylum!'

'Let me first put you straight about myself,' Louis intervened. 'I am Louis Arnold. Does that mean anything to you?'

'No, I tell you . . .'

'Louis Arnold,' persisted Louis. 'Arnoldi?'

'My oath!' mouthed Ziegler. 'Arnoldi!'

'The same,' said Louis. 'The same. Am I starting to make myself clear?'

A thin patina of sweat filmed Ziegler's face.

'What do you want from me?' he said, less arrogantly now. 'If it's Rick's diamonds, we can make a deal –'

'Diamonds! Rick!' echoed Louis contemptuously.

'What *do* you want from me, then?'

Louis answered unhesitatingly, 'Your life. The Stones of the Sun.'

Ziegler uttered a half-hysterical strangled noise and finally got out, 'There's not much left, after that.'

Louis went on remorselessly, as if reciting by rote a speech hammered out during lonely hours of agonizing.

'There was not much left when your Prussian grandfather had finished with my uncle. He died a couple of days after von Keller pistol-whipped him. I never knew him. But I knew my father. He was a craftsman and von Keller blinded him. It robbed him of everything he wanted. They named me Louis after my uncle, as a reminder that I should be the bearer of vengeance.'

Ziegler said wildly, 'These are old, forgotten sins by old, forgotten people! They have nothing to do with me!'

'No?' asked Louis. 'Let us come nearer in time to you, then. Jost Keller, the U-boat captain.'

'He only did his duty. U-boat captains were regarded by the other side as pariahs . . .' Ziegler blustered.

'Was it his duty to play cat-and-mouse with a prisoner and try to drown him for the amusement of his crew? To sink a shipful of women and children? Leave them to the sharks?'

'These are fairy-stories,' broke in Ziegler. 'British war-time propaganda.'

The gun held very steady on Ziegler. 'Not so,' said Louis. 'Jost Keller did it to me.'

'You? *You!*' Ziegler was thoroughly shaken now.

'There is more. Jost Keller also stole the Stones of the Sun.'

'That's a lie!' responded Ziegler. 'I know it's a lie! My father himself told me how our family came into possession of the necklace. It was put into my grandfather's safekeeping by the Empress of Germany . . .'

Louis laughed; Ziegler didn't like the sound.

'Did he not tell you how your grandmother stole it from the hunting-lodge at Allenstein and how it was stashed away for eighty years on a remote farm in Namibia? Did he not tell you how, when he came back for a brief while when his mother was dying, he tried to kill his sister with Bushman poison?'

'That's another lie!' burst out Ziegler vehemently.

Louis eyed him. 'If I didn't know you knew the real story, I would feel almost sorry for you. It wasn't a lie. You see, he tried to kill his sister, who became my wife.'

Ziegler's mouth gaped and he sagged against the safe.

'Stop!' Louis ordered. 'I've told you enough for you to know why I am here.' He raised the revolver.

'No, no!' mouthed Ziegler. 'I'll take you to it! It's down below, on the lower deck of the flotel. I keep it in a tank . . .'

'A tank?' For a moment Louis was curious, his killer impulse momentarily checked.

'It's weathering, so that, so that . . .'

There was a silence, and then Louis said slowly, 'Weathering, eh? I see now what you're up to with the *Nova Scotia* wreck! *My* ship! But you'll never get your hands on the *Nova Scotia* to write another chapter with the Stones of the Sun, Ziegler! I'm going to see to that – now!'

'I'll take you to the necklace – don't shoot!'

Louis eyed him contemptuously. 'We are not going out into the public corridors.'

Ziegler indicated. 'I have a private lift. It goes down to the old missile control centre and the hydropower chamber.'

'Don't talk round it,' snapped Louis. 'The Stones of the Sun — where is the necklace?'

'In the hydropower chamber. They've got their own special container and hooking device . . .'

The elevator was fast, silent. It seemed only seconds before it reached its destination.

The door slid open onto the dereliction of the old missile-tracking control centre with its array of abandoned steel desks, disconnected computer consoles and empty telephone cradles.

Louis shoved the big revolver into Ziegler's back. 'What are you playing at? This isn't a buoyancy chamber!'

'Give me a chance! This chamber is part of the previous army security system — blast-proof, flame-proof, sound-proof . . .'

'Then no one will hear the shot,' interrupted Louis.

Ziegler's eyes were riveted on the base of the fire-control console. There were several electric buttons, one slightly more prominent than the others — the panic alarm.

He had to get to it! Its sound-and-flash alert was located in a couple of key areas of the Lodge: in his own suite, in Romira's reception office adjoining the helipad, and in Buks's private quarters.

He had to get his hand to that panic button!

He said to Louis, without turning, 'The buoyancy chamber door is over there, to our left, part of the wall. It's got an electronic opening system — ' he produced the hand-held radio switch from his pocket ' — this is part of the gadget. But it has first to be activated from over there.' He indicated the fire-control console. His mouth was dry.

In the silence, a bubbling, gurgling sound reached them from the buoyancy chamber.

Louis hesitated, but Ziegler strode forward to the console, reached down . . .

Romira stared in astonished disbelief as the harsh note of

the buzzer screeched insistently and a companion red light started to flash. She was immobile for a moment then sprinted down the steel steps from the helipad to Ziegler's quarters and the private lift. In his suite, Buks, too, reacted to the alarm. Adrenaline poured through his veins, and he grabbed what first came to hand – the speargun and spear he had been checking.

Clutching the weapon, he ran along the seemingly endless corridor, up two flights of steps, and burst into Ziegler's quarters.

He was already too late; Romira had beaten him to it; the lift light showed it was heading into the bowels of the flotel.

It landed with a soft thump in the fire-control chamber. As the doors swung open, Romira had already convinced herself it was a false alarm.

The place was empty.

Ziegler and Louis had made their way, gun to back, through to the buoyancy chamber, along the steel catwalk, past the double standing control consoles with the 'driving seat' between them, to the big lighted glass tank near the far wall in which hung the incomparable Stones of the Sun. The necklace picked up the light from the overhead strip with translucent loveliness.

Louis' back was towards Romira; she did not see the revolver.

'Ken! What . . .!'

Louis swung away, startled into a half-crouch next to the ugly, gaping mouth of the access and ventilation shaft.

'You fool!' ground out Ziegler. 'You bloody little fool! Why didn't you wait?'

'What's going on here?'

Louis gestured with the gun. 'Get alongside him – quick! Any games and – '

'I thought it was a false alarm . . .'

Louis said in a low, menacing voice, 'This is for real. I am here to kill this man.'

'Am I hearing right . . .?' Romira was incredulous.

'Move!' rapped Louis. 'I don't want to have to shoot you too, but I will if you try and interfere.'

She stood mechanically next to Ziegler, stunned more than terrified.

'Further round by the tank!' ordered Louis. 'Get the necklace out! And don't try anything!'

Ziegler held the loop and 'fishing rod', ready to hook the necklace out of the water.

As Louis moved half a pace nearer, perhaps for a better view of the magnificent jewels, a 500-mm spear took him on the left side, between neck and shoulder. He collapsed gurgling to the floor, his gun discharging as he fell.

Buks hadn't rushed his fences like Romira. He had pulled off his boots in the lift going down, and moved swiftly and silently through the buoyancy chamber to stand concealed by the consoles before taking his shot. It is doubtful whether Louis ever saw the avenging figure with the strange weapon clamped to his shoulder, and his convulsing body now twitched to rest on the edge of the access shaft, the spear projecting obscenely from a wound already pumping blood.

Ziegler froze, the colour draining from his face. Romira stood transfixed, staring at the exquisite masterpiece in the tank.

Buks approached Louis' body, a pleased, lop-sided grin on his face. He jerked a thumb at the corpse.

'That skewered the bastard, all right.'

Ziegler's immobility snapped. 'You stupid, blundering sonofabitch! You've ruined everything!' he thundered, savagely.

'What are you bitching about? I got him, didn't I?' Buks was truculent, bristling at Ziegler's hectoring, ungrateful tone.

Ziegler indicated the body. 'Think, man, think! How are we going to explain that? *Why* did you kill him?'

'He had a gun on you, didn't he? He looked as if he could pull the trigger any moment, and all the bloody thanks I get is a mouthful of crap!'

'Oh, for crying out loud, use your bloody brains, if you have any!' burst out Ziegler. 'For eighty years that masterpiece there has been kept from anyone but one or two of the family, but now because of this a public spotlight will be thrown on it!'

Buks walked across to the tank, eyed the necklace, and gave a long whistle of astonishment.

'And a murder!' Ziegler ranted on. 'With a bloody speargun, for Christ's sake! *How will you account for it?*'

'How the hell was I to know what you had stashed away here?' Buks was indignant now. 'The fuzz needn't know he was nailed here. We can get rid of the body.'

'Take it out, and let me wear it . . .' Romira's strange, faraway voice cut through the argument. 'It's beautiful, beautiful . . .'

'Hell's delight!' exclaimed Ziegler. 'Does no one want to listen to me or help? We're in deep trouble! *What do we do?*'

Buks pulled his attention away from the tank. 'We'll make a plan,' he muttered. 'No one will be any the wiser.'

'Don't be so bloody stupid!' screamed Ziegler. 'I tell you we're in the *shit* – right up to our necks!'

He rounded on Romira, still abstractedly eyeing the necklace. 'Haven't you any contribution to make, damn it?' he ground out. 'You're in this, too!'

Romira smiled, gestured at the necklace.

'Up to the neck, you could say, couldn't you, Ken? For a long time now, ever since the Tintenpalast days.'

'This isn't a reminiscing session,' he cut in roughly. 'Think, damn it, *think!*'

'If you take the necklace out of the tank and let me wear it, I'll tell you what to do.'

Ziegler was stopped by the tone in her voice.

'What are you up to?'

She shrugged her elegant shoulders. 'It's your neck. It's your past. It's your family skeleton.'

Ziegler went to her, his face suffused with anger. 'You bitch! You heartless, uncaring bitch!'

'All that crap doesn't help,' she retorted levelly. 'The necklace.' She stretched a languid hand towards the tank. 'I wear, I tell what to do.'

Ziegler grabbed the 'fishing rod' and thrust it into the tank. Buks's attention was riveted on him. His hands lacked full control, and he missed his target the first time. Finally, at the second attempt, he hooked it out.

Romira came forward, took it from his hands and slipped it, still wet, round her neck. She half-knelt to the tank to see her reflection in the water.

She gave a secretive, self-satisfied smile.

'Here's how we get rid of the body . . .'

22

'It's a dream, I tell you! My old man's fixation about the Stones of the Sun is in his mind only – it doesn't exist in reality! He's chasing a will-o'-the-wisp!'

Rick's voice, roused and angry, filled the small flat on the shoreline of Mossel Bay. The apartment was functional, one of a cluster of similar 'Meccano'-type buildings gridded down on a bleak stretch of shore to house the men who came and went to the offshore production platform, seventy kilometres away over the horizon.

It was Friday afternoon and Gareth had waited for Rick all day, fretting away the hours, knowing that Pernelle would now be due in Durban on her way to Bangazi.

Rick was still in oilskins and working overalls. His hands were filthy and he smelled of oil and burned chemicals. Days of fighting the elements had scored fine marks under the line of his untrimmed beard and he was dead beat, irritable.

'Listen, Gareth, I've had a shitty week, and I'm knackered. All I want is a bath and a stiff drink, and then you confront me with a load of crap the moment I set foot ashore! You could have knocked me down with a feather when you sprang from nowhere – I thought we'd agreed that we'd do no more than keep in touch until I finished my list of small diamond men.'

'I wouldn't be here unless I thought it vital. It's a matter of life and death. Your father's life or death.'

Rick pitched his oilskins over the back of a chair and headed towards a drinks cabinet.

'A drink?' he asked impatiently.

'Scotch, thanks.'

Rick splashed whisky into glasses and flung himself down in a chair.

'This whole story of revenge at the point of a revolver is simply an over-dramatization of something which has festered in my father's mind over a lifetime,' he said abrasively. 'Now Pernelle – and you – have provided him with a focal point in Ken Ziegler. No wonder he's rushed off like a lunatic. I'd shoot Ziegler myself, for completely different reasons, as you know. But not for an airy-fairy story like the Stones of the Sun. Empress of Germany's necklace! Hidden in the desert for a lifetime! Mineral unknown to modern science! No longer around, so that it can't be proved! What a load of bullshit!'

'You're fencing, Rick. Face up to it. Your father's rushed off, gun in hand, to kill – '

'He won't kill, once he discovers the mistake he's making. And if he does put a bullet into Ziegler, good riddance, I say!'

Gareth went on quietly.

'Okay, you say it's all eyewash – '

'Listen, Gareth,' continued Rick roughly. 'I've been fed this story ever since I was a kid. The priceless inheritance which was mine, except for the vicious ways of a Prussian officer. Then Allenstein, the faithless serving-girl, the lonely farm, the love-hungry daughter, the wicked U-boat ace . . .'

'You'll be telling me next that Jost Keller didn't sink the *Nova Scotia*.'

'That old rust-bucket!' sneered Rick. 'I've had that tale of walking the plank thrust down my throat until it's choked me!'

'You're saying it didn't happen?'

Rick took a stiff pull at his drink. 'It could have happened, I suppose, but I'm sick and tired of hearing about it.'

Gareth said, 'Pernelle is an extremely conscientious researcher. She can document anything I'm telling you.'

Rick shrugged. 'I'm not rushing off and spending my

week's special leave, which I've bloody well earned out there on the platform, rushing up to Zululand to try and stop my father making a fool of himself.'

'Ziegler is a dangerous man,' Gareth reminded him. 'He disposed of Samsonov. He's running a smart, dangerous diamond racket.'

'Yeah, yeah, I know!' retorted Rick. 'But you have concrete proof of your part of the story. You handled that diamond in the abalone. You've seen my receipt signed by Ziegler, alias Dehn. *Proof.* I accept that. I don't, however, accept a load of stuff eighty years old which has been passed through the mental resentment systems of my family until it has been blown up into a superheated collection of psychological traumas.'

'All that I'm asking is that you come with me to Cape Town and we go to your father's flat and talk some sense into him, stop him exposing himself to the danger of Ziegler.'

'What danger? Ziegler won't listen to my father.'

'How deeply are you estranged from your father, Rick? Every skittle I put up, you bowl over.'

Rick got up and went to the drinks cabinet, pitched a mind-bender into his glass.

'Look, my father considered the way I came unstuck over the trusteeship scam a shame and a disgrace to the good name of Arnold, or Arnoldi, whichever you like.' He smiled crookedly. 'These bloody Sicilians and their pride! Their goddamn family pride!'

'And their revenges,' added Gareth.

'Why do you say that?'

'Because that's plainly and simply what this is all about. All I'm trying to do is to stop a fine old man running into trouble.'

'What sort of trouble?'

'If I knew, I wouldn't be here. But I know enough about Ziegler to make a guess.'

Rick said quickly, 'It would be impossible for me to crawl cap in hand and say to the old man, listen, Dad – '

'If his life was in danger?'

'Ziegler simply won't listen to him.'

'Listen or not listen, I believe he means to kill.'

'Ziegler will never part with the Stones of the Sun . . .'

'So, the necklace is only a dream, is it, Rick?'

'Jeez, don't tie me up in knots! I'm not answering questions in a law court.'

'No, but you may have to.'

Rick got up, his heavy boots echoing on the steel floor.

'We could motor back tomorrow,' Gareth said. 'Pernelle has already tried to phone Louis in order to stop him. But there was no response. We don't know whether he's already left or not.'

'See here, Gareth, it's not as easy as you make it out to be. I can't walk in on the old man with hand outstretched and a big forgiving grin on my face. Things don't work that way. Not with the sort of background both he and I have to get past. If I were a religious guy, I'd say he regarded my deal over the *Namib Dawn* diamonds as the nearest thing in the book to ultimate damnation. And *his* son involved! No, Gareth, your reason's not strong enough for the sort of climb-down it'll require from me.'

'You'd rather see him die?'

Rick shrugged. 'He's got to take his chance.'

Gareth went on. 'I think I could be the peacemaker between the two of you, if you'd let me. I already know and respect your father. That's a starting-point.'

'How, Gareth? This thing's deep.'

'If I tell him about the abalone diamond racket, how I broke it open. Paint Ziegler just as black as I believe him to be. Tell him – although I can't prove it – about Samsonov's end. Ziegler was behind it, whatever. It'll be some confessional, but we could save his life, this way.'

'In other words, poor little Rick was put upon and

double-dealt by a super-crook! Okay, I suppose it might work.'

'And we'll leave Romira out of it.'

Rick grinned lop-sidedly, the first time since he had come ashore. 'Yeah, no Romira. Speaking of women, what about Pernelle?'

Gareth glanced at his watch. 'She'll have just about arrived in Durban. She's staying overnight there at a hotel and going on to Richards Bay and Bangazi tomorrow. If I'd been at her place at Hout Bay, she could have phoned me there.'

'You could try her from here.'

'I don't know her hotel; she didn't book any place in advance. But she'll be back in Cape Town on Sunday. I'm meeting her plane. She's spending only tomorrow night at Bangazi. I'm sure Ziegler won't stretch his hospitality once he hears what she's got to say to him.'

It was early on Saturday afternoon when they pulled up at Louis' flat in Rondebosch, Cape Town. A yellow police car stood in front.

A blue uniformed warrant officer waited at the door, smoking. From the number of stubs on the ground, he must have been there for some time.

He tossed away a cigarette as they approached.

'Is this the home of Mr Louis Arnold?' he asked formally.

'Yes,' answered Rick. 'What's this all about?' He threw a quick, nervous glance at Gareth.

'Who are you in relation to the . . . ah . . .' He stopped short of the word deceased. But his heavy-handed approach left little to the imagination. 'There's been an accident,' he added cautiously. 'A bad accident.'

'Involving my father?'

'You're his son?'

'Yes.'

'And you, sir?' The question was directed at Gareth. The man was clearing his decks for what both men guessed was coming.

'I knew Louis Arnold – slightly.'

'Get it out, man! What has happened to my father?'

'Are you the next of kin?'

'I said, dammit, I'm his son.'

The man pulled a small notebook from his pocket with agonizing deliberation.

'Then I have orders to ask you to phone Sergeant Joubert at the Richards Bay police on this number as soon as possible . . .'

Rick had no key to the Rondebosch house, so Gareth took him to Gil's Cottage to use the phone.

Sergeant Joubert said, 'I regret to have to tell you, your father is dead.'

'Dead? Dead? How?' The patina of estrangement had fallen from Rick to leave only a distraught man gripping the telephone with a shaking hand.

'An accident, we think.'

'What sort of accident – a car?'

'Nothing like that.' Sergeant Joubert's voice was cautious, official. 'In fact, it is a most unusual accident. He was killed with a speargun, a scuba diver's speargun.'

'Speargun?' echoed Rick, gesturing to Gareth to come closer to overhear what Sergeant Joubert was saying. 'He couldn't have been diving, at his age!'

'He was killed on land,' replied Sergeant Joubert. 'At least, that's what we think happened. The body was found on the beach.'

'On the beach? *What* beach? *Where*?'

'Listen, I don't consider this is the kind of conversation for the telephone,' said Joubert. 'How soon can you get to Richards Bay so that I can give you details?'

'I'm in Cape Town,' said Rick.

'I need positive identification of the body as well,'

went on Sergeant Joubert. 'I warn you, it may be painful.'

'There's a lot of organizing to be done at short notice,' said Rick, clinging to the logistics of the journey rather than going further into details of Louis' death.

Sergeant Joubert said, 'We have the body here in the police mortuary at Richards Bay, pending identification and investigations.'

'Investigations?'

'A man isn't shot in the neck with a speargun without the police asking questions. But, as I said, it would be better if we talked this out face to face.'

'It'll be some days before I can get to Richards Bay,' answered Rick. 'I can't wait that long to know exactly how my father died. You said the body was on the beach. Where?'

'Where the *Nova Scotia* memorial is being built, near Bangazi lake.'

Gareth watched Rick's knuckles whiten as he clenched the receiver. His mouth twisted under its camouflage of beard.

'Bangazi?'

'Your father was staying at the Lodge at the time of his death.'

'*Staying at the Lodge?*'

'There's nowhere else close. He apparently wanted to do some checking at the *Nova Scotia* memorial. Ken Ziegler flew him there in the Lodge chopper, and dropped him off. When he went back to fetch him a couple of hours later, he found the body.'

'Ziegler – ' Rick got the name out with difficulty ' – Ziegler was alone?'

'No. Buks van As from the Lodge staff was with him. He corroborates all this.'

'You say he found the body – how, where?'

'It was lying half-in and half-out of the water, on the

shelf of rock which forms the base of the memorial. There was no sign of anyone who might have fired the spear.'

'The beach – footprints – ' said Rick.

Sergeant Joubert said off-handedly, 'There were no footprints apart from those your father had made as well as Ken Ziegler's and Buks's when they landed from the helicopter.'

'So they – '

'Ken Ziegler acted with great correctness,' cut in Sergeant Joubert shortly. 'On the second pick-up flight he landed on the beach, saw the victim was beyond immediate assistance, flew back to the Lodge and telephoned here to report the tragedy. He asked for police instructions. I told him to leave everything as he had found it and come and collect me at Richards Bay.'

'You say he was shot in the neck? Then his attacker must have come from the beach – '

Sergeant Joubert sighed long-sufferingly. 'He was shot in the neck, half from behind. The obvious deduction is that the spear was fired from the sea, from shallow water. We haven't been into the pathology yet. There hasn't been time.'

'But how . . .'

'Sir,' said Sergeant Joubert ponderously. 'I know this must have been a very great shock to you and I feel it would be better to go into detail when you arrive in Richards Bay.'

Rick realized it was useless to continue trying to get information over the telephone and hung up after promising to get to Zululand as soon as possible.

'Listen,' Gareth told Rick, 'I'm coming with you. Pernelle knows too much for her own safety with a bastard like Ziegler. Two killings! Two clever killings! He'll stop at nothing!'

Anger burned Rick's eyes and Gareth saw in them the hot glow of Sicilian vengeance.

'I'm going for him,' he said thickly. 'I'll be glad to have you along.'

Gareth glanced automatically at his watch.

'I can't get in touch with Pernelle now to warn her not to say anything to Ziegler with that bloody radio-phone being out of action at weekends. She's bound to hear about Louis at Bangazi and I just hope to Christ she gets the underlying message. All I want now is to get her safely out of there.'

'She's due back here tomorrow,' Rick said. 'Surely Ziegler won't try anything.'

'I keep telling myself that,' rejoined Gareth. 'But what if he does? What if . . .'

He got up abruptly and looked out across the grand view of the bay.

'Before we do anything crazy,' said Gareth quietly, 'let's wait and see what Pernelle has to say when she flies in tomorrow. We can base our strategy on that.'

Next afternoon, Gareth watched the file of passengers arriving at Cape Town airport. Pernelle was not among them.

He waited with sickening apprehension for the next aircraft.

Again, there was no Pernelle.

He drove back to Gil's Cottage like a man in a dream.

'Our sortie against Bangazi Lodge takes in Pernelle as well now,' he told Rick. 'I've got to find out what's happened to her.'

'That makes two scores we have to level with Ziegler,' replied Rick.

'We can still check first thing tomorrow when the radio-phone opens.'

Pernelle was before Gareth's eyes all through that interminable night of waiting. As he wandered the cottage in the early hours, he heard again her soft, explosive laugh, remembered the passion with which she had unrestrainedly given her body . . .

Rick found him watching the sun come up over the sea and the mountains.

He said, 'I had an idea in the night. Let me do the speaking. It'll probably be Romira who answers, and she could recognize your voice. The less she knows or guesses about us, the better. I'll put on a bit of an Italian accent, just to throw her off the trail.'

'Pernelle Clymer?' asked Romira when they finally established contact with the Lodge. 'Yes, we had a Pernelle Clymer staying here, but she remained for only one night – Saturday night. She's gone now.'

Rick swallowed hard. 'Gone?'

'Yes. Went with the ferry helicopter to Richards Bay. I don't know where she was headed after that – we don't keep tabs on our guests. Especially,' she added, 'when there's romance in the air.'

'What are you saying?' asked Rick, eyeing Gareth.

'She went off with a man.'

Gareth shook his head. 'Romira overplayed her hand,' he told Rick. 'What you've just told me makes me more desperately anxious than ever.'

'I know Romira,' added Rick thoughtfully. 'She had to exaggerate in order to make it sound good. I don't believe it, either.'

'It was a cover-up for the fact that Pernelle's still at Bangazi and Ziegler wants the world outside to think she's left,' Gareth answered slowly. 'If it hadn't been for Romira's bit of romantic embroidery I might almost have believed that she had gone. But she hasn't. She's there. I'm getting to Bangazi Lodge as quick as hell. I'm going to get Pernelle out of there.'

23

'Master of the Daystar, Lord of the Equinox.'

The ancient Chinese inscription from a fragment of Ming pottery off a Dutch East Indiaman wrecked in Table Bay kept spinning round in Pernelle's brain like the whirl of the helicopter rotors above her head. Little dancing shards of sunlight confettied their way through the perspex of the cockpit on to her lovely hair.

Daystar. Daystar. Daystar. Stones of the Daystar.

What had happened to Louis? she wondered. Would she find him at the flotel, or had he thought better of revenge and returned to Rondebosch?

It was now Saturday lunch-time; she had left Cape Town the day before, stopped over in Durban, and then flown on to Richards Bay where Ken Ziegler had picked her up in the helicopter to spend the night at Bangazi Lodge as his special guest.

There had been something odd about Ziegler when he had met her. The scorings between his hard slivers of eyes were more pronounced, and his mine-host banter seemed forced, although he was amiable enough and clearly out to please. What she did not know was that Ziegler had come directly to the airport from the police mortuary. Sergeant Joubert had tried shock tactics to re-test Ziegler's previous account of finding Louis' body on the beach: the sight of a frozen body with a spear projecting from the neck could loosen a chink in any man's armour, however well prepared he might think himself to be. But Ziegler had stuck to his story and Sergeant Joubert had had to accept it.

Ziegler now gestured at the face of the calm sea. 'It's changed a bit since you were here – look!'

Four danger lights were grouped in a rough rectangle on the sea's surface. Two of them, to the east and west, had curious double metal vanes – like a bird spreading its wings on take-off. These were Tideland solar-powered lanterns. The 'vanes' were solar batteries. To the north and south of the rectangle were two older-model conventional gas-powered lights.

'The *Nova Scotia*'s grave is well marked,' added Ziegler.

He was obviously pushing home the point she had made so strongly that his application for salvage had to state the exact position of the wreck.

'It must look pretty dramatic at night,' was all she could find to say. It was a poor way of expressing what she knew in her mind's eye would be a scintillating cerement of light gridded on the surface of the sea by the son of the killer who had sent so many innocent victims to a watery grave.

Ziegler turned the machine's nose westward towards the land, heading for the distant mirror of the lake behind the green wall dividing it from the sea.

Pernelle felt tongue-tied. How, she asked herself, was she to tell this big powerful man next to her in the pilot's coat that she didn't consider him to be trustworthy or well-intentioned, two of the stringent conditions which were necessary to secure a salvage permit? She almost wished she had taken the easy way out and hidden behind a paperwork barricade in Cape Town. But that wasn't her way – what Ziegler had to be told, she would tell him to his face.

The red-and-white latticed phallus of Bangazi Lodge reared above the forest. Pernelle saw the circle of sweat under Ziegler's arms and smelled his fear as he went straight in, unlike the delicate dragon-fly approach Lance was accustomed to making. With about a metre of altitude to go, he seemed to let go, clumping and bumping to a halt as if Buks's boots had been attached to the landing-wheels.

His face was moist when he turned to Pernelle. 'Neat landing, eh?'

There was no one about the helipad-reception area, except Romira, exuding sex in baggy harem pants, her raven hair hanging loose around her shoulders.

'We're delighted to see you again,' she told Pernelle throatily, fussing over her luggage. 'Ken, if you wouldn't mind taking the bags to the Coelacanth Suite ... It's a little late for lunch in the dining-room,' she went on. 'But I've arranged for a snack to be brought to you.'

Ziegler took Pernelle's luggage and escorted her into the lift. She wondered what his reactions would be later in the afternoon.

Alone in her suite, Pernelle felt suddenly isolated and afraid. She only toyed with the hot seafood sent down for her lunch and didn't touch the half-bottle of Veuve Cliquot standing in the ice-bucket. Just how nasty would Ziegler turn once he discovered she was the main obstacle in the way of his objective? And what had happened to Louis? she asked herself again. If only Gareth were there!

She wanted to get the confrontation over, and ahead of time made her way to Ziegler's private suite.

The meeting had an air of unreality, of discussion on two levels: the big executive desk behind which Ziegler sat, covered with documents and several maps, gave the sense of a business boardroom discussion, while the revelations she would be obliged to spring to justify her refusal of his application floated in the background like an amorphous ghost. Less amorphous was Romira, now dressed in man-alluring sharkskin pants and revealing silver blouse.

'This shouldn't take long,' Ziegler said, consciously relaxing his thickening features, 'but I thought it worth everybody's while to have you here, with the deadline date so close, so that any possible errors could be ironed out in advance. I greatly appreciate your coming.'

Not for long, thought Pernelle. She found it hard to keep up the charade.

Ziegler rushed on. 'Let's get some of the minor details out of the way first, or,' he was greatly deferential and solicitous, 'would you rather deal with the points your way?'

'The National Monuments Council requires certain conditions to be agreed upon by the applicants – '

'Yes, yes,' intervened Ziegler. 'We've dealt with all that previously.' He consulted a typed list of notes. 'I presume that you're satisfied that the salvage work will be undertaken in an approved scientific manner and that proper marine archaeological excavation methods will be used?'

'I thought you wanted the wreck as a scuba-diving attraction for your guests?' asked Pernelle.

'Partly, partly,' Ziegler covered up. 'But you know my interest in the historical aspects of the *Nova Scotia* ... We know how and when the *Nova Scotia* was sunk, by a U-boat on November twenty-eighth, 1942, which is another fact the application requires.' He held his pencil ready to tick off the point on his list. 'Satisfied?'

Pernelle inclined her head. She said nothing about knowing it was Ziegler's own father, Kapitänleutnant Jost Keller, who had sent her to the bottom.

He went on quickly. 'A plan of the wreck site must be prepared and all finds must be related to a grid system or fix-points. Naturally I am willing to do that.'

Pernelle said, 'You haven't said anything about an agreement which must be entered into between yourself and a recognized museum to whom you must be affiliated, and with whom you must be willing to share, amongst other things, the finds you make – '

Ziegler cut in. 'Of course, of course. Only there hasn't

been time. I'm being squeezed for time, that's why I wanted you to come here in person.'

Ziegler found himself looking into a pair of steady grey-blue eyes whose large lids shadowed their pupils of all but their purpose and solemnity. Her voice was charged.

'Let me warn you now that your application will founder on a major consideration. We require that you should be trustworthy and well-intentioned, someone of integrity. Unfortunately for you, this is not what my investigations show.'

Pernelle found herself almost admiring the way the man could ride a knock-down punch and still come back for more. There was a tight silence, broken only by a nervous cough from Romira.

And for a moment, a strange light, which Pernelle did not understand, flared in Ziegler's eyes. Had it appeared also to signal Samsonov's end?

His only outward reaction was to snap his pencil in half.

'That's a very damaging statement, Pernelle. Actionable in law, too, I'd say. I wouldn't advise you to repeat it in public.'

The threat lay across the desk like a naked dagger.

There was an overtone of menace, like distant thunder on the horizon, when he went on. 'I demand to know your reasons for questioning my character bona fides.'

'I don't believe you want a salvage licence for the *Nova Scotia* for the reasons you give but for something else. Something else far less worthy.'

Ziegler barked laughter. 'That's an old-fashioned, out-of-date word! Explain yourself!'

'I have reason to know that you – and your family before you – are involved in a racket involving treasure. Priceless treasure.'

'What nonsense have you got hold of? Where did you hear this cock-and-bull story?'

'I think you know Louis Arnold. Louis Arnoldi.'

Ziegler's face jerked like a missile launcher spitting its deadly cargo, but he caught himself in a flash and managed to hold his voice level.

'Louis Arnold?'

'He came to see me in Cape Town.'

'He also came to Bangazi Lodge a few days ago. You won't meet up with him to feed your fantasy any further. He's dead.'

Pernelle had not the control over her face that Ziegler had. For a split second her eyes closed as if they had been slapped with the back of a hand, her brain screaming that Louis had come to kill, and yet it was his victim who sat, unharmed, in front of her.

She asked unsteadily, 'How did he die?'

'I don't know, the police don't know. I went to pick him up in the helicopter on the beach at the memorial site and found his body, with a speargun dart through his neck.'

The stark brutality of the method jerked her back to full awareness of the heavy man sitting across the desk. *He* had done it, *he* had killed before – Samsonov! If anything were required to prove the Ziegler–Dehn–Keller background and the sinister history of the Stones of the Sun, Louis' death was it.

Romira said from the sidelines, 'We were all very shocked about it. Can I get you something to drink?'

Pernelle shook her head. With Louis out of the way, who would – could – substantiate the story of the theft of the masterpiece, except by way of hearsay? She couldn't let Ziegler get away with it!

She pulled her thoughts together and asked incisively, 'I want to know more about the Stones of the Sun. That is a key stumbling-block to your application. It falls down over that.'

Ziegler's face resumed its guarded, tight lines.

'The Stones of the Sun? Is this another one of Louis Arnold's fabrications?'

'You know what I'm talking about. A priceless necklace. Stolen by your grandfather. Originally from the Arnoldis, and subsequently from the Empress of Germany. Smuggled into the colonial territory of South West Africa. Hidden for half a lifetime on the farm "Allesverloren". Stolen by your father Jost, who tried to kill his sister for it, and nearly succeeded. Got away through a slick change of name to Dehn. The son Dehn inherited it and made another slick change of name to Ziegler. Kentrat Ziegler. What, I ask myself, is Kentrat Ziegler up to? Why should he go to such extraordinary lengths to salvage a wartime wreck his father, a U-boat devil captain, sank? It kicks back – it always kicks back – to the Stones of the Sun. Wrecks have been salted before, you know.'

She found herself shrinking from the savage, enfilading look he threw at her. She knew then her account was right.

It lasted only a split second before he regained his composure.

'You have certain information. Dangerous information, I may add. Tradable information. It is only natural that you should try to push me into a corner and capitalize on it.'

He got up abruptly, went to the cocktail cabinet with the false façade and pushed the secret button. The door swung back to reveal the battered old pre-World War One safe. He took the Makarov from among the bottles.

Like a well-drilled puppet, Romira moved round from her position behind Pernelle's chair to the cocktail cabinet. Ziegler passed her the Makarov.

He said thinly, 'Security.'

Romira held the gun, not aiming at anything in particular.

Ziegler addressed Pernelle. 'Everyone has their price.'

In the tight silence which followed, he reached into his

pocket and pulled out a banknote, which he drew, almost by reflex, through his teeth. If Romira could have shot him, she would have.

Ziegler unlocked the old safe with a key on a chain from his pocket, and swung the heavy steel door open with an almost histrionic gesture.

The light caught the little heaps of diamonds.

24

'Are you trying to bribe me with Rick's diamonds?' demanded Pernelle, disdainfully eyeing Ziegler's expectant face.

The offending banknote dropped as if a violent wind had blown it away with a savage surge of anger. His right hand arced out and slapped the Makarov out of Romira's hand into his own. He threw its sights on Pernelle. His voice came hurtling at her like an Exocet missile.

'You bloody interfering, meddlesome, probing bitch!' he yelled. 'Investigations! My arse! Who is paying you to check on me, eh? Tell me, you'll tell me, before I've finished with you! So you know about Rick, too! You know about Rick's diamonds! If you know all that as well, you know twice too much! I'll see you don't blab it any further!'

This was the reaction Pernelle had long been expecting.

She managed to hold her ground and replied levelly, 'Rick's diamonds. The Taiwan diamond route. Abalone.'

The Makarov made jerky little arcs as Ziegler's out-of-control hand muscles tried to make a show of keeping it levelled at her. They stood there, the three of them, the tall bull-necked man with the pistol, Romira, white-faced and empty-eyed, Pernelle, riding the broadside of vicious anger.

'Abalone!' She punched home the word. 'You should have been more careful with the packing, Ken Ziegler.'

Ziegler's voice was rough, primed with menace. 'It would take an expert to know what you're talking about.'

Pernelle played a bad card. 'Gareth Ridpath's an expert.'

'Ah!' he breathed. 'I won't forget that, either. Which

means he also knows too much.' The threat hooked the corner of his lips away from the line of his beard. A killer's lips. Perhaps he had looked that way at Louis. At Samsonov, too. Pernelle went cold.

Ziegler had his voice under control now. 'You know too much. It wouldn't be safe to let you go free, both for what you have stashed away in your mind, and for what you have tucked away in those papers of yours there.' He indicated the desk.

'I can document everything I'm saying – '

'Then more's the pity, for you.' He gestured with the gun. 'Get over there.' He steered her to the private lift.

Ziegler addressed Romira. 'The buoyancy chamber door control – bring it. The hook too, there in the safe.' He rounded on Pernelle. 'So you want to know about the Stones of the Sun, do you? Well, you shall. But there's a price on the viewing – your life.'

Ziegler pressed the lift button.

'No one saw her arrive today, did they?' he asked Romira.

Romira shook her head.

'And she had lunch alone – none of the guests knew . . .'

'No, no one,' answered Romira.

'Good. Then we have nothing to worry about. No witnesses.' The lift door opened. 'In there!' he ordered. 'No monkey tricks, eh? I'm right next to you with the gun.'

The three of them crowded into the small lift; it smelled of old paint and oil, mingled with Ziegler's sweat.

'Out!' ordered Ziegler, as the lift stopped with a faint thump.

Pernelle stepped into the airless atmosphere of the former missile-tracking control centre.

'Get on!' snapped Ziegler, prodding her in the back with the Makarov and steering her half-left out of the lift towards what seemed to Pernelle to be a solid steel wall. Romira slipped ahead with the hand-held radio control and went through the ritual of opening the buoyancy chamber door.

'Inside!' ordered Ziegler.

If Pernelle felt she had stepped into a world of unreality in the fire-control centre they had just left, the man-height consoles, the array of pipes, the bulbous 'brandy stills', glassed-in 'cockpit' and bank of turbines on the far side gave this place an air of dream. But, unlike the tracking centre, the buoyancy chamber was alive, pulsing softly. Light came from strips of flickering green-and-black computer dials on the two tall consoles, and pale violet illumination emanated from a large rectangular water-filled glass tank near the far wall.

'Over there,' Ziegler ordered. 'Romira, light!'

Pernelle felt the steel catwalk through the soles of her thin shoes as they crossed the floor. There was something in the tank apart from the light.

Then she saw the Stones of the Sun. Even the dulling effect of months of submersion in water had not wholly clouded the reflective glory of the heliodore. It looked stunning in the violet light.

'You pushed your way in where you weren't wanted, mouthing about the Stones of the Sun,' said Ziegler abrasively. 'You and Louis. Now take a good look – there they are!'

Romira stood to one side, looking into the tank, a strange affinity between the violet of her eyes and the colour of the light. For the first time Pernelle saw them come alive.

Pernelle said, 'I can understand a man would kill for it.'

Ziegler lifted the pistol purposefully. 'What my grandfather did, he did.'

'Louis –' interrupted Pernelle.

'Leave Louis out of this!'

'I can't, when I think of that spear through his neck.'

'Shut up!' snarled Ziegler. 'Shut up, I say! You'll have plenty of time on your own later to think about Louis.'

Ziegler said brusquely to Romira, 'Go and fetch her suitcases from the Coelacanth Suite. Look around, and bring anything she may have left lying around. Bring it all.'

Romira couldn't take her eyes off the necklace. 'Let me dry it off and wear it, Ken, just for a minute or two.'

'Don't try and hamstring my plans with your damn childish whims,' Ziegler retorted. 'What do you think this is, a fashion parade?'

'It's the most beautiful thing . . .' began Romira.

'If it wasn't I wouldn't be risking my neck,' answered Ziegler. He half-waved the gun in her direction. 'Quick!'

'Don't threaten me,' said Romira. 'You have a lot to lose if I go sour on you.'

'Get the suitcases, and perhaps you can wear the necklace when you come back,' Ziegler said placatingly.

Romira hung back for a moment, glanced at Ziegler, and then hesitantly at the Stones of the Sun.

She said to Pernelle, 'Don't you think it is too lovely?'

'I've never seen anything like it.'

'For Pete's sake!' burst out Ziegler. 'Get up to the Coelacanth Suite!'

The venom in her look was as pervasive as the strange light in the buoyancy chamber.

Ziegler watched Romira make her way to the lift, deliberately taking her time, waited for the door to close, then turned to Pernelle.

'I want you to get your options clear.'

'Options?' Pernelle was derisive.

'I'm giving you a last chance. You can either accept, or take the consequences – down here.'

'The list of unexplained disappearances at Bangazi Lodge is building up,' Pernelle responded. 'First, Samsonov supposedly drowned by accident. Louis – I don't know how you explained his death to the police. And, next, I go missing – the police aren't dumb, you know.'

'It's my problem, leave it to me,' he answered harshly. 'I know what I'm doing.'

'Do you?' Pernelle asked. 'Do you? You've tied a ball and chain to your ankles with that – ' she gestured towards the Stones of the Sun ' – it has a long history of bloodshed, and you're adding to it.'

'Don't lecture *me*!' Ziegler snapped. 'I'm not going the route my father went. He sat a whole lifetime on a god-forsaken dump of a farm out in the desert, afraid to move for fear that someone would discover his hidey-hole. Talk about a ball and chain! Scared to mention it, scared to make a move to sell it, scared – oh hell!' he spat out. 'I never knew about the Stones until my father came clean after terrorists had killed my mother and he had his heart attack which finally killed him. I couldn't credit what he told me, fifteen million dollars for the taking!'

Ziegler was thoughtful. 'I saw, after he died, why he'd kept quiet. I approached some dealers on the Continent. Questions, questions, probing questions! Bangazi Lodge was a much better bet. It's been worth staking a couple of million. And neither you – ' he pointed the pistol ' – nor anybody else is going to stop me. If I have to lock you up until you rot, I'll carry out my plan. Perhaps you may feel differently after a spell down here in the darkness alone.'

Pernelle said nothing.

'I'm offering you a simple alternative. Endorse my application for a salvage permit, and keep your mouth shut. I'll guarantee you don't lose out. Otherwise . . .' He waved the gun menacingly.

'You won't get away with it,' retorted Pernelle. 'Other people know I'm here at Bangazi Lodge. Gareth for one. He's due to meet me tomorrow afternoon at Cape Town airport. When I don't show up – '

'There's an answer to that one,' interrupted Ziegler without humour. 'You're a woman, a very attractive woman. He's not the only man around.'

Pernelle turned away. 'You're loathsome!' she exploded. 'You'd actually say . . .?'

'I'll say anything, for the sake of the Stones of the Sun,' he snapped back. 'Do I make myself clear? Anything! I have a fifteen-million-dollar stake on the table. I intend playing the benefactor at the memorial service and showing an admiring crowd what I've raked in from the wreck of the *Nova Scotia*.'

'The *Nova Scotia* is to be declared a war grave and therefore out of bounds,' said Pernelle.

'That had got no further than Louis' mind,' Ziegler sneered. 'Nor will it, now. What are a few old bones, alongside what I will offer the remaining survivors, who can't number more than a handful anyway? I'll offer them a retirement village for themselves, built at my expense, wherever they wish. I'll become Number One hero at the opening ceremony when I announce that.'

Pernelle drew back a little. 'You're trying to cut corners, the same way as you're doing over the salvage rights.'

'The end will justify the means,' retorted Ziegler. 'All your bureaucratic red tape will evaporate once it's confronted by the reality. The reality of that.' He pointed the gun towards the Stones necklace. 'What if I am in advance of the paperwork? Who's going to fret? I'll have the media, the experts, all lined up, public opinion too. You can be part of it, if you choose. Your opinion on the necklace would set the seal on it, so to speak, but there are other experts in the field if you won't play along.'

'And if I don't? My office knows I'm here. You can't talk your way out of that.'

'Can't I?' His mind was twisting and turning like a speared shark. 'Can't I? The opening's next week – what could be more natural than that you should have decided to stay on for it, as one of the honoured guests? That's what I'll tell your office.' He thrust his powerful head forward in a gesture of menace, his lips tight behind the short black beard.

Pernelle backed away, nearly tripping over the thrown-back lid of the water shaft.

'What's your answer?' he rapped out.

'You can guess.'

'You stupid, stubborn bitch! You're only making it difficult for everyone. It could be so easy!'

'I don't buy your sort of crooked scheme.'

'Is that your final word?'

'Yes.'

'It mayn't be, after a couple of days in solitary confinement. You asked for it!' His voice was as turbulent as a thunderhead. He ran his left palm down the side of his chest and on past his stomach, as if wiping it free of sweat and responsibility.

The sound of the lift came from next door and Pernelle found herself almost welcoming Romira's return. 'Our guest has decided to stay on a few days more at Bangazi – down here,' he sneered. 'You and Buks will see that she's fed and looked after. And – ' his voice was loaded with menace '– if anything happens to her, I'll hold you responsible.'

'And the necklace? You're not leaving that in here with her!'

'Do you think I'm plain stupid?' demanded Ziegler. 'Get it out and dry it on a towel – careful! It comes upstairs with us.'

Romira held the necklace in front of her breasts and said impetuously, 'Ken, let me wear it! Just once again! Now! Let me!'

'Cut the crap!' he retorted. 'Damn your ego! Here, give it to me!' He snatched the towel and the necklace from her and closed it in his left hand.

Romira stood immobile. The animation was gone from her face, and in its place a sullen, frightening anger. Other people had killed for the Stones of the Sun. Romira was another candidate.

'Lights. Get the lights off!' ordered Ziegler.

Romira made a circuit of the chamber, switching off various lights, until all that remained were the indicator lamps on the computers and the tank's violet glow. At least, thought Pernelle, she would be able to find her way without falling over anything or into the water pit.

The door giving on to the missile-tracking centre swung to behind Ziegler and Romira, shutting out the last traces of normalcy, leaving her to the surrealistic light and the soft sound of gurgling water as the automatic pumps cut in and out.

Ziegler hadn't been bluffing. A prisoner might go mad before finally capitulating simply in order to get away from the place, away from the silent gaolers which stood watching with their pinpoint cyclops-eyes.

Or die.

Down here, death did not have a chilly prognosis. It was warm and clammy, chuckling in the pipes.

25

'Bangazi Lodge is like a castle guarded by a moat – there's no way in or out once the drawbridge is pulled up. And in this case substitute helicopter for drawbridge.'

Gareth banged down his glass so that the ice in it made tiny reverberations in minor imitation of a portcullis chain.

'And that's tightly in the hands of Ken Ziegler,' added Rick. 'No one can move in or out of the flotel without his consent. Shut as a virgin's legs.'

The two men were sitting in Gareth's mining-company flat at Richards Bay. It was Tuesday evening. They had flown up that morning from the Cape. They had chosen to use the major airport at George, only fifty kilometres from Rick's base at Mossel Bay, and had motored there from Cape Town the previous day, after making contact with Bangazi Lodge when its switchboard had opened again following the weekend. After hearing Romira's statement that Pernelle had gone off with a man, a counter-check with her office in Cape Town threw up a conflicting account: Pernelle had decided to stay on at Bangazi for the opening of the *Nova Scotia* memorial the following weekend.

Neither Gareth nor Rick could wait to get within striking distance of Bangazi Lodge. They had opted for Richards Bay because Rick was required there by the police for the identification of Louis' body, and Gareth's flat was the ideal jumping-off place for their plans.

They had left the Cape with a burning determination to get Ziegler in their sights.

Sights! Gareth remembered the way Rick had run his

finger along the streamlined foresight of his Colt Auto and back along the blue barrel to the backsight, then down past the breech to the hammer, showing just how deep the revenge-lust had bitten its way into him since Sergeant Joubert had explained the method by which Louis had been killed. Gareth had watched him pack his Excalibur fighting-knife as well. Then Rick had gone to a cabinet and unlocked it.

Gareth eyed the contents. 'What in hell is all that?'

'Two T-1 Russian hand grenades,' replied Rick. 'We don't know what we could come up against with Ziegler.'

'The other's not a hand grenade,' said Gareth.

'No. Soviet mini limpet-mine.'

'First, what do you want a limpet-mine *for* at Bangazi, and, second, where did you get it?'

'Plenty of them floating around in Namibia; backwash of the terrorist war,' rejoined Rick. 'What for? I don't know, at this stage.'

'We're not going to blast our way into the flotel, are we?' demanded Gareth.

'We'll play the situation by ear. Who knows, at this distance?'

Gareth indicated the last object in Rick's 'armoury'.

'And that? It looks as if it came out of a museum.'

The ornate hilt of the small dirk was chased with flowing lines and a coat-of-arms, inlaid with gold and silver. But it was the thinness of the tiny blade – perhaps seven centimetres long – which gave the weapon its sinister look.

'Medieval Sicilian steel,' explained Rick. 'Very much sought after.'

'What do you intend to do with that, plus all the other hardware you've got lined up there?'

'In this case, it would be appropriate to use the dirk against that bastard Ziegler. Sicilian revenge, with Sicilian steel, if you like.'

Rick overrode Gareth's further questioning. 'Have you got a gun yourself?'

'Yes. I inherited it from the Rössing security people. A Walther P38. A snub-nose job, smaller than your Colt.'

'It'll do,' retorted Rick tersely. 'Especially if we get to close quarters.'

At Richards Bay, they had gone straight to Sergeant Joubert at the local police station.

The policeman could not conceal his surprise at the sight of Gareth. For the moment, he bypassed Rick.

'You! Gareth Ridpath! What are you doing here?'

Before Gareth could answer, Rick intervened. 'I asked him to come with me.'

Sergeant Joubert eyed Gareth. There was something different about him, something he could not put his finger on – for the moment. The firm lines of the man's jaw and cheekbones seemed more severely etched; the full-lipped mouth showed no trace of the smile he had seen in the Bangazi dining-room and his skin seemed tight-drawn, shadowed, as if an artist had put a faint smudge of charcoal across the features. The eyes looked wider apart, too, under the somewhat more brooding brows.

The man had something on his mind and Sergeant Joubert jumped straight to the wrong conclusion.

He said suspiciously, 'It is extraordinary to me that every time we have a body round here, you are in the front line.'

There was a sudden flash of flame in the brown eyes, quickly snuffed, as if to give nothing away. The man had perfect control of himself.

'Meaning?'

'First, a visitor to Bangazi Lodge dies by falling off a bird-watching boom in the middle of the night. You are conveniently there first thing next morning to haul the body out of the water. Then another man dies by a most unusual method, shot through the neck with a speargun dart. The first person who's here to identify him is – you.'

'I don't care for your innuendo.' Gareth held his voice level.

'I want to know where you were on the day of the killing.'

Gareth saw the trap at his feet.

'I don't know when he was killed, so I can't answer.'

Sergeant Joubert sighed.

Gareth added, 'But I've been in Cape Town for the past few days. I've just flown in with Rick. We came straight here.'

'Can you prove that? An alibi?'

Rick said impatiently, 'Oh, for Pete's sake, man! I was eighty-five kilometres out to sea on a job for Mossgas and Gareth was waiting in one of the guest cottages my outfit has – he's been in my company ever since Friday afternoon late when I came ashore.'

The policeman seemed disappointed. Gareth now knew from the exchange that, even if he had had any thought of involving the police in Pernelle's disappearance, it would be impossible in the light of Joubert's attitude. He had been let off the hook for the moment, but the sergeant, it seemed, had a long memory.

Joubert, too, officiously declined to allow Gareth into the mortuary while Rick identified his father's body, and Gareth, on seeing Rick's shocked, white face when he emerged, was relieved he hadn't been in himself.

For a brief while, after their visit to the police station, Rick's rage had ignited like a magnesium flare; now, in the comfort of Gareth's flat, the sobering realities of the situation were having a dampening effect.

'Somehow, I don't know how yet, I'm going to get that bastard Ziegler,' Rick swore softly. 'Here we are bumping our gums while he sits behind what you say is an impassable barricade.'

Rick helped himself to another drink and went on impatiently. 'You make it sound as if Ziegler is holed up in a bomb-proof bunker.'

'Listen, Rick,' replied Gareth. 'You don't know the area that well. Bangazi is one of a chain of lakes which stretches along the Maputaland coast, locked away behind what are reckoned to be the highest compacted dunes in the world. The nearest point of the lake is roughly a little more than a kilometre from the sea . . .'

'Then what in hell are we waiting for?' demanded Rick. 'We can start our attack from there.'

'I said, the dunes are high. They are also covered in impenetrable bush, shrub and small trees. Impenetrable is the operative word.'

'It can't be as dense as all that,' Rick interrupted irritably.

'If Louis had been alive, he would have backed me up. He damn near died on the beach trying to find a way through the thickets; he guessed there must be water on the other side. But he never succeeded. He told Pernelle and me that night when he came to Gil's Cottage that he was so crazy with thirst that he tried to shoulder his way on all fours through the narrow tunnels the jackals had made in the undergrowth but they ran dead and he had to turn back. Other desperate people have tried. The memorial itself commemorates a Portuguese noblewoman and her family who died in the same way.'

Rick still wasn't persuaded. 'A boat's the answer.'

'How do you think you could convey a boat, if you couldn't get a human body through the undergrowth? In any case, you couldn't even get as far as trying,' went on Gareth. 'The whole length of the beach which includes the shoreline opposite Bangazi lake for about forty-five kilometres encompasses the St Lucia Marine Reserve and the St Lucia Marine Sanctuary. You can only get in under limited permit. The restrictions and beach patrols would make it impossible to launch a sortie against Bangazi. It's out, Rick. Not a chance. The authorities only agreed to the *Nova Scotia* memorial because Louis hit on the brilliant idea of prefabricating it and flying it in.'

'There *must* be a way in to Bangazi!' went on Rick wildly. 'We could charter our own chopper . . .'

'And try and land it on the flotel's pocket-handkerchief helipad next to the space already occupied by Ziegler's Jetranger?' mocked Gareth. 'This isn't a pirates' cutting-out expedition, man! This thing, if it is to be done at all, has to be done silently, secretly, with flair and speed if it's going to succeed. To start with, we don't even know where in the flotel we have to look for Pernelle. She could be anywhere.'

Rick said quietly, 'If she's there at all, Gareth. It's something you may have to face up to.'

The only clue in the drawn face in front of him to a hard-kill counterblow was the slight twitch of the muscles under his left eye.

Gareth said, in an inflectionless voice, 'I'm going there for her, whatever.'

There was a long pause, and then he said, 'I've nearly blown a fuse in my computer trying to think of a plan. There's nothing.'

'We could try swimming – I'd be prepared to give it a go.'

'Swim – from where?' responded Gareth. 'There's no springboard at all for any kind of sortie. That's the whole basis of our problem.'

'Water!' exclaimed Rick in disgust. 'Nothing but bloody water on all sides! In the east, a whole oceanful of water, and in every other direction swamps, rivers, marshes . . .'

Gareth sat up so abruptly he almost knocked the drink off the arm of his chair.

'Water! Rick! You've got it! Water, water, water! Glorious water! All the water in the world!'

'But that's our biggest enemy!'

'No, Rick, you're wrong! Water is our friend, our biggest friend!'

Gareth jumped up and pulled a chair over to a cupboard, on top of which was a litter of hiking gear. He grabbed the backpack and removed a crumpled, plastic-covered map.

'What's bitten you?' Rick asked, curiously.

'"Madonna", Rick, the cyclone. That's why I missed Samsonov – I was turned back by the floodwaters.'

Gareth went to a table and spread the map.

'Here! Look!'

It was a large-scale chart showing the coastline and immediate adjoining interior from St Lucia in the south to Sodwana Bay in the north. The star-shaped outline of Bangazi lake was heavily outlined. Lakes, innumerable streams and waterways were coloured blue, interspersed with strips, dots and patches of green. Forests were indicated and named.

'This shows the swamp forests surrounding Bangazi, mainly to the south and west,' Gareth explained excitedly. 'Here, look, these colourings are my own, to show where Madonna's floodwaters spread outside the usual swamp-forest boundaries – '

Rick interrupted. 'I can't understand your sudden burning enthusiasm for the very thing which is stopping us getting at Bangazi Lodge. Okay, okay, I accept your map and newly flooded areas – so what?'

'Water!' Gareth's words tripped over one another. 'Do you know what a swamp forest means, Rick? It's a wild, dangerous conglomeration of stagnant pools, small streamlets which scarcely flow, tiny islands of firm ground here and there, and for the rest you're up to your ankles or waist in stinking, foul water. Your way onward is barred by impenetrable forests, fallen trunks of every shape and size, huge trees tall enough to block out the sun, low trees that catch and pluck at your clothing, luxuriant undergrowth

– ferns, orchids and creepers which thwart you as you try to push on. These aren't tame mangrove forests, Rick, they're killers, and prison to a man trying to make a way through . . .'

'I ask again, so what? You're only underlining our problem. We know already that Bangazi is effectively shut off on the landward side in every direction by swamp forests, and on the remaining side by the sea. So what?'

Gareth pointed to a demarcation of swamp forest blocking Lake Bangazi from the west, and to a smaller, arrow-headed patch on the south-western corner.

'This is a kind of natural Maginot Line protecting Bangazi.' He grinned at Rick. 'That bit there is about twelve kilometres long, and neither man nor beast can get through. I know. I tried. I also tried the gap between its southern extremity and this arrow-head-shaped patch. No go either. The place was under floodwater.'

'Listen, Gareth, I may be a dumb engineer, but I don't understand what you're driving at.'

Gareth stabbed his finger on a line running along the landward extremity of the barrier of swamp forests.

'This is a road, of sorts,' he explained. 'Look, it passes just south of the Mkuzi game reserve. It was somewhere in this area that I hoped to hit on my Mountain of Green Stones. We could use this road as a springboard to put us on course to reach that Maginot Line of swamp forest.'

'It's just the thing to avoid, if you ask me.'

'Water!' Gareth rolled the word round his tongue. 'Madonna left her water there, flooded the place so that the main drainage channels started to flow, instead of being an endless chain of stagnant pools. We now have channels, *waterways*, Rick, don't you see? *Waterways* pointing at the heart of Bangazi! We can get past the fallen trees and creepers and undergrowth which would normally bring us to a standstill. We needn't attempt the impossible – we can outflank Bangazi Lodge this way!'

Rick stared at him, and then asked quietly, 'This isn't just morale-boosting talk, is it, Gareth?'

Gareth's excitement died as if an electric switch had suddenly cut it off.

He replied harshly, 'Pernelle's in that flotel. I don't know what Ziegler has done, or is doing to her.'

'We'll need a boat.'

Gareth indicated the paddles on top of the cupboard.

'I've got a rubber dinghy in my four-wheel drive in the garage. It's the thing for the job. We'll have to portage it over the rough bits, but for the rest we can paddle our way.'

Rick gulped his drink. 'It looks good, Gareth, almost a stroke of genius. How far is it from Richards Bay? How long will it take? What's our plan when we reach Bangazi?'

Gareth made a quick calculation. 'It's nearly 300 kilometres from Richards Bay to our starting-point in the swamps. For the first part of the journey we use the ordinary main road to False Bay, the northernmost part of St Lucia lake. From there we pick up a track which eventually goes through to Sodwana Bay. No problem. We have a four-wheel drive.'

'And then?'

'That's the fast section behind us. We carry on on the track until we pass the southern boundary of the Mkuzi game reserve. One of our biggest barriers then lies ahead – the Mkuzi river, one of the four big rivers which drain into St Lucia lake to the south. Once we're over the river, the way's open to the east and Bangazi lake.'

'If we can get through the swamp forest.'

'You said it.' Gareth studied the map.

'How long do you reckon the sortie will take?'

'No knowing. We don't know at this stage how much will be footslogging and how much will be dinghy.'

Rick said reservedly. 'It's a damn fine plan, and it dropped into place like a computer program. It'll be tough, though.'

'Something's bugging you, Rick?'

'Yeah. What I want to know, Gareth, is once we find ourselves on the shores of Lake Bangazi and see the Lodge there in the lake ahead of us, what do we do? Where do we start?'

'You know the flotel lay-out and the vulnerable points, Rick. You worked on the missile platform when it was being built in Durban.'

'It was an army project when I worked on it. It's now a five-star hotel. So, like I said, where do we start?'

'The flotel's sleeping accommodation, the dining-room, lounges and so on are all at the top.'

'Okay, then. We cross the lake in the dark in the dinghy. You swing your rope and its grapnel on to one of the lower decks near the lifeboats and the bird-watching boom. We climb up, guns in our belts, grenades on stand-by, limpet-mine ready to prime . . .'

'Why the tone of mockery, Rick?'

'It isn't the way to make this thing work.' Rick shook his head. 'The whole place was security-proof when I helped build it. There were bulkhead doors which divided off the various sections so that each one could be isolated. The guys manning the facility were always on the look-out for a terrorist attack.'

'That was the Cold War. This is a peacetime wilderness lodge.'

'Maybe, maybe,' said Rick. 'I don't know how many of the original precautions still work. But one thing is for certain – I'm damn sure you won't locate Pernelle in the Coelacanth Suite!'

'What's in your mind, then?'

'It isn't only Pernelle we're after, never forget. I want that bastard Dehn or Ziegler or whatever he calls himself at the point of my pistol.'

'Okay. But it's going to take time. It won't – can't – be a quick in-and-out snatch.'

'Exactly. As you plan it, we scramble up a rope, force our way inside the Lodge, winkle out Pernelle, and make a break for it – we don't even know what sort of physical shape she'll be in. I wouldn't put anything past Ziegler, especially if he's had her locked up.'

'I come back to my original point, you know the detailed lay-out of the flotel, the ex-missile platform. We must cash in on that knowledge, somehow.'

Rick said thoughtfully, 'What we need is a diversion of some sort – something spectacular that will give us time to operate and stir up the guests to the extent they're going to piss themselves with fright rather than try and stop us.'

'Throw a grenade at one of the upper windows.'

'They were all armour-plate originally and I don't see Ziegler having replaced them just for fun. So, if a grenade goes off outside a window, there's a flash and a bang – and then what? We need something which will involve – threaten – everyone.'

'Something to stir up a hornets' nest, something to rock the boat, so to speak?'

Rick said, 'You wouldn't rock that boat easily, man. It has probably the most sophisticated buoyancy and stabilizer system afloat. I know, I helped install it. It was built to offset the listing effect of the prevailing north-easterly or southerly winds. The flooding valves are opened in sequence to offset the extent of the list and electronically compensated for. The whole structure is kept neutral by means of the buoyancy tanks . . .' Rick suddenly tailed off.

'What is it, Rick? What is it, man?' Gareth exclaimed.

Rick's torrent of words fell over one another.

'If suddenly everyone in the flotel felt they were going to be hurled into the lake – that the whole damn Lodge was toppling into the water – that they'd be drowned – panic stations! Like a ship being cut in half and everyone stampeding for the boats . . .'

26

'They're like the tits on a man's chest – they don't have any function, but they're there, just in case.'

Rick was grinning and laughing, stalking up and down in Gareth's flat, sketching pictures in the air with his hands of what he was trying to communicate.

'It's a piece of cake, and we've got the means here. The limpet-mine and two grenades are enough blasting power. The tanks are only lightly welded because they're *meant* to be blown off! We do it all the time with new oil platforms. Only in this special instance the army didn't want to follow the usual drill once the base module had been launched on the lake!'

'If I'm going to be part of this operation, I have to understand what you're aiming to do. Now Rick, in simple terms . . .'

'Okay, okay.' Rick grinned. 'It's the way the two of us can create one hell of a panic and under the ensuing cover get in there and haul Pernelle out! Everyone will be rushing around, yelling, trying to get through the exits, maybe going for the boats. The chopper will be non-operative because the helipad will be at an angle – '

'You're going to blow – *what*, dammit man, *what*?'

'Auxiliary buoyancy tanks, nothing to do with the main system. Look, it works like this: when the jacket, that is, the base plate of the whole structure in layman's terms, is first manoeuvred into position, it's upended from a barge for flooding. The whole thing is controlled by valves which are opened in sequence based on a control centre which comes into operation built into the jacket. Before that, the buoyancy is statically controlled by small auxiliary buoyancy tanks, one at each leg. When the jacket is up-ended to take its final position, these small tanks are normally blown off with explosives. They've served their purpose. They're lightly welded into position and we know exactly how much explosive force to use. In the case of Bangazi, however, the army didn't want the small tanks removed. Why, I don't know. They're redundant anyway – like those male tits I was talking about. But, nevertheless, the small tanks have to be taken into account as the system automatically compensates for any list caused by exchange of weight or the wind.

'Now, if we blow off one of those tanks, the whole flotel will go over at that leg until the list is automatically corrected by the main buoyancy system.'

'How long would that take?'

'I can't say, but I'd guess anything up to half an hour, depending on how far over the superstructure leans. That's a completely unknown factor. The Lodge now has all the tophamper on the upper floors which wasn't there in the days of missile launches.'

'Won't it lean right over and sink?'

'Not a chance. I reckon the loss of one of the small buoyancy tanks might provoke a list of half a metre, which would be enough for everyone to feel they were falling right over into the lake, the same sort of effect as a small earthquake shock in a high building. Everything will shake and slide all over the place, which is what we want. Under the cover of the upheaval we'll rush in and find Pernelle.'

'As you say, there'll be a stampede for the exits, Rick.'

'More than likely. The crowds will hamstring Ziegler's movements.'

Gareth said, 'I'll bring Pernelle out, even if I have to shoot my way. We'll use the dinghy as our getaway boat, as well as for the attack.'

'Return journey through the swamps?'

'Listen, Rick, the return journey is something we'll have to play by ear. We can't work out every minute logistical detail in advance. We simply don't know. Neither do we know how long it will take us to get through the swamps, once we've parked the four-wheel drive ...'

They left Richards Bay on Wednesday morning, and travelled nearly 250 kilometres northwards up the main tarmac road running through Zululand before turning off on to a track – the main route to the northern resorts. Their four-wheel drive vehicle looked similar to scores of others to be seen in the fishing and scuba-diving regions of Maputaland, loaded with a two-man inflatable dinghy, a couple of pangas, a clutter of gear and some provisions in the back. However, concealed out of sight under the front seat was their armoury: Rick's heavy Colt Auto, the Excalibur knife, his finely chased medieval dirk, along with Gareth's snub-nosed Walther. They had carefully packed the mini limpet-mine and the two Russian grenades to cushion them from the bumpy ride.

They jolted and splashed slowly for another thirty-odd kilometres until they reached the Mkuzi river. Slipping, sliding and bucking, Gareth put the off-road vehicle at the terrain until finally it ploughed to a standstill facing the first section of swamp forest. They stopped, nose to trunk, against a twenty-metre-high waterberry tree, swathed in a tophamper of creepers and ferns.

They swung out of the cab and sank ankle-deep in the spongy turf. Ahead lay not one defined waterway but scores at random, interlaced with fallen trees and branches; small islands stinking happily in the sauna-like heat; irregular herringbones of innumerable roots; beautiful orchids illuminated by the pinky-purple light filtering through the powder-puffs of the Barringtonias and wild frangipani blooms.

Rick stood in silence, daunted at the setting: immediately in front of them was what seemed at first glance to be a stagnant pool from which rose the trunks of grotesquely entangled trees, fighting for sunlight and survival. But the slowly drifting blossoms of the powder-puff tree gave evidence of some water flow, too slight, though, to be called a current. But it was movement, movement southward, and, later, Gareth hoped, eastward towards Bangazi lake.

It was impossible to see, let alone judge, where the far boundary of forest lay because the men's line of sight was blocked by slender pillars of massed stilt roots growing vertically downwards from the long horizontal cross-members of the swamp figs.

Rick asked in an awed voice, 'How far have we got to go through this?'

'Not through, but down,' corrected Gareth. 'It's the whole object of our exercise. To try and force our way to Bangazi through fifteen kilometres of this sort of tangle would never work. See those swamp figs? They're a pretty good indicator of the main drainage channels, and that's what we're looking for. It's like getting into a fast-flowing river and allowing oneself to be swept down in the general direction by the current, and eventually hitting the other side at more or less the right spot.'

'Hoping against hope that the other side is at or near Bangazi.'

'Right. Hence the dinghy.'

'It looks about as certain as Russian roulette to me.'

'There's no other way to do it. What we're looking at here is part of the western fringe of the barrier shutting off Bangazi from this quarter.'

Rick shook his head at the ecological mess in front of his eyes.

Suddenly his reverie was interrupted by a wild scream from high above, the blistering intensity of the cry making him reach for the seat of the four-by-four where his Colt was stashed.

Gareth laughed. 'Hey, relax! It's only a samango monkey! He's objecting to us intruding into his territory. You won't spot him, he keeps out of sight. His fur has been a part of Zulu tribal dress for centuries. He's nearly been exterminated.'

The strange light disturbed both men. The pool ahead had a sorcerous shine, its mystic, luring quality enhanced by the curious purple-grey of the foliage hanging from the branches of trees and creepers. Here, death and life flourished side by side, and death was a dynamic thing, only a gaboon viper's fang-strike away, the swifter-than-sound whiplash of a mamba's jaws.

Gareth said shortly, 'The sooner we get cracking, the sooner we'll locate Bangazi. Our first job after we've got our kit off is to camouflage the four-by-four.'

'Camouflage? What in hell's name for? No one's going to come searching for us from the air.'

'No, but there could be a flash off the windscreen or windows which might catch the eye of a fisherman along the track,' said Gareth. 'I think we're committing an offence by being in these parts, anyway; it could well be a protected nature reserve and our firearms alone are enough to land us in trouble with the authorities.'

Gareth took a panga, stood on the cab roof and chopped down a large piece of fern growing against a waterberry tree so that it fell and half covered the vehicle.

They dragged the dinghy from the back and inflated it from the gas bottle, then heaved in their equipment and wetsuits. Last of all, they loaded the explosives and firearms.

Rick retrieved the Colt and thrust it into his waistband. 'I feel luckier with this close to me.'

Shoving off from the rotting bank, they picked their way between stilt-root pillars, their movement stirring up decayed vegetation and a cadaverine stink. Gareth piloted from the bows.

Suddenly, the water along the right bank churned to white, like an old-fashioned torpedo wake.

Rick lifted his paddle clear in astonishment. 'What . . .!'

A V-shaped formation of mudfish, hideously black and ugly, their long antenna-like whiskers erect in front of their vicious eyes, moved on a shoal of smaller fish with the accuracy of a homing Tomahawk missile and herded it against a broken log. The beak of the formation struck home, tearing, ripping, spearing the trapped victims, while the flanks closed in from left and right.

'Christ, Gareth! Will we have to sleep anywhere near those bastards at night?'

Gareth answered truthfully. 'I don't know where – if – we're going to sleep tonight, but I'd like to be in sight of Bangazi.'

They paddled on in silence. It was impossible to calculate distance or speed, but most of all direction. The sun disappeared in an amorphous mist of leaves and branches at the topmost level of the forest canopy. The light, as it filtered through endless creepers and blossoms, lost still more luminosity, until finally it became hopelessly diffused.

The paddlers' vigilance became dulled by their surroundings, the suffocating heat and humidity, the pervading stench. Their clothes, boots and socks were streaked with a patina of black, cloying mud. They stank. Yet they put off as long as possible changing into their wetsuits. The waterway seemed to be getting narrower and more overgrown; soon they would have to.

The waterway became impassable for a stretch, and the men pulled into the bank. They hauled the dinghy out and, with the lead-rope, handed the craft across the top of massed ferns towards clearer water.

The savage jerk at the rope, Rick's yell, and the crash of the shot were almost simultaneous.

Gareth wheeled.

Rick stood, legs splayed wide, body doubled forward, the Colt held in a reverse grip.

Between his ankles jerked a black-and-yellow gaboon viper, less than half a metre long. It was headless.

The mess of flesh which had been the reptile's head kicked and thumped harmlessly against Rick's boots.

'Get out of the way! Move, man, move!'

Then Gareth realized that Rick could not. His muscles had frozen and were taking no signals from his shocked brain.

He gasped out at length. 'I trod on it – you must have stirred him up . . .'

'Did he . . .?' Gareth was afraid to ask. Deadlier than a mamba, only slower in reaction, there is no antidote to a gaboon viper's venom, and the nearest hospital was hundreds of kilometres away. Rick would be dead before he got him there.

Gareth saw the answer on Rick's boot. A thin stream of venom ran down it, from a score in the leather where the fang had struck, but had failed to penetrate.

Gareth found the strong spirit they had christened Angel's Teat among their gear and handed the bottle to Rick for a stiff pull. He had a slug himself.

They pushed on.

The heat intensified. Instead of the channel widening and gathering momentum from feeder side streams as Gareth had anticipated, the extra supply of water seemed only to evoke more luxuriant growth, higher trees, thicker undergrowth. The pulley-hauley of paddling a short distance, then heaving their soaking, sweating bodies out of the dinghy, slipping, sliding and tripping over the plethora of roots, was both muscle- and energy-sapping.

Mosquitoes accompanied their perspiring, hatted heads like a fighter-bomber escort. Their khaki clothing was a dirty, smelly mess. Every slip, every fall into the slimy mud brought a fresh layer of muck out of the turgid stream-bed.

After a while, they decided they could make better progress by changing into their wetsuits. These armoured them against the mosquitoes, bringing merciful relief, but they paid the penalty in heat and sweat. It was almost a deliverance to fall into the stinking water.

By the middle of the afternoon, Gareth became worried about their progress. He checked with the compass: the general trend of the waterway was still southward.

'I haven't a clue where we are, or how far we've come,' he told Rick.

'What about a tree-top for a look-out? We might spot the flotel.'

'How'd you get up those smooth trunks without crampons? You'd need to be a samango monkey to attempt it.'

'We could overshoot the Lodge,' Rick warned soberly.

'Not yet,' replied Gareth. 'It's an eastward-trending waterway we're looking for. The map shows a big tongue of swamp forest pointing due east where the main tree barrier starts to thin southward. That's our dagger at the heart of Bangazi. Let's get on.'

Rick bumbled forward like an exhausted marathon runner – head down, elbows drooping, legs and feet like lead. Neither man had yet felt cramps, but it seemed only a matter of time.

The swamp began to assume a wash of softer light. They heard creatures snorting and blowing. Hippos? Was the channel wider ahead?

As the heat died, other animals, inyala or reedbuck, splashed in front of them.

Half-dark fell.

Gareth didn't see, only felt the gradual change.

'Rick! The channel's swinging east! East, man, east! And it's getting wider!'

Rick lifted his head like a boxer responding to the bell after a knock-down.

'The flotel – do you see it?'

Gareth handed him the water-bottle they had been hoarding all afternoon.

'No, but the terrain is opening up! We're on our way, man!'

The channel was deep enough to propel the dinghy forward without the continual obstacle race. Their paddle-strokes became rhythmic, determined. They progressed.

They passed on until the light finally faded. Gareth, in the bow, used their powerful hunting-lamp sparingly, trying to fend the dinghy from floating logs, roots or overhanging branches.

They hit the island before they saw it.

The ferny, shrubby mound lay right across their path and Gareth jumped ashore, hauling the rope fender behind him. 'We'll hole up here.'

'Great! I thought the Skeleton Coast in a catamaran was bad, but it has nothing on this ride,' Rick commented, exhausted.

'Hold the light, will you. I want to secure the dinghy.'

Gareth half staggered, half walked, to a small tree overhanging the water. Suddenly, his face was plastered with a white, sticky, meringue-like substance, and a chorus of furious croaking came from the water at his feet.

Rick held the light on him, dumb-struck.

'What in hell's name . . .'

Gareth clawed the white-of-egg from his eyes and nose, then burst out laughing.

'Somewhere above my head is a frog having a whale of a sex-act,' he exclaimed. 'This – ' he shook the white mess out of his fingers ' – is frog's eggs – '

Rick directed the lantern beam into the water. It was a churning mass of writhing, squirming frogs.

'Those are the guys the boffins call sneakers,' Gareth went

on in amusement. 'The female up here on the branch is being mounted by one male only, and as she drops the eggs, they fall on those guys below, who actually fertilize them.'

'Sneaker is the word!' Some animation came back into Rick's voice. 'Not my idea of good sex, letting the other guy have the fun while you do the work.'

'We happened to land up just at the wrong party spot,' said Gareth. 'Let's move, and leave them to it.'

They drank strong coffee, brewed over Gareth's small climber's gas stove, and consumed cold iron and high-protein rations. They pulled the dinghy clear of the water on to a slope of marshy island so that it served as a pillow for their heads.

Rick laid the Colt, naked and loaded, next to him, and Gareth a panga, haft close to his hand. The hunting lantern was between them.

They slept.

Gareth jerked awake from a sweat-soaked, mosquito-plagued attempt at rest. From close by came a mewling, keening sound. He jumped to the conclusion, in the no-man's-land between sleep and waking, that it was Pernelle's cry – torture! Ziegler!

His hand clamped the haft of the panga, he half-sat up. It was with relief that he shook off his sub-conscious agony and tried to see. It was as dark as Dante's Inferno. What had he heard? The swamp had a furtive, sinister life of its own, moving, seeking, killing. Was the mewling a sign of pain or a signal to a hunting-mate? Gareth refrained from putting on the powerful light for fear of waking Rick, who lay like a dead man.

He tried to sleep again, but his thoughts were more of a torment than the mosquitoes. Had his navigation of the swamp been hopelessly at fault? What he dreaded was that they had bypassed and overshot Bangazi Lodge without spotting it. But how was it possible to miss its high red-and-white latticed control tower rising above the swamps and trees?

That fear overshadowed their start next morning. Daylight was a timid affair, but even in the wan light they realized their main heading was still south, not east towards Bangazi.

After an hour, Gareth said, 'A look-out is vital. When we spot a suitable tree, I'll give it a go with the rope and grapnel.'

'The problem's the same as yesterday – it all looks the same to me. But I reckon we could still be okay, Gareth.'

Gareth shot a fingernail impatiently against the face of the compass. 'Then this is lying. We've got to make our landfall at the Lodge while it's still daylight.'

'We've got the whole day ahead of us.'

Gareth replied tersely. 'For you, yes. It's okay if you level the score with Ziegler today, tomorrow or next week. Meanwhile, what is he doing to Pernelle?'

'I can guess how you feel.' Rick's warmth belied his tough-man appearance. His face had a stubby growth of beard and he was dirty; but his energy had been recharged – unlike Gareth's – by a night's sleep.

After a while, they spotted a tree taller than the rest and edged the dinghy to its base. Gareth had difficulty swinging the grapnel on the rope-end, the thick clutch of foliage impeding him on every side. Eventually, the iron caught a branch and he pulled himself up.

'See anything?' called Rick.

'Less than from down below,' replied Gareth. 'Seems thicker up here.'

He tried climbing higher, but it was impossible. Finally, he abseiled back to the ground.

'Let's get on,' he said tightly.

For another hour they paddled in silence. The channel grew inconspicuously wider. Every metre of width meant it was opening up – towards St Lucia.

Finally, Gareth said in desperation, 'Stop! We're throwing away our chances! Look, the countryside is starting to open up – '

They didn't see Bangazi, then.

They heard it. As the wind-break effect of the forest diminished, the sound channels clarified.

Thud-thud. Thud-thud. Thud-thud.

Gareth spun in his seat, facing half-left, back the way they had come.

'Rick! Rick! That's the diesel! That's Bangazi's power-house diesel! Listen, man! That's it!'

Rick swivelled his head like a radar antenna. 'By all that's holy, you're right! We're nearly past, though – the sound's coming half from behind – '

Thud-thud. Thud-thud. Thud-thud!

'It's in the bag!' Rick exclaimed excitedly. 'Steer for the sound of guns, as they say! We've got the bastard nailed, fellah!'

It wasn't as easy as that. Between the channel and Lake Bangazi lay a welter of swamp forest, innumerable lakelets, pools and tributary waterways, all trending south, not east or northeast, the way they wanted to go.

It took hours of muscle-stretching exhaustion to work their way through the swamp forest. Pulley-hauley, rise, fall, splash, stagger. They homed in on the sound of the diesel as a lifeline to salvation. Without it, they would have been lost. Once, when they struck an open patch of country where the trees and shrubs oddly levelled out, they spotted the distant red-tipped summit of the helipad like a church steeple rising from a flat plain.

At last they found landfall on the star-shaped south-western tip of Bangazi lake where there was a particularly clogging section of swamp forest – they went forward cautiously, silently, crouching to avoid any chance detection. They worked round gradually to the northern side of the flotel towards which the bird-watchers' boom projected, the place from which they would launch their sortie.

By late afternoon, they were on station.

They sank down into their foxhole, out of sight in the waterlogged mess, checked their armament, and mounted watch over the tall tower they intended to half-topple tonight like the Leaning Tower of Pisa.

27

'It's the disposal of the body that's Ken's problem, or else I guess he'd have thrown her to the sharks long ago,' said Buks comfortably. He might have been discussing a blocked pipe or a faulty switch in the flotel.

'Sharks?' demanded Romira. 'Sharks? Is that what he says he's got in mind for her?'

'It's not that easy,' went on Buks in the same casual tone. 'He's got to talk his way past the two previous killings, and he can't repeat a success, so to speak. Both Samsonov and Louis were pretty original jobs, you must admit. The fuzz mustn't smell a rat over the third: it might open up the other two cases again.'

Romira's violet eyes remained screened. 'You killed Louis, never forget. Ken didn't ask you to. You did it on the spur of the moment. You wouldn't talk your way out of that in a court of law.'

Buks continued contemplatively. 'Sharks have a lot going for them – no bits and pieces for the pathologists to nail evidence on. No blood to show the time of killing, and no remains to indicate whether she was alive or dead when she went into the water. Seems a pity, though, to throw such a beautiful lay to a bunch of sharks.'

'Oh shut up, you callous sex-mad bastard!' snapped Romira. 'It's all you can think of.'

The lift came to a standstill with its usual muted thump and the door slid open. Romira led the way through the ghostly remnants of the former missile-control centre, carrying a tray laid with food under stainless steel covers and a vacuum flask. Incongruous among the dishes and cutlery was Ziegler's Makarov automatic. Over the past six days, ever since Pernelle had been thrust at pistol point into the buoyancy chamber, this had become a twice-daily routine.

Buks hung back for a moment, shifting his right-hand grip on the Stechkin 9-mm machine-pistol slung from his shoulder, and gave his braces a slap against his singlet-clad chest.

He said, 'I've got bad vibes about this set-up, Romira.'

She jerked her head impatiently at the machine-pistol and the panga hanging from his wrist by a thong. 'Afraid of the dark, with all that? Want your nappie changed, dearie?'

Buks didn't rise to the taunt. 'Listen, what worries me is that Ridpath doesn't seem to have shown the slightest interest in her disappearance. Not so much as a phone call.'

Romira eased the tray on to a desk. 'How would you know? I take all incoming calls to Bangazi.'

'And there hasn't been anything from him?'

'The only one I can't account for was early last Monday morning asking for her. It sounded like a foreigner. He wasn't very insistent. In fact, he sounded pretty casual.'

Buks put the machine-pistol next to the tray and slapped his braces again.

'Ridpath wouldn't act this way, just leave his honey-bunch without his honey . . .'

'You make it sound so romantic,' she scoffed.

'He was – is – crazy about her,' retorted Buks. 'And Ridpath could be a mean opponent. Remember how he went down to Samsonov's body at the end of a rope? He's got lots of guts.'

'Is that why you patrol the bird-watchers' boom every night with all that heavy armament?' she asked mockingly. 'Scared of Ridpath coming aboard?'

'It's a good vantage point to see and not be seen,' responded Buks. He indicated a steel roll-up type double door on the far right wall. 'That leads to the boom. We used it to recover the misfires and duds; brought them up with a hydraulic crane and on through that door once they were rendered safe.' He gave a throaty, unpleasant laugh. 'Nowadays the order's reversed – we make 'em safe inside here first, then move the bodies out, not in.'

Buks gathered up his machine-pistol. 'Let's get this food routine over with. It gives me the willies. Then I'll do a spell round the boom. I've got a spotlight rigged there too, just in case.'

Romira shrugged and stopped at the buoyancy chamber door, pointing the impulse switch at the seemingly blank wall.

The door swung open. Pernelle, sitting in the 'cockpit' chair, threw up an arm to protect her eyes from the sudden shaft of light. Buks had the Stechkin on her in a flash. She got to her feet, squinching her eyes, and fumbled forward to find the dark glasses retrieved from her luggage.

'Hold it! Hold everything!' Buks rapped.

'Oh, for crying out loud, don't be a fool,' snapped Romira. 'She can't see.'

Pernelle jammed the glasses hastily on her nose against the harshness of the incandescent light. She had spent six days and five nights in the darkened chamber, her only light the violet glow emanating from the weathering tank, the only sounds the muted hum of turbines and the whisper of water in the hydraulic pipes. Alone with her thoughts, and with no dividing line between day and night, she had held to her sanity by devising a game based on the flickering computer lights, and following an exercise routine, using the pipes as an improvised 'gym'. She had slept on a canvas stretcher used by the emergency shifts in the missile days, and had washed at the handbasin in the toilet between the console and the wall.

Her only hope was Gareth. He was all she had to hold on to and she knew he would not let her down.

Romira went forward and put down the tray on the

casing over the nearer of the 'silt domes'. She removed the Makarov and let it hang loosely at her side.

'Supper. It isn't what you were getting in the Coelacanth Suite. And no Veuve Cliquot either. Hot water instead. In the jug. Take you through the night.'

'There's no knowing which is day and which is night down here,' Pernelle retorted.

'Listen,' said Romira. 'You could make this all very easy for yourself. Stop being so bloody-minded . . .' She took a step forward.

'Keep that gun out of her reach!' There was an abrasive echo in Buks's warning. 'Stand well back!'

Romira shrugged impatiently. Pernelle could smell the waft of expensive perfume that came from her body.

She went on. 'You've got twenty-four hours to make up your mind, do you know that? Saturday's the day of the memorial opening, and it's Thursday night now. Get this quite clear. With or without your say-so, Ken intends announcing at the unveiling that he has recovered the Stones of the Sun necklace from the wreck of the *Nova Scotia*.'

'My say-so!' echoed Pernelle.

'This is his final ultimatum,' continued Romira. 'Ken intends to cut clean across all your piddling bureaucratic red tape and petty carping. Who do you think is going to listen to all that niggling crap when Ken produces that stunner of a necklace and dangles fifteen million dollars in front of their eyes? More so when he announces that part of the money is going towards a retirement village for the remaining survivors of the *Nova Scotia*. You can go along with his proposition – or else.'

'Or else what?' asked Pernelle.

Buks sketched a sighting tracery over her body with the barrel of the Stechkin. In the silence, the background hydraulics chuntered soft warning.

'We have several options.' His words were ambiguous, calculated to run a red-hot needle along her nerve-endings.

'You'll never get away with it!' Pernelle fired back.

'No?' he sneered.

He patted the Stechkin almost affectionately. 'This is one option. But it has disadvantages. It's noisy and messy, and that's what we have to avoid. I myself prefer the Samsonov route.'

'Shut up, Buks,' Romira cut in sharply. 'This sort of chat isn't getting us anywhere. You – ' she addressed Pernelle, ' – have a straight choice. Forget about your knight in shining armour. He's forgotten you already. It happens all the time, here at Bangazi – just like the shipboard romances. When you get your feet back on land and reality, you'll realize that it was a weekend dream. Ridpath has gone off on a fishing trip – did you know that?'

Pernelle shook her head.

'I must admit I didn't expect him to dump you as soon as that,' Romira needled. 'So I checked with his flat supervisor at Richards Bay. Gone for a few days' fishing, he said. So you see, you're all alone, duckie. Face up to it.'

Pernelle saw through her tactics. By getting at her from a different angle, she was hoping to soften her up, to get her to fall in line with Ziegler's ultimatum. Pernelle simply took off the dark glasses and did not reply.

'You stuck your nose into a family secret which wasn't your business, and you've burned your fingers. No one but you knows all about the Dehn–Keller background.'

Pernelle nearly let it slip but stopped herself in time. Rick! Romira did not know that Gareth had been in touch with Rick, or that he had met Louis in Cape Town, and the interchanges that had taken place. Ziegler must believe that she was the sole repository of the secret which would deny him acceptance in the eyes of the National Monuments Council. She had strong cards yet! She could play them when she and Ziegler came face to face at that final inevitable confrontation.

Pernelle said incisively, 'You're wasting your time. My answer is no.'

'All the guests are at dinner. All together in one place. Good for a panic stampede.'

Gareth checked the luminous face of his watch and eased himself above the rim of their foxhole.

Bangazi Lodge, roughly a kilometre away, stood out like a Disneyland fantasy etched in light on the dark waters of the lake. All activity now concentrated behind the long windows of the dining-room, with its superb view facing eastward towards the sea.

Their hours of watching and waiting had not been idly spent. Rick had brought out the mini limpet-mine, the two Russian grenades and a squash-bag of specialist tools. He secured the three explosive charges, any one of them by itself capable of killing half a dozen men or more, into a compact bundle for fixing to one of the flotel's auxiliary buoyancy tanks by means of the mine's adhesive apparatus. The plan was that the discharge of the mine would detonate the two grenades by sympathetic explosion.

Rick had also checked the mine's setting device, a tube-like affair sunk lengthwise into the body of the metal casing.

He said to Gareth, 'I'll use a zero setting, then we'll have to move like hell.'

'What does that mean?'

'The mine has several settings, up to a couple of hours from the time it's activated,' he explained. 'We need one for almost immediately we put it into position. We can't hang around and risk detection in the dinghy.'

'Almost immediately – that sounds ominous,' commented Gareth.

'Thirty seconds.' Rick was tight-lipped. 'Trouble is, these Russian timing devices are never very accurate. We could blow ourselves to kingdom come even before starting the countdown.'

'Sounds dicey.'

'Also, I don't know how old this mine is,' went on Rick. 'It could go off in my hands as soon as I activate it. The older the mine, the more temperamental it becomes. Just shut your mind to what may happen till we get on target.'

He had seemed to want to divert attention away from the lethal package and had indicated the flotel.

'See how easy she rides. That's the automatic stabilizer system compensating all the time. If the north-easter gets any stronger, it will compensate all the more.'

'Where's your target located?' Gareth had asked.

'We'll go for the tank on the waterline just below the bird-watchers' boom,' he replied. 'It's connected to the main system by some big pipes you can't see from here. The whole flotel structure will tilt over as the water rushes in and before the main hydraulics have time to compensate. Inside the flotel, it will be like an earthquake shock.'

'For how long?'

'Twenty minutes, perhaps half an hour. While everything is still falling about everyone's ears we'll have to get Pernelle out and I have to settle with Ziegler.'

Gareth had run his finger over his climber's rope. 'I'm going to get her out, Rick – whatever.'

'The flotel will steady up, Gareth, before our time is up. Maybe the panic will die down as it does so – or maybe it will have taken too much of a hold by then. The strategy is simple: we create a major diversion, go for Pernelle first, then Ziegler.'

Now they thrust carefully and pulled clear of the shoreline, heads down, shoulders up, to present as small a profile as possible. 'Careful with your paddle!' breathed Gareth. 'Keep your stroke deep and steady – no reflections off a wet blade!'

There was no giveaway overhead light, no moon. It was too early for Orion seaward in the east; the bulk of Bangazi Lodge blocked the glory of the Southern Cross.

Fifteen strokes, twenty strokes.

The avernal dark between the steel pillars low down under the flotel's waterline deck was split by a tracer of light, as swift and momentary as summer lightning.

Gareth and Rick froze. '*What was that?*' Rick breathed.

'Looked like a door opening and shutting,' whispered Gareth.

They were too far away to have seen the brief reflection on the barrel of the Stechkin or on the blade of the panga. Buks was enjoying his watchdog role, down on his hands and knees so as to present no silhouette.

'There's no door in that area that I know of – ' began Rick, then suddenly he broke off. 'It's been served up to us on a plate, Gareth! A bloody plate! I'd forgotten! There is a big door the army used for retrieving dud missiles! We needn't go for the upper part of the flotel for our entry! This is it! It's what we want – an Achilles' heel clean into the heart of Bangazi!'

'You sure?'

'Positive. It's just what the doctor ordered!'

'Keep your voice down, for Pete's sake!' cautioned Gareth.

'If that *was* the door opening, though, it means there's someone around.'

'Where does the door lead?' Gareth demanded in an urgent whisper. 'Does it lead anywhere at all? Are you sure we won't find ourselves at a dead end?'

'It leads right into the old fire-control centre and hydraulics chamber. We can take it from there. And get out again that way, too.'

'Those steel legs look damned smooth. How do we manage to get up and in?'

'The grapnel. Hook it on to the bird-watchers' boom. Then up we go!'

'Press on!'

The dinghy came from the rear at the flotel's lowermost

deck, the platform on which the whole massive structure was balanced like a steel house of cards. By this approach, they unknowingly put the bulk of the flotel between themselves and Buks.

Buks stood up. The night seemed as unthreatening as any other since he had taken up his nightly vigil.

The dinghy drew closer. It headed for the slimy criss-cross of pipes, heavy support legs and strengthening cross-members which the bulk of the module on its shoulders turned into a dark pit.

In front of the pit was the boom.

In front of the boom was Buks.

He stood for a few moments and tried to penetrate the darkness towards the swamp forest shore.

Nothing.

He turned back, relaxed, sauntered along the boom. The panga dangled from his left wrist. The Stechkin sat comfortably snug against his braces.

The dinghy crossed into the first line of blackness under the flotel. Neither Gareth nor Rick could see anything immediately in front, although there was a luminosity on the far side of the shadow zone like the twilight end of a tunnel.

'Take over,' whispered Rick. 'I'll feel my way and guide you.'

'Can you manage?'

Rick's voice vibrated. 'It's like a woman – you do it by feel.'

For answer, the dinghy thumped softly into an invisible steel leg. It was slimy, cold, even in that benign climate.

'On – then turn left,' murmured Rick. 'Nearly there now. She bulges here on the corner.'

Gareth felt the rounded above-water bulge of the tank, shaped like an aircraft wing auxiliary. He could not distinguish where it began and ended.

Rick clawed and felt his way along.

He whispered excitedly under his breath, 'Here – I'm going for it here, where the tank joins the leg, on the inside. Once I start counting, go like a bat out of hell towards the boom. The blast from this close could finish us.'

Gareth's mouth was dry. He crouched tensely, ready to plunge the paddle at the first getaway stroke.

'Ready?' Rick's voice wobbled throatily.

'Ready.'

'I'll activate and fix the charges in place, then count.'

'Okay.'

'Stand by!'

Gareth could not see, only feel, as Rick went forward to attach the mine.

'Now! One! Two! Three – go, go, go!'

Gareth plunged his paddle deep. As the dinghy made a flying start to cut clear, the superstructure above groaned slightly, as if guessing at the outrage in train against it.

The dinghy cannoned into one of the flotel legs, slewed, half-stopped.

Rick counted on.

'Eighteen, nineteen, twenty . . .'

A cold hand grasped Gareth's stomach. The whole device could fire or misfire at any second. He dug the paddle savagely, deep. The craft bumped off another obstruction, but swept clear of the black steelwork trap.

'Twenty-eight, twenty-nine . . .'

28

The mine and the floodlight detonated together.

From darkness as deep as hell they were suddenly subjected to light as piercing as a laser beam, and a hail of 9-mm Stechkin bullets which whanged and whined off the agglomeration of steelwork.

At the same time, there was an outsize burp as water rushed into the ruptured buoyancy tank.

The entire superstructure of the flotel, towering high into the night sky, trembled slightly then lurched in the direction of the bird-watchers' boom. The boom itself, long and unwieldy, jerked downwards at its extremity towards the water. Its metal housings, where it joined the base deck, ground and groaned, steel against steel.

As the flotel lurched, Buks was thrown off balance and the slugs went pouring indiscriminately into the underside of the steel legs, the racket of the volley adding to the chaos and panic sweeping the dining-room five floors up. He reeled back, clutching at the boom's railing, hamstrung by the cumbersome weight of the Stechkin in his right hand and the heavy panga swinging from his left.

'The whole thing's falling down!' Gareth hissed.

Rick grinned lop-sidedly. 'Not yet! Now – your grapnel! Get at him!'

Gareth jumped up in the bow, swung the grapnel by its rope like a lasso.

His aim was good. It hooked fast where the boom linked the main deck. He pulled the rope taut.

Now the flotel gave a second, bigger, lurch.

On the summit, the Jetranger pulled free of its overnight mooring and careered down the canting helipad. It slammed to rest half-on, half-off, against a small crash barrier. Alongside, the latticed-steel launcher crackled and buckled with the strain.

Objects – unseen in the darkness – fell with huge splashes into the water like depth charges.

Buks had just lined up the Stechkin when the big lurch came. He staggered backwards again as the boom tried to dip its nose, lost his footing. The cumbersome weapon flew from his grasp as he clutched for safety, joining the other splashes in the lake.

But Buks still had the panga.

He saw Gareth coming hand-over-hand up the rope.

Buks yanked himself up with an oath and headed for the grapnel at a half-shambling crouch.

Gareth's head was level with the lower edge of the boom when Buks reached him.

There was nothing he could do. His hands were on the rope, the Walther thrust into his waistband.

There was a heavy crash from below as Rick risked a snapshot at Buks with the Colt. But the steel bottom plate of the boom was as good as armour, and Rick's aim was dicey from the dinghy's unstable platform. He could not risk hitting Gareth with further fire.

Buks switched the panga to his right hand, swung the heavy steel blade at Gareth's lifeline. It was nylon rope, the best, designed to hold when a climber's life depended on it.

The panga threw up a shower of sparks as it chipped the hand-railing. Gareth felt the rope start to fray. One more blow like that and he'd be in the water below.

Buks swung again.

As the cane-knife whanged against the railing, Gareth let go, threw up his right arm, grabbed for the underside of the boom.

He heard the rope part and lash, but the grapnel remained in position, hooked over the safety-rail.

He saw the savage flash of delight in Buks's face as he hefted the panga to slash a third time.

They both knew the target.

Gareth's hand.

Buks swung. In the act of descent, Gareth switched grip to his left hand, his body dangling by one tenuous fulcrum.

The panga smashed against the steelwork.

The force of the blow threw Buks forward and he fell on his hands and knees.

The flotel seemed to list again. The high red-and-white guidance tower, Bangazi Lodge's landmark, started to angle like a sinking warship's mast. Screams and shouts rose from the living area.

Gareth jerked his body in half-pendulum motion to give himself momentum, then swung himself up, his feet kicking and scrabbling for a hold. He pulled himself upright and started to haul himself over the rail when Buks came at him with the panga.

The blade came in a wide, swinging arc, meant to decapitate or at least to chop off an arm.

Gareth was astride the rail. He leaned forward, snatched the grapnel free of its anchorage, and angled its wicked hooks upward. The blow landed on the open end, nearly jerking his arm off.

He hurled himself from the railing, thrusting the hooks into Buks's face.

Buks didn't give up easily. He half-threw Gareth off, but couldn't claw his way past the grapnel spurs. He flailed helplessly with the panga, but his range of movement was too cramped to do any harm with the weighted blade. He tried to gouge Gareth's eyes with his free left hand, but was eluded.

Gareth doubled in agony as Buks jerked, wrenched and

kneed him to the floor, viciously swinging the panga like an old-time executioner at the kneeling figure gasping and clutching his groin.

Rick's shot took him as he went for the *coup de grâce*. He had pulled the dinghy clear to get a better sighting with the Colt in the hope of a snapshot. When Buks leapt up for that final blow, he got it.

'Gareth! Gareth!' called Rick from below. 'Are you okay?'

Gareth pushed Buks's body, rank with sweat and blood, aside. 'Okay,' he panted. 'Come up – the rope . . .'

'I've got it. Can you fix it there somehow?'

'Give me a moment.'

The world spun. What was his own dizziness and what was the drunken angle of the flotel, he could not distinguish. Wild mechanical noises, shouts, screams, falling debris, clanged and roared through his ears.

He stood up, felt easier.

'Rope?' he asked Rick.

Rick tossed an end. He made the wet, slippery cord fast to the railing. Rick joined him.

'This is the time!' Rick said so urgently. 'This is the time to go for Pernelle – while everything's still falling about their ears.'

Gareth hung on to the rail for a moment, sucking air.

'Look!' he said suddenly.

The flotel had tilted over towards the boom. The extraordinary angle had caused the missile retrieval door to swing on its hinges and it now hung wide open like an invitation.

'That's the way in to the missile and buoyancy chambers,' rapped out Rick. 'Where's your gun?'

Gareth shrugged. 'Gone.'

'Here, take this.' Rick passed him the long Excalibur knife. 'Follow me.'

*   *   *

The dining-room with its concentration of humanity was in chaos. The first shudder of the explosion had rocked the room like an earth tremor. The second, when the buoyancy went haywire, was the earthquake.

Plates, crockery, soup, wine, food, had all taken off and flown towards the far left-hand corner.

The band joined the rest of the shambles, the mad jangle of the instruments adding to the falsetto screams of terrified women.

Ken Ziegler grabbed Romira as she tried to steady herself by hanging on to the harp and its tall stand.

'Let that damn thing go – come!' His powerful voice hardly carried above the din. He clamped a vice-like grip on her shoulder and used his weight to propel her through the crush towards the main doors. At the doorway itself, a scrum had developed in the desperate attempt to get clear.

Ziegler didn't spare his guests. Gone were the mine-host niceties. He shoved, pushed, elbowed, stamped, shoul-dered, until he and Romira finally emerged in the passage outside.

'Quick! The necklace first! Then we'll get down to the buoyancy chamber and see if we can't fix it . . .'

They snatched the masterpiece from the old safe, along with little bags of raw diamonds, which they stuffed into their pockets. Ziegler passed the Makarov to Romira, and kept Louis' Service revolver for himself.

'We may need these,' he said tersely.

'Ken – *what is happening?*'

'The devil alone knows! Let's get down to the control room and see!'

The place was in darkness. Ziegler didn't bother with the lights of the old missile-tracking control centre but rushed towards the security door of the buoyancy chamber, the radio impulse switch for the locking system in one hand and Louis' big revolver in the other.

Romira knelt to retrieve a diamond bag and her hyper-sensitive, sharpened eyesight caught a faint, half-obscured movement beyond the last of the big control desks near the door leading to the boom outside.

A door swinging because of the list? People?

Romira didn't wait to evaluate it. Her dominating instinct for self-preservation told her she was in silhouette against the lift's light to anyone out there in the darkness. Get out of sight! Quash the light!

She stayed down, reached up with one hand and pressed the operating button so that the lift door slid shut, then cut the power with the master-key next to it.

Darkness fell like an axe.

She got to her feet, the Makarov thrust towards the door.

What had she seen? Had she herself been seen?

She waited.

Three minutes.

Five minutes.

Then she cautiously turned the power activating switch again, blinking against the sudden light.

She pressed the 'open' button and, preceded by the Makarov at full-arm stretch, headed at a crouch for the beacon of light coming from the buoyancy chamber door.

And the sound of voices.

Only a few minutes before, two figures had moved with similar stealth across to the buoyancy chamber. Clad in black wetsuits with close-fitting caps, weapons held at the ready, they looked like fiends spewed from the rank debris of Bangazi lake.

They had padded silently past Romira's shut lift door, attaching no importance to it. No danger. No poised Makarov on the inside.

'Kentrat Dehn!'

Rick had to pitch his voice above the frenetic fibrillations of the hydraulics, which pulsed and pounded like a patient with a terminal heart attack. Water tore through the valves and monitoring pipes as the automatic system tried to compensate and stabilize the havoc which Rick had wrought down below in the buoyancy tank. The bank of turbines on the other side of the access and ventilation shaft whined and shook at full revolutions on their mountings. The previously staid faces of the man-height computer consoles were a frenzy of flickering lights and wildly oscillating needles.

Ziegler crouched in the cockpit 'driving seat', his right hand flicking the eight switches of the 'dashboard', his left manipulating the 'gear lever', his face rapt in concentration on the computer lights. Almost within touching distance of the open glass 'windscreen' was one of the two transparent illuminated 'silt domes'.

On it, spread out in all its glory, was the Stones of the Sun necklace. The craftsman-cut jewels attached to the gold chain stole the light to themselves, and each tremble of the 'silt dome' threw off coruscations of fire. The cross at the extremity lacked only the swell of a woman's breast to complete its perfection.

At Rick's words Ziegler began to reach towards a small table near the windscreen for Louis' revolver.

'Leave it!'

Now, standing back from the 'silt dome' was the still, tall figure of a girl, her eyes still trying to adapt to the brutal light slapped into them when Ziegler first burst into the chamber.

'Leave that gun!' repeated Rick. 'You know my voice. I'm not bluffing.'

'Rick!' The word was an accusation.

'Aye, Rick.'

Gareth paid scant attention to what was going on between Rick and Ziegler. His gaze went across the pulsing instruments to Pernelle. She did not move, or say anything. Only her eyes spoke volumes. The residue of the hideous past days and nights was in the slightly swollen lids, and the deathly pallor of her cheeks. But her eyes themselves were vibrant with a luminous fervency.

Then, as if the other two players with their lethal weapons did not exist, she walked slowly and fixedly towards Gareth, her eyes embracing his.

'I knew you would come.'

Then she was in his arms. The noises in her throat could have been sobs or her own soft, characteristic laugh.

Rick had waited too long for the moment of reckoning with Kentrat Dehn to be distracted by anything.

He rapped out yet again, 'I said, *leave it*!'

Ziegler remained sitting, but Rick said harshly, 'Get out of there! I have things to say to you, Kentrat Dehn!'

Ziegler got up slowly, reluctantly. As he passed the 'silt dome', he edged over slightly towards the necklace.

But Rick didn't miss a single trick.

'Stay away from that, too!' he ordered.

Ziegler spoke for the first time. 'If I leave the hydraulic controls, we're lost . . .'

'Don't give me that – I know better than you do what's happening. It'll stabilize itself automatically soon – sooner perhaps than you think.'

'You bastard, Rick. You did this.'

'What did you do to me? What did you do to my father?'

He gestured towards the Stones of the Sun. 'This is a reckoning, Dehn. A long reckoning from both the past and the present.'

Ziegler's voice took on a false note of accommodation.

'I've got your diamonds safe, Rick. In fact, they're close by now.'

'Stuff the diamonds. This thing is bigger than that. You

can't talk your way out with the offer of a few diamonds. They're mine, anyway.'

'Not a few, Rick. A lot. We could talk turkey . . .'

'You make me sick! You're worse than the rest of your family.'

'What exactly have you come for? I don't know what you're talking about . . .'

'Yes, you do.' Rick indicated the necklace. '*That*.'

Ziegler's eyes swivelled sideways past the array of instruments and consoles, as if he hoped to win time. Where was Romira with the Makarov? He had been a fool to have rushed off from the lift leaving her with a fortune in diamonds. His gaze returned to Rick's gun, steady on him. He swallowed hard and said, 'It's my birthright. I inherited it.'

Rick's laugh was not a pleasant sound. 'Ask Pernelle here how the Zieglers, otherwise the Dehns, otherwise the Kellers, otherwise the von Kellers, manage their inheriting. There's much more on the table between us than a necklace. There's blood.'

Ziegler tried switching his defence. He addressed Gareth: 'So you're in on this racket, too? Is that why you're here? And – ' he indicated Pernelle with a sneer ' – her also? After all the fictitious muck-raking she did to hamstring my salvage application . . .'

'There was not a word of fiction in my researches on the von Kellers and the Arnoldis,' retorted Pernelle. 'I can document it all.'

Rick broke in abrasively. 'Can it! I haven't come here to argue or listen to your lies. What I know, I know, and that's enough. I'll make it brief.'

He raised the Colt so that it pointed square at Ziegler's head.

'You killed my father, Louis Arnold. Your father also half-killed him during the war with a filthy U-boat skipper's piece of sadism. It's easy to judge where you get your talent from. Jost Keller also tried to kill my mother, *his own sister*, with Bushman poison. All her life she remained half crippled from it. Why? For that?' He gestured towards the necklace.

'It belonged to him – '

'Bullshit!' retorted Rick. 'It was no more his than it is yours. Jost's own father and mother set up a racket together and stole it. That was after the Prussian had himself stolen it from the Arnoldi brothers. The brothers were my grandfather and grand-uncle.'

'It was all a long time ago.' There was almost a wheedle in Ziegler's voice. 'Eighty years.'

Rick replied with the voice of an executioner. 'Eighty years is not a long time when it comes to a Sicilian blood-feud. Some of our vendettas go on for centuries. I have come to claim my family's blood.'

He lifted the Colt and sighted.

'*Nobody move! Stay where you are!*'

Romira stood in the doorway, the Makarov at full stretch in a double-handed grip. The whine of the hydraulics had masked her stealthy approach from the lift.

'*Drop that gun! Drop that knife!*'

Rick said, without turning, 'Romira!'

'Drop it – quick!'

Rick's gun fell with a clatter on the steel catwalk. Gareth's Excalibur joined it. In a flash, Ziegler snatched up Louis' big Service revolver, trained it on Rick, Gareth and Pernelle.

He said with savage menace, 'Never leave your ace where it can be trumped.'

They hardly paid attention to him. Their eyes were on Romira. In her long midnight-blue skirt and black top, her byzantine earrings a kaleidoscope of flickering lights under the piled-up black hair, she was strikingly lovely. But it was not her beauty but the expressionless, deadpan face which riveted them. Even the violet eyes seemed to have been leached of colour by overwhelming inner emotion.

Still holding the Makarov aimed in the double grip, she walked slowly across to the 'silt dome' on which was spread the necklace. There was an exalted abstraction about her, as compulsive as it was frightening. Laying aside the gun, she clipped the necklace around her neck, and stood back. She took the cross at the end of the chain and rubbed it in the cleft between her breasts.

'We have an affinity,' she said in a strange, unreal tone.

Ziegler broke the spell with a wave of the revolver.

'That's fine,' he said roughly. 'You've had your fun, Romira. We've got other business to settle, stern business.' He reached out his free hand and snapped a finger. 'Here – my necklace.'

'*It is mine.*'

She picked up the Makarov and calmly shot Ziegler between the eyes. The crash of the shot in the confined steel cage was as stunning as an artillery shell.

Shocked surprise was in Ziegler's eyes as he lurched forward, the revolver flying from his nerveless hand. He flung out his arms reflexively to save himself and landed half-kneeling, half-clutching, against a batter of hydraulic pipes.

Romira turned to the trio still reeling from the shock. She addressed them with the impersonality of a tape-recording, fingering the exquisitely cut stones.

'It is mine.'

She stood considering for a moment, then said to Pernelle, 'A pity. I would have liked to have seen you wearing it, just to compare with myself. But it can't be. We can't have three witnesses to a killing, can we?'

Gareth tried to get a hand to his belt. One lightning snatch and he could have one of the heavy karabiner buckles he had linked with the climbing rope to hurl at

Romira, but the cold, watchful madness in her face told him his fingers would never get there.

Romira gestured with the gun towards the 'weathering' tank.

'Here!'

She stood with her back to the tank near the edge of the shaft in which Samsonov had died.

'First, Rick – I always had a soft spot for you.'

The Makarov started to come up into a firing position.

Gareth, desperate now, began to ease his hand towards his belt.

Romira's eyes caught the slight movement and, for a brief fraction of a second, her glance flicked away from Rick's face. It was enough.

Rick snatched the medieval dirk from his belt-pouch and whipped it into Romira's heart.

She stared down in disbelief at her left breast between the loop of the necklace chain and the lacy black top. The small gold-and-silver inlaid haft of the tiny dagger stood out as a perfect foil to the byzantine colours of her earrings.

Romira's fingers released the Makarov. It crashed to the floor as she clasped her hand around the dirk, blood pumping through her fingers.

She staggered to the left, crashing her head and shoulders against the tank. As she pitched forward, the necklace caught on a corner of the tank and tore free, toppling Romira over the edge of the access shaft into the yawning black pit below. All that remained was a length of gold chain, and on the end of it, the Arnoldi craftsmen's greatest triumph, the cross inlaid with the Stones of the Sun.

Rick seemed at first not to understand what he had done. Only the dangling cross bore witness to the consummation of the blood-feud. Then he went forward, plucked loose the broken necklace and looped it over his hand. Still without speaking, he turned in silent mime and offered it to Pernelle.

She didn't have to shake her head in refusal. Her eyes told him everything.

Rick stood for a moment, contemplating the glowing heart of the masterpiece. Coming to a sudden decision, he twirled the cross on its gold chain and let it fly from his hand. It flashed lightning as it arced towards the shaft, where it seemed to hang for a moment before vanishing from sight.

The public memorial ceremony scheduled for Saturday was abandoned. Instead, Pernelle and Gareth flew by themselves to the cupola on the beach.

Pernelle tolled the bell.

One for the *Nova Scotia*.

Two for the Stones of the Sun.

The Fighting Man
Gerald Seymour

IT WAS A FIGHT HE COULD NOT WIN,
BUT COULD NOT AFFORD TO LOSE.

Thrown out of the SAS for insubordination, Gord Brown now lives in disillusioned exile on a failing salmon farm in the Scottish highlands.

Yet to the three Guatemalan Indians who track him down, he represents the last hope of freedom. They have come to recruit a fighting man to lead an uprising against the brutal military dictatorship which is killing their people.

Gord flies with them to Cuba, then on with a small band of men to a rough landing strip in the rain forest of Guatemala.

As the ragged army marches through the jungle and across the high mountains towards Guatemala City, a hopeless dream becomes a burning reality. But the forces pitted against them are formidable.

'It's time for Gerald Seymour to be recognized as ranking right up there with Graham Greene' *New York Times*

'Unstoppable momentum' *Daily Telegraph*

'Moving and gripping. Seymour's characters are all beautifully drawn. The dialogue is so real you can hear it and the plot is as tight as a drum. It is tempting to say that Seymour is at the height of his powers . . . He just gets better and better'
Today

ISBN 0 00 647714 3

Let Not the Deep
Mike Lunnon-Wood

A stricken ship, an impossible rescue attempt . . .

The MV *Caledonia*, stricken by engine failure, her cargo shifting as a hurricane-force storm approaches across the Atlantic.

The *Maeve Corrigan*, a superbly designed lifeboat based in the Scillies, heading through tumultuous seas for the casualty.

On board the *Caledonia*, a passenger whose fate will command the attention of the news media from all around the world.

On the *Maeve Corrigan*, a crew that will be tested to the limits of courage and beyond in the longest night of their lives.

Exciting, suspenseful, moving and thrilling, *Let Not the Deep* is destined to become a classic of the sea.

ISBN 0 00 647590 6

☐	REBEL. Bernard Cornwell	0-00-617920-7	£4.99
☐	THE DARK SIDE OF THE HILL Rodney Stone	0-586-21738-X	£4.99
☐	ALPHA 7 Mark Joseph	0-00-647260-5	£4.99
☐	HIGH HUNT David Eddings	0-00-647593-0	£4.99
☐	CORMORANT Douglas Terman	0-00-647309-1	£5.99
☐	DUE NORTH Mitchell Smith	0-00-647642-2	£4.99
☐	NIGHTWING Martin Cruz Smith	0-00-647908-1	£4.99
☐	ALONG CAME A SPIDER James Patterson	0-00-647615-5	£4.99

All these books are available from your local bookseller or can be ordered direct from the publishers.

To order direct just tick the titles you want and fill in the form below:

Name: _____

Address: _____

_____

Postcode: _____

Send to: HarperCollins Mail Order, Dept 8, HarperCollins *Publishers*, Westerhill Road, Bishopbriggs, Glasgow G64 2QT.
Please enclose a cheque or postal order or your authority to debit your Visa/Access account –

Credit card no: _____

Expiry date: _____

Signature: _____

– to the value of the cover price plus:

UK & BFPO: Add £1.00 for the first and 25p for each additional book ordered.

Overseas orders including Eire, please add £2.95 service charge.

Books will be sent by surface mail but quotes for airmail despatches will be given on request.

24 HOUR TELEPHONE ORDERING SERVICE FOR ACCESS/VISA CARDHOLDERS –
TEL: GLASGOW 041-772 2281 or LONDON 081-307 4052